REBEL

The American Iliad

REBEL

The American Iliad

A novel in verse

by

SCOTT WARD

Adelaide Books
New York / Lisbon
2021

REBEL THE AMERICAN ILIAD
A novel in verse
By Scott Ward

Copyright © by Scott Ward
Cover design © 2021 Adelaide Books

Published by Adelaide Books, New York / Lisbon
adelaidebooks.org
Editor-in-Chief
Stevan V. Nikolic

For any information, please address Adelaide Books
at info@adelaidebooks.org
or write to:
Adelaide Books
244 Fifth Ave. Suite D27
New York, NY, 10001

ISBN: 978-1-954351-39-4

Printed in the United States of America

This book is gratefully dedicated to

Professor Bert Hitchcock
Who taught me belles lettres

Acknowledgements

Undertaking such a project as this one, requiring years of research that includes visiting relevant historical locations, one would be lucky indeed to have a friend to drive him to battle fields, hang around while he traipsed back and forth taking pictures and notes on the geographical minutiae, and listen to interminable discourses on Civil War history. I was profoundly lucky to have two such friends, Preston McGill and Ken Folsom. I will always be grateful for their support and friendship. I wish to offer warm regards to Carolyn Johnston for her kindness and thanks to Lee Irby, Helen Wallace, Michelle Brulé, Jared Stark, Jon Chopan, and K.C. Wolfe for commenting on portions of the manuscript. I would like to extend special thanks to my colleagues Julie Empric and Wayne Flynt for reading the entire manuscript. And finally, special thanks to my wife Jana Napier for proofreading the manuscript and for her liguistic and literary judgement (any surviving errors are all mine) as well as her love and good humor regarding the aforementioned interminable discourses. I wish to thank Eckerd College for granting me sabbaticals during which considerable portions of the poem were composed. Excerpts of *Rebel* have appeared in *Tampa Review Online* and *Critical Pass Review*.

October 10, 1862 Eufaula, Alabama

Exultation of the blood reveling winter
night before the inkling of dawn, thriving
from solstice to solstice, driving forward all
the lusts for earthly labors. As he was young,
this beating desire, this thrust and blood-calling,
even cold sogging his skin like wet
clothes, pricking and tingling his vital heat,
made him feel the more his own blood's heat,
so it was nothing to unbutton in strict winter,
the blood demanding release, dawn time inheritance
from some ancestral animal, this marked frenzy
of wanting, this bestial thrusting on. He was only
a dollop of time's metaphysical fluid, surging
vital heat into frigid darkness, that urges
and gets, creating men and the world of men.
Above the indecipherable dark horizon,
ringed with quick drawn strokes of fine October
branches, expressive of human lineage, from roots
incomprehensible, diverging outward to myriad
points, each to bud and leaf and fall,
a fire behind them rising beyond the snaking
Choctawhatchee, swinging its head toward the Gulf,
its flowing the whispered hiss of wind in branches,
his blood infused in the current, making the earth
and all things living radiate translated flames.

He burned for the exultation of joy, aching
for soft embraces, purity of glimpsed crinolines,
devout endearments, perfumed tresses, lips
to kiss. Desire rose to bursting, breaking.
He gasped at stars, and the fit passing, his back
fell soft against the barn's unfinished boards.
Duke the ox breathed out a bellows sigh.
Sweet hay, ox stink shifted in the stall as he dreamed
historical meadows, the cow's scent, the urge.
A hunk of darkness, crow shaped, launched into air,
the rhythmic, brittle beat of tapering laughter.
He took a stout oak branch, ice crusted, beat
a stone, showering hoar frost, unsheathed his camp knife,
and pared the soggy bark, piling the dry
shavings, whistling in pleasure's aftermath.
He struck two stones at the tinder. His breath touched off
a yellow blossom, growing in leafy effulgence
as if he held a live coal to his lips.
He added kindling and fuel, stoked a blaze,
then crushed the flames with a syrup kettle and filled it
with water. That vessel arranged, he boiled some coffee
in a small pot and heard his mother stirring
about in the kitchen. The woods were wet and shadowy,
his childhood happy inside those forest annals.
This was peace. His mind was giving him lessons
in relishing peace. Now from the dark and fracturing
cold came frost crunch and brogan scuffles.
Dean's voice struck him first, shrill and insistent.

"The Yankees want us subdued. It's slavery!"

"Dean,

we got slavery, and slavery it ain't. The whole
damn thing could have used a little patience"—

                                                       "But Carl,
you know that's not what I mean to say. I'll say
tyranny, then. It's tyranny straight up and down." —

"But the silk hankies and gold fobs have led
the ways to parting, and now we're at blows, and Southrons
is gwine to carry their truck alone, and they's going
to be hell and thunder and lightning to a mint julep,"
and Carl scuffing his words like a man stepping
in shucks, Garland chuckling at his irked tone,
common to those conversing with Dean Wallop,
hawk nosed Dean, whose chief joy and pastime
lay in the manufacture of contrary opinions.
Carl came, leading four men, Dean at his elbow,
tenacious.

                   "I think tyranny's a better word,"
said Edward, standing behind the two and winking
at Garland over their shoulders, setting Dean on
again like a blue jay diving a drowsy cat,
Carl, broad shouldered, thick as a stump, and Dean
thin as an August scare pole in his airy clothes.

"I just cain't see why folks in the Wiregrass don't
support the Southern cause."

                                   "I'm all for Garland,"
said Carl, shaking his hand. The others followed,
and Garland poured each man a steaming cup.

"How's things, Garland?"

                               "Fair to middling, I reckon.

Carl. Ed. Roland. Stu."
        "Garland."

"Dean."
      "How's it going, soldier?"
                  "Good."
His neighbors warmed their hands on hot coffee.

"I bet Garland's been star gazing. What you seeing
up there?"
        "Show us country boys some stars."

"There's old Draco, his tail caught in a post oak."

"The serpent is the subtlest beast of the field," said Stu.

"I hear Garland's been offering the serpent to some
of our local Eves." Garland went wide eyed
at Roland's suggestion, his abashed look intensifying
the mirth.
        "Garland Cain, whose petticoat you chasing?"

"They ain't no pretty girls to study me.
What woman worth having wants a man dirt poor
and covered in dirt?"
           "You can always take a bath,"
Edward said, "for a space of incorruption
till your next good sweat."
           "Garland's too dirty," scoffed Roland,
"too much busting sod like the first Adam."
Garland stoked the fire, and the sparks flew up.

They watched them swirl and die on the updraft, the heat
warping mythical anatomies in the fixed stars.

"Look long," said Stu. "They ain't no celestial bodies.
The longer you look, the more the dark contends."

"Lordy Stu," said Dean, "you best not let
the preacher hear you saying blasphemy or he'll be
speaking to yore momma again."
                                        "Can you believe
that streaked-neck Baptist going behind my back
to my mother? Like I's some clod hopping farm boy, wet
behind the ears. To be a man of God,
he sholey covets the tall hog's spot at the trough."

"Looking at him, I'd say he getting hit
with the slop oftener than not," Roland chuckled.

"Garland, you studying God at East Alabama?"

"The Lord's too much of a lesson for me to get up.
It was my aim to study agriculture,
before, you know…" Just then approaching footsteps
on the path, a handsome mulatto appeared, short
and broad in the shoulders, the hair about his temples
starting to tarnish like sudden withering frost
on resurrection fern. His name was Levi,
and he was loaned from a large plantation interest
fifteen miles up county every autumn
to help the Cains and their neighbors kill and cure
their winter pork. His owner, Mister Pinkerton,

had been a friend of Garland's father, Patrick,
who died July thirtieth, two summers ago.

"Massuhs," the slave said, smiling, his eyes trailing
along their brogans.
                              "Good to see you, Levi,"
said Garland. "Help yourself to some coffee and biscuits."

"Be right smart if I do say, and I thank you."
The man unwrapped a biscuit from the flour sack
and took the cup of coffee offered him.
He was middle aged, not as old in years
as appearance, having worked his age on lugging sacks
of black belt cotton.
                              "How you doing, Levi?"

"I'se 'bout two to the hill, and how you is,
Massuh Stu?"
                              "I allow I'm fair to middlin.
Shore is nice of Mister Pinkerton to let
you come and help us out."
                              "Yassuh, massuh
is a goot man, a rat goot Chrustian man."

"We best stop giving tongue and work," said Carl.
Now Garland brought around the first porker
from the muddy sty of a dozen piney woods rooters,
the pig quick trotting with squeals and honks, guided
by a rod of oak switch big as Garland's finger,
which he used, come to the killing ground, to scratch
its mud caked shoulders, stroking the bristly hide,

so the watchful, quivering hog exhaled a satisfied
hoink, closing his heavy eyes. The men,
moving and speaking softly so not to get up
his fear and stir his blood, flipped a coin
to see who'd deal the first blow of the slaughter.
Stu won the tosses, hefted the long handled mallet,
stood a bit to the side of the pale white hog,
and stretching his arms high, he brought the hammer
down in a swift arc on the pig's brow,
dead between the eyes, so the braincase popped,
and the sound told the swing was good, the hog
collapsing onto knees, rolling over, legs quivering.
Carl stepped up, slipping a knife deftly
between the back of the jawbone and the left ear,
severing the jugular, and when he drew out the blade,
the wound gushed, spurting in pulse time
as the heart slowed and stilled. Edward split
the back legs, pulled the hock strings out, and he
and Carl threaded the heels on a gammlin stick
as chickens waddle-ran to peck the spattered
gore, clucking and squawking. When the flow ceased,
Levi touched three fingers quick to the water,
and finding it right, nodded, so Stu and Carl
lifted the splayed hog by the stick and lowered
him in, water displacing to the brim, the boiling
slowing down almost to a stop. The work
was Levi's now, he giving his whole attention
to the great carcass in the pot and tossing in busted
pieces of pine resin knot. The men stood back
and admired his skill.
                          "We'uns gots to git

him hot jess so. If'n we don't, dem bristles
be setting in dat hog's hide, and we be scrapin
all de day and de night too." At last
he gave the sign and they hoisted the pig, heaving
the pouring corpse steaming into frigid air
to a flat stone. Levi straddled the pig,
and taking a knife, he commenced scraping the loosened
bristles out of the pinkish hide. His hands
knew the work, the turning knife blade flashed,
crossing, recrossing, but never touching a patch
already scraped and leaving everything clean.
The slackened hog jowl quivered under the knife,
gathering and going taut with each quick stroke.
He wondered about the dead scattering fields
from Shiloh to Malvern Hill. Were men different
than slaughtered animals? Did they exist somewhere?
Had their mauled terrestrial bodies become celestial?
Now Stu and Edward lifted the gammlin stick
and hung the hog on a forked branch, its flesh
pristine as a newborn's. Then Levi took a knife,
worked it deep in the hog's belly at the groin
and slid it down in one swift motion, all
the way to the chin, opening the swaying carcass.
Two quick strokes with a hatchet split the breast bone.
He tied off the anus, removed the bladder, tossing
the toy to Henry, a cousin of Garland's, just
arrived with Lila Belle, his mother's sister.
Levi grasped a clear tissue, hauled down
hard, and the compact guts slid out, slapping
a coiled rhythm in a number three washtub. He divided
livers and lites, sweet breads and tangled chitterlings.

Garland brought the cistern bucket, lifting
it over his head with muscular arms, the workers
looking up from several tasks, admiring
his strength as he tipped the long unwieldy bucket,
pouring water and cleansing the carcass gore,
running with crimson stain, then coming clear.
Now he positioned himself behind the pig,
hefted an axe, rocked back on his right foot,
feeling the swing's pleasure, muscle shifting
on muscle, cleaving the backbone away from the butt,
careful to trim as close to the spine as he could,
cutting along the joints of the meaty chine.
Then he and Levi propped the stick on their shoulders,
toting the sides to a wagon bed where they blocked
the meat with butcher knives. Even as a boy,
he'd always enjoyed watching Levi work.
The slave was ten years older but just as strong,
his eyes tainted yellow but his teeth still good.

"I declare, Massuh Garland. These hams is gwine to be smart
as any Massuh Patrick ever did."
The skin of the servant's hands was a cured leather,
the rising suns in the nails, rosy and slick.
Levi was the only Negro of Garland's acquaintance,
and now that he was grown he found himself curious
about Levi, realizing for the first time what a mystery
the servant was.
                    "Levi, how old are you?"

"Don't rightly know, young massuh. They says I'se born
on Easter Sunday, if'n you can cipher hit out."

Garland could almost envy the man, could almost
believe the South was right on slavery, believe
what preachers preached, what the Bible said, and yet,
interdicting such formidable persuasions was a lingering
impression, a hilum cicatrix on the curved seed
of his brain. Summers his father always hired
Levi to tend the fodder corn, and once
Garland, age seven, was sent out to work with him,
and Levi was hoeing, leading down the row,
Garland moping along pulling the suckers.
The field was swirling hot, so Levi stripped
to the waist, tossing his soaked shirt on top
of new stalks half leg high, and Garland saw them,
cross hatched over the Negro's rippling back,
large raised scars, pale as glow worm bodies,
obscene marring of his ebony skin. He stood
in the whispering nave of corn, in cool soil,
confounded. Levi was twenty feet ahead
before he noticed the boy, standing stricken,
silent. He smiled, showing his large white teeth,
face streaming sweat, leaning on the hoe handle,
his black arms lithe and muscular, the scars turned
away from Garland's eyes. "Hyar, young massuh,
I's gwine to be in Selma fo you ketch up."
Then his smile faded into understanding.
Levi approached him, Garland retreating a step,
his eyes fixed in Levi's gaze, which expression
he could not read, fear welled up, the urge
to bolt, but Levi knelt in the row, placed
his hands on the boy's shoulders with a gentle touch
and searched his eyes for a moment before he spoke,

"Nobody ever toll you how they beat us?
Hit's what a nigger gits fo running, running
to be free, like you is free." Garland was struck,
incredulous as Balaam. These were the only words
he'd ever heard Levi say that carried heat,
emotion, and the reminiscence trembled his mind
in tectonic shock of recognition of the great
pantomime, the slave's ridiculous grinning mask.
He looked at Levi again. Of course he possessed
a greater self-knowledge than he was letting on,
and what is a man without the freedom to speak
the truth about himself to other men?
But then he was only an ignorant boy. He bent
back over the row, pulling another sucker,
the crisp snap, the cool red earth on his feet,
lash of sun biting his shoulders, aware
of Levi, his eyes on him still, until the rhythmic
scuffing of the hoe resumed, Garland aware
of a question arising, moving in him and through him
unbidden, *Why would people be mean to Levi?*
His anguish stunned him, pierced him through, on account
of childish self consciousness. Because a bad person
had treated Levi with cruelty, he felt that cruelty
perpetrated on his own person, and anguish mounted
to outrage, and his soul took in that refuge emotion
and secreted that hurt away. And now he knew
what he could not know then; when he raised up,
he witnessed empty sunlight, an ordinary garden.
Stu and Dean joined them around the wagon,
butchering the blocked meat, first trimming fat
for the big wash kettle, carving out hams, butts,

the middlings, shoulders, ribs, the side meat and roasts.
Already another hog was hoisted up,
and Levi and Garland went to take the chine.
The oak limb mallet was poised in Carl's hands,
cracking another hog's skull and driving him down
to knees, mouth stretched in a faint fading squeal
as his hooves kicked and trembled in death's agony.
"Git ready wit cho axe, Massuh Garland,"
said Levi, taking handfuls of leaf fat trimmings
and dropping them in the kettle's roiling oil,
where cracklings rose and sputtered in rendered lard.
Levi kicked some glowing sticks from the fire.
"Yassuh. Hit's looking nice."
                              "Levi, help
yourself to cracklings," said Carl. The Negro reached
to the large, cloth lined platter where they lay,
golden-hued and bubbly, draining fat.

"Thanky suh. Don't mind if'n I do."
When Garland had severed another chine, his mother
appeared on the stoop, tall and wiry in cotton
smock and blood stained apron. She carried a steaming
bowl of brains and eggs, balanced atop
a stack of plates, a passel of forks in her hand.
Stu said,
            "Missus Cain, won't you join us?"

"Mr. Harris, a Christian cannot stand by
and hear the bodacious lies I know you men
are telling. Just don't you be telling any,
Garland." She reached to his face and put her fingers

20

lightly on his cheek and the unexpected gesture
touched them all and all of them looked away.

"*I'm* another young Washington, Mother. I never
tell a lie." Everyone laughed and protested.

"Besides, Stu," she said, serious now,
"I've got to tear and sew the sausage sacks."
Garland let the other men help themselves
and took a heaping plate of eggs and brains
to Levi, sitting astride his third hog,
whetting a knife blade back and forth on the hide.
His whole countenance quickened, seeing the food.
He wiped the scale and bristles from his hands, leaving
dirty streaks on dirty trousers and taking
the plate said,
                    "Pow'ful thanks, young massuh," his fingers
searching first through the egg for hunks of brain.
He ate all greedily, running his fingertips
around the empty plate and sucking off
from them last bits of egg and sweet grease.
The women arrived, having finished their morning chores,
Patricia, Beth Anne and Merle. They assumed the blocking,
prepared the smokehouse, filling the saltbox bottom,
splitting oak kindling in a pile for fuel, sweeping
the floor, and making skipper rub with pepper
and molasses. His cousins, Mary and May, raced past
screaming, vanquished by Henry, wielding his pig bladder.
Their shrieks put an edge on winter air and carried
around the house, pursued by Henry's laughter.
He chuckled, picked up a bucket of innards and one

of hooves. On the stoop, he heard the women singing,
as was their custom, corn songs or brush arbor hymns,
their voices a flock of finches, combining and swerving.

Some glad morning when this life is over
I'll fly away. To a land where joy
shall never end. I'll fly away.

He set the innards by the kitchen hearth. Nestled
in embers, three Dutch ovens boiled a hog's head
each, grinning pearl-eyed through bubbles,
ears waving. His mother would grind the head and cheek meat
with pepper and sage, press them in a stone crock,
to make exquisite head cheese, delightful morsels
suspended in jelly, quivering as he sliced a helping.
He stared at the heads submerged in boiling water.
He wouldn't get to taste a bite. Not this year.
A big stew bubbled on the hook with melts, sweetbreads
and hearts. The savory aroma wafting into the yard,
twisting the guts of working men in knots.
He thought with rue of the bread and dried beef
he'd eaten for two months now at the Rebel camp.
At the kitchen bench, his mother tore sausage sacks,
and Merle fed a grinder with shoulder meat
and fat, and Sarah and Hattie, their faces lovely,
poised between childhood beauty and a young woman's
first pristine flowering, stood over bowls,
their small hands kneading the ground pork, mixing
in allspice, sage, fennel, and hot red pepper
in even batches to get the seasoning right,
these recipes passed from mother to daughter for nigh

a hundred years. Farther, at the dining table,
Beth Anne turned the sausage grinder with strong
arms, laughing with Mary and May, who held
the filling sacks and twisted them into links.
Seeing Garland, she stopped her work.
                                    "Let's get
these hooves in the other hearth," she said, wiping
grease from her hands on a rag tucked in her belt
and following. She was a sturdy Alabama farm girl,
with sensuous breasts and muscular haunches, like a prize
mare, her countenance full of joyful mischief.
I bet she can go like a calf licking yeller jackets.
At twenty-two she was a widow, her husband
drowning a year ago, and when she had learned
of Garland's conscription, she had begun to express
an interest in him in terms which were not subtle.
Before he'd left the first time for Camp Watts,
he'd been so blue he hadn't responded to her.
For the last two months, he'd regretted it every day.
"I'll hold the bucket, Garland. You set the hooves
in the fire." He felt his face go crimson. She smiled,
her eyes intent on his, she gripping the bucket
in straightened arms so that her breasts, bound
in homespun, strained the buttons in their buttonholes.
He thought they might pop off and reached in the bucket
below her waist, taking handfuls of bloody
trotters, inserting each stump hoof first into coals,
his face by turns scorched with throbbing embers,
then by smoldering ardor in Beth Anne's eyes.
She whispered, "Come see me tomorrow to say goodbye,
I'll give you a jar of wild cherry preserves."

He glanced at the kitchen, aware the women had fallen
silent.

     "Thank you, Beth Anne." He took the bucket,
sloshing its lees of blood and held it before him,
catching a snigger or two as he passed the women.
He stood on the back stoop. Tomorrow morning
he'd visit her, robust and winsome, her skin immaculate,
her eyes a greening motion in pine top breezes.
After her husband passed, she'd managed her farm,
performing some work herself, hiring others
to do what she could not and always paying
the men who came to help from neighborly regard.
In a year she'd earned a profit and wide respect.
Yes, he'd pay her a visit, and if he survived
the war, well, Beth Anne was a likely woman
for a man to hitch his wagon to, and the thought
of marriage eased his scruples, vexed by proprieties.
He sat to whittle a spit, and Henry came
and joined him, watching him handle his knife as the point
took shape and shavings curled away from the bevel.
"You fair to middling, Henry?"

                   "I reckon I am."

Henry's face was almost perfectly round,
his eyes brown as slash pine, his ears protruding
from his head like little wings, just like his daddy's.
"Garland?"

     "Yes."

       "Momma and daddy says
you going off to fight in the war."

                   "I am."

"I'd be scairt. Air you scairt, Unc?"
                                "I guess
I'd be a fool not to be scared a little."

"My daddy is afraid you might git kilt, but momma,
she says God is gonna watch after you.
Will God do hit, Uncle? I don't want
you to die." His voice broke, his eyes clouding
with tears. He gathered Henry up in his lap.

"Henry, I think the Lord takes care of us
whether we live or die."
                        "But I don't want
you to go. Why don't you just stay home, stay here
with me and Aunty Cain?"
                        "I would if I could,
Henry. But the government says I have to go."
He set the boy down, turned him around and faced him,
freeing his pocket knife from where he'd stood
it up in the stoop planking and folding the blade.
"Henry, I need a favor while I'm away.
Will you oblige me?"
                    "Awe Unc, you know I will."

"Take care of my pocket knife while I'm off sojering.
Keep it oiled and the blade sharp on a good
whetstone."
            "Uncle Garland, do you really mean it?"

"Sure Henry. You can tell your friends your uncle
is a Rebel sojer fighting in the war. But Henry,

you've got to promise me you'll tell your ma
and pa I give the knife to you and ask
their permission to tote it around."

        "Awe, Garland,
do I have to let them know about it?"

        "Yes,
Henry. If we want God to provide for us,
we must do as he says, and he says we should respect
our parents."

    "Yes sir." The trial of virtue raged
in the boy's mind, but the knife's weight in his hand
and the beautiful antler scales dyed red brought
him round to boyish happiness. "Thanks, Unc,"
he said and trotted off to employ his gift
before he should have to make the required disclosure.
He smiled at the boy, watching him go, and thought
how pleasant life would be raising a chit
like Henry, but wearing the look of his father's face
and his and a hint of Beth Anne's. Carl climbed
the stoop, crouched beside him and surveyed the yard
for a moment.

    "Garland, they's something I need to tell you.
Every year when Levi scrapes his last
hog and has our work nigh under way,
your dad would give him a dollar for helping out
and let him have the afternoon free, to walk
the seven miles to Brady's Farm up there
on Lick Creek. He got him a Negra gal
up there he fancies. Your father also let him
take a ham as a little present to give her."

"Do you know his woman's name?"

                                    "I think it's Myra."
Levi knelt at the well curb, cleaning knives.

"You get the meat, I'll give Levi his money."
He had the dollar on him. For years he'd watched
his father take the money from his bureau. Till now
he hadn't known what for. The discovery pleased him,
made him a little envious, knowing Levi
enjoyed a woman's consolations. He noted
his walking papers and put him out on the road
from Beat 14. "Thank you for helping us, Levi."
But the slave did not reply, and Garland was startled
to find him looking, holding his gaze like a man,
not like a servant, causing the ghost of noon
sun to bear down on his neck, the memory
of surging fear and earth cool on his soles.

"They says you gwine off to fight, young Mars?"

"Yes, Levi."
            "Young Mars always good
to old Levi. Levi will pray to the Lord
to keep the young Mars in his strong protection."
Garland's throat went parched and dog days dry.

"Thank you. I'm obliged."

                          "Goodbye, massuh."
On impulse, he offered his hand. The servant took it.

"Good bye, Levi. God Bless you." Levi turned

and Garland stood for a long time watching him walk
between the pine tree columns lining the road,
his bare feet flashing pale above the dust.
Now the neighbors set up saw horse tables,
draped with clean, white cloths. Riley Chiles
arrived as if on cue, in shabby suit,
his ham sized hand clutching a black Bible.
If one stood back from him a little ways,
he might discern, buried under corpulence,
the limned suggestion of a young man's musculature,
who buckled hames and choke straps and held traces
before the sun and handled an ax till dark.
But years of poundings, dinners on the ground, and supper
in every parish matron's home with chickens
to fry or hams to boil had so compounded
his flesh, the mass of it could find no purchase
on the scant circumference of his whippet frame, so sagged,
dropsical, cheek and jowl, arms and belly,
always a portion of pendulous flesh was swaying.
The women set out skillets of crackling bread,
barbecued ribs, fried chicken, pork chops, butter beans,
fresh milk warm from the cow and hot coffee,
cathead biscuits, a mess of steaming poke salad
seasoned with fat back, bowls of candied yams
and mashed potatoes, dotted with pools of butter,
red eye gravy for meat, sawmill gravy
for bread, boiled and fried okra, sweet
potato pie, pecan pie, and blackberry cobbler,
fried apple pies, like quarter moons, the round sides
tracked with fork tines. Now the men were seated,
the women standing behind like sentinels, to hear

the grace and serve them after. Garland's mother
stood behind him, her hands resting on his shoulders,
which made him feel the other men were watching,
and they were, as Brother Chiles was shown to the seat
at the table's head, his father's seat, and everyone
bowed his head. The preacher said,

                        "Let us pray.
Dear Lord, for what we are about to receive,
make us thankful, make us thankful for a table
of bounty, set before us in the presence of our enemies.
Defend and lead our president and our armies, imbue them
with holy might, O Lord, that the children of earth
may see as of old, two nations born of a single
womb and two manner of people, the elder to serve
the younger. For those who have put their trust in you
rejoice, for the righteous thou wilt bless, O Lord,
and compass them as with a shield, Amen."
And everyone seated at table responded,

                        "Amen."
The neighbors helped themselves, passing bowls
and plates and baskets of bread. The preacher spooned
a dollop of mashed potatoes and looked about.

"Garland, I hear you're doing your Christian duty
in service for your country. When do you leave us, son?"

"I been at Camp Watts up in Notasulga
training for the past two months. They give me a furlough
to come back home and kill the hogs for momma.
I return to my unit tomorrow." The preacher shoveled
some butter beans and bit a piece of crackling.

"May God go with you, son. If he fights for us,
no power can prevail against us. Remember that."
Stu said,
              "I read where the Reverend Beecher says
the institution of slavery is incompatible
with the spirit of the Bible." The words were a fuse hizzing
to the packed keg of the preacher's convulsed belly.

"Aughw now, there we have the Yankees!" The preacher
sprayed chewed bits and shook his finger. "The spirit
of the Bible indeed! Let them read the words
of the Bible, sir. When a man forsakes the words
of the Holy Bible, he makes a god of opinion.
Let arrogant Yankees speak for God up north,
but let the Southern man attend to the Word.
If God sees fit to place the Negro in our charge,
our duty lies in the execution of that charge."
He gruffed another aftershock from his maw.
"Yankees got all them public schools and all
that education and nary a one will read
the Bible or the Constitution of the United *States*."

"Amen to that, Brother Chiles, amen to that,"
said Stu, nodding to all around the table,
but Carl was solemn.
                    "I don't allow I know
what God is thinking, but I wish the South had given
a sight more time to pondering. I worry, what
with New Orleans is fallen, Federal troops
lodged in north Mississippi and Alabama,
and General Grant—he's a determined man—

coming south, and it don't take no genius
to guess where he is headed, to do the job
that Halleck should have done last summer and open
the Mississippi River. And when he does,
then we'll be cut in half and then we'll howl."

"Terrible what they did to the people in Athens,"
said Dean, "and them's the folks up yonder what's on
their side. Just shows it ain't no government to tie to."

"Terrible things is always done in wars."

"That happened to our own, Ed," said Merle.
                                        "That's right,"
agreed Patricia, "The Yankees are a godless lot.
If they fighting for Negroes, why do they rape their women?"
Brother Chiles grumphed,
                        "Yankees is godless fo sho."
Beth Anne winked at Carl, funning him.

"Mister Johnson, he's a repentant Rebel,
but Garland's gonna teach them Yankees Gospel."

"I fear I was never borned again in the first place.
And I ain't sure the Southern people are ready
to fight the kind of war it's going to take
to win. I think a lot of folks have sworn
their solemn oath to Dixie from the teeth out."

"Dark days for our young republic," the preacher said,
sucking meat from the knob of a chicken leg.

"But we will lift our eyes to the hills from whence
our help cometh. The Yankee is no fighter.
Without his ironclad ships and machines, what is he?
A Johnnie Reb will whip him every time.
Could you pass that bowl of snap peas this way, Carl?"
He felt a movement behind him, saw his mother
stepping toward the house, hunched forward, shoulders
heaving. Merle went bustling to comfort her.
With Mrs. Cain out of earshot, Carl muttered,

"Yes, but Yankee's got a lot of both."
He recalled how many times that day she'd touched him.
Fire plunged his throat and garroting fear.
The thought of dying troubled his mind but worse
was imagining his mother alone. The prospect confounded
him with shame. But why? He was being forced
to go. Conscription had reached him at last, coming
in the person of an aged officer in trig butternut
with a German goatee and eyes that begged forgiveness.
His meat turned dry and sour on his tongue. He excused
himself to fill two jorums with water for his guests.

"I'll help," said Stu, following him to the well curb.
"Say bud, you know how the Baptist preacher retrieved
his greasy chicken leg what slipped his fingers
and fell straight through the jake's hole?" He shook his head.
"He lowered his false teeth down on a piece of twine,
and they bit that chicken bone like they's alive."
His eyes danced. He slapped Garland on the back.
"Don't let the old fool bother you, son. He ain't

speaking for God. He speaks for Mister Pinkerton,
who gave him the screw to build his brand new parsonage."

"Oh it's not him. It's leaving momma, mostly."
He regretted the words as soon as they left his mouth.

"I'll watch out for her, Garland. I give my word.
You let your mind rest easy spang on that score.
They's no pains I won't take for her, no pains."
He regarded Stu, who was staring off at his house.
He knew his mother was young enough to remarry,
but sorrow darkened his heart to imagine her
with a man who was in any way less than his father.

Carl had worked the hardest and stayed the latest,
helping him stow the tables in the barn, wash away
blood pools, clean and whet the knives, and pack
the salt box with scrap trimmings. They knelt in the smokehouse,
striking a fire, and banked it to waft its smoke
around the hanging racks of hams, bound
in croaker sacks and swabbed with skipper rub.
Their muscles slackened, weariness came on sudden.
Carl produced a demijohn and looked at him
across the embers' pulsing glow, his own face
losing its lines and furrows in the scanty light.
He twisted a few quick mouse squeaks out of the cork.

"Your father and me, we always finished this day
with a little taste of red eye. Patrick was my good
friend, Garland. I miss him powerful, but as sad
as that is, it's just as much a pleasure to offer

a drink to his son."

"Thank you, Mr. Johnson."

"He'd say, *Ain't nothing like a swig of bust head*
after you've worked all day like two peckered dog,
and by the way, it's time you called me Carl.
You not a boy any more, Garland, and you going
to a place where only men are called. I know,
I been there." Garland took a pull and felt
the whiskey kick against the bottom of his eyes
then canter out to pasture in his middling parts.
He sputtered a bit and handed the demijohn back
to Carl, who took a pull without the slightest
change of expression.

"What's it like?"

"Hell.

That ain't original, but hit comes nearest the mark.
I had my fill of Mexico and Diamondbacks
and never been so thirsty in all my life.
You going to see some hard things. You got
to keep yourself collected, keep yourself calm."
The embers turned. His mind turned with the whiskey.
"That war we fought with Mexico was a great injustice.
You know that?"

"No."

"Our President Polk used it
to gobble up a passel of western land,
land where Mexicans were living and dying for ages.
And I'll tell you now, I don't think much of this war.
Governor Moore—what a piece of work.

34

He should have let us vote."
                                    "Do you think we can win?"

"The South can't win. We can only wear 'em down.
And I pray God we do, 'cause there'll be hell
and high water if we are conquered." The two fell
quiet in the smolder glowing.
                            "Carl, do you think
I'm doing right by going?"
                            "I'm sure y'are, son.
The Yankees are here amongst us, and they got to be
invited to leave, and what else could you do?
Join the Federal Army and kill your neighbors,
friends, and family?" He stared at mesmeric embers.
"I'm going to give some unasked-for advice."

"No—I want advice, I'd be obliged."

"Heroes are found in stories, poems, and graves.
Don't let your blood get up to do no foolishness."
Smoke writhed upward in a twisting djinn ecstasy,
layered around the hanging shanks and hams,
macabre ornaments to postpone want. The notion
of war was suddenly absurd. He suppressed a giggle.
Then Carl regarded him the way his father
used to, with quiet pride, paternal admiration.
"Garland, your life was the aim of your father's life.
All the sweat that he had spent to wrestle
order from this crowded wilderness, to keep the brier
off the fencepost, cow bloat out'en the field,
what would his life amount to, losing yours,

losing his son to carry on his work?
The peril we face has spurred a lot of men
to make great sacrifices; such ain't for you.
Your duty's to go and survive and come back home.
Surviving ain't easy because the sort I mean
means a lot more than just not getting killed."
He chuckled. "Carl Johnson making speeches.
Like he thought he had a lick of sense." He offered
the jar to him then thumbed the cork back in.
"Always loosens my tongue more than's good.
It's late, old Garland. I ought to mosey home."

"Saddle up Dash—he needs a walk."
                                        "I'm obliged.
Tomorrow when you heading out for Notasulga,
stop off and say goodbye."
                                        "I'll see I do."
Hearing Carl ride off, he walked outside,
his mind in a euphoric whiskey drift, his first time
drunk, regarding the cabin, dog trot like a weary
yawn, the cistern, the well pump's handle poised
and cock's comb scarlet, pens and troughs and roosts,
the barn's rooftree, swayed like a mule's back, all
evoking goodness. Even the burial plot
suggested a certain permanence, a building on the work
of fathers and mothers, as Carl had said. A fear
stabbed him—the chance his bones might never lie
in earth he owned. He'd read about Shiloh, Sharpsburg,
open pits of flung and rotting corpses.
Where was the glory there? Glory was stock
and trade to boys at camp, but Carl had mocked

the notion wholesale—heroes in stories, poems,
and graves. He shuddered, raked by a crest of bitter
wind. He walked beyond the barn to a rise
of ground, considered the scattered Milky Way,
a dusty cow path cutting the cosmos in two.
There the Northern Cross, a sign post or sword,
shimmering from a black lake's silty bottom, Aquila
with wings thrown open wide, and Pegasus midstride
in flight above the road. He thought of summer
when the starry way would run from north to south,
how all the houses of light would swing around.
Then from the northern sky Ophiuchus will come
brandishing the serpent toward Boötes, a fanged
whip, a poisoned cudgel. His father had taught him
a passion for names, trees and birds and stars,
how they turn and change from season to season.
His father had never taught him how to fight,
but he'd been learning that at camp. So far,
it all seemed harmless; for two months now he'd drilled,
tramping to and fro on a field of hay,
a pine stick propped on his shoulder, and once or twice
the absurdity delivered him fits of suppressed mirth.
Tomorrow a three day walk to Notasulga,
so he could get more practice walking. He yawned.
His body was tired, his mind fatigued from all
the apprehensions of leaving home. Though always
along with the dread, there was a tickle, a whisper
of interest to get away and see the world,
but then the news of battles, the Seven Days,
Malvern Hill, the bodies of young Americans,
tangled limb for limb in pits. Enough.

He had to sleep. When he passed the barn, Duke
snorted and exhaled, dreaming summer meadows,
the joy of mounting, lovely drudgery of rows.
He entered the house with care should his mother be
in bed, sat in his father's chair, staring
at soporific embers and the darned toe
of his sock. A delicate treading, he turned to find
his mother standing in her gown, holding a parcel
wrapped in brown paper and a bow, tied
with purple ribbon. She smiled her grief and handed
him the gift.
          "Momma. I told you not to.
That coat, I know, cost a fortune and now another
present?"
          "Don't fuss at me. Besides, I may
as well spend my money before it's completely worthless.
So cease your grousing and open your gift." He tore
away the ribbon and butcher paper to reveal
green covers of a cloth-bound volume, the title stamped
in gold, *Southern Botany*.
          "Oh Momma, it's wonderful."
He stood and put his arms around her. "Thank you."
She buried her face in his shoulder a long moment.
They sat in silence and when speech came, they spoke
of trivial matters with familiar words, evoking
memory's architectural powers, so the heart
can span its recollections from days to come
formidable in loneliness, creating certainty that where
today there is the void of absence, yesterday
there was affection, true to its promise and somehow
thriving still. During the weeks before

his first departure, stories tumbled out of her,
of her family and his father, many of him as a child,
and now, the last goodbye at hand, it seemed
to him his mother was being overburdened,
not by grief or dearth of things to say,
but the need to express a heart too crowded with love.
"I don't want you to worry about me, Momma."
She gave a high pitched laugh that startled him.

"A mother who doesn't worry is not a mother."
Her face was weighed with care, her eyes aggrieved.
For the first time ever, his mother looked old to him.
"I'm tired. I'd best to bed." She gripped both arms
of the chair to rise, the way her mother did.

"Good night, Momma. I love you."
                              "Good night, son.
I love you too. And Garland"—
                              "Yes, Momma?"

"Don't you ever forget it, no matter what."
She hugged him again and held him a long time.

"I won't forget it, Momma." She smiled and retired.
He thought that smile the saddest look he'd ever
seen on a woman's face. He whispered to the ash
embers, "I feel like a bully with a glass eye."

October 11, 1862

Dawn light's beveled edge wedging eyelids,
perhaps the last Eufaula dawn he would ever
see, the window forming in his vision, cross frames
parceling tangled frost flowers. A recollection
touched his mind, he shaded from roiling summer
by a gate of luxuriant honeysuckle, his cousin
Emily teaching him to milk nectar
from a flower's ivory horn. She pinched the calyx,
pulled the pistil through, and gathered clinging
to the stigma hung the clearest pearl of light.
She placed the drop on his tongue, and when he closed
his eyes in abandoned relish, she pressed her lips
to his. That sweetness slackened his knees, troubled
his sleep for many nights since. He'd only kissed
one other girl, Mary, in a dogwood grove
after a dinner on the grounds. Her lips were soft
and warm, but he'd imbibed no blossom wine.
Beth Anne was a rare vintage indeed. The prospect
of visiting her stirred his blood, blunting insinuating
fears of coming dangers. He pulled his clothes on
quick in cold, shrugged into his frock coat, shouldered
knap sack, and glanced about. In the sitting room
the clock ticked, the sun slanted level in the window,
the shaft revealing writhing motes, a poignant
emptiness.
      "Momma." Silence. When he stepped outside,
she was there, gathered with neighbors and family, Ester,
his mother's friend, with a son in Bragg's army camped
at Murphreesboro, Aunt Mary and Uncle George,

standing holding hands and several members
from the Baptist church. His mother stood in front
of the little group, all of them working up smiles.
"Y'all forgot the band but not the pretty girls."
The women laughed and chided, the men stared
at their boots. He went to each of them, shaking hands,
receiving murmured "good lucks" and "God blesses,"
then hugged the women, first his grandma Cain.
Renowned for austerity, she'd always frightened him;
her austerity vanished, she frightened him all the more.
She was pale, seemed almost undone as she took his face
in her hands, stroking his cheeks with leathery thumbs.
He knew she saw her son's face in his as she spoke,

He that dwelleth in the secret place
of the most High shall abide
under the shadow of the almighty.

I will say of the Lord, He
is my refuge and my fortress, my God,
in Him will I trust. Surely He
shall deliver me from the snare of the fowler. . . .

Her voice weakened and ceased. She reached behind her,
accepted a proffered hand, which bore her back
to the comfort of those staying home, standing now
in tableau with dooryard, house, and fences. His mother
grasped his coat lapels and pulled herself close.

"I loved you, Garland, from the moment you were born,
and you are not obliged to me for aught.

I cannot ask any more of God, being blessed
so much, and if He require you back," her speech
was measured with weeping, "it is a debt I owe,
but it is hard. Oh Garland, I fear too hard.
Be careful, Garland. Promise me you will."

"I will, Momma," he said in an idiot stammer.
He'd thought up brave and eloquent things to say,
but now their stupidity made him burn with shame.
Now everyone made a circle, joining hands,
and Tom Harkness, the Baptist Deacon, prayed.

"Our Father, we come before you today, begging
mercy and forgiveness for foolish deeds men do,
despite of your son's sacrifice and command to love.
We ask you, Lord, to be with Garland Cain,
and shelter him from the wiles that harm men's souls.
And if it be your will, then bring him home
again, where he is loved and wished for by family
and friends. All this we ask for the Lord in the name
of your beloved son our savior Jesus Christ."
The women wept, and helpless and small, he wanted
escape from all this overwhelming love.

"I thank all y'all. I'll always remember your kindness."
He turned and faced the road away from home,
but he had not gone far when a wailing broke
behind him, fierce, blind, indignant keening
of a creature hurt beyond its will to endure.
He turned, the men were restraining her, hair wild,
mouth stretched round in her altered face, and terror

stabbed him sickle cold, and before he knew
what or could command himself he was running,
his panic high, his swift feet churning dust
in puffs blowing across the road behind him.
He did not turn again to look at the group
but ran and kept on running until exhaustion
dropped him to hands and knees, he clutching dust
as his lungs labored, desperate for freezing air.
A farmer on a cart drove past, the oxen's shoulders
plodding machine like, the codger's watery eyes
gleaming under straw brim shadow. A chaw
protruded his cheek.

              "Hankering for a ride, Sonny?"

"Thank you. I'm good." He touched his hat as he passed.
His cart was filled with pumpkins. Ripe for pies.
He shifted his sack, thought of the dried beef
and biscuit with molasses. Thought of his mother's howl,
of her alone on the farm, seed time and harvest,
how she'd fare. He saw her opened mouth,
her wail pierced his chest, its frigid agony.
Why did I not go back? The wind bulled
against him. Gratitude for the coat welled in his throat,
it might have fallen from clouds upon his shoulders.
Another pang. He'd run by the turn in the road
to Beth Anne's house. Now it was far too late
to go and see her. He cursed himself. He had longed
to have her and squandered the chance for sheer cowardice.
How could he be such an ass? And now another
goodbye confronted him. He decided he'd write
his mother, ask her to convey his excuses to Carl.

He didn't want to show him disrespect,
but this was hard, taking leave, and Carl
would understand, but when he turned the bend
where he could see the way to Carl's place,
the man was waiting on the sunlit side of the road.

"Price of seed's near 'bout doubled. We gone
be living hand to mouth 'fore too much longer."
He scraped a brogan toe in the dust, looked down
the road that Garland would take. "'Fore I forget,"
he produced a small felt bag from his overall's pocket.
"I got this together for you. Keep up with it.
I know for a fact this kit will serve you well."

"What is it?" he asked, peering inside the sack
at a small vial and a dark blue cake of something.

"Every soldier arriving at the front almost
always comes down with a bout of the flux or camp itch
or both. The glass is potassium sulfide. You mix
some fifty grains of that with a hand full of lard
and rub it on your camp itch, and four or five days,
it'll kill that little critter what's dealing you grief.
The wad is called blue mass. That's for flux.
It's a waxy base infused with mercury. You take
some two small plugs," he gestured holding his thumb
on the last joint of his pinky, "every day
until you're right again."
                                        "Thanks, Mr. Johnson.
I'm mighty obliged." He stowed the medicines away.
Carl shook his hand with a strong grip.

"Garland, be a man." The admonition
took him aback.
                    "All right. How do I do that?"

"You decide. Decide and then stick to it.
It's the sticking to it more than what the *it* is.
God bless you, Garland. Get yourself back here soon."
Eufaula to Camp Watts was a three day walk.
Every field of wiregrass, dog trot shack,
each stalk of brittle goldenrod and ruined
sumac, every bird that stayed to strive
with the Alabama winter, all were burdens.
The day was silent, winter vacant, sun
smothered to a struck match in dense cloud lowering
above the naked sweet gum and long leaf pine
hemming his course in the road. The wind was driving
head on. He shivered and buttoned his coat's top button.
His mother must have paid double what it was worth.
The blockade up and many railroads fallen
into Yankee hands, staple goods were scarce
as hen's teeth and prices rising by the day. He saw
her face once more, wild, contorted in anguish.
Later he stopped outside the town of Midway,
finding a clearing behind a screen of pines.
He chewed a hard biscuit and stared long
into flames. He rolled out a blanket, threw more fuel
on the fire, then pulled his other blanket over him.
There were no stars. The wind hissed in branches,
brushing away the fire's heat. A screech owl
trilled her tocking purr from a far off shelf
of dark, a strange clock run away with ticking.

Amorphous images of terror and suffering oppressed him,
and because they had no form, there was no help.
At last fatigue subdued his mind's writhing
nest of apprehensions with sleep's oblivion,
a weird and lonely purling vibrating dreams,
the future's black face smiling behind her veil.

October 12, 1862 Midway

He was up on his trotters already when dawn light coaxed
the hamlet of Midway from dark. He chuckled at the one horse
tied to a gallery post, passed some shops,
a boarding house, a stable, and the empty street
played out to an empty road. A mile from town,
a rider drew up, sitting a pretty bay mare
with a sprightly canter. The man began addressing
Garland's back.
          "Charles Ketchem, from Scraggins,"
he smiled, leaning out of the saddle to shake
his hand. "I wish the clouds'd move and allow
the sun to knock the chill off things. I own
a shoe factory back in town."
          "How is business?"

"I'll swany, since this war commenced, I can't
make shoes enough. I got a dozen ladies,
sewing from can till can't, six days a week.
I'm heading up to see the quartermaster
in Montgomery about another wagon load
of leather. What about you, son. Where you headed?"

"Headed to Camp Watts. I been on furlough."

"Ah, that's fine. You'll do our country proud.
If only my position did not preclude me from service
on the field of glory." The man sat rapt in a fancy
of martial attitudes, hoisting the Rebel banner,
dispatching the last beleaguered Yankee on the field.
"I reckon you'll make Union Springs by evening?"

"That's my aim."
                        "Do you know the Bateman place?"

"Never heard tell of such as I recall."

"Bateman owns a fine plantation house,
which he's made a hostelry for soldiers on army business.
You'll get fine treatment for ten dollars—here,"
he said, reaching in his pocket, "I'd be honored
if you passed the night on my largess." The crisp
Confederate bill waved in the freezing air.

"I'm obliged, but I have money. . ."
                                    "Sure you do—
but I'd be honored—The least we men of means
can do for the young brave boys who hazard all
for country and liberty," and saying that he leaned
out of the saddle and thrust the note in his pocket.

"Well, I thank you kindly, Mr. Ketchem."

"Thanks to you, for what you're going to do."

He spurred his mare and she whinnied shrilly and leapt
to her gait, pounding crescent hoof prints in the dust.
He was grateful clouds were holding back the rain,
grateful for a spate of company, even with cobbler
Ketchem, diverting him from troubles. Having spent
the last two months in a tent in Notasulga,
the thought of one more night in a cozy bed
made Ketchem seem a pretty decent fellow.
He took the first road past the depot leading
out of Union Springs, turned west at the stone
marker Ketchem described as a tombstone. The light
was dying, but three more miles brought him there.
The moon ignited clouds, the fluted columns
with Greek capitals pale behind the oaks.
He climbed the swell of ground and entered a funny
wicket gate, rickety and nothing resplendent
like the mansion, and made his way to the back door.
A Negress, her deep obsidian eyes commingled
with night, answered his knock.

                                   "May I hep you, suh?"

"Evening, Ma'am. I hear the Master of the house
will provide a room for fellows off to war?"
The woman's vision touched his coat and collar,
then concentration slipped, her sight rolled past him.
She was coal black and fat, her ponderous breasts
cinched with a belt, whiff of breath a piercing
odor of spirits. Her head fell soft on the doorjamb,
and her eyes began to close, languid as jalousies
in smithy dog days August. "Ma'am, ma'am."

"You is gwine to fight fo Mistuh Bateman."

"What? I'm fighting for the South. For home. Now look"—

"Privates," she said in a drowse, "we's all be working
fo Mistuh Bateman." She smiled an exaggerated, motherly
tenderness at an imbecile child.

       "Where *is* your master?"

"He be in Montgomery heping fix de laws."
Weariness of a day's trudge, the road in grit
and dirt around his neck enervated patience,
made him resent this fleshy obstruction, exhaling
brandy fumes, while the house breathed warmth around her.

"So are you going to let me out a room?"

"Yassuh, Mars, ten dolluh fo de night."
He gave her Ketchem's note. She beamed at him,
suddenly revived, and shoved the bill deep
inside her bosom. Had the dark not been complete,
she would have seen him blushing. She took his arm,
drew him in the foyer, took a candle from a stand.
"Dis way, Mars," she said as they mounted the stair.
He walked behind her enormous shifting backside,
whisking thigh friction, her breath short,
the candle throwing her ponderous shadow and his slender
one at comic lopsided angles on the wall.
On the second story landing, they passed a room—
he had a glimpse—servants at tasks, women,
one sprinkling the floor with water, others sweeping,

several on hands and knees scrubbing floors
with something making scratchy sounds and fragrance,
pine needles it must be. The fat slave passed the room
shouting an admonition at the door, unveiled
threat to stop their lollygagging and work,
"Heyna now, don't you be no foolish virguns.
What I tell the massuh when he get back?"
The girls had come to attention like soldiers—uncanny,
just like soldiers, standing in darkness, a breathing
sullenness, broken at last by a voice compliant
and weary with burdens bearing down generations,
exacted by institutions, hypocrisy, greed,
law and politics, even scripture's edicts;
out of this history, a voice indomitable by its very
weariness, though from which slender girl, he could not
tell, spoke from the darkness.
                                            "Yes Miss Hattie."

"You, Serrie, get down and says Hattie says
to hurry supper. Whatever will I tell massuh
'bout these sorry niggas?" She looked at him
dumbfounded by humankind's propensity for slackness.
Her authority perplexed him, yet it was real, why else
should fellow servants be tractable? "Clancy! Clan--*see!*"
her booming voice resounding. As if on cue,
a Negro appeared on the landing.
                                            "Yes Miss Hattie?"

"You lights a fire in the east bet room, Clancy."

"Yes Miss Hattie." And he disappeared into shadows.

Hattie left him in a washroom. A stove with live coals
heated water, which he poured in a basin steaming.
The air like a soft robe enfolded him. Such luxury—
a washstand and perfumed soaps and towels. What splendid
luck. He stripped and washed with vigor, dousing
his head and drying by the stove. Miles of road
settled in the basin. He admired the brass appointments,
the polished mirror, ignorant of gadroons or names
like Phyfe or Chippendale, but recognizing one thing in the rich
accoutrements, the wainscoting carved in frieze with ships
and soldiers in cuirass and greaves raising swords,
others marching in files to a city consumed
with fire, women beating their bare breasts.
In another scene, soldiers on a wall were pitching
a child from the rampart. What was his name? Astyanax.
He enjoyed school. He was sorry he'd had to leave.
In the hall, Clancy appeared and bowed, led him
to a dining room and seated him at table,
alone. From a room close by came laughter and music,
women's voices, but the spread before him was sumptuous,
the side board groaning with dishes—boiled ham, fried quail,
herrings, eggs and greens and oysters and potatoes,
fresh bread and biscuit, chicken and dumplings, corn bread,
and a tub of bottled spirits enough for a regiment.
"Would suh like a glass of Madeira?" Clancy droned.
And he, who had not the slightest clue of what
Madeira might be, guessed from the bottle's shape
it must be wine.
                          "Thank you much, Clancy."
The butler poured the lightly tinted amber
in a crystal wine glass. Garland, pushing away

a bowl of watery soup garnished with rose petals,
was conscious of any solecism he might commit,
even—especially—before the servant. He ate
slowly, taking small bites, and used his napkin
after every one. Around his plate was arrayed
an arsenal of silverware of every configuration.
He chose his implement according to its apparent capacity
to heft the desired amount of food to his mouth.
He sensed or thought he sensed Clancy's scrutiny
each time he made to select a new utensil.
By his third glass of Madeira, he turned expansive,
reminding himself this house, after all, served
as a soldier's hostelry; he could hardly be the first
yeoman at table who lacked a little polish.
"So Clancy, this war is big doings."
                                        "Yes suh."
A servant brought more cornbread, returned to the kitchen.

"Clancy, tell me, if things go your way, what
will you do?"
                "Oh suh, I's stay with Massuh Bateman."

"Why?"
        "Massuh Bateman treat me well."

"But don't you want to be free?" Clancy's aspect
altered with the question as if a roguish proselyte
had spoken ill of the god in the holy of holies.
He looked at the servant, the servant looking away,
who had been regarding him, his bald head pointed
at the crown, a gray ash dusting his tonsured hair.

He measured out his words to the kitchen door.

"Well now, if thangs falls out the way suh says,
I reckon I would be free." He allowed that thought
to settle. How many millions of Negroes must be
thinking Clancy's thoughts? Their race was showing
a steely patience.
            "But wouldn't you be tempted
to leave this house? Get yourself shut of Hattie?"
The Madeira made him highly amused with himself.
Muffled convivial laughter rose and subsided.

"Suh, old Clancy's been a butler now
these forty years, fo Massuh Bateman and his father
befo him. I's too old and gots no hankering
to plod behind no mule in the pouring sunshine."
And now he gathered his voice to keep his words
in the room— "As fo Miss Hattie, I knows how
to hitch Miss Hattie's wagon. You can bet
old Clancy do. And 'sides, Miss Hattie, she gots
them favors from Mr. Bateman what old Clancy
don't be wanting no how." Mirth lit up
his eyes, but Garland did not comprehend
and his look which did not comprehend doused
that light. Where a moment before the genuine Clancy
had stood, now stood Clancy the servant. The pantomime
had resumed. "Will suh require anything else?"

"No thank you."
            "Enjoy the rest of yo evening, suh."
He negotiated the stair, yawning and pulling himself

along by the banister, reflecting how hard it was
to get to know the Negroes. But why should Clancy
be forthcoming? A slave had obvious reasons
to dissemble, but what he'd said about plowing seemed true.
His life must be a decent one if freedom
wouldn't change it. Yes, he was glad they'd chatted.
Gaining the landing, he realized how tired he was,
how delicious sleep would be in a warmed bed.
A light from down the hall and heavy breathing,
Hattie, trundling forward, candle in hand.
Baa baa black sheep have you any wool? He sniggered.

"You be finding everthin you need in dis room,
Mars. Deuces is gwine to take care of you."
She pushed the door open, a chasm of light
obtruding between them, blunting vision, he wondering
what in the world was a Deuces. A toasty crackle
and oaky tang mingled with another scent,
faintly sweet, bunched and tangled, pendulous
flutes in dappled summer languorous afternoon.
He spread his hands to the fire. Then turning to warm
his hinder parts, he beheld a woman seated
in a chair like a burnished throne, posed with imperious
grace, a bronze seraphim, her flesh gathering
light yet supple; a regal artifice, yet breathing.
Astonishment hushed his mouth. She smiled almost.
Her scarlet silk, cut off the shoulders, flowed
from waist and hips in streams of anguished desire.
Her skin was twilight's first encroachment on evening,
the elegant yellow of honeysuckle flowers;
exquisitely delicate, forbiddingly strong, her mien

exuding assurance he'd never encountered in any
woman, making her incomprehensible, yet asking
no comprehension, demanding only adoration.

"What is it that they have sent to me? A colonel,
a brigadier, a captain?"
                                "No Ma'am, I'm just a boy."
The hames connecting mouth and brain had come
unbuckled. He felt humiliated and stupefied.
But her countenance softened, a bellows blow stoking
beauty's intensity, radiance suffusing his face.
"Hattie said you are Dueces?"
                                "I am called Duessa.
The Negroes alter my name to suit their speech."

"Duessa. That's an unusual name for a woman so. . ."

"For a woman so what?"
                                "Lovely." During their talk,
he found her forward gaze unnerving, but now
she appeared abashed and looked away and whispered,

"Tell me how lovely am I?"
                                "If I had faith
enough to see beyond the world's dark glass,
I know there would be angels kneeling at your feet,
to guide Duessa's way and preserve her life."
He was so pleased to extricate a compliment from the knot
of teased up thinking in his head, and yet her face
betrayed a sudden distress. She went to a tray
lifting a crystal decanter and poured two glasses.

"What are you called?"
                    "My name is Garland Cain."
She offered a glass. He decided he loved wine.

"Have you ridden far?"
                    "Nome, I've walked from Eufaula."

"Mon Dieu, my boy, you must be very fatigued."
Her smile tingled his skin like the fire's heat.
He glanced around the room, the poster, the couches,
an odd sort of room, both bedroom and sitting room,
but his whole attention was fixed by the woman's beauty,
lending focus to his mind's lethargy, her placid
chestnut eyes, her breasts thrust high in her bodice,
she thrilling his senses electric.
                    "Where are you from?"

"Until it fell last April, I was of Nawluns."

"I reckoned from your French accent you were a Creole,
and I hear the city, not the country in your voice."
She laughed at this, a laughter full of high
joy with no care in it, nor even the history
of care nor near acquaintance, and the fact he pleased her
stained his self-regard with sophistication.

"Born and bred in Nawluns."
                    "Did you like it there?"

"There was never a city like Nawluns and never again.
The whole world knocked on its door. Paris of the Delta!

The elegant houses, the streets alive all hours
with brass bands and ballade singers and cotillions!
Every night was a ball. The happiest thing
on earth is to dance in the arms of a man you love
while all the world limps on its wretched way.
The matrons said at fifteen I was more beautiful
than Helen. I was Nawlun's most renowned
duenna, and all the young men wanted me."

                                        "I'm sure
you're still no less a prize." But she didn't hear.

"Our lives were so gay before the Yankees came.
I thought the wine would pour forever, the music
never stop playing—the roasted partridges, lamb chops
and thyme at Dassons, silk dresses and river boats.
Now all those wonderful times have flowed away."
She saw the city staged in gaiety, a prophecy
in reverse, the nights of trysts and luxuries a farm boy
couldn't fathom, so many worlds removed
from him. She rose, sat on the floor at his feet,
a move which might have discomfited him, were it not
for the wine, he reveling in her passionate flights, her grand
emotions, the lost exuberant longings for her city,
distilled, invigorate in her flesh, laced and corseted.
He whispered so not to draw her away with violence
from the welter of memories she loved,
                                     "What's a duenna?"

"Quadroons and Octoroons, we were—not slaves,
no more slaves than any man is prisoner
of his birth or destiny, no more a slave than any

woman become a wife. Duennas were chosen
for our superlative qualities, beauty of face and form,
native intelligence, and schooled in the finest houses,
taught every refinement of manners, Parisian dialect,
and every dance known to cultured society.
Before the war, society of Nawluns was a nuanced
affair and dreadfully intricate. That world demanded
complete devotion from men who set themselves
the task of negotiating advancement in rank or fortune.
A man of means might take a duenna to wife
because we graced that world and knew its secrets.
My husband owned two cotton plantations and slaves;
he won a seat in the legislature. His name
was Vann, Captain Ambrose Vann. When the war
broke out, he enlisted right away, in spite
of me, who begged him to serve by other means.
The day he put me on the train for Alabama,
I knew I would never see my city again.
And what has my life become in Alabama?"
She paused and sipped a long slow draught of wine.
"He was killed somewhere on the Atchafalaya, fighting
with General Taylor. They didn't even pause
to retrieve his corpse. He worshipped me like a queen.
We had been happy such a little while.
They sent a Corporal to tell me he died facing
the enemy guns, or some such." She clutched her glass
in her hands as if she might be swept away.
Desire and pity and wine snarled his thinking.
The focus of concentration kept tumping over
as if he were trying to stand in a canoe. Her exquisite
longing, her suffering, its high tragedy, intensified

her already formidable charms. He wanted her,
but she bore indelible marks of a class above him,
beyond her race, of sophistication and wealth.
He ached for her but scruples mocked his desire.
He could not allow mere bestial conjugation,
the way a boar hog struggles to jump a sow's back,
that pitiable and comic sequence that keeps its eyes
pressed shut, stubby legs dancing for purchase.
Every time he looked at her, her eyes
were driving into his, vanquishing courage but kindling
hope, fantastic, implausible hope. His hands
were calloused and brown, so much darker than the dropping
honey of her Negress arms. What history imbued
blood of two races mingling the curse of Hamm,
for some primeval outrage between a drunk
father and a son of questionable sexual proclivities.
And here was Duessa, scion of myth and misery,
her body caressed by oils and fragrant soaps
every year of her life—how many he wondered,
twenty-three or four—by satins and silks,
she hardly venturing out of doors and never
unless a slack-jowled Negro servant, quick
as her shadow followed behind down vernal streets
of the Old French Quarter, the great mysterious vacuity
behind the affable clown's grinning demeanor,
holding a parasol above her expensive coiffure,
shading this cultivated wonder, who apprehended
treacheries so subtle that all good people lay them
down as the keelson of virtue and put their backs
to the oars. She had eaten the best cuisines, been borne
in exquisite traps, had reigned, a dark queen,

governing a world that was society's shadow,
practiced beauty and grace in fractured light
of cut crystal chandeliers, dispersing and revolving
fabulous visions as dancers stepped their elegant
quadrillions, and young Negresses swooned in dizzying
circles, the young whites standing by, holding
them in predatory patience, who had learned patience
on their inexorable way toward all they wanted in life.
But Duessa's man got a Yankee bullet in his brain.
Perhaps a bullet was racing toward him too,
already fired in time's metaphysic and he
on a course to intersect its mortal trajectory,
poised as he was to step inside an apocalypse
the likes of which the world had never seen?
Were it so great a sin to enjoy a woman?
To have one woman? Would not God forgive?
Perhaps when he got to Virginia, he could buy one.
He trundled attention back to the staring woman.
"Could you love me, knowing what I am?"
Her invitation struck him, a fiery bolt.
Knowing what? Octoroon, duenna?
Part white, part black, a widow, why should I care?
Before she took his hand, before he was able
to form a yes in response to her invitation
to her bed, even while his sense was stupefied
at the prospect of touching her body, Duessa raised
herself, planted hands on his knees, and pressed
her lips to his. Joy came rushing, warm,
golden as September muscadine, whose plump
rind he presses to his lips and sucks till the taut
skin breaks and sucks through teeth so meat and juice

are pulled away from seed, reeling the eyes
with vintage savoring the dizzy store of summer.
That kiss invested him with heavenly powers
and an idea—for possessing her and preserving honor.
We will become one flesh in the sight of God.
I have the will to make this union true
as it was in Paradise and remains for the backwoods husband
remote in Alabama wilderness who jumps
the broom and keeps his new wife's honor dear.
Her instant kiss became his great commandment
to follow the bidding of this woman's warm embraces.
All his pent up worries of first time solecisms
vanished in a flood of joy, savoring languorous
draught on draught of her kisses, spring essence wet
on the honeysuckle's elegant corolla, shock
of her tongue, the taste of yearning; he forgot war's chimeras,
his fear, forgot his name. She was out of her dress
and turned, he pulling the knot of her corset laces,
feeling her pent up breasts push out from confinement.
He must be dreaming, and yet he placed his farm boy
hands on her hips, her flesh a cloth of gold,
traced the curve of her waist, impressions of ribs,
his right palm holding a moment her heart's passionate
rhythm, as if he held her life in his hands,
and such a privilege made him humble and glad.
He pulled her close, feeling along his length
her body's subtle mysteries, arms, breasts,
the catch of her thighs, her sturdy hucklebones nested
in his palms. She drew him down on the bed above her,
he kissing her as if to break that delicate
spell of her lips on his might cause her to vanish,

she coaxing him forward, shifting underneath him,
he concentrating only on the paradise wine
of her kisses, until he felt a hot wet flower,
her body supple as a silk stocking, responsive
as a raft of wind shuddering through golden oak leaves.
He felt himself reborn, component with her body
motioning responsive beneath him, their two forms making
a fragile hull on a wide and perilous river,
man and woman swept on a torrent of pleasure,
a shimmering, astonished journey, full of youth
and youthful fury, each urging the other to the brink
of passion's abyss, gasping at the height, she reaching
and cradling his face like a child's. Never would he
have guessed the act of love might generate such meaning,
creating commingled hearts, the generous intention
of placing another life ahead of his own.
After love, they lay in the four poster's enormous
satisfaction, tangled in fragrant sheets, whispering
in intimate darkness until they were vanquished by sleep.
As night advanced, a drumming barrage roused him
from pleasant slumber, this gorgeous woman nestled
warm in his arm, orchestral tiers of rain noise
beating roof and window glass, the bass notes
of thunder reverberating, the window flashing alarms.
Duessa opened her eyes and shifted for comfort.

"I want to tell you something," he said, "but you
　must promise not to laugh at me."
　　　　　　　　　　　　　　"Mais oui."

"I feel like you've made me a man." She laughed anyway,

a mellifluous rich and joyful noise, consonant
with rain, which made him feel the more a man.
"Duessa, you're unlike any woman I've known.
I want you to be my wife." Her eyes widened.
She laughed. And stopped.

                  "Mon Dieu, we cannot marry.
Nowhere outside Nawluns could you and I marry,
and now the city is fallen, not even there.
One part of eight of my blood makes me a nigger.
You're having relations with a nigger. You understand?
And if you win this war you're off to fight,
I'll stay a nigger. And Garland, if you lose the war,
I'll stay a nigger. That law will never change."

"There are higher laws that supersede man's law."
She propped herself on an elbow, looked at him.

"What do you think I'm doing here—in this house?"

"A Negro, you are legally the white man's trust.
But look at the world, who knows how things might change?
A moment ago, while we were practicing love,
a memory came to me from years ago
when I was a chit. My folks had taken me
to Natchez to see some family there, and one day
we crossed the Mississippi on a creaking steamer.
The boiler's heat was surging up through the decks,
and odor of pitch and oil and burning fuel.
The great wheel slapped its water music, the flood
a mile wide where we were crossing, dwarfing
the land. Midstream, the side wheeler, laboring astride

that muddy highway, was jostled by currents, cavernous
whirlpools churning implacable violence. I was sure
we would be swallowed down. Three times those whirling
tornadoes turned our prow, each time the helmsman
righting her course, and I was so afraid,
I clung to my father's knees while he laughed at me.
At last, he peeled me off his legs and set me
on his shoulders where I could see the Father of Waters.
That river taught me what a great country was mine,
and when I took you to myself, Duessa, I felt high
and lifted up. I remembered the Mississippi,
my safe passage, felt its natural omnipotence."
Her eyes widened in understanding, and he knew
for certain she warmed to his affectionate proposition.
"Duessa, you and I have found ourselves
in extraordinary circumstances. If I can carry
your promise of love to war, then I will know
my actions can never compromise my honor
for I will only be fighting for the woman I love."
She looked at him long and long.

          "My dear Garland,
you just don't understand the way things are."
He laughed.

         "You're right, Duessa. I don't understand,
but you can teach me." She gave a wistful smile,
and he lay and watched her sacred face ease
into sleep, reveling astonished with his glorious fortune.

October 13, 1862 Union Springs

A mud-caked wagon wheel was spinning out
of round in his head, his belly whirling nauseous.
Vision burned his eyes with surgical incisions.
The woman was gone. He recalled her rising earlier,
standing naked in the morning window stretching,
clothed in the aftermath of the storm's weak light.
He felt like he'd been kicked in the head all night.
He had to get dressed. He sat up and lay back down,
taking deliberate breaths. A quiet knock
at the door, he braced his head in hands and whispered,

"Come in." Duessa stepped inside with breakfast.
Griddle cakes and bacon and coffee. He sipped
this first, surprised to find it sweet. But sweetest
of all even through raging eyes was vision
of Duessa, flowing about the room in crimson
silks, gorgeous as the phoenix preening fire,
an enthralling, sensuous liquefaction, assuaging
his heart. Appetite returned. He ate with rapine
and marked her every gesture, using his eyes
to write her in memory's book, which he would con
to the end, holding her dear, her bare feet whispering
floor boards, coiffure disheveled by sleep and passion.
Not since he'd met the conscript officer on the stoop
with his father, had his spirits redounded to such ecstatic
heights. He propped in bed like an oriental king,
stuffing his face and wondering what a magnificent
beauty Duessa was. When the late hour came,
they walked together as far as she could go

to the edge of Bateman's fields. They stood close
in chill light fractured by a thousand needles sighing,
and he bent and kissed her queenly lips, one
last time, a bliss to preserve his soul in battles.
He held her hands and thinking to give her a token
of the union they had conceived in their night of love,
he produced a monogrammed kerchief, gift from his mother,
which he had been prepared to give Beth Anne
had a roving fate not cast itself between them.
She bowed her head.
                              "You, boy, you don't know
what you're about." But saying this, she drew
from her hand a wadded kerchief, inside a diminutive
leather pouch, tied fast with rawhide laces.

"What is it?"
                     "It is a charm of powerful luck,
given to me by Mary Laveau herself
at Maison Blanche, a terrible and wise woman.
The sachet binds together mojo and juju."
He squinted at the bauble.
                                        "Mojo and what-what?"

"Equal parts of magic black and white.
She told me you were coming. I didn't believe."
She reached behind his head and tied the strings
around his neck, he closing his eyes to relish
pleasured tingle of her fingers straying in his hairline.
"Wear it in battle. If aught can give you aid,
this will." An eloquent kiss, then she whispered,
"Garland, you don't know what a chance love is."

This sentiment startled him, provoked assurances.

"Just give me a chance to love when I get back."
They kissed again, his tongue touching hers
in shocks of ecstasy, and then she wet his face
with weeping, and he was sad but buoyed by the irrefutable
sign of affection. As he walked away, he screwed up
his courage once to turn and look at her,
and she was there, her eyes priceless with sorrow.
Love's certainty made him feel his worth enlarged,
the very sky an arch through which horizons
gleamed receding. Death's terror mitigated, diffused
like light at dusk, the meaning of war was reduced
to love of her who'd ushered him into manhood.
Now hope of reunion, tender spoils of longing,
would attest his powers, and effort, expectation,
and desire would lead through trials and on to infinitude,
his end, this blossoming, being's heart and home.
He turned the final bend, foot sore and thirsty,
to Camp Watts, busy canvass village drawn
on perpendiculars at bottom of a winter field
where cows and horses inclined their heads to hay
between phalanxes of marching Rebel soldiers.
He passed a sorghum press, a drowsy mule
pacing a muddy rut at the sweep's circumference,
rousing sometimes to eye the bagasse with longing.
Beside the press, a young girl tended a fire—
a beautiful child with eyes of black molasses—
and a large flat pan, boiling the long sweetenings.
Wielding a great wooden spoon, she stirred and scooped
the foam, laughing and flinging it high in the breeze,

imbuing autumn air with aromatic savor,
sweet odor of sorghum molasses; his stomach twisted.
He went to the commandant's office, saluted the sergeant,
gray around his balding crown with a thin
mustache, diving down from his mouth and bursting
into protuberant mutton chops, his small lips pursed.

"Welcome to Camp Watts, Camp of Instruction One.
Your name and city?"
                          "Garland Cain, route one,
beat fourteen, Eufaula, Alabama."

"A conscript?"
                  "Yes sir."
                                "One of the few with brains,"
he mumbled. "I have your record here. A miracle.
All is in order." He puzzled and scratched his head.
"I cannot fathom how such a thing might be.
I'll have your furlough paper. Thank you, private.
You'll find your billet remains tent sixty-one."
Outside his tent, he found stacked arms, new issued,
shiny stocks and barrels with gleaming bayonets.
He stood before the tripods, sobered. In camp
so far, he'd wielded nothing more dangerous than an axe.
Beyond the weapons, lounging before their tent,
were men of his mess he'd met two months before.

"Garland Cain of Eufaula, reporting for duty."

"Your name is Johnny now."
                              "It's Fresh Fish Garfish."

"Welcome back to the Spotswood." The men were huddled
around the fire, intent on a stew kettle hung
from a tripod. Caleb got up and shook his hand.

"Good to have you back. How was the furlough?"

"Right fine. We killed and butchered fourteen hogs.
Howdy Greasy, Patty, Titus, Preacher.
Fellers, I'm ready for a blowing spell, and I'm
so hungry my stomach thinks my throat's been cut."

"We having Confed'rit stew."
                                "What's that, Hog?"

"A dollup of this and that."
                                "Possum and corn pone."
Four men around a crate were studying cards
with eruptions of despair or exultation depending
on the way that luck was running.
                                "That's a Euchre!"

"A lot of men fancy losing all their money
to make one soldier happy," Caleb said.

"If I can just stay drunk for two days running,
I'm happy soon enough," said Apple Jack,
laying his trumps and sweeping away three tricks.

"Caleb is a moralist."
                        "Snake, that's just not so.
I object to games of chance in that they do not

afford an accurate representation of the world."

"Hell and scissors it ain't accurate. I've had
no luck in wives, in the army, and I'll be damned
if I can get a hand of cards."
                    "Now Snake,
you don't get cards, hit's easier fer me to win."

"Well thank you kindly fer showing me the bright side,
Guide Post."
                    "The reason Orator don't take to cards
is he parted company with twenty shinplasters his first
night here and now he's shy."
                                "A man must learn,"
Caleb winked. "It's men who never learn
who generate all the world's great aggravations."

"Private Cain, hit is an intoxicating pleasure
to interduce a new galoot. This here's
Private Buzzard from Chalk Farm, Alabama.
Private Cain, Private Buzzard." Guide Post
made an effusive gesture, indicating a lanky
soldier, his limbs pulled over a blanket's edges
like a dead spider. His black eyes were deep set,
his face rough hewn and ligneous. Garland nodded,
Buzzard nodded back. "Mr. Buzzard
is convalescing from his first swaller of pop skull,
compliments of Co. H." The man's face
was impassive as stone, his eyes fixed on nothing.
"The Buzz come right near puking his stockings up."
This was a company prank—the men would offer

a jar of whiskey to recruits upon arrival
at the Spotswood Hotel, a bottle filled with Ipecac.
Garland and Preacher were the only men of the mess
who hadn't fallen for the trick, who hadn't lurched
themselves behind the tent on hands and knees
vomiting hard tack and creek water. As Garland stood
before the smiling mess urging him to gulp
a swallow of the army's "best damn rifle knock knee,"
Caleb spoke up,

    "Just like a Garfish—he doesn't
take the bait easily." And the name stuck.

"Don't take it hard, Buzz. They get everybody."
Garland dropped his pack, set himself down,
allowing ease to fall through all his muscles,
smelling with relish the grub Oscar was cooking.

"Where's Corporal Corpus?"

      "Plaguing other folks else."
Caleb wandered over.

     "Supplies come in
at last. I reckon you'll want to get yourself
to the quartermaster. I'll tag along if you like.
He'll give you your Rebel issue. Be good to get
an extra blanket 'fore Taps is beat tonight."

"I'd be obliged," but Patty got up and followed,
and once the three of them were out of ear shot
he whispered,

    "Beware the Buzzard, laddie. He'd steal
the dimes off a dead man's eyes and slap his jaws

because it warn't a quarter."

      "He'd do to watch,
for sure," said Caleb.

      "And they've moved the blessed sinks
again. Be Jazus if we won't have to strike tent
and march a day just to move our bowels."
He and Caleb walked the cow path avenues
between the tents, hearing laughter and singing.
Caleb, intelligent and voluble, had finished college.
He seemed a good man and a good man to tie to.
Garland gathered his issue from the quartermaster,
a slight man darting from box to box like a chipmunk,
he having checked and double checked his lists
so not one item might be misdirected
of two wool blankets, haversack and cartridge sack,
canteen, uniform of handsome gray, a rifle,
a dozen cartridges, and a twist of fresh tobacco,
which Garland didn't use.

      "Save it," said Caleb,
"later you can swap it for something you need."

October 14, 1862 Camp Watts

Dawn light platted out in jaunty reveille.
Fatigue duty filled their days, digging latrines
and chopping trees; even farm boys inured
to rigorous work complained of aches in back
and arms, felling oak and ironwood. But the duty
men hated most was guard detail. Nothing
provoked a spirit of mutiny or ushered forth

a red faced employment of oaths than the order to walk
a beat for half the night on a Notasulga cow path
with the nearest Yankee two hundred miles away.
A man was clapped in the guardhouse for cursing an officer.
Hog confessed to Garland,

                         "They done put me
in at guardhouse for leaving camp without'n nary
a pass. Don't be a muggins and get yoreself throwed
in air, shivering all night without'n nary
a fire. Hit's colder than a widow woman's step-ins."
The week before a man was arrested for sleeping
on guard detail. He escaped confinement, took
French leave, was captured two days later, drunk
in a Montgomery boarding house. A court of officers
sentenced him to thirty-nine lashes and branding.
Today all companies mustered to witness the punishment.
Two ropes were tossed across a post oak limb
and tied the prisoner's wrists, stretching him out,
fat and haggard, till he stood on the tips of his toes.

"That codger must be nigh of sixty years
if he's a day," said Garland.

                         "I heared tell
from a feller in his mess he warn't none too smart."
The air was sullen with cold and consternation.
About five hundred men described an arc
around the oak tree, the man in ridiculous posture,
his torso bright as a peeled potato, arms
and neck dark as a Negro's, the dugs pointed
and feminine. Another guard marched out, forming
an opposing arc behind the prisoner, faced

the recruits, and presented arms. Of all the soldiers
they looked the most distressed. An officer on horseback
read the charges, produced a leather whip,
the braided popper tied off in three thin strops.

"Ain't no justice air," groused Apple Jack.
"The court martial give him thirty-nine lashes, but at air
whip'll give him three time thirty-nine,
at air's, at air's"—
              "A hunurt and seventeen."

"A sight more'n thirty-nine. No justice air."

"Ain't no cause to whip an old man, neither,"
said Preacher.
           "I'd be damned if I'd let 'em beat me."

"Shit, Buzzard, you see that row of muskets
fornenst that sonna bitch? Who you think
they put them there to guard—him what's hog tied?"

"They're beating him for us." He spoke the moment
the words occurred to him, and the soldiers standing
around, their faces hangdog and rooster furious,
stared at him as if he'd spoken in tongues.

"He's right, sholey." Caleb's voice somewhere
among the ranks. "The Major's tired of us shirking
our duties, sneaking off, and sleeping on guard.
Now take a look at where you parked your rifles."
A few of the soldiers turned to see the neat

tripods of stacked arms, some forty yards
behind them, guarded, not by a detail of enlisted
men, but a group of mounted officers, their stern
gazes fixed. A friction in air turned
their heads again, the slap of leather on flesh.
After the second round house stroke, the prisoner
slackened, body falling forward, toes
bent under, all his weight depending now
from his bound wrists. The men were counting silently,
all of them bracing, praying he wouldn't cry out,
in a gruesome contest the host of men had pitted
against the officers. On the tenth spattering stroke
he did cry, a keening shriek, which was arrested
by the following lash in convulsive intake of breath.
Well before the thirty ninth lash had cut
across his back in spattered gouts of blood,
the deserter was swaying deep in shock, having spoiled
his trousers. Two guards cut him down, and he collapsed
in a writhing wallow of bloody mud. A surgeon
withdrew from a blazing fire an iron tipped molten
half-moon. The guards sat on the heap; the doctor
knelt and holding the brand in blacksmith's gloves,
touched the glowing iron to the prisoner's face,
his groaning sobs an abandoned, animal lowing.

October 15, 1862

"We larruped the Yanks like the Devil beating tan bark
at Manassas," said Corporal Howell.

>   "And run old Pope

plum all the way to Minnesota."

                            "You said it,
Preacher."

        "Better he up there killing Indians
than killing Rebels."

                  "But Pope and his army escaped,"
said Caleb. "The Seven Days, Front Royal, Winchester,
Sharpsburg, Second Bull Run, and Yanks are thick
as cow peas in the hull."

                        "And Yankees know they can fight us
Rebs to a draw and win the victory."

                      "You're right,
Patty. Stalemates and encroachments for us are the same
as losses."

         "As long as Richmond is ours, we the tall
hog at the trough, and as long as she has Lee
defending her gates, the South will stand."

                        "I disagree,"
said Caleb. "There are no strategic places. Richmond
may fall, but as long as we have rifles in our hands
rebellion lives. Lincoln understands
this fact, which is why he continues shuffling his deck,
drawing a different general. He's after a fighter,
one who knows that by attrition from aggressive assaults,
we must be destroyed. He exhibits a Christian
humility which seems profound and worthy of the name,
yet his guiding hope, each hour, each day, is our quick
and comprehensive annihilation."

                  "Let us pray
God grant him the wishes of his heart, granting also
each Rebel sojer lives to see 'em fulfilled."

"Well hail and storm, Patty, Orator allows
that President Lincoln feller wants us dead,"
said Buzzard. "God cain't perform no contradiction."

"What's prayer for if not for miracles," smiled Patty.
Caleb regarded Malone with a bemused look.
"Whiskey eloquence. 'Tis why we Irish are all
of us great lovers."
                    "With God, all things are possible.
If I take the wings of the morning and dwell in the uttermost
parts of the sea, even there shall thy hand
lead me." Snake scowled,
                    "God can't have me dead
and alive at oncet, Preacher."
                    "Why it's the marrow
of Christianity. I am the resurrection
and the life. He that believeth on me though he
were dead, yet shall he live."
                    "Well," said Ainey,
"I'm trusting Jesus but watching out for my chances."

"I say our chances is good. We done turned out
and showed a Rebel sojer can whip a Yankee
ever time."
          "But Hog, the question is,
Can a Rebel whip ten Yankees every time?"

"All we'uns got to do is follow the Word
of God. They's nothing to think about at all."

"But is God leading to the Land of Canaan or the Wilderness?
How do we know we're not his stiff necked people?"

"A pertinent question, Snake."

                           "God works in history
and always has, and it don't make a difference one
to two or twenty. If'n we Rebels unbutton
enough of their collars, they'll turn around and mosey."

"Watch out you don't get yourn unbuttoned, Corpus."

"I'm ready for death. And it's Corporal, not Corpus, Private
Buzzard. I love the South and I have faith
in our prospects."

                     "I do not advocate despair, but I think
it becomes a man to set the facts on the gum stump
and be apprised of sacrifices he'll have to make
and the character required to obtain a righteous success."

"I'm with Corpus Howell," said Buzzard. "Lee
is gwine to lick them Yanks like a cow licks salt."

November 30, 1862

The fire smoldered in embers, and men relaxed
before taps, writing letters, smoking, and chatting.
Garland was rearranging his kit out of boredom.
He tossed the tobacco in his sack and happened to glance
at Buzzard's face, a steely look in his eye.

"Do you chew?"

                  "I allow I likes to take a chaw."

"Well here, I don't use it," he said, tossing
the twists in his lap.
                    "You got a heart in you, mister."
He heard camp chatter catch around a question.

"Ainey, what's the biggest fish you ever
caught on a trotline?"
                    "Well sir, I have to say,
while he warn't the biggest fish I ever caught,
the best I ever caught was my cousin Eugene."

"Yore cousin?"
                    "Yes sir, old Eugene." Ainey
put his hands behind his head, leaned back
on his stump. The edges of a deck fluttered together,
the embers sighed.
                    "All right, Ainey, tell us
all about it."
                    "Well, we was younguns,
and my Aunt Rebecca, she was the oldest among us,
twelve or thirteen, and momma put her in charge
of looking after Eugene, who was just a chit
round about six month old. So we decided
to have a Baptism, and since we all was Methodists
and Eugene was just a squirt and had no say,
we decided to baptize him. All we needed
was a dab of water for sprinkling, but none of us
had the sinew to winch the cistern bucket, so Becky
allowed we could use my daddy's catfish barrel.
When we'd go fishing and bring a stringer home,
what we didn't eat or give to neighbors,

we'd keep in the barrel for another catfish fry.
We gathered round and sang *Amazing Grace*,
just like the grownups did. Then Aunt Becky
held fussy Eugene over the barrel and preached
a sermon from *Genesis* about the Spirit moving
over the waters, about how when one repents
they is joy in Heaven. Hit was purty good preaching
for a youngun. She had a lot of words in there
what we was wont to hear in church, but then,
just as her discourse was winging up to the Lord,
something shot out from Eugene, glinting in sunlight,
and we'uns turned to watch it puff in the dust.
And then they was a splash and we turned back.
Becky's hand was holding a limp piece of diaper
over the barrel. We crowded around to look,
me pulling my chin up over the rim, and there
in the black well was Eugene's pale shape circled
by writhing shadows. Becky screamed for momma,
but all the rest of us chits just stood like stumps.
She thrust her arm in the barrel to the shoulder, straining
to reach the baby, terror wide in her eyes.
I grabbed Aunt Becky's shoulders, pushed her aside
and threw my weight against the barrel, and the others
caught on and commenced to pushing too till we got
a rhythm going. Turley went to the other
side and tugged and soon the water was swaying
back and forth until with one great heave
we pushed the barrel over, water gushing
and catfish slapping and baby Eugene sulled up
like an old toad and squalling to wake the damned.
I've never heard a happier sound than that.

I was sore relieved till I saw Turley, his right foot
crushed and bloodied where the barrel had fallen on him."

"I bet chew got a thrashing."
                                 "Shoot I reckon.
But Turley, all grown up, 's glad he got him
a bum foot—it kept him out of this war.
And poor Eugene, no worse off for his dousing,
dead on Malvern Hill."
                         "The Lord, he sholey
work in mysterious ways," said Hog. The men
fell silent. Snake, inspecting a hand of cards,

said, "At least he died a Baptist." But no one laughed.
They'd gotten orders today for active duty.

December 7, 1862

He sat by a splendid fire, Corporal Howell
reading an old *Montgomery Advertiser.*

"Listen to this one boys, *A Female Soldier:*

*Mrs. Amy Clark volunteered with her husband as a private, fought
through the battles of Shiloh, where Mr. Clark was killed—she performing the burial rites with her own hands. She then continued
with Bragg's army in Kentucky, fighting in the ranks as a common
soldier, until she was twice wounded—once in the ankle and once
in the breast, when she was taken prisoner by the Yankees. Her sex*

was discovered by the Federals, and she was regularly paroled as a
prisoner of war, but they did not permit her to return until she had
donned female apparel. Mrs. Clark was in our city on Sunday last,
en route for Bragg's command. —*Jackson Mississippian.*

I swany, the world is turning upside down."

"I fancy I'd like to meet that lass," said Patty.

"What sort of man wants a woman to be a man?"
said Apple Jack.
        "True," said Caleb, "but then,
she told her husband goodbye and knows where he died
and how, a great consolation, while many folk
will suffer lifelong torment because their loved ones
left their homes one day and simply vanished."

"Life is not an adventure. We have our places,"
said Howell. "Men must do what honor and duty
prescribe, and combat is no place for a woman."

"Well Corporal," said Ainey, "If Private Clark could say,
he mote say combat ain't no place for a man."
Later the mess cleared out to go to preaching,
and Caleb and Garland lagged behind to cook
some coffee, fry some hoe cakes, and enjoy a time
away from a crowd of soldiers. The evening was cold
but peaceful, and both were silent for a long spell,
relishing the breeze's exhalations through winter
branches and muted soldiers' voices, singing
hymns, Caleb with his kepi over his eyes.

"Caleb."

　　"Yeah Gar."

　　　　"Do a woman's breasts make milk
all the time or only when she's pregnant?"
Caleb chuckled,

　　　　"You find a drink of ninny
round here somewhere?" Garland saw him smile
under his hat brim. "And what a question to ask
and you a farm boy!"

　　　　"Well, they's a lot of differences
between the human animal and other animals.
A woman can get a baby any time,
but an animal has to be in the state of estrus."

"Well, old son, I'm hardly an expert on sex,
but I think that after a woman has a baby,
she begins giving milk and continues as long as she suckles."
The wind gave a long sigh through a stand of pine.
"You find a good girl somewhere round here to spoil?"

"No. A feller's just curious about women is all."

"Whatever you do, don't suggest she enlist."

"The woman I fancy's not the soldiering type."
So she has a child, but the fact remained she'd ushered
him into manhood, had nourished him at her breast,
an act that weighed his mind with mysterious import.

December 8, 1862

Dawn recurred to a back and forth mechanic
chuffing, echoing scream tearing through crisp
air and billowing smoke routing through treetops,
snaking its way to the camp. A locomotive,
its brakes screeching agonies, labored to a stop
and sat expending steam, venting tremendous
pressures in fits and hisses. The engineer
was talking to some of the boys.

                                  "How fast will she go?"

"Thirty miles an hour on level ground."

"Durn. Can you believe it?"

                              "T'ain't no way."
The men lined up in companies, then entrained
and chuffered off to Auburn. As the engine lurched
forward and got up steam, the pistons quickening
their rhythmic push and pull, the boys' excitement
mounted. The coaches rattled track music,
and the keening whistle caused the boys to whoop.
They pulled the windows down and put their heads out,
squinting in driving wind and drunk with the rush.
Who would have ever conceived an age like this,
the great iron stallion conveying glory of passions,
joy of side rods and driving wheels, the freedom
of uninhibited travel? They sensed the world
contracted as the train sped on. They reached Auburn
and tumbled onto the platform north of town. The spires
of Old Main's towers rose above the oaks,

its Flemish Bond stark in December twilight.
They marched to a colors ceremony and were sworn in.
It never occurred to him he would have to do this,
but the oath presented his mind with a consolation.
As he raised his right hand and spoke the vow,
he sealed his fate. He was wed to the Southern cause.
It was done though he had no idea what it meant.
Their unit called themselves the Wiregrass Grays.
They'd been assigned to General Cadmus Wilcox,
Eighth Alabama, Army of Northern Virginia,
which was at present encamped near Fredericksburg.
He watched the boys tossing their slouch hats and beegums,
wringing each other's hands, each man's exuberance
at a pitch. He was almost swept away by it all,
yet something held him back. He watched the wild
exultation and wondered how many men were marked
for death, wondered if he were marked for death.
And now a parson escorted a girl to the stage
to confer the company colors. The cheers intensified,
changing the way the rush of a wildfire changes,
consuming timber enough to reap the whirlwind.
The girl was a homely brunette, blushing furiously
when a burly color sergeant stepped on stage.
The parson raised his hand, quieting the din.

"Brothers and Sisters, allow me to introduce
Miss Anna Collins who will present the colors,
sewn by her hands, and make appropriate remarks."
Eyes intent on her sergeant, she unfolded the flag,
much like the battle flag, but red, with thirteen
stars, two cannon crossed in a blue crux.

Along the top of the banner, she had stitched,
Company H, 8th Alabama Infantry.
She cleared her throat with a soft coo and recited
her speech by rote, the ancient parson standing
a few steps off, mouthing it word for word.

"Receive this flag from sisters and mothers whose affection
greets you in this guidon of martial honor, constructed
by our poor and feeble but faithful hands. When this banner
floats before you on the field of battle, stirred
by breezes of freedom, may it inspire you
to daring and glorious deeds, and be a patriotic
remembrance that cherished ones at home appeal
to you for salvation from a fanatical and godless foe."
She handed the sergeant the flag with a blush and a curtsy.

"Lady, with high beating hearts and pulses throbbing
with patriotic ardor, we receive from your hands
this emblem of our young Republic. To those who are destined
for homecomings robed in victory, may it lead us back
to loves we left behind; and to those who shall spill
their blood in the strife, sacralizing Southern soil,
may this holy banner cheer their souls to Heaven."
The sergeant regarded the woman hardly at all
but directed his mustachioed attention to the hall,
                                        with his left leg
thrust forward, his right fist gauntleted, resting on his hip.
Some laughter. Snake was mimicking the soldier's stance,
holding a red bandana folded triangular.
Pressing it to his nose, he blew a resounding honk.
Garland just contained a braying laugh.

Chuckles rippled about, but some boys threw him
hostile glances.
       "My apologies to all," said Snake,
dabbing his eyes, "closed spaces make me rheumy."
The sergeant took Miss Collin's hand and kissed it,
his lips lingering, stoking the lady's face
and the pastor's discomfiture. Garland smiled at all
these virgin antics as the reverend hurried the dismissal.

"May the God of Battles favor our just cause
and the love and mercy of Jesus Christ our Savior,
keep you in his might and care and protect you from evil,
troops whom we have bedizened, bedighted and bedecked,
in thy honor and glory, Amen."
       "Well I'll be danged,
durned and damned, if that warn't a fine prayer,"
said Snake. A band had crowded in back of the hall,
and they started the party off with a quick step Dixie.
The soldiers began to mingle with civilians, crowding
the walls and leaving a spacious dance floor in the midst,
which filled with orbiting couples, young men twirling
girls, their hooped crinolines turning circles
within circles, under the wary eyes of matrons.
The men too old and boys too young for service
hung on the exulting soldiers like heroes, a few
in natty gray, but most in homespun dyed
in copperas and walnut hulls. The soldiers' spirits
were high and soon another kind of spirits
appeared outside behind the hall. Confederates
were ever more convinced of their martial prowess,
boasting of deeds they would perform for God

and Southern womanhood.
                              "I'm gonna shoot
ever Yankee they is in the state of ol' Virginny."

"We gonna chase em all the way to Maine."
After midnight, the fandangos sputtered out.
The crowd dispersed, many young men having coaxed
young ladies away for promenades in the quiet
under scribbled branches of live oak and blackjack oak.
Soldiers not persuasive with the ladies or unable
to procure an invitation to a private home
untied their bedrolls on East Alabama's campus,
wrapped themselves in blankets and shivered till dawn.
He lay down, covered in stars, feeling superior
to all this boyish striving after females,
recalling Duessa's womanhood and warm
caresses, opiate desire whelming thought.

December 9, 1862 Auburn, Alabama

Next morning by no small miracle, all the boys
were gathered for inspection, made a brisk march back
to the station platform, cheering girls, and music.
Patty Malone came shambling up, singing
an Irish ballad, puffing a large cigar,
and offering his canteen.
                              "I'm all right."
                                        "You'll be wanting
a swig of this here, laddie. Best blessed red eye
I swallowed this week." He made a generous pull,

the whiskey describing his gulping apparatus with delicious
fire, the heat going down as the fumes went up.

"At's mighty good, I'm obliged."
                              "'Tis nothing, lad.
And now a sweet specimen of Alabama
womanhood awaits on the platform yonder."
He tipped his cap and chuffed cigar smoke through the crowd.
The people of Auburn had loaded the soldiers down
with every conceivable thing, from hard biscuits
to rolls of lint bandages. A homely redhead
offered a package of these, a rather uncheerful
gift, confronting the mind as it did with unnerving
prospects that blunted the cerebral dervish two pulls
of spill skull had started up in his brainpan. The girl,
however, led no crowd of boys, was protuberant
about the front teeth, yet her eyes exuded
a wistful compassion, and he felt an abrupt pity
so took the bandages and kissed her cheek, smelling
soap and bottled blossoms. The soldiers packed
their persons and impedimenta into cars. He boarded
and realized the redhead had followed along the platform
as he made his way through the coach, calling to him
through the window.
                              "My name is Ida Mae. I live
on Gay and Thatch Street. Yellow house with the porch!"
He sank in a seat on the opposite side of the car.
Boys were hanging out the windows in the sunny
cold air, kissing the girls' hands and laughing.
And then they vanished in swirls of steam and smoke.
Caleb called him to a seat in back of the car.

"Sit down and put up your dogs, cousin. We taking
a long ride." And it was. A few polite miles
from town, the soldiers rifled packages and parcels,
and items deemed uneatable were tossed out windows.
Pistons and side rods knocking, sway of cars,
and rhythmic clacking bled away excitement.
For many men, unused to modern travel,
the rocking back and forth, the rushing of livestock,
fences, and tree lines, rising and falling by windows,
made their innards queasy, so they tried to sleep.

"How many stops you reckon we'll make, Caleb?"

"Not many, I hear. We rushing to Fredericksburg."

"I guess if the brass is getting us there on the gad
that only means one thing?"
                            "I reckon they got
to get us there before the dance commences."
For hours the train rocked on, first to Atlanta,
then Chattanooga, Knoxville, through Cumberland Gap,
a bare deciduous beauty shrouded in fog,
the somber, December desolate Appalachians,
and then the long slow eastward journey to Lynchburg.
Here Garland's face grew hot; he required frequent
recourse to the slop jar. He fumbled a piece of blue mass
from his pocket but shaky hands dropped it in the jar
to his disgust. The fact he was a prisoner in the car
compounded misery. He suffered and tried to sleep.

December 11, 1862 Fredericksburg, Virginia

Caleb toted him weak kneed to the field hospital
and reported him ill to General Wilcox's adjutant.
His bed was jammed in the back of an upstairs hall
in a commandeered house, the reek of slop jars putrid,
the suffering quiet. A nurse came to take his symptoms.
Her eyes were new leafed hazel gold, her voice
a river lazy, summer languid drawling.

"Has there been a fight already?"
                                        "No," she smiled,
"these poor fellers is just the sick. It happens
every time a passel of sojers comes
together—dysentery, inflammation, small pox,
or measles. You got all the symptoms of the flux.
Doctor Britt will be along to put you
on the medicine list. Don't worry. You'll be strutting
your onions in no time, honey. What company you in?"

"Company H, Eighth Alabama."
                                        "Oh,
I got a sister lives in Alabama.
Down in Demopolis. You know where that place is?"

"Yes'um."
                "She's a nurse like me. They sent
a bunch of Yankee prisoners down there for parole
after the fracas at Shiloh, and they all got sick
'cause northern boys ain't used to warm, moist air.
Sister helped 'em get better." Then she lowered

her voice and took his hand in hers. "Her name
is Pearl and bless Pat if she didn't fall
in love with one of them durned old Yankee sojers
what only had one leg. Law, I thought
our daddy was going to have a smothering spell.
My name's Ruth. If you need me, just call out."
He laughed but his cheer was quashed when she turned away
and he saw her blood stained smock, its washed out smudges,
a terrible atlas, rivers and oceans of blood.
When next he opened his eyes, Ruth was standing
above him with Doctor Britt, whose entire visage
sagged around his blood shot eyes, hammered
deep in his head. Ruth recited his symptoms,
and the doctor put his foot beneath the bed
and slid the slop jar out.
                              "Correct as usual,
Ruth. This brave lad's doing the Tennessee Quick Step.
Tartaric Acid and water, quinine and morphine.
If there's no morphine, give him a plug of blue mass.
You know the dosages." He passed to the next bed.
Ruth squeezed his arm, smiled and followed the doctor.

December 13, 1862

Dawn light trembled frost flowers etched in windows.
His eyes shot open, the battle was on. He hurried
outside. The ridge muted musketry's humming,
and along the crepuscular hilltop, illuminations
stabbed the palls of smoke from Rebel batteries
in eerie halation, followed by staccato reports.

A rider came over the crest, urging his mount.

"Give this order to Colonel Britt immediately"—
and jerked the reigns around and spurred away.
He jumped the steps and leapt the wide front stoop,
past brittle, denuded roses, fresh painted jalousies,
found Doctor Britt in his kitchen office, reclining
awake, covered in a frock coat, sock feet propped
on the servants' table amidst a gallimaufry
of documents, glass vials, horrific surgical implements,
stacks of folded lint, a half filled bottle
of wine and a single tallow candle guttering,
causing the room to list from port to starboard.
He set the order down on a stack of forms.
The doctor neither stirred nor regarded the missive.

"The wounded men need bringing up to hospital.
Tell Assistant Surgeon Hals to enlist
his usual detail of abler patients. You go
with him. You're well enough to tote a stretcher.
Hals is the irascible Irish fellow asleep
on the back stoop. Nudge him good with your foot
when you go to wake him, and if he's holding his side arm,
first get a grip on the pistol, hold it tight."
He kicked an unarmed Hals, arresting rattling
snores. A dead soldier stood beside him. When his eyes
opened, he was wide awake, sprang to his feet,
and cocked his head toward rumbling of Marye's Heights.

"It's a tinker's breakfast for us, me laddie."
                                        "What's that?"

93

"A piss and a look about." Hals was curt,
  short, and quick, with a breath of rotten cabbage.
In no time he mustered his squad, and all were trudging
up hill toward roar of guns and noise of muskets
changing from the hum of bees to the rapid fire
rattle of myriad rifles. Approaching the clamor,
he trembled, but gaining the ridge they stopped in awe.
The hill's eastern face was burnished with proscenium
sunlight, burning off an early fog,
  showing a steep slope scored with parallel shelves
of Confederate entrenchments, ripping the air apart
with fire and bedlam. They were standing behind artillery
on the height's crest, the batteries taking punishment
from Union gunners. Below, a road described
the hillside's base, bounded on either side
by a low stone wall. The Rebels had shoveled spoil
on the far side of the east wall, constructing
a breastwork's glacis, adding protection for infantry
and concealing their line. In front of this, an expanse
of brittle grass and farther a shallow depression
where a mass of men in blue lay flat for cover.
As Union infantry rose, he caught his breath,
their long line surging across the naked swale,
gaining speed in a gadarene plunge toward the wall,
behind which hunkered a double line of Rebels.
The Federals, come within fifty yards, one line
of Rebels fired, stepped back to reload, the second
coming forward to take their place and fire.
Front ranks were scythed away. The troops behind them,
stunned, milled about, then turned to run,
  dotting the field both ways with sprawling rag dolls.

He felt an irrepressible urge to cheer them,
but Hals was shouting, "We'll leave the ambulances here,
out of range. The mules are ancient and can't pull
nary a load." They descended to a row of batteries.
The ground he stood on vibrated. A dozen horses
were stationed behind each gun, many killed
or wounded. The gunners served their pieces with quick
efficiency, unflinching amid the shrieking missiles.
He knew he'd die in an instant. The battery captain
sat his horse behind the nearest gun,
before him and after couriers also on horseback.
He was taking note of a target through field glasses, drawling,

"Depress the number two muzzle one degree."
Around the weapon's carriage, two men lay.
A missile's whine emerged from din of muskets,
he flinching as Hals strode over one of the bodies.
A band of metal thin as a hat brim protruded
the soldier's forehead, shading astonished eyes
as if in all this raining iron, death
had been a surprise. He made to close them, but someone
spun him round, the surgeon glaring contempt.

"This man needs your help, that one doesn't."
Hals stood unheeding air electric with bullets
and rents torn in early light by shells.
Over Hal's shoulder the other man lay in dirt
and blood, groaning, his legs pumping slowly,
rutting two little mounds of loosened earth.
A fragment, spinning vicious as a rip saw blade,

had sliced his belly open—
                                        a stupendous blast,
his blouse almost torn off him, the percussive force
come near knocking him over, his hearing thinned
to a whine, his senses receding, then trickling back.
In dream vision, he saw the captain holding
an empty bridle, the horse's head and neck
converted to bloody spray which the captain wore
on his front, wiping his mouth with his hand. The shell
had sheared the hind legs off the horse in front,
the front legs off the horse in back, and both
were slanted down on nubs, their riders tumbled
from saddles. The captain's horse kept standing, its breast
ejaculating blood in slowing rhythms, then quailing
down to its knees. A chuckling gunner helped
his captain up.
                        "Sir, you're a dreadful mess.
Have my kerchief." One of the couriers produced
a side arm and shot the legless horses in the head.
They turned attention back to the bleeding man
who screamed when the stretcher bearers lifted him.
Hals knelt and cut his breeches away from the wound,
the gash not opening across the stomach, but lower
down near the groin.
                            "Lucky for you, me laddie,
it missed yer bladder." Hals folded a bandage, slapped it
in Garland's palm. "You keep the pressure on,"
Hals locking a vice grip on his hand, shoving it
in the wound, he jerking away when the man screamed
in perfect pitch with a falling shell that struck
a man of the detail, showering all in blood,

Garland the only man who went to ground.
Hals, smiling, yanked him up by his collar,
"Laddie, a shell is every bit as liable
to kill you where you weren't as where you were,"
thrusting again his mud flecked hand in the wet,
hot wound, provoking another scream. The air
was thick with shells, pressing breath from his lungs,
his face prickling, the surgeon yelling "Pressure!
You want this man be bleeding to death?" He shook
his head in answer and to clear his wits, his fingers
cupping quaking flesh, feeling corporeal
heat like a hog's but touching the languishing rhythm
of a man's pulse. At every foot jolt, the soldier
screamed, his own nerves recoiling. When they dropped
                                        the patient
groaning in an ambulance wagon, he asked the others,

"What do I do now?" A fellow answered,
trotting away,
              "I reckon he'll have to hold it."
The lout descended the hillside laughing, the crown
of his white kepi bobbing.
                          "Listen to me.
"You've got to press your wound to stay your bleeding."

"Mother of God—just go and let me die."

"Listen to me"—
                "I don't want to go to the surgeons."

"Listen to me—you've got to do this to live."
The patient regarded him with inflamed hatred.

"It doesn't mean I'll live and why should I live?"
He grabbed the man's right hand in his right hand.

"Maybe folks back home are wanting you to."
And saying that, he had an inspiration.
"Tell me the name of someone back home, someone
who wants to see you again?" Pain scowled his face,
but then his rage was doused, his countenance changed
like a hound dog striking trail and giving tongue.

"Clara," he muttered.
                              "A sweet name. Is she your wife?"

"Clara's my daughter."
                              "All right. Do it for Clara."
He shoved his dirty hand in the wound, deftly
drawing out his fingers as the pulsing mat
of hot flesh slid away, leaving him startled
with his bloody hand. The man moaned long and low.
Still terrified by the shells' malicious ululations,
he met the stretcher bearers coming up,
mien and countenances light, cheerful as nitwits,
as if life's chief pleasure were a crowded rain of grape
and canister, and trotting past they called,
                                                      "Flicker,
Flicker, Alabama Yellowhammer!
Flicker, Flicker, Flicker," laughing and huffing
on the breathless steep, gleeful and impertinent as fiends.
I have held together a body and soul in my hand,
and to these devils, I'm yellow as egg custard.
At noon he found himself in the sunken road
in a train of about a dozen men, trying

to move three stretchers. He couldn't believe this haggard,
scarecrow lot of soldiers. Many were shirtsleeved,
half were barefoot in full teeth of December
searing cold, a rabble, not an army.
Above their heads, the vicious hizzing of bullets,
and often he heard the zing and repercussive slap
when a Minie ball struck flesh. But nothing stopped
the work of the men in two long lines, sheltered
by the wall—not men it seemed but demons, impervious
to bullets as to cold, some grim, mouths set, eyes burning
with battle fury, others strangely becalmed
as if combat were any quotidian occupation.
He hugged the ground, his arm flung across a wounded
soldier to keep him writhing from the stretcher. A ragged
man stepped back and knelt to tear a cartridge;
a thin beard, grown from sideburns, shadowed his jaw line,
framing a delicate mouth. He set the percussion
cap with studied cheerfulness.

                                    "Best you stay down,
cousin," he drawled. "The Yanks is getting ripe
for another charge. When we turn them fellers round,
you'll hear the fire slack up some, and then
you mosey on out'a here. I'll tell you when."
With a dirty hand he gave a woman's caress
to the wounded man's face, a ball having punctured his throat.
"These men are gonna take good care of you, Howard,"
but Howard was alone in agony's narrow world.

"I'm obliged. I watched their first charge from the hilltop.
How many more have they made?"

                                        "They done made four

and each one's been damn bloody. I has to say
these damn Yanks got grit."
                  "Got dammit, Dale,
air you gonna fight or stand there talking about hit?"
said a soldier coming down from the fire step,
winking at Garland and spitting a cartridge top.

"I'm trying to give you a chance to get caught up,
Smash. You been keeping the Yankees safe
all morning." Dale went up on the step and fired.

"Now Dale, don't you start yore lying, you won't
be able to stop. You know you ain't shot nary
another Yankee than me. Pore Dale," he confided,
"he thinks he knows how to shoot a rifle." Smash grinned,
showing the single tooth that tore his cartridges.
A cresting thunder fractured air, a palpable
racket, hell advancing, batteries weaving
a roof of streaking smoke and brimstone, provoking
a deluge of shells from opposing Union guns.

"These ball's got shucks tied to they tails," Smash shouted,
"and coming down like 'simmons after frost."
The air above his head was thick as a quilt
with riot's warp and woof of shot and shell,
crowding trajectories of death, pinning him down.
He knew if he did not concentrate, if he
did not, by force of will, exercise the utmost
self control, he'd surely pee like a puppy.
An outraged shout went up, a calling down
of Jericho walls, resolving to a gleeful jeering.

"C'mon blue belly. Bring 'em boots and blankets."
All up and down the line the mockery built
and faded.
   "Bring 'em boots and blankets h'yar."

"I's cold last night Yank—bring at blanket,
 bring it on!"
   "Git it up hyar close!"

"Sue-ee. C'mon, Yank. Sue-ee, sue-*ee*!"
The racket broke against the first volley
like a catastrophic wave, and when he thought
his head might jar from his shoulders, the wave receded.
Clamor bled down to commotion. Dale stepped back.

"They taking off. You'uns better get on."
He and the other stretcher bearers moved out
at once, crouching beneath the humming air,
the road erupting desultory with spherical case.
When he stood on the heights again among the coming
and going of ambulances, a detail was posted there
to relieve them. The swatch of ground before the road
a hundred yards deep and spanning the scarp's foot
was strewn with blue clad bodies. Beginning thirty
or forty yards from the wall, a man could walk
to the enemy lines on a pavement of Yankee dead.
This far off, he could see the wounded crawling
among the clotted piles of dead and fallen
stands of colors. Ambulances clambered the hill,
bearing screams and prayers and imprecations,
wagon beds pouring streams of blood on the road.

At the hospital, wounded spilled from stoop to dooryard.
Some lay on the ground, a few reclined on tree trunks.
He'd never seen so many ruined faces.
The jambs of the wide front doors were daubed with blood
from traffic of stretcher bearers brushing against them,
and from every door and window so many saws
zipped and dragged in human bones, the whole house
trembled like some fantastic nightmare hive.
He had not eaten anything all day long,
so hunger impelled him to fetch his sack. He stepped
over bodies crowding the parlor floor. A boy,
terrified, gripped his ankle tight, holding
him still, his other arm shred formless and bloody.

"Don't let 'em take my arm. Please don't let 'em!"
He wrenched free of the boy's grip and found
his bed upstairs. All down the passage, men stood
holding candles over prostrate and bespattered forms
of human wreckage. Their screams stuffed the hall.
At the foot of a bed, Britt was sawing a bloodied
leg, a flap of skin laid bare and hinged
at the knee. His arm was working furious, but his eyes,
skewed away from the task, looked almost vacant
as if he guided the saw's work not by vision,
but like an expert carpenter, by the song-tones
of its back and forth sighing and biting of bone.
Behind the working surgeon, the patient's terrified
visage gaped, a wood stick clamped in his teeth,
his whole face streaked and sweating runnels of crimson
as a river stone sweats in a summer lazy current.
The hizz of the saw ceased. The leg came off

in assistants' supporting hands, was borne away,
at his feet a washtub of abscised arms, the hand
of one poised, still wearing its gold band.
Another patient occupied his bed, his staring
eyes empty cisterns, a neat hole drilled
in the temple, the brain matter puffing in gray gouts.
He reached across the gently breathing corpse,
gripped his sack and made his way to the porch.
He stumbled beneath a convenient oak, wrapped
himself in a blanket, and lay, trying to keep still,
but jerking like a drunk with the fantods. *How do they do it,*
Dale and Smash, cordial and calm as store clerks?
He shook himself then closed his eyes and breathed.
You're in it now, old son; it's root hog or die.
He rummaged his sack, ate two pieces of hardtack,
lay his head on the ground and tried to sleep
as repercussive battle shocks pulsed in his mind.
In the middle of the night he shivered himself awake
and somewhat rested went back to offer help.
Behind the house, he found a congregation
of surgeons, bloody to elbows, passing a bottle,
all their faces skyward.
                "What is it?"
                         "Look,
just there. A rare sight in Virginia skies—
the Northern Lights!" It was wondrous and strange, a blue
and green diaphanous curtain, its billows arrested.

"Heaven waves its banners for Lee's great victory,"
slurred an officer, both hands gripping the porch rail.

"What makes you sure it ain't divine encouragement
for the Yankees?"
                    "I find the suggestion impertinent, sir."

"*You* the one what said they's the *Northern* Lights."
His fellows laughing, the drunken officer whirled
to face him, sneering, his eyes burning with liquor,
but a rasping cackle distracted the officer's ire;
the gathering turned. Dr. Britt intercepted
the bottle, passing from hand to hand, and took
a long pull with his right eye fixed on Garland
as he chugged the whiskey.
                    "Beware a true prophet!
This country Calchas may know more than you.
What's your name and where do you hail from, prophet?"

"My name is Garland Cain. I'm from home."
Raucous laughter seized the doctors like flame
in cord wood. These officers were inscrutable, open
mouthed and chortling. He stared at the heaven's ominous
fires with discomfiture. Groans of wounded were simmered
to whimperings, and he retreated into night to regroup
his spirits, telling himself to steel his nerves,
It's root hog or die, old son; it's root hog or die.

December 22, 1862

Hoarfrost crusted his blanket, numbing flesh
in chilling currents, swirling him towards dawn.
Pulling his blanket tighter, he purposed to go

and speak with Dr. Britt about returning
to his company. Walking through early mists, he approached
a towering pile of offal dumped since yesterday.
He admired the spacious porch, its ornate posts
and railings, a restful spot to sit in evenings,
and now the soldiers tossing odiferous garbage
right in the dooryard for mere convenience's sake.
A gray dog tore at something near the bottom
of the pile, rolled his eyes at him, growled
low through clamped jaws and gave no ground.
He whiffed a vile odor in spite of cold,
tasted its sour tang. Then vision resolved,
a mound high as his chin of legs and arms.
Staggering backward, he quailed at bloody stumps
showing raw, cut clean as hams on a kitchen bench.
He dropped to a knee, retching out the acid
plunging up his throat, scorching his nose,
another convulsion, like taking a whack to the gut,
a hard dry heave, resolved in a spasm of coughing.
He waddled back to his feet, knees free as hinges.
Balancing himself, he dealt the cur a savage
kick, which somersaulted, shrieked and bolted.
He shuffled away from reeking human meat,
sat on porch steps, holding his head in his hands.
Pine boards creaked behind him, the doctor's voice.

"I've got another mission to give you, prophet.
Can you tell me what it is?"
                                    "I reckon not."

"Well, a prophet can only read the auguries,

which only come from God, and God is fickle.
It's burial detail, and you won't thank me for it,
I can assure you."

        "Why are you sending me then?"

"You're near to hand and able bodied, and no one
should get to turn his back on the death he deals.
He should see the mangling, breath its stench, bury
the offal. In time to come it might prevent
his doing something shameful." Patients were waking,
raising a groaning chorus. "I could requisition you,
prophet, for medical staff. It's dangerous everywhere,
but safer here than the ditches."

        "I'm obliged, but I can't
abandon my friends."

        "Ah yes, devotion to comrades.
War always thrives on such like notions of honor."
The doctor turned on his heel, entered the infernal
rooms. He rose, glanced in disgust at the pile,
then struggled up the height, exhaustion vitiating
stick and sinew, in a column of eight, including
two Negroes, one of them mumbling over and over,

"Sho don't want to do dis hyar thang, sho don't,"
till one of the soldiers said,

        "Ain't none of us wants
to do hit, but hit's got to be done. Now hush yer fuss."

"But massuh, what if one a dem corpsis haints me?"

"Treat the dead with respect, and they won't haint you."

The Negro cast his companion a dubious look,
who appeared, not fearful, but disgusted, saying,
                                        "Napoleyun,
you ain't got sense to last you ovuh night."

"Don't want no sense. Just don't want to be hainted."
George Athey from Tennessee shambled beside him,
his gaunt face shadowed with stubble, his mouth slack.
His head was shaped like a stirrup, round and bald,
the jawbone thin as the stirrup iron. He'd gummed
his chaw till the leaves were spent, his spit clear
as spring water. The Negroes, hangdog, pulled a dray
loaded with shovels, pine poles, and spoiled blankets.

"Why we taking stretchers with us, George?"

"Easier to move 'em bodies; 'em corpsis sometimes
falls apart when you go to grab aholt."
He shook with laughter at this, his head bobbing.
"I ain't had nary a furlough in six durn month.
You reckon at's fair?"
                        "No George, that's not fair."

"Ain't nothing but red tape in this here army,
and I fought in ever battle since the Bully Run."
Gaining the summit and looking over the field,
he was astonished at the cast of white bodies.

"My God. What happened?"
                            "I reckon Rebs been prowling
'em corpsis." George shivered laughter, holding his arm

and lifting a new leather sole to Garland's sight.
"I done been three month barefoot till yestiddy.
Now don't you reckon old Jeff Davis ought
to give us fellers a pair of boots to march in?"

"Yes George, I do."
        "And Garland, lookee h'yar.
I got 'em boots and a tintype from out'n his pocket.
Look at 'at Yankee gal. Ain't she right purty?"
His porcine eyes were squinched, his slack face close,
his reek of breath staggering rancid, he holding
his purloined treasure. Her hair was glorious brunette,
her countenance fraught with proleptic sorrows, and now
she was somewhere enduring husks of longing all people
else call hours. The notion shot him through
how when you take a bead on a man, you're aiming
at lovers, friends, families, wives and mothers,
and it struck him aghast that he should author such cruelty.
"Wooden chew like to tup a purty Yankee
gal like 'at?"
        "Yes George. Now please, put up
the picture." He chortled and clung to Garland's arm,
using him like a crutch as they snaked downhill.
Inside the earthwork, a platoon had fallen asleep,
their injuries dressed, bandages wrapping heads
and arms in slings, many leaning in postures
of repose, the putrefying stench assaulting his nose.
Two young men reclined against the wall,
their cheeks pristine; the head of one was bandaged,
the other's breast, a scarlet blossom blowing
in the lint. The Negroes commenced hefting corpses,

among them one of the pair of friends. He stepped up,
lifted the other, grunting his body on the fulcrum
of his back.
                    "What chew doing?"
                                        "Massuh, you gwine
to wear yoself to the peaked end uh nothing."

"I want these two to lie together in their ditch."
George blinked, his eyes wet with incomprehension,
like a coon dog's eyes. He broke in squinting laughter,
hiccoughing, his frail shoulders trembling.
                                        "Let's mosey."
Napoleon, pulling the dray, gazed behind him.

"O why did massuh hire me out to the gen'rals?"
They finished work, produced canteens and crackers,
slumped in the trench and leaned against the stones.
Then as when a farmer is sowing a field
and notices the calming sough of wind in pines,
he thought he heard a cry far down the swale.
He closed his eyes, the syllables forming, *water*.
He threw up a leg and stood atop the wall.

"How far can I walk before I get in range?"

"At's no consarn today; they is a truce
for burying all of them what's gone up the chimbley."
He made a tentative step on the glacis, pocked
as if from a raging hailstorm, nerving himself
for the mortal crack of a rifle. "Air you gwine
to do a mite bit of Confed'rit commissary work?"

George was snorting. At forty yards lay the brave
closest the breastwork and beyond them bodies massed,
white and black and blue like macabre quilt blocks.
In the silent town, buildings were shivered and charred.
Two yellow balloons swayed the hostile air
on the Federal side, tethers bobbing their noses.
Inside a wicker basket slung under each,
a minute figure, holding glasses, watching.
The call came again. He started, boot soles breaking
brittle grasses. His breathing quickened, gorge rose
hot and vile, and nausea hollowed a nest
in his queasy innards. He expected air to shatter
like a glass, his body shatter. Nothing happened.
A murder of crows clambered up into wind,
wings and crow call sawing frigid air.
Turkey vultures covered many corpses,
rending putrescent flesh, erupting in sudden
wing beating and beak stabbing squabbles
each time a shred of meat was shorn for consumption.
A bird was firking an eye from its socket, a brood
of hogs lined up at a body as if slopping a trough,
the corpse shaking as snouts tore meat from bone.
He looked to heaven to steel himself, but there,
a revolving stair of scavengers in a sky profound
with silence. Before him stretched a highway of dead.
Spoilage and gases attendant to decomposition
bloated torsos. The stench was enough to knock
an ox down. He held his breath until the need
for air yawed vertiginous in his head and exploded
in a violent intake of breath and taste of decay.
The naked youth were the most obscene, the shrunken

sexes, appendages burst or sheared, revealing
bone and organ, the pale flesh marred by bruises
of multiple bullet wounds, many bodies
rent, the entrails strewn. Here a man
cradling intestines, the blue guts having oozed
through fingers, uncomprehending horror lurched
the face, the eyes a hog's eyes stunned to death.
Here a hand clamped to a shoulder stump,
here a torso, legs shorn off, the arms
flung up and back in shocked and outraged surrender,
there a man without a head, and there
a head had rolled to a stop, stump side down,
the features peaceful, composed as if he slept.
The harrowing bulge of thousands of eyes scanned
the arching opaque gray, betraying pain
and shock, the musculature of each dead visage
framing madness, desperation, agony,
torment of death's excruciations, which filled him
with revulsion for this hell of human manufacture.
The Federal balloons waggled and tugged their tow lines,
inscrutable, amorphous eyes, ascending foundations
of air, a towering hostile Babel omniscience.
He gathered the fullest canteens and promised himself
he'd be a good man on the field of battle, but the words
revealed him to be a stooping hypocrite. *My God,*
my God, nothing I know is any use here.
The field was strewn with trash, cloth and paper,
splintered stocks, dented canteens, and ever
so often, a diary, a Testament, a dead bird,
and here and there a photograph a dying man
had produced for his final mortal recollection,

the lifeless eyes of wives and children staring.
To traverse the Champaign meadow, he was forced to tread
on bodies. The sufferer called, he found the man,
his languished eyes beholding him from a distance.

"Oh God. Please dip your finger in water to cool
my tongue." He pulled a canteen strap from his shoulder,
raised the sufferer's head and gave him a sup.
His lips being wetted, a spasm of gratification
coursed his body, the way an axe, striking
a knot in the grain will send the blow's shock
backward through the haft, tingling hands and forearms,
shoulders and pectorals. The man had unfastened his trousers
and held a bloody hand below his belt.
Many corpses had their pants undone.
The man's dark hair was mussed, his face rough hewn,
a smile lingering, and he was amazed the sufferer
preserved good humor all this terrible while,
awaiting hideous death with a stalwart heart.

"I'm going to leave a canteen. You can use it again
when you're thirsty." He stood on the island of dead and turned,
but his foot stuck fast. The man was gripping his ankle
though weak with loss of blood and exposure. He knelt,
"I've given you water, soldier. What else can I do?"

"I want to see Genevieve. I want to go home."
Dismayed, he gave the ruined one another
drink.
      "What's your name, soldier?"
                        "Erskine."

Two hundred yards or so near the Federal lines,
a Union burial party was digging, three soldiers
and half a dozen Negroes with shovels and drays.
He struggled to scooch the wounded man on shoulders,
he gasping through clenched teeth a breath that Garland
prayed was not his last. Then burdened but steady,
he stepped with care on the treacherous way of corpses,
a terrified equilibrist. Spotting a man's broad chest,
a sure foothold, he stepped—a hollow crump
and puddle gush, like crushing a rotten pumpkin,
throwing him off his balance. He shifted his left foot,
and looking down at his right, he saw black blood
seeping up through cotton broadcloth and pooling
over his boot. He couldn't move fast, his left foot
being behind him, so he had to let his right foot
sink for purchase. Then he stepped, and the ooze
pulled his boot almost off till suction
broke, and he was free, his sock squelching,
he thinking all his life to this day a delusion
of crass fantastical hours, filled with getting
and spending for needs, rendered now to pitiable
distractions, which proved him a ramshackle, slipshod creation
of biscuits, chitterlings, chickens, yearling pigs,
ploughshares and wagons and boots and coats and hats
and land and crops and coffins; was it for these
he raced and grasped, a child catching at soap bubbles,
the soul laboring to support an appetent creature
rapt with the seen, the unseen never minded,
and all the while it beseeches an angry God,
dangling millions over blazes of spirit perdition,
unaware his hand is poised to let them drop?

The Yankees, bemused and aghast, watched him stumbling
beneath his load, canteens hanging on his neck,
and had he not been blown and scared, he might
have laughed at the astonished faces.
                                        "This man's alive.
Could you fellers unfold that stretcher there?" They sprang
into action, and he knelt and slid the hurt one off
his shoulders, bumping him hard on buttocks but cradling
the back of his head to lay him gently down.
"His name is Erskine. He says he wants to go home."
He turned and started making his way over corpses.

"You murdering bastards shot these men like dogs!"
Over his shoulder one of the Yankees, eyes
narrowed, face contorted in rage, brandishing
a pistol, and the lieutenant—he'd seen his chicken guts—
moving to interpose himself between them,
gripping the weapon, shaking it loose from his hand.

"That man's a soldier just like you, goddamnit.
Holster your piece." He heard him mumbling threats
but decided to put more space between them in case
the private turned out to be a persuasive man.
He hadn't gone far when the lieutenant shouted again,
"Thank you, Secesh. It was a fine thing you done."
And he turned a final time, lifting his hat
in salute, then made his way across the field,
hearing beneath his unsteady tread, the bones
of the enemy popping loose from sockets, the gush
and bubble of gases when his feet met rotting flesh,
spewing in wheezes noxious and odious miasmas.

Already the sun was low, the shadows long.
He thought with rue how the light had just sufficed.

December 23, 1862

Britt released him to Company H, sliding
the order across his desk, not speaking. He visited
a sutler's wagon, one of dozens clogging
each muddy cow path leading to camp and purchased
pencils and paper and a shank of nice dried beef.

"Garland Cain reporting from Company Q
to Anderson's corps."

        "Ain't seen you in a coon's age."

"Where you been, Cain?"

        "I been shitting like a goose."
Caleb bounded from the tent and threw his arms
around him.

        "I's powerful worried about you. The veterans
say the surgeons are a sight more dangerous than Yankees.
What was your diagnosis?"

        "Sawbones says
I had the Tennessee Quick Step."

        "I reckon a wagon
load of men have done come down with that,"
said Oscar. "The boys will acquaint you now with mud
and lice and camp itch."

        "I'm much obliged to y'all."

"Garfish, these fellers is our new mess mates from the old
   company," said Apple Jack. "This here's Yancey.
We call him Papa. This here's Deke or Critter.
This feller's Hiram; he's our First Shirt.
And this is Bill Mordecai, our new lieutenant.
We voted for officers while you were taking things easy."
Hiram, reading the paper, gave him a nod.

"Try not to get your ass shot off," said Papa.
"And by the way, the boys call Mordecai Left Tenant."
Mordecai's face grew stern at this introduction,
   but though he outranked Papa, he did not rebuke him.

"Always pleased to meet a fresh fish.
I hope that none of you boys are white washed Yankees."
With a dubious look around he took his leave.

"Pleased to meet you gentlemen."
                                        "Mordecai brays
like a colicky jenny, but he's rock steady on the line.
That's the time you'll want to pay him attention.
Oscar has got our supper fixing. We'uns
is tickled to death to have him cooking fer the mess.
He beat the man what killed hisself frying corn pone."

"What we having?"
                        "Cush."
                                        "Would some beef help out?"

"Sholey," said Oscar, tearing butcher paper.
"I swany if this ain't good dried meat, a sight

better'n the blue beef we've been issued." Some soldiers
crowded the fire, enjoying aroma of victuals,
admiring Oscar's skill. He'd covered a crate
with a white cloth, where he kept his utensils in order.
And now he carved the marbled flitch into rashers,
added them spitting to grease, then poured in water
to cover. Stewing the meat a while, he crumbled
in two pawns of corn bread and stirred as the water
cooked a way. When the Cush was dry, he lifted
the pot from the tripod and set it down on a stone.
"There y'are, boys. A mess of Confederate Cush.
Come and get it." Men lined up with mess kits,
circling like birds, stomachs tight as twine,
and Oscar spooned a dollop of cush for each.
Hospital fare of hard biscuit and creek water
hadn't stuck to his bones. With every spoonful
of cush, he felt improved, savoring the grub.
Wagons and horses moved through camp, far off
music was playing, conversations lulled
as spoons scraped tins and dusk gave way to dark.
They took out bedrolls and blankets, arrayed themselves
around the fire.
                    "Critter and Hog, where y'all
going? The sinks is that a way." Hog laughed
and Deke said,
                    "I ain't never used any sich thang,"
and disappeared with Hog into outer darkness.

"A Rebel sojer's near a Sooner dog."

"Damnation, Snake," said Yancy, "you read the paper

and fart a sight more'n any man I've served with."
Snake's back was turned to the mess in order to keep
the firelight full on his page.

           "It is written, Papa,
a vain knowledge fills the wise man's belly
with the east wind."

         "Where's that from?" asked Caleb.

"Smells awful like a northerly wind to me."

"Snake's a clever feller," put in Buzzard.
"Before the fight, him and me was bumming
by the river, bumping our gums with some Mississippi
boys when a Yankee picket come down to the bank.
'Hey Sesech!' one hollered, 'We gonna be coming
to see you soon on our way to Richmond. We hope
you fellers won't take it nothing personal like.'
And Snake, he shouted back, 'If'n you boys
is wanting to get to Richmond, you gwine to have
to get up early, come down a long street,
leap a stone wall, and climb two hills,
and you jest might wind up wishing to be on the lee side
of all the grape and canister you commence to find.'
The Yank thought that was funny, and then Snake says,
'I been to Richmond. Ain't nothing to see there no how,'
and the Yank just couldn't stand no more. 'All right,
Secesh, I hear what you're saying,' but them two fellers
with him, they warn't laughing atall; I recollect
they's green and looking kind of spotted, what
like all the peas in they cornfield's done been spiled."

"We whupped the Yankees purty good this time,"
said Ainey. "You reckon they gonna quit, Papa?"

"I reckon not."
                          "The thing we got to do
is go full chisel and make the Northerners tired
of war and fetch us some political recognition
from France and England."
                                        "How come is 'at, Snake?"

"They leaders'd recognize our independence."

"What do they care 'bout our independence?"

"Nothing, but they care a heap 'bout all them bales
of cotton they ain't getting on account of the blockade.
The mills in France and England what makes fabric
are quiet as churches, their folks is out of work.
Mister Napoleon is especially uneasy and Davis,
I read, is working him like a blind dog
in a meat packing house." Caleb glanced about.

"You know why that recognition's not forthcoming?"

"I don't know," said Garland.
                          "Because of slavery.
France won't act without England's acting first,
and England won't act because her folk are loath
to condone our peculiar institution." Left Tenant
scowled at the fire.
                          "Well, we'll have to tote

119

our truck alone. We have our right to property
and honor, and the Yankees mean to deny us both.
I for one will fight them to the knife. Liberty
is a dead thing if Yankees win this war."

"Doesn't it fret you at all that your notion of liberty
depends on keeping other men in chains?"

"Nothing is going to alter my view on this matter.
Opinion, argument, Yankee blood in endless
quantities, nothing will ever convince us we are
wrong on slavery. Sanctioned in holy writ,
central to Southern economies, strip it away
and our very lives are undone, and this is exactly
what the Yanks are about. They wish to go on spoiling us.
God a mighty. I thought I joined the *Rebels,*
and here I am in a company of abolitionists."

"Hell, Mordecai," said Yancy, "I ain't fighting
for no rich feller's right to flay another
dollar outen my hide nor a nigger's either."

"I'm with you, Papa," Guide Post said.
Snake began to chuckle.
                              "What's so funny?"

"Sisters, I hate to offend your refined sensibilities,"
he glanced at Caleb, "but this here war has one
root cause, slavery. Slavery created the sections
and drove them apart. And here is something new,
the rise of your mercantile class as political actors.

They pitting free labor against remunerated labor.
Rich man's war and poor man's fight? It's worse.
All of us—we just the rich man's niggers."
The soldiers burst out laughing, but Snake pressed on.
"Money ain't a fancy thing to die for,
but Rebel sojers are fighting for the peculiar institution,
will or no, and if you don't reckon it's true,
you beating the Devil and running round a stump."
Caleb's face betrayed grave consternation.

"But the situation's more complex than that.
Sumter was our mistake, but the North invaded.
They made to levy us to coerce our neighbors."

"What kind of man would I be if I wouldn't turn out
to defend my mother and father, my wife and chits?"
said Apple Jack. "But I don't think they's anything
wrong with slavery itself. I got me two slaves,
Bess and George, and I learned right off the only
way to get 'em to do any work without me
standing over 'em ever minute of the gol durn
day was to treat 'em like I'd want to be treated."

"But many masters do mistreat 'em," said Caleb.

"And the fault is with them, not with the institution."

"The institution places a man's happiness
in another man's hands. That is a great evil,
whether an owner treats them well or not.
I'm sorry Apple Jack, I didn't mean"—

"No, Caleb, I see what you're saying. If a man
would own a slave and be a moral man,
he must assume that awesome responsibility."
Oscar stood.
    "Well I got one thing to say.
Damn the French if they don't get a move on.
I'm set to quit this folderol and mosey home."
He put some water on to scald the vessels.

"Papa, what would you be doing if you
was home right now?"
     "What? I reckon I'd be
happy again in my bed with sweet Miss Sally,
God defend her and bless her pretty ways."

"If I's at home, I'd be sitting around
with molasses in my britches waiting to get to the river."

"What river is it you wasting yore life on, Ainey?"

"The Tallapoosa near about Weedowee.
Best place to fish on God's green earth they is."

"Ainey, tell the one about the moccasin."

"Oncet on a dog day July afternoon,
my woman caught me swigging pop skull and run me
out'n the house. Hoofing across the stoop,
I grabbed my pole and line and sprinted for the river.
But since I'd gotten off like one possessed,
I didn't have nary a thang to use for bait.

I started walking up the river bank
and presently I come across a cottonmouth
and brother he was monstrous—long enough
to stretch from now until the morning—lying
there working his jaws around a fat old bull frog,
so I step on his neck and pluck that bull frog out.
Then I give him a good long pull of whisky
and kick him splash in the river. I cut up my frog
and bait my hook and have a sip myself.
The sound of the Tallapoosa flowing south
is the usefullest music this side of Heaven they is.
I got my back again a sweet gum tree,
it's a lazy shade around me and a sleepy noise
in the breeze, and I'm almost nodding off when they come
a tugging at my britches' leg about my ankle."

"What was it, Ainey?"
                                "Hit was at same snake.
He'd brung me another frog." Garland laughed
with the men, listening to stories until their words
were faint murmurings, and he drifted into sanctifying sleep,
dreaming Duessa's twilight arms around him.

December 25, 1862

Twilight milling, reclining, the mess retiring,
he huddled with Caleb to stave off winter chill.
A boy came wandering up from another mess.
They'd met on a stint of fatigue duty, digging trenches
for new latrines. His name was Henry Barkloo,

and he hailed from Samson, Alabama. He approached
the two men tentatively, carrying a folded paper.

"Hey Garland."
> "Hello Henry. How's it going?"

"Fair to middling, I reckon." He looked around
to see he was out of ear shot of other men,
"Hey Garland. I needs to axe you a favor."
> "Sure."

"My momma done wrote me a letter. I puzzled on it
some. You reckon you might read it to me?"

"Sholey, Henry. Sit down and put up your dogs."
He unfolded the letter, kept this voice low.

Deerest Henry:
> *I rekon you hev got*
yore self off to Verginnia by nauw. I hope
the long trip did not tir you out to much.
Henry, war is terribl, but I gess we hev
to hev a war. But Henry all ways remember
that there are worser thangs then for yore body
to die. I wood rather you hev to die Henry
than to know yore mortal soul had been corruppted.
I been married to yore father twenty years, and I know
what men are like when a passel come together.
I know there will be cussing and drinking liker
and gammling in the army. Henry don't you hev nothing
to do with any of that. Go to church

when you can and read yore Bible Henry and pray.
Pray ever nite before you go to sleep
and all ways say a prayer before you go
into battel. Repent yore sins each day and axe
forgivenes for them things what all you mite could hev dun
to displeese the Lord. Don't get no notions, son.
We are a simple folk and amongst our lot
you aint the sharpest blade in the drawer Henry,
so don't you go and get yoreself no notions.
When you come home I want to greet my Christyun
boy, and if you die then I want God
to greet yore sole in Heaven, where someday in the sweet
bye and bye I two will see you again.
Take cair Henry and remember yore mama loves you.

He folded the letter and handed it back to Henry,
who was looking like he might begin to cry.
"I'll help you write her back if you want me to."

"I'm obliged, Garland. Maybe tomorrow. I got
to think what all I wants to say." He buttoned
the letter in the bosom of his blouse. "Thank you Gar,"
and he strode away, Caleb regarding him.

"Now there's a Christian dame severe as any
Spartan mother ever was—'*Henry,*
come back with *your shield of faith or* on *it!*'
We've never turned away from our pagan ideals
but cobbled Christianity above the lintel,
not even stepping back to see if love
could thrive with honor. There our religion sways,

a shingle hanging off the temple of Mars."

"But Caleb, what consolation does a mother have
to shore against the fear of her son getting killed?"

"She has nothing but faith, yet we must square our faith
with the Word of God. Are Christians being honest?
You'd think not a soul in this country's ever read,
For all have sinned and come short of the glory of God."

"That verse would make us humble. We are not humble."

December 26, 1862

A biting and sighing, silencing dawn's first bird,
hauling saw blade back and forth, sweating
hard and grunting breaths, they hark and spit.
Ironwood growling lance tooth's musical snagging,
stroke and backstroke, sawyers heave, their muscles
aching. The trunk ticks and both men straighten,
scramble for mallets and wedges, pounding them in,
forcing the thin cut open to prevent the blade
seizing, striking in rhythmic swing on swing.
The man on the other end of the cross cut saw
was quiet in camp, tall and blond; the boys
had dubbed him Count because of his Dutch accent.

"What's your real name, Count?"
                              "Charles Kreuger.

But I don't mind you call me Count. Dem boys,
dey give me name because dey like me."
                                    "All right.
Where you from?" They leaned on mallets, panting,
sweat on their bodies turning instantly chill.

"I come from Puzen in Bavaria."
                                "What I meant
was where in Alabama are you from?"

"Close to Montgomery. I lives on my brodder's farm."

"What made you want to find another country?"

"After forty eight, things not good
  for Jews in Bavaria. I write my brodder and he say
come to South. People eez good to Jews."

"Do you own any slaves?"
                            "My brodder he owns slaves,
but when the people come to Montgomery and he rent
his lands, he sets his Negroes free. I don't
think it eez right for a man another man
to own, but I don't think eez right for North
to sell the slaves then say to southron, 'you
are bad man, you give up your property now.'
But I do not fight for slavery. I fight for South."
Count gave him a wily smile. "You know, Garlunt,
every man he fight for different reason.
Why you fight, Garlunt?"
                            "I fight because they made me."

"That is bad. Mens should have a choice."

"Life doesn't always come to men with choices.
I don't suppose you had much choice when you
left your home, and I can't see why God would curse
his chosen people to suffer endless wandering."

"God I think no longer choose the Jew.
I think that now God has choose the Negro."

"Why's that?"
         "Negro suffers more than Jew."
That afternoon when he returned to camp,
a parcel and letter from home was waiting for him.

Dec. 12, 1862

Dear Garland,
       I take my pen in hand to write
my beloved son. O Garland, how our home
is changed without you here. I work all day
and the only sounds I hear are the cluck and lowing
of the beasts I tend. Stewart and Carl, true
to their word, have stood by me. They are kind men
but they can never make up for the men I've lost.
Garland, I'm ashamed of the leave I took of you.
I should have been stronger, son. I owed you that.
A mother must be strong in ways a man
can never hope to understand, but it's hard
faced with the prospect of losing a son. But I
will trust and pray. Frost has killed my collard

greens and finished off the okra. The meat
in the smokehouse is curing nicely. Wish you were here
to share it with me. I bought an extra barrel
of flour this month. Things are more expensive.
Our country torn in two, sundered in violence.
Oh what anxiety and care.

Your loving mother.

P.S. I'm sorry to be a gossipy old woman,
but some of us had the impression you and Beth Anne
might have an understanding. I don't mean to meddle.
I will only say the obvious, Beth Anne is a woman
of considerable feminine charms and strong character,
and were you inclined to direct a letter to her,
I think your thoughts would find a soul companionable.

Beth Anne. Duessa had driven all thought of her
from his mind. And heart. He regretted he could not write her,
but he could not give her hope, nor was it wise
to alert the folks back home his heart was surrendered.
Time would have to carry them different ways.

January 19, 1863

The mess at supper, Deke beside him, grumbling.

"They's so much goddamned cob in this here cornmeal
I can't say whether I should eat hit or wipe
my ass with hit." Now a man from the Seventeenth

stumbled over with a bottle and glairy eye,
sloshing rifle knock knee into cups and slurring,

"Boys, today is Mars Roberts's birthday,
fitty six yare old. Even a bunch
a conscripts like yoreselves has got to drink to Mars."
He stepped on top of Oscar's cartridge box
in new Yankee boots, holding his tin cup high.
"To Mars Roberts, Army of North Virginny.
In ten months and twelve fights, only
a single draw at Sharpsburg—the rest—ass
whuppings for the Yankees!" His voice choked, his face
contorted in emotions novel to his sensibility. "God Bless
Mars Robert," he sputtered, wiping his nose on his sleeve.
A Yankee frock coat swallowed this stick of a man,
adorned with sacks and belts, all lettered *U.S.*
This woodsman lived beyond the reach of society,
fishing and hunting and drinking, performing only
those labors essential to keeping body and soul
together or those which wife and whelp refused
to do or could not do for lack of sinew.
Robert Lee had taken in hand this promiscuous
rabble from piney hollows, wiregrass bottoms,
swamps, and gulley washes, Appalachian foothills
and gained from them a near religious devotion,
hurling them vicious against the longest odds
and holding them up, not to the nation only,
but to the whole world, incomparable, invincible men.
And here was such a one on his rocking pedestal,
subdued by rifle knock knee, leading as much
of the camp as could hear him in a sonorous Rebel yell,

rising to a pitch as revelers unstacked arms
and fired celebratory discharges. The orator, reeling
with whiskey and breathless from yelling, his eyes rolled up
like jalousies as he stiffened and tipped like a broken mast.
Before the soldier crashed flat of his back,
a hand reached out and caught the whiskey bottle.
The musketry brought out officers, and they, applying
various expedients, quelled the firing. The yell
subsided like the dying of a sudden violent wind
into ranged voices, a fiddle, singing, laughter,
the usual hummadruz of camp at night.
A drunken detail staggered from the Seventeenth
and retrieved their rhetorician, bearing him
away like a slaughtered hog. Oscar stood
by the cook table, staring disgusted at two clay boot prints
on the cloth he laundered every day in a bucket.

January 20, 1863

Garland's mess had built a chimney back
of their wall tent, framing a box with thin boards,
and stacking three sides with blocks of cut sod,
allowing the frame to burn away with successive
fires. Yancy, Caleb, and Oscar were snoring.
He lay beneath his blanket with paper, pencil,
and passions, writing another letter to Duessa.
She hadn't responded to any missives. Though he longed
for reassurance of returned affection, he wasn't
too troubled. Mails were slow, but love proved worse
than war for frustration. He erased a phrase and surrendered,

fishing the juju bag from his shirt and breathing
its strange scents deep. A shower dappled the tent fly,
peaceful, languorous, and soporific, and he
was lost in her wild notions, in the dark continent
of her womanhood, in exotic jungle exuberance.
But after remembered passion, enacted in solitude,
he recalled the grave disquiet of her parting words,
Garland, you don't know what a chance love is.
What did she mean by that? He could not say.
Drifting into sleep's inexorable current, he recalled
a memory of hunting with his father, he a boy,
having never shot a deer. They lay on a hillock,
a stream beyond and a copse of oak, choked
in fog, when out of the heavenly mist a heavy
doe came stepping to the water. Before his father
could stop him, he brought her down with a clean pull
of the trigger as laughing crows flapped up and away.

January 21, 1863

Dawn and frigid words were rousing him.

"Come quick, Garland," Oscar sputtered and sprang
from the tent. He pulled a blanket over his shoulders
and threw the tent fly open onto ground patch worked
with reflections of the queasy sky.
                                    "I reckon it must
have rained pitchforks last night." He stretched and yawned.

"Like a cow pissing on a flat rock, and just wait

till you see how deep the Yanks are bogged down in it."
Scaling the heights, they joined the Eighth, soldiers
sitting on stumps, cooking coffee and perusing
with high amusement the travails across the river.
Caleb handed Garland some borrowed glasses.
The scene was indescribable. For a mile and more
than he could see, the Federal Army was stalled
in a highway of mire. The big pontoons they'd thrown
across the Rappahannock were lashed to wagons
with great double wheels, each of them rutted to axles.
One had several tow lines tied to its front hounds
and dozens of men tugging the end of each
to no avail. Scores of cannon lined
the road; the horses pulling them were gaskin
deep and struggling toward exhaustion. One gun
had sunk out of sight. Men with shovels were laboring
to exhume it, throwing up filthy muck that oozed
back down the hole. Others had pine poles shoved
under axles, attempting to leverage it out. Caissons
and ambulances clogged the road, the mules, fleshed
icons of despair, refused to struggle, just raised
their heads and brayed, baring teeth as they sank.
There were legions of wagons, medical and ambulance, slung
with hospital wreathes, wagons loaded with tents
and arms and rations, wagons with blacksmith furnaces.

"My Gawd, the Yankees got a lot of truck."

"Now look at that train of wagons," Oscar pointed,
"east of that line of caissons. They brought 'em up
last night. Appears that Burnsy, feeling sorry

for his boys, who had to sleep a-lying in the mud,
is pouring them all a glass of whiskey for breakfast."

"Mary and Joseph," someone whispered. Sure enough,
brigades were congregating at commissary wagons,
so many having forgone their futile work.
And now two regiments marched to face each other,
striding determined, their leaders gesticulating ire.
At the end of his tunnel vision, he saw a motion,
a man recoiled. Someone had thrown a punch.
The effect was like tossing a piece of bread in a pool
of bream. Every man hurled himself at once
to that point, compressing the mass with bodies and fury.

"Let me look," said Oscar. "If this ain't a regular
shindy, I'll never see one." Without the glasses,
he could still make out the minute forms stacking
the writhing mound of combatants. Men grappled in mud
and came up brown and slick as river otters.
Catcalls and cheers rang out from Marye's Heights
from Confederates gathered on the terraced amphitheater,
down to the pickets skirting the muddy river.

"This here must be the biggest whiskey brawl
in human history," snorted Ainey, peering.
The ground was stomped to an oozing daub filled wallow.
From the grinding hub, violent spokes stretched out
to felloes of shouting gawkers ringing the melee.
The officers had mounted, were striking soldiers with flats
of sabers, some firing in air; yet such expedients
were slow in subduing the Yankee pandemonium

to lam a neighbor's skull or bite his thumbs.
The dead still lay on the field in contorted postures.
Houses in the town below were gutted and charred.
Caleb said,
   "The men and produce of a great
civilization, weltered in a mire of drunkenness,
their works in sorry disarray. I fear the Yankees.
Such Sloughs of Despond we enter because of pride."
Hog, who was standing just behind Garland, whispered,

"I never know what that feller's talking 'bout."
Some Georgia boys on picket made a sign.
It read *To Richmond*, with an arrow underneath,
pointing the opposite direction of the stalled march.

February 18, 1863

"You fellers been to preaching?"
      "How can you tell?"

"The boys are pious to build a church house just
for a winter. How'd jew find hit?"
       "Well Ainey, I'll say
it's curious," said Caleb. "The house is shaped like an L,
with the altar in the crook. The pews are reduced in length
as they approach the pulpit—this to provide
some standing room for altar calls and such—
until at the front they's only a pew the width
of a dunking chair spang in front of the preacher.

It gives a fellow the distinct impression that every
word of the sermon's meant for him."
                                        "Sholey,
Jesus sat you there to convict your sins."

"And I guess Jesus let you hide behind me,
Garland, or just you running me over in a dad burned
rush."
            "Cal, at durned old gallinipper,
was solemn as a jasack in a snow storm with the fodder gin out,"
Buzzard laughed.
                        "Snake, why didn't you join us?"

"I don't need reminding I'm fixing to go back to ashes.
To a Yankee sojer, 'at cross is just a bull's eye."
Preacher looked grave.
                            "If it should happen you're lying
on the field in distress of your life, you'll want the Lord."

"Papa, what's the tightest fix you been in,"
Buzzard asked. Yancy blushed a little.

"Gaines Mill. Lee rode out and asked us in person
to break McClellan's line. The sun was set
behind the trees when we were ordered forward.
We carried our rifles at right shoulder shift and made
long strides downhill. At the edge of Boatswain's Swamp,
we stepped over A.P. Hill's shattered brigade,
what had failed to take the position, and saw entrenched
on the slopes ahead three lines of Yankee infantry
and rows of guns emplaced on Turkey Hill.

I knowed the game was up. I commenced to whispering,
Yea though I walk through the Valley of the Shadow of Death,
over and over I spoke it. Their guns opened,
a thunderous racket pitched and bearing down,
missiles so crowded wind from them fanned my face.
Not a single man of us dared to look behind,
afraid we might get squirrely at sight of soldiers
falling from our ranks. They screams was cold enough.
We left a thousand men sprawled over that ground
and halted across the swamp and fixed bayonets
and dressed the line"—

                "You dressed the line? My God."

"In a rain of grape and canister like I ain't never
seen, Hood and the officers standing before us,
their backs to the enemy guns as unconcerned
as anything. When one would drop, the man who was next
in rank would take his place. And then the charge,
and General Hood was the first man up that hill,
the Yankees raking us with shot and shell.
Twenty yards from the line, we let out a yell,
our arms at charge bayonet. Ten yards, and blue coats
scattered like grackles, scuffling up hill and hurling
onto the second line, what broke and swamped the third.
At last we fired at the milling, piled up men.
And that was the push that sent them over the top,
and we followed across the plateau and fired again
mostly at horses as gunners was trying to limber
their pieces, just before we swamped the lot of 'em.
We gobbled up fourteen guns and two whole regiments."
He marveled at the cool detachment in Yancy's voice.

"That charge was the first I seen a man git hit
dead on with a canister shell. He was trotting along
a bit in front of me, and there come a shriek
and sizzle like spilling water in hot grease.
My eyes was clapped right on that feller, Hicks
was his name, from Company K, a good old boy.
He was running and then he smudged away, like a match
blown out, an instant nothing, without no trace."
He looked around. Apple Jack, Préacher, Oscar,
and Snake were looking right spotted.
                              "My God, Papa,"
said Snake. "How do you muster the pluck for such?"

"Don't be troubled, fellers. We'uns all felt
like you at first—me and Left Tenant and Hiram.
But another fight or two, you'll make your peace
with the elephant."
                        "How's that Papa?" Yancey looked
around at the mess, aware of a sudden how all
were intent, uneasy, and a shadow crossed his face.

"Well," he hesitated, "fellers, they's a fact
as big as all outdoors and part of the house
you got to face and that is, your death is a thing
accomplished. Every sojer starts out worrying
if he's gonna die and then he realizes, sholey
I'm gonna die. How could I not die?
And then your mind gets easy." Snake's countenance
was bland and hopeless.
                        "Is that yer good advice?"

"When you get up something better, tell it to me."

"Well Papa, you've survived so far, can't you
tell us the reason?"

           "'Course I can."

                  "All right?"

"Luck."

     "That's it?"

             "What else could it be?
Why Hicks and not me? Hit's chance. Every bullet
has its billet, and when your shot is fired,
they ain't no dodging it. I could name a hundred
names of men what bit the dust while charging
right beside me."

               "But Papa, I think what the fellers
is looking for is any sort of practical
consideration to help 'em get through battles."

"That's right," said Snake, "some of us want to live."

"Well Snake, I reckon ain't no harm trying to live.
If you fall off a cliff, you may as well try to fly."

February 25, 1863

Dawn of strangled winter light, and he rose
to revenant silence and threw the tent fly open
on a blinding land, smothered in Heaven's change.
Oscar had stoked his cook fire.

                  "Morning, Garland.

Coffee's ready," his whole attention focused
on frying bacon. The white transformed the streets
and fretted houses of the town below to a peace
of ordinary habitation. The fall had hidden
the rotting dead, and he was glad to be spared
the sight for a time; he plunked himself on a stump
and enjoyed the fire, the coffee, the ministrations
of the cook among his vessels.
                              "How'd you make
the coffee today?"
                    "Diced a sweet potater
and roasted the bits."
                        "That's clever, Oscar. It's tasty.
Like sweet potato tea." All the sprawling
line appeared abandoned, except for a few men
gathered by fires, and all the camp—cannon,
glacis, and curtain were lavished in wholesome unreality.
And now a platoon appeared with crunching steps.

"There you are, skulking behind the lines—
storm and hail! The tented field awaits,
man! To arms, to arms!" He tossed his coffee
and made a dash to fetch his rifle. "Wait
old son," Caleb laughed, and he saw the squad
of men was unarmed. Caleb led the company
behind Marye's Heights and charged the men
with words of battle, one hand tucked in his blouse.
"Recall the beautiful belles who kissed you goodbye.
Recall their honor and their maidenheads."
                              "I like
to call on maids for that," laughed Apple Jack.

"Should we be vanquished here, the invading foe
 shall touch them with begrimed mechanic hands."
                                                "Scandalous!
Let us touch them first," Ainey guffawed.

"Let us hold before us our duty to God and country,
we happy few, we band of brothers, for he
today who sheds his blood with me shall be
my brother, even should he be vile as most
of you are." A cheer sputtered. "A rhetorical banquet
squandered on starvelings," he muttered, standing on a crest
of rock and gesturing below with a black birch saber
at a line of men crouching behind a heaped
white breastwork, snowballs stacked like solid shot.
He noticed the boys had even brought the Negroes.
"See below deployed in the vaunted field
Stile's brigade of Georgians, our comrades in arms;
beyond in the forest's margin with pennants rude,
General Hoke's brigade, the baleful foe.
God and fate have placed us here to fall
upon their flank and rout them." The Georgians were posted
in the wood in careful formation. Skirmishers shook out
ahead of the line. The officers barked out orders,
and the ranks obliqued left; another bark
and forward again with the delicate, rhythmic whisper
of boots compressing powder, and he saw what precision
meant and recalled, *terrible as an army with banners.*
"Listen men, execution and courage are key.
Have patience, wait for their flank. Don't surge forward
too soon and give them time to refuse their line.
When I give the command, don't stop. No plundering the dead

or aiding comrades. And don't bunch up for safety—
it's not safe." The armies came on. He patted
several snowballs till his fingers ached and noticed
Regis in the ranks.
                              "You're Colonel Herbert's man,
ain't you?"
              "Yassuh, massuh."
                              "You like snowballing?"

"We'uns don't get much snow in Alabama,
do we suh?"
              "No we don't."
                              "Hit's right
pleasant to see. Hit makes these grown up mens
behave like little chirrens." He hadn't seen it,
but hundreds of veteran faces shone with glee,
including Regis's, he dressed in a new woolen frock coat,
the lot of soldiers sporting shirtsleeves and galluses.
The order to charge, and Caleb led the way,
birch saber drawn, and the Eighth galloped downhill,
fracturing winter stillness with a crooning yell
and—incredible!—a volley of missiles churned in air
like ginned cotton or snow falling upward, defying
natural law. The enemy flank folded
like a bellows, and Hiram in the van pursued the routed
Mississippians till they were run to ground.
A fierce melee ensued. Garland brought low
many men, and once, poised to hurl
a missile, was struck at the belt line, a pang at the groin
as powder sifted down his pant leg. They captured
two captains, twelve slouch hats, a pound of bacon,

and four fresh pawns of cornbread they carried in triumph
to Oscar. Their casualties were low, three bloody noses,
two boys with blackened eyes, and one poor fellow
hit by a snowball loaded with stones that smashed
his front teeth out. The officers were so impressed
with Caleb's generalship, they brought a jar
of rifle knock knee, mellowed with a veal, raising
elaborate toasts and singing Rebel songs.

Whenever we go out to fight
   The Southrons give us lickings,
But then we strive to get revenge
   By stealing all their chickens.

Come throw your swords and muskets down
   You do not find them handy
Although the Yankees cannot fight,
   At running they're the dandy.

For weeks, Caleb was called the Snowball General.

March 21, 1863

Feb. 18, 1863

Dear Garland:
            I take my pen in hand to write
my beloved son. I trust you are well and pray
for your safety. The news from home is Mr. Pinkerton
has passed away, and whether his soul passed up

to Heaven, I shan't presume to say, but the only
interest people seem to have is where
his money passed to. People love nothing more
than gossip. I chance to know his money went north
with two mulatto daughters. I've seen them, comely
girls, plump as plums, who could pass as white,
and surely five hundred thousand dollars will buy
their emancipation (in specie of course), and though
their engendering were shameful and sin that pays its way
can travel freely, still I think it right
good fortune go with them and protect those girls
from wicked lusts of wicked men who stoop
to such depravity. It's disgusting in a man and rank.
I would rather a white man take a Negro wife
than use his serving women as prostitutes.
Such free lust has proven the downfall of many
a good man, the resort of many a bad one.
That lust is countenanced and defended by the slave system,
and should it pass away, I will not mourn it.
Oh Garland, what a world we live in now.
In all my life I never would have dreamed
of such anxiety. I love you, Garland.

                                                Mother.

March 27, 1863

"Air you going to church?"

                              "We got to, Buzzard?"

"Hit's *strongly urged* in the orders."

"Well I swany,"
said Hiram, "I gots a stronger urge to nap."

"Hey," said Ainey, "I'll take fasting and prayer
instead of fatigue duty quiker'n a pig can swaller
turnip greens."
    "Wisht I had me a mess
of turnips," said Buzzard. "Why so blue, Patty?"

"There'll be no whisky ration on a fast day, lads."

"Well Patty, we got to act like Christians sometimes,"
said Preacher, whose scoured hands were wringing a blouse
in a sudsy bucket.
    "You're all good lads, but I'm grieved
you've made no careful study of orthodox theology.
There's spiritual proof we Irish have heavy souls.
A round of bumpers it takes to lift our spirits
to realms of divine communion."
      "They's proof in the spirit,
Patty, ain't no doubt about that," said Caleb.
Soon the men cleared off to church or places
less accessible to those with power to assign
them duties and chores, but Caleb and Garland stayed
behind and boiled some coffee from parched wheat.

"The boys are quick to pray as they are to pull
the trigger on a man," said Garland. "Though given a choice,
I reckon I'd just as soon pray. All I did
was scuttle about the first battle toting wounded,
and it pert near scared the dog water out of me.

And it troubled my conscience. Do you think we're doing right?"
Caleb's visage grew stern and wary.
                                        "Old son,
this ain't just any pea patch you tearing up.
It's a dangerous question folks will kill you for asking."

"If I'm to be a man, I have to ask.
I promised to fight, I gave my word. That fact
I cannot change. Though looking back on that moment,
it seems the men who bade me swear were hardly
being forthright as to what my oath would mean."

"The prince of this world is also the father of lies."

"And I know if I'm to act, to endure this war,
I must be honest. I cannot lie to myself."
Caleb leaned forward, his voice enthused and intimate.

"You're right, Garland. A man must know himself.
While you were saving men at Fredericksburg,
I dispatched them."
                        "You did what you had to do."

"I tell myself it's the case, but Christ keeps nagging."

"What does Jesus say?"
                        "His word is simple.
Love God and your neighbor. We make him complicated
and prance about with honor like pagan heroes
to conquer and subdue, knowing Christ contends
a man is exalted to the measure he humbles himself.

Our courage must lead us in conversation with grace."

"That grace convicting your acts?"
                                        "The very same.
An untroubled grace can have no power to save."
Garland's stomach purred a feline growl.
His coffee, bitter bread smelling sop, was frigid.
He slugged it back. He felt betrayed by grace.
Religion offered no consolation but compounded
terrors, the God of men revealed in the instant
to be a creation of men, a papier-mâché,
wearing the hideous, lifeless grin of a manikin.

That night in camp, men read, wrote letters, plied
their housewives, wrapped themselves in blankets, traveling
country byways, woods and hills and rivers,
along the Black Warrior, the Tombigbee,
the winding Tallapoosa or Chattahoochee,
Alabama a beautiful state for rivers,
toward Gobbler's Crossing, Dixie Springs, Parrish,
Warrior, Pocahontas, or Coon Creek;
perhaps they lounged in arms of women they loved
or stalked with a favorite dog through jeweled grasses,
expectant for quail trilling the startled air,
or tasted food they were now denied, fat winter
sausages, beefsteak, and venison, recalling any
and all these haunting components of good life,
which thoughts have followed armies since there were armies,
sustaining the soul through desolate hours of tedium,
recalling happiness binding lives together,
of home and what is meant by patriotism,

once all the gaudy abstractions are peeled away.
But waiting on sleep, Garland's imagination
made a bee line for a white plantation house.
The redolent juju bag conjured her vivid
phantom, casting her magic, they reenacting
love's impassioned unction, leaving his heart
the vessel of her grace. Though life were driving him
like a rented mule, Duessa's love annealed
his soul with moral confidence, his spirit with peace.

April 1, 1863 near Guiney Station

He skirted the Rappahannock north and west,
passing an eyot parting the current, taking
delicious April air in keen advertency
for birdsong and myriad, twisted buds, each knotted
twig annealed by winter, shivering on the verge
of green. He wandered far and aimless, pursuing
every pip of kinglet and woodpecker's trill,
his copy of *Southern Botany* under his arm.
He relished spring's expectancy, driving winter
away like a peddler with sacks, reviving flows
of sap and roots in earth's spongy nourishments.
A streak at vision's periphery, a piping whistle,
a wood thrush sat him down in deciduous airs
at the bottom stair of sunlight. He closed his eyes,
as the gates of Heaven were rolled away to allow
his humble access. Her arms embraced him. The spell
of gris-gris scent and music summoning her phantom,
he tangled in her sheets and her caresses, reliving each

angelic touch and kiss and thrust. The singer
skittered away. Duessa's image vanished,
replaced by a wood, the stairway slanting steeper.
He followed the sighing river back to camp.
Behind the heights where the Eighth had built their huts,
he found two regiments sprawled in a sunny swale.
The boys had limbered up a battery of guns,
put them in park along the meadow's edge,
and started a baseball game. The soldiers whooped
and called, and horses and mules were grazing the outfield.
Garland's mess comprised the team at bat,
and Hiram served as their captain.
                                        "Garland Cain!
Where the hell have you been? We've got a powerful
need of you if you can swat a baseball.
These Mississippi sons-a-bitches are licking us."

"Fortunes of war," said Oscar, hefting the hickory
stick. "We beat them at snowballing, and they
beat us at baseball." Hiram went apoplectic.

"Just hit the damn ball, Oscar. I ain't losing
nothing to no Yazoo Mississippi hillbillies."

"Get 'em Dog Robber!"
                          "You can do it, Greasy."

"Use that bat like hit's a wooden spoon."
The pitch came straight and Oscar laid it on,
cracking the ball away in a hard line drive
over the first base man's head, who leaped up,

149

brushed the ball with the fingertips of his gauntlet
a cavalry unit had lent them for gloves. So touched,
the ball arced downward, took one bounce and struck
a mule in the haunches. The startled creature brayed
and made two passes at the fielder, trying to bite him,
allowing Oscar to take an extra base.
Cheers and chortles went up from company H.

"Bless him for an Alabama jasack," cried Hiram.
Oscar, now on second, was the tying run.
Someone called,
        "Let Regis bat," and all
eyes turned to Colonel Herbert, who took his pipe
from between his teeth.
              "Regis may bat if he wishes."
As Regis was wearing a shirt of brand new homespun,
he stripped to the waist. He was not especially tall,
but his musculature showed lithe and manly articulations,
a bronze god, animated and stepped from his pedestal.
The soldiers had to show him how to hold
the bat, but Regis had been observing the game
and was eager to try his skill. The pitch came straight
and fast. His swing rent the air, barely
kissing the ball, which dribbled across the grass.
The defenders raised a cheer which caught in their throats,
for though a fielder was quick to retrieve the ball,
Regis's feet seemed never to touch the ground,
and he beat the throw by a step. With runners at first
and third, Hiram handed the bat to Garland.

"Come on, Garland. Don't let these Mississippi

mudpuppies make us tote an ass whupping home."

"Knock it over the Rappahannock!"
                                        "Whip
these mud waddlers," and Barksdale's boys were chanting,

"Alabama Yellowhammer flicker,
flicker, flicker." He stepped to home and took
a practice swing and drove the first pitch high
and beyond the centerfielder. When he rounded first,
the fielder had run down the ball, pivoted, took one
step forward, hurling his body into the throw and sprawling
flat of the grass. He saw the ball propelled
like a cannon shot and the flashes of Regis's feet,
knew he wouldn't stop. The catcher came up
to guard the base for the easy out and crouched
on haunches to scoop the ball's low bounce and make
the tag. The company moaned prolonged despair.
Everyone knew that Regis was out, except
for Regis, who never slowed his pace or looked
away from home, the pound of footfalls shaking
the torso, the thigh's large muscles. When he turned third,
Garland glimpsed his face, his eye becalmed
as if there were only this running, now and forever.
A sudden consternation as both teams thought
there might be contact, the baseman put his shoulder
down to meet the blow, and Regis leapt
high, his winged feet striding once, twice,
purchasing air, arms pumping, his face an agony
of rapture. The boys of Company H in the act
of moaning their loss, gave sudden voice to the meadow,

151

the way a flock of myriad robins alters
direction in flight—a sudden shift, eclipse
of shadow sifts across the flock and passing,
their course is changed. Just like that the cries
transformed from despair to wild exhilaration.
The Mississippi unit left the field
heads hung low and swearing.
                              "Goldamn."
                                        "Beat
by a got-damned nigger." The Alabama boys
cheered till they were hoarse and kept on shaking
Regis's hand and many gave him gifts—
a pound and a half of bacon, a homespun shirt,
a plug of tobacco, a demijohn of spill skull.
Hiram was overjoyed to have subdued
the state of Mississippi, and so he presented
Regis with a pocket knife, a drop point blade
that folded, with antler scales and brass bolsters.
Garland rummaged his sack, regrettably spare.

"Regis, you saved the day, please have this,"
offering the servant a pound of fresh ground cornmeal.

"I thank you, massuh," Regis said, not meeting
his eyes, but Garland could see his stifled pride.

April 5, 1863

Sunday morning and Caleb and Garland sat

together on a split log bench under a clean
spring sky, attending to the regimental chaplain.

"The watchful hand of Providence is always acting
in human history. A belief in Providence is essential
for true manhood and the conduct of true religion.
Wellington claimed the issue of every battle
depends on Providence solely. Napoleon declared
when he crossed the bridge at Lodi, he felt that God
were ushering him toward greatness. His invisible will
determines the ebb and flow of events; his power
spurs our revolution with force inexorable.
Providence sundered churches South and North,
thus showing the path for our civil body to follow.
And just as Colonial citizens, grown exasperated
at being denied their rights as Englishmen, sundered
their ties to the Mother Country and took their place
among the nations as free and independent states,
likewise the South has spat the bit of Northern
tyranny and drawn her sword for nationhood.
Each of us knows our attachment to the union was fervid
and pure. It was a magnificent dream, of one
great empire stretching sea to sea. The splendor
of that dream ennobled our hearts, but the ties of affection
were spurned again and again, the illusion fractured,
and we have come to ourselves in tents and trenches.
Washington wished to remain an Englishman, but Providence
made him a Rebel. Luther did not wish
to spurn the Papacy, but reviving Providence drove him
beyond the Wittenberg Church to the Diet of Worms;
his courage to follow God's law emboldens us still.

So let our conscience be captive to the Word of God,
which compels and supports our struggle for independence,
preserving the vision of Jefferson, Madison, Paine,
justifying our course of action to our fellowmen
and worldly opinion; howbeit, brothers, in spite
of the confidence history and scripture inspire, yet we
are sinners and should be ever mindful of our slight
position in the presence of God Almighty, proceeding
in fear and trembling. For we are vile as Job
and should remain on our knees, begging his mercy
and repenting our manifold sins in sackcloth and ashes.
We celebrate today our redemption in Jesus Christ.
Hold in your minds the image of him on the tree,
the son of God given ignominious death
between two thieves, by soldiers who wagered his garments.
If you have not been washed in the blood, won't you
come forward now and give your life to him?
Secure your eternal soul in the love of God,
in the compassion and grace of his only begotten son?
The altar is open now. Won't you come?"
The soldiers sang a hymn and after the prayers,
Garland and Caleb wandered off to the shade.

"What did you think of the preaching?" Caleb asked.

"These chaplains are cribbing the same old pasture gate.
Pretty soon they gonna chew it to pieces.
Momma sent me a pocket Testament for Christmas.
Since then, I've read it twice. If that's supposed
to be the tactics, I sho don't get the drill."

"We want a God who approves our will and so

we fashion a God who approves. This is the subtlest
form of self deification because it wears
the dress of honor, patriotism, merit of law,
society's hallowed mores, but here's a fact;
preachers can preach politics till they's enough frost
in hell to kill snap beans, but the will of God
is the will of God. *He* knows what it is,
and we do not. To claim we see him moving
in human affairs is a fool's arrogance."

                              "And trying
to urge a Christian humility, he undid his sermon
with mention of Job, whose patience wrecks his message."

"Job's greatness derives from his understanding that God
is always more than what men say he is.
This causes him not to act but suffer with integrity."
He felt that Caleb was urging him on to a strange
rebellion, but if God had given men scripture that argued
with itself, one way to God must be through argument.
Left Tenant appeared.

                         "What are you lay abouts doing?"

April 21, 1863

"I hear the Yanks is on the move."

                              "I reckon
at means we'll be moving fore too much longer."

"Yep. Hooker's got to do something to show
he's got more fire in his belly than Burnsy had."

"Which way they going, Papa?"

                     "They got a bridge
throwed over the river up yonder at Franklin's Crossing.
The Yanks have gotten across the Rapidan Fords
behind us. Stuart done galloped off east with his boys
yestiddy."

           "Where do the roads lead from the fords?"

"Don't rightly know."

                  "I reckon Mars Robert'll get
them Yankees figured out," Left Tenant said.
"Fellows, I got to make some Yankee tea."
The nights were warming, intensifying stink of latrines.
The dog stars shone in frolicsome poise with their master
as he plunged headlong over the western horizon.
Campfires parceled darkness as if the stars
waved in reflection on a wide expanse of water.

"Here's an item in the paper, boys," said Oscar.

*"Matrimonial—A gentleman belonging to the service, now absent
from his command on account of wounds received in battle, twenty-five years of age, fair personal attractions and moderate income,
wishes to make the acquaintance of a young lady with a view to
matrimony. The young lady must be of medium height, handsome,
intelligent and educated. Wealth, although not objectionable, will
not be considered essential. Address Frank R. Summerfield, Mar-
ietta, Ga."*

"I wonder how bad he's hurt."

                  "Likely's none

too bad since he's coming back. He probably trying
to get him a marriage furlough to add to his leave."

"Summer's the time to stay shat of the army."

"I hope the Lord will bless the poor soldier
with a good wife. A godly woman is the pith
of all life's sweetness is what I think," said Preacher.

"But a man can't really know that till he has a wife,"
said Hiram. "It's a thing you discover as you get to know
a woman."
    "Or when you go to war," said Yance.
"I's married four years when I jined, and Sally and me,
we got along just fine, but I didn't see
what my marriage meant till I left my wife behind
and little Edward. I miss that feller awful,
and all this death and ruination—hit's exactly
opposite of having a house, a wife and chit."

"You mean a home and family makes men civilized?"

"Preacher, I reckon they must."
      "Why every man,
what does he want as soon as he comes of age?"

"To take hisself a ride!"
    "Shut up, Critter.
You ain't no gentleman."
      "Hell and like I care."

"My wife's a parish of sweet milk and honey," said Hiram.

"A farm, a good woman, an income, with a little
left over to sell in town for a few amenities,"
said Snake "will keep a man from working hisself
to death and give him time for books or church."

"Or fishing," said Ainey.
                              "But what about this farm wife,"
Garland said.
              "She's got to make a good
blackberry cobbler," said Apple Jack.
                                    "She must
possess a sweet nature and an ample bosom,
which is meet for a husband's pleasure and nurturing children."

"Patty, all's you want is a good milk cow."

"Be Jazus, I fancy the bosoms more accessible."

"The ideal woman is handsome and virtuous," said Snake.

"If the love of Christ inspires her heart, she'll be
transformed in godly beauty."
                              "I'm with Preacher.
A virtuous woman is more precious than rubies," said Caleb.

"And all the things thou cans't desire are not
to be compared unto her."
                          "Yance!"
                                    "Well don't be
astonished, Preacher."
                        "I just didn't know you read

the Scripture."

    "I don't. But Sally used to read
the Bible every evening." He smiled at the fire.
"She always read them parts about good women.
I thought that was all the Bible had to say."

"She's giving you your education, Papa."

"Sholey, Garland. I was at my best as a man
every time I gave her virtues sway."

"Yeah," said Deke, "but I bet yore gal's a right
purty woman. Hit's easy to see the good
in a purty woman."

    "You got it backwards," said Preacher.
"Virtue has to be there first. It's the fire
behind the glass."

    "I reckon she's got to be womanly,"
Left Tenant said.

    "Wives submit yourself
to your own husbands as unto the Lord."

    "Good luck
getting my wife to submit."

    "Doesn't she read
the scripture, Ainey?"

    "I guess the parts what suits her."

"Only a mucker ripe with shilly-shally
would hitch to a woman what was too obedient,"
said Patty.

    "If virtue is the light of woman's soul,

then spirit is the fire of her character. Give me a gal
what's got a touch of fire in her blood," said Snake.

"Not one that wants to be a man, but one
who could do a manly thing if circumstance
required," said Caleb.
                    "Just like that Sally Tompkins
down yonder in Richmond, running the Confed'rit hospital,
saving hundreds of soldiers' lives a day,
and the papers say when the army took it over,
Davis made her a Captain to keep her on."

"Wish we had a gal captain."
                    "Shoot I reckon."
Deke spat,
          "You fellers is full of more shit
than a livery stable. If we'uns had yore fiery
Christian gal and her face looked like the south end
of a north bound mule, ain't a single one of you fellers
would have nary a thang to do with her."
                              "I would."

"And hell I reckon it's so, Preacher, 'cause you
is God crazy. Crazier than a duck on a June bug,
crazier'n a damn peach orchard boar. But the rest
of you'uns is full of more shit than a blocked bull.
You know what all men want, and they don't have to marry
to get it. A fool will tie a knot with his tongue
he can't untie with his teeth when all's he wants
is a little puppy nose. And he wants it for the same
damn reason he goes to war—because he likes it."

"It may be true with women but not with war,"
said Garland. "I've only seen a smattering and I don't
like it."

   "Awe boy, you'll take to hit, you mark
my word." Deke leered, his face above the fire
amiable as Satan's.

      "Stop your foul mouth, Deke,"
scowled Left Tenant. At this Deke turned, pulling
his blanket over his shoulders, his back to the fire.
He cut a stuttering fart. Tattoo sounded.
Yancy snuffed the air.

      "Damnation, Critter.
Something done crawled up inside of you and died."

April 29, 1863 toward the Wilderness

Crowded darkness, funk of soldiers dizzying
his stomach, three days' rations in sacks, the abandoned
heights somewhere behind their backs. He shivered,
waiting for units to pass them, batteries, ambulances,
wagons starting, halting, drovers swearing
the most articulate and rhythmic curses, knowing
only curses can move a train of mules,
their black, bowed heads and flattened ears impassive
with dejection. Now it was coming, and he was beset
by terrors. The darkness weakened, light resolved
the landscape, revealing shadows slanting westward.
They marched an hour, halted for ten minute's rest.
He sat by Caleb and went to take a drink,
holding his shaking canteen in both his hands.

"Ain't no use bucking the halter," Caleb said.
"We come for the Monkey Show, and besides, I reckon
  it's still a ways off yet."
                              "That's what's irksome.
If it's got to be, I'd just as soon get it done."
The files scuffed the road, describing miles
of verdant and undulant country. The sun bore down,
the dust rose up, and they marched in a parching tunnel.
The wayside was scattered with sinful pleasures, cards
and dice. Sometimes a soldier would toss a bottle,
and a thirsty wag broke ranks, sprinting to fetch it.

"The Good Lord may not want me to gamble," one said,
"but he can't begrudge a feller a little swig
  to settle his nerves before he meets the elephant."
Now voices stirred, directing attention down
the road behind the march. It was Colonel Herbert,
leading his horse by the reins, a hayseed straggler
in the saddle, a stick of a fellow with bulging eyes.
The colonel's face wore its usual affable look,
and the private's back was ram rod straight, one
of his hands on the pommel, the other poised on his hip
as he passed like a Sultan regarding desert minions.
Heat and exertion wringing their bodies dry,
soldiers began disposing of martial items,
blankets, spare canteens, belts, haversacks,
and among the clutter, he noticed bayonets glinting
in the nervous dust. Many rifles lacked them.

"Say Brutus. Why're some fellers throwing away
  they pig stickers?"

"Well, I reckon the boys
ain't throwing 'em away exactly—at's against regulations.
They losing 'em."
                    "I see you lost yours. How come?"

"In a fight when you reloading fast as you kin,
it's a hindrance. Some cut they hands before they learn,
and lose 'em."
                    "What do you do in a close encounter
with a Federal?"
                    "Grab holt of the muzzle and swang the rifle
like a club. It'll give you reach and keep you getting
jobbed."
          "I'm obliged."
                    "Shoot, t'ain't nothing, old son."
Then he added. "Besides, you really want to stick
a man? At's nasty business."
                    "Thanky, Brute."
The two friends reconnoitered up and down
the column, and seeing no officers, they detached bayonets
from barrels, and Caleb handed his to Garland,
who hefted the irons, regarding blood gutters cut
along the blade's triangular shank, a shape
designed to deal a wound that will not close.
They were repugnant. He tossed the things in a ditch.
After parched hours of marching, the column slogged
past trains and caissons, parked in a fork of the way.
The leading regiment kept to the Plank Road
while Garland's unit veered away on the turnpike
and marching another mile were ordered to halt.

"Spades out!" cried Hiram, and Colonel Herbert rode up

and dismounted, his uniform worn but clean and pressed,
with one or two patches showing, his hair, mustaches
barbered and combed, his face sun burnished and handsome.
The men were proud of him as a thoroughbred stallion.
He and his junior officers walked the trench.

"Good day to you, Colonel Herbert."
                              "God bless you, colonel."

"Colonel, you and Billy Fixing just flush
them Yankees out, and we gone give 'em a hiding."

"Don't worry men. The Yankees will come to us.
They never seem to learn." There were hoots and cheers.
Now the spoil was leaping out of the trench.
Company H was close to the turnpike, and as far
as he could see their line was formed on the outskirts
of a dense forest.
                 "At'air is called the Wilderness."
Sunlight snuffed in crowns of stave oak and post oak,
here an elegant red maple new leafed and fine.

"The Yanks will have a struggle to come through that,"
Oscar mused.
              "Sholey. But they'll get through,"
said Yancey, who kept on digging. He loosened spoil
and tossed it but couldn't stop wondering if he were digging
his grave. Then one of the diggers straightened his back
and pointed.
              "Lookee y'all." A rider galloped
a hanging pall of dust and reigned up hard.

A conference of officers snapped to attention.

                                     "It's Stonewall!"

Murmurs rippled the trench, hushed, enthused,
and men began stepping out of the ditch, gathering
around the brass but keeping respectful distance.
The general's smock was coated with dust, his back
a fencepost, his eyes a blue wavering flame,
shadowed under the brim of his dirty cadet's cap.
He was speaking to General Anderson, division commander.

"McLaws is not an hour behind me, general.
When he arrives, see he keeps to the turnpike
and move your lines forward. We must find the enemy
and drive him, sir."

                       "I'll pass your orders along,
General Jackson, and make the preparations
necessary to advance, and may God grant us victory."

"May Providence grant us a great victory." His voice
was sonorous, cadenced as if he were reading Scriptures
in sunday school. He turned to the bunch of soldiers.
"Men, your country relies on you to drive
the enemy from our hallowed soil. Press him, overtake him
and give him the bayonet!" His eyes were stoked.
He reached in his blouse, produced a lemon wedge,
and jammed it between his teeth. He saluted the men,
wheeled his sorrel around, igniting an exuberance
of cheering. Though Garland felt a twinge for throwing
away his bayonet, he added his voice
to the mad exaltation, careering down the line
as Stonewall vanished in a blur of hooves and dust.

Most soldiers kept on digging well after dark,
he among them, watching Papa and thinking,
If you fall off a cliff, you may as well try to fly.
In his dread, he recalled Duessa's precipice pleasures,
the joy of being slain in delight's high places.

May 1, 1863 The Wilderness

A box of forty dead men thudded the ground.
His eyes flung open. He rose and grasped a handful
of cartridges. Shovels thrust in glacis spoil
slanted like shorn crosses in a vandalized graveyard.
Soon the men were formed and ordered forward,
scrambling out of the ditch and striding through sunlight,
hopper's wings scuffling papery, wind-up rattles
till Wilderness canopies brushed the light from his shoulders.
Clutching his rifle, he moved through complacent shadows,
making leaf meal ruffle and twig snap,
in their wake no mockingbird or jizzywitch.
In his chest, a lithe wild creature hurled itself
against its cage, each lunge making him gasp.
They halted and officers made adjustments to the line.
Every forest shadow held its bead.

"Easy men and keep yourselves together,"
Left Tenant encouraged, strolling along behind them.
"We fixing to show these Yankees Southern manhood."
Forward again, his hands slick on the stock.
A rustle in front, a brown shape bolted from thicket,
dodging zigzag behind them, and he could feel

the guts of fellow soldiers clench and unclench
amid some rippling laughter. Buzzard said,

"Go'n, old hare. I'd run if I's a hare."
He near jumped out of his socks when musketry broke
in front, a cascade of angry balls swarming
the high branches. They returned fire, breech smoke
engulfing the line. They were ordered forward out
of the blinding cloud toward pop and grumble of rifles,
changing from long ripping sheets to distinct cracks,
desultory, then crowded together. He tried to go
in a hunker, yanking feet through thicket tangles.
The racket was now a presence, pummeling him,
disorienting sense. They strode through smoke embankments,
hanging in boughs like storm clouds, breathing acrid
scorch, and weird with spinning hizz of bullets,
zinging air *and tack tack tacking* tree trunks.
They emerged in a clearing. The man on his left had vanished,
but Caleb still on his right. A volley sheared past,
and they flattened, he hearing Yankee accents in front,
their blue shapes advancing. Captain Blackwood appeared.

"Pull back, but fire. Keep it brisk for the Yanks."
He discharged five or six rounds, edging backward
through Wilderness thickets until they joined the regiment,
sheltered in a slight declivity, the officers working
to get them back in line. Caleb mopped
his face, shining with sweat and powder burn.
The newest recruits wore keenly alert expressions,
their fear lending a measure of consolation
as he strove to steel himself to keep from trembling.

Again they were ordered forward. The line surged
toward the hellish nest of musketry. Blackwood ordered
them to hold their fire, and they sprinted ahead
as best they could through bramble and woven brush.
A Yankee volley burst in their faces, showering
rachis and twig. On his left he heard a wail,
prolonged and piteous, everywhere swearing and groans.
They halted and returned fire, Blackwood again,
the order to charge echoing down the line,
"Charge 'em boys. Let's give 'em goss on a stick."
The men rose in a body, surged through the wood,
struggling through thickets in retarded dream motion.
The Yankees got off a volley, wild and high,
shredding oak debris and spiraling leaf meal.
The charge had knocked the Yankees back on their heels.
They pushed forward and fell in a shallow run,
the bank behind him littered with cartridge tops.
His mouth was pasted shut. He emptied his canteen,
pushed leaf litter away from the water's surface
and filled the vessel. The fire had died a little,
his stomach roiled. An abandoned U.S. haversack
lay in the mud. He crawled through water to fetch it,
tossing a pocket diary, a sheaf of letters,
and finding crackers, a baked Irish potato,
and fried bacon, which he portioned out to Caleb
and offered to another soldier who shook his head.
He gnashed his ration. Blackwood scuttled up.

"Are you loaded?"

                    "No," he croaked through a mouthful of spud.

"Well goddamn, load your piece; don't you know

what's coming?" There needed no response. Through brush,
the deep chested *huzzah* of Yankee infantry, the chanting
rolling forward. The Captain scampered off,
hoiking Rebel soldiers back into line
and steeling them. "Hold fire. Keep your barrels low,"
but the Yankee charge was bark knife savage, and they pressed
with valor. "Pull back slow. Stay in line.
Now load for bear and fire!" But Rebels were peeling
away from the line, dodging for cover and swinging
round trees to shoot. He leaped a fallen pine,
behind which Henry Barkloo made a redoubt.
He laughed at Henry's powder blackened face,
its sweaty sheen, appearing swart as a Negro's.

"Come on, Henry, let's mosey, it's too hot here,"
yelled Caleb.
                    "You boys go ahead on. I'll keep
the Yankees busy for a spell and then catch up."
They took off, Henry disappearing in hanging smoke
as they leapt tangles and regrouped in a hastily dug
entrenchment where a fresh brigade was waiting. Their spirits
rose, grim and glad for reinforcements,
reforming behind these men, waiting with iron
patience. When Yankees burst from underbrush,
a Rebel volley shocked them, spinning them round,
reeling them back to refuge of forest shadows.
Blackwood again, ecstatic,
                    "All right boys,
we gwine to give these Yanks a gaub of trouble."
Surge and forward. Garland stepped over the line
of dead, lying still as manikins. No charge,

but they went on the trot, making a steady, relentless
drive, taking them deep into woods and pressing
the enemy. Advancing thus, they discovered Henry
behind his log. He turned him over, recoiled
at the misshapen face, left eye and cheekbone shorn
away leaving a raw and clotted mass.
A few steps away, Caleb looked on, appalled.
Far down a palisade of elm and oak, the captain
was waving his arms and calling, "Back in line!
Get back in line!" The hour was creeping toward dusk,
and dusk already darkness inside the wood.
When Rebels surged across the Furnace Road,
they raised a high pitched keening, a wave of madness
rolling through the wood, his own voice forcing battle
racket out of his head and stoking his blood
as they drove the Federals back. Across the lane,
the line swagged, retarded by bramble and brake.
And now above the musketry, a bump and whistle,
flowering down in shrieking trajectory—a shot
crashed through branches, hollowed a shaft of weakened
twilight. Now more distant coughs, racing
like a heartbeat, become a steady roar, and shells
and terror broke in an iron rain above them,
ice in his blood, as oak crowns shivered in splinters
and ground before and behind heaved into air,
some shots caroming off trunks in mortal ricochets.
The prodigious racket pressed his body down.
He was watching the man to his left, heard a piercing
whistle, saw a flash where he stood, a spray
blow crimson on leaves, his body evanesced into air.
A wide eyed soldier was pacing about as if lost,

toting something. He was clutching his severed left arm,
his eyes black stones. A patch of his skull sprayed out
in front of him. He shivered to knees, then fell.
Left Tenant came behind them urging speed.

"Forward, men, on the double quick! For God
and country! Independence lies ahead."
The order regrouped and reinvigorated will
and strength. *This must be the decisive battle.*
The line went sprinting forward, raising a boisterous,
crooning yell, he running in a hunkered crouch
and screaming, the clamor filling him with dread
of himself, he leaping roots and grasping briers.
Do the thing. Do the thing and go home.
A volley shredded branches. He threw his back
against a trunk and panted, seized by infernal
thirst. He spun and sprinted farther into shadows.
Another lead wind sweeping past, he dove
hard on the ground, scuffing elbows and knees,
his face slashed by briers, fear contracting
his whole musculature, his animal heart heaving,
another volley ripping air, but coming
from behind, inciting panic, men's voices crying
inarticulate and bestial. He raised his head
from brambles. Yards ahead, a Yankee soldier
was strolling away, loading his rifle in slow
deliberate motions. His heart was knocking in every
extremity. He raised his Enfield, sighted the bead
between blue shoulders, gripped the sweating trigger,
the pressure building to decision's crux. He could not
do it. He could not shoot a man in the back.

He raised the sight, put his ball in a pine trunk
inches from the Yankee's head and dropped back down
in thicket cover, watching the blue shape hasten
into shadows. He reloaded, calling,

                              "Yankees in front!"
He rammed a cartridge home and raised himself
in a penumbral copse of trees. He was alone.
A blade of nausea stabbed him, panic encroached,
all bearings lost in this forest abattoir, racket
of guns and cries and musketry hemming him in.
A battery opened on his left. He commenced a backward
prowl, scrabbling tree limbs and staring corpses.
After a long scuttle through briers and bramble,
a voice called out from a thicket,

                              "Yank or Reb?"
and the Georgia drawl was sweet and reassuring.

"Reb, and lost," he called and ducked into brush.
"Lost as a goose. You fellers know where we are?"

"Got nary idear where I am, but I know where you are.
You with the Third Georgia, Wright's brigade.
We and McLaws is fencing off a bulge
of Yankees on at hill up yonder, to sweep 'em off.
So you best buckle up and get yerself ready to plow."
But whatever the reason, they got no orders to move.
The night was final. He wanted to find his unit,
but he was afraid of moving around in the dark.
So he shared the rations of his Georgia friends and slept,
thankful for having survived his first day of combat
and wishing to God he were any place else on earth.

May 2, 1863

Timbre of voices fluttering like leaves forced
his eyes from dark to arborescent shadows, diffuse
and cool. The Georgians struck a fire and cooked
some coffee. Officers nearby were deep in conference.
He approached a major with curly mutton chops,
a slim, triangular nose a boy might have cut
with a compass.
                    "Major," he saluted, "Private Cain.
Could you direct me back to Wilcox's brigade?"
The major studied him with warm brown eyes.

"I believe that General Wilcox was ordered back
to cover our rear at Banks Ford. You, however,
must be an aggressive soldier to have advanced
so far ahead of your line. Did you bag many?"

"Sir?"
        "Did you shoot many Yankees?"
                                "Oh, it's hard
to get a bead in such dense brush, but one came
close and I surprised him." The Major's face shone.

"Superb, smashing. Why don't you remain
in line with us? Georgia can use you today.
This will keep you in Anderson's corps and you'll
meet up with Wilcox soon enough. Where's home,
sir?"
        "Barbour County, Alabama."

"Superb. Alabama men make fine soldiers,

keen for difficult work. I'm Major Jones.
Welcome to the Georgia line. Let's fotch us some Yankees."
He made to salute, but the major shook his hand,
so he returned a foundling to his Georgia mess,
marking how officers never answered a question
head on or consented to give you exactly what
you were asking for as if accommodation were some
inherent form of weakness always to be eschewed.
But now whole regiments were coming out of line,
leaving the ditches almost bare of soldiers,
and rumor worked the trenches like a widow killing
snakes with a hoe blade.   "Jackson is moving his corps—
they going round the Union right by God!"
The man in line by Garland, by name of Folsom,
was not transported by the rampant enthusiasms.
His eyes were wide and watery, his face foul,
unshaven, his brown slouch hat cocked on the crown
of his sweaty head.   "I reckon at means we got
a line of not near fifteen thousand Rebs
holed up in front of ninety thousand Yankees.
Ninety thousand. Jesus God all muddy."
He wiped his brow with open palm and screwed
his features up as if his skull were splitting.
"Boy, if Yanks come charging out'a them woods,
you take my advice, you turn tail and run,
I mean run screaming like you's fixed for the Devil."
This knowledge put him on edge. Each time a bullet
snicked the brush, he started, jitters drawing out
abrasive hours, till late afternoon when guns

on Fairview Hill let loose, fluttering shrieks
high and gathering fury downward, thrilling
electric expectations of instant death.
"Damn Yankee flour barrels," Folsom muttered,
the projectiles' birling whirr churning earth.
The incommodious Georgia major sprinted
to their position, ordered them from under the cannonade.

"Press them, but don't engage too hotly. We want
Sickles and Slocum held at bay but not
pushed back. If they should begin to fade, the order
will be given to charge that we may bag them entire.
But for now, let's nail 'em down." The company moved,
made about fifty yards toward Union skirmishers,
blue shift and shadow, which they started pushing back,
yard by contested yard, toward Sickles' line,
the guns' apocalyptic magnitude displacing
all sounds, shot and canister blistering air.
Spiraling limbs, leaves, and leaf meal showered,
and earth heaved up, spattering boughs, then raining
maelstroms. With every incoming shriek, his nerves
recoiled; with every deafening burst, his heart
heaved. He crawled from under the hellish rain
of iron and brush, discovered boot soles protruding
from a bower. Folsom. He lay on his stomach on top
of his musket, crushed by an oak limb bigger around
than Garland's thigh. A solid shot had sheered it
off, and falling, it had broken the poor man's back.
His face was turned to the side, his eyes still glassy
with astonishment. Garland closed them and lay for a while,
allowing garboil of boughs and leaves to cover him,

battle racket humming in his teeth. The eruption
rolled away to the west, still raging. He shook
from under his camouflage and fired at the roiling
commotion in front. In deep dusk, a ragged
corporal found him.
            "Who in hell are you?"

"It's a long story, sir."
                  "Well come with me,
we fixing to get our lines contracted and ready."
The line was thirty yards behind him, but he doubted
he could have found it in a year. The mass of soldiers
fortified his calm. A boy wearing a raccoon
mask of powder burn fell down beside him.

"Stonewall and Bobby Lee done done it again!
They rolled the Yankee flank like biscuit dough,"
he crowed, guffawing and slapping his Enfield's stock.
"They saying that Howard's dirty Hessians ain't
stopped running yet. Hot damn! I can't wait
to write my pappy. Carl Cleburne, by the way,
from Noonan, Georgia."
                  "Pleasure to know you, Carl.
Garland Cain from Eufaula, Alabama,
down in the Wiregrass."
                  "Damn, if I ain't starved.
I et my victuals the first day's march."
                              "Here,"
he rifling his sack, "have a Johnny cake."

"Hey thanks. You got a heart in you." A layered

smoke feathered and densed beneath the canopy,
far off the erratic sputter and pop of rifles.
Behind them came the clopping of battery teams,
and cannoneers fumbled by lantern light to unlimber
and drop trail. The guns trembled darkness,
and muzzle lightning showed a line of Rebels
in instant red refulgence, some half-buried
in trenches, some raised to fire, and among the battery
pieces, a gunner stabbing a barrel with sponge rod
or worm rod, an officer poised behind the Napoleon,
one foot propped on a stack of canister, and again
the catastrophic fracture, the noontide flash
slamming night in his face, so before his eyes
the gunners' forms pulsed weird, scarlet and floating,
till the next ignescent burst revealed them again
in different postures consequent to rote exertions.
He plugged his ears and watched the guns spark visions
until the fury died, and the Wilderness was burning,
casting strange halations reflected in ghastly
unreality on smoke woven like broadcloth.
At last the noise of battle receded, replaced
by the piteous groaning of wounded. He lay unsleeping
and thought how pain, the tooth and claw of suffering,
belied man's spiritual nature. He recalled a boy
in school, who made to cultivate a roguish superiority
by means of his learning, espousing a certain Englishman
who proposed that men derived from simian ancestry.
Some students received this information quietly,
but most mocked it wholesale, deriding the boy,
making monkey sounds when he entered a room.
These screams of agony ushering from forest dark

bespoke a legitimate history of animal lineage.
And now on the sudden, one of the fleshed cries burst
through brush, tripping over Garland and striking earth,
he hearing the shadow of substance make involuntary
exhale, then struggle to heave breath back.
                                                    "Shot!
He's been shot! The general. It's treachery!" Soldiers gathered.
Garland stood the man up.
                              "Who's been shot?"

"God's sake don't say Lee."
                              "No, not Lee,"
the man was shaking his head, gasping for air,
"Stonewall. Shot by his own men. He's hurt.
He's hurt bad." The man was clutching his sleeve,
still panting. Walking shadows swelled the congress.

"Hail and storm in Beulah land."
                                    "How bad
is it?"
          "Shot oncet in the right arm, twicet in the left."

"If this ain't sucking hind tit"—
                                    "If Jackson dies"—

"He ain't a gonna"—
                        "Hell, we might as well say it.
If Jackson dies, we're whipped."
                                    "And ain't that why
we know he'll live? God won't take him from us."

"It air a fact that Jackson's a Christian soldier.
God won't let him die."
                              "Don't you reckon
Christians died here today by hundreds, by thousands?"
No one responded. He wondered if men were thinking
or merely trying to place a stranger's voice.

"Sholey. But they ain't important men like Jackson."

"The Rebels ain't never gone be whipped as long
as we got Mars Robert leading the army. That's all."
But men were distressed God had forsaken the general
and so the South, leaving her people to the mercy
of the champion of Gath.
                              "Who shot him?"
                                             "They say some green
Tar Heels, what'd just been spooked by Yankee cavalry
blundering into their lines in the dark." A consequent lull.

"He might come back," said Garland, "He could lead as well
with one arm."
                    "Sholey," a voice chuckled, "but most
what have an arm or leg sawed off, don't live
to tell the folks back home how bad it hurt."
A doom of stupefied silence held them rapt
as if they stood in a field after thunder clap,
so with nothing else to discover, the shadows dispersed.
Men slept on arms and rested for next day's action.
He lay for a while till he could hear the soft
exhale of soldiers' rhythmic snoring. He rose
with care. He had to be able to find his way back

without getting lost or shot, so he hung his rifle
on a tree stob, making a cross to mark his location.
He stumbled over branch litter, kit and corpses,
guided by pitiable moans and cries for water,
and within a few yards, discovered some wounded men.
Night was so strict, he had to touch their faces,
feel the pulses of some to know if they lived.
One man's ruined face was covered in blood,
which gave him a shiver, sopping his hands, but he didn't
feel the ants, already feasting on moribund
flesh until they began to bite his fingers,
which he slapped cursing, wiping on trousers and leaf mold.
Zephaniah Thomas had a painful wound in the calf.
He tied a tourniquet on and gave him a drink.

"We'll get the Yankees tomorrow and it will be over,"
the wounded man kept repeating. "Tomorrow, we'll get them,
you'll see." Recalling the same fond thoughts he'd had
that morning, he felt foolish, embarrassed by fear.

"Yes, I feel it too. Tomorrow we'll get them."

May 3, 1863 Chancellorsville

Picket of Wilderness boughs repulsing dawn,
he struggled through crepuscular corpse gardens in a line
of men, discerning tension in faces, nervous,
staring expectancy. The Yankees had moved their guns
from the hill left of their position, and Rebel batteries
were firing the other way, urging them forward

with hoarse and apocalyptic admonitions.
Musketry was light, their movement steady. Federal
lines were fading back to the Rappahannock.
Past Hazel Grove, they halted. They started and stopped.

"Hell and high water. Why don't we move?"

"They keeping the line in order. Keeping us ready
to repulse a counter attack or make a push."
The soldier was cheerful and handsome. He'd dug a twist
of tobacco from his sack and cut himself a rasher.

"Care for a chaw to soothe yer nerves?"
                                        "No thank you.
The thing for my nerves is to get this Monkey Show done."

"Well don't you worry, old son. She's a coming."
He felt like a shunted engine bleeding steam
through vents and valves, killing motion, and force
of action the only thing to hold his mind
and heart to this savage purpose. His knuckles were white.
He closed his eyes, breathed in, relaxed his hands.
He checked the hammer and counted his cartridge sack.
Twenty rounds. He wiped his forehead and took
a sip of water. Then the commands of officers.

"Forward. Forward! Guide center." The line
surged. The Georgia major came riding up.

"Keep your line together, men, and keep
the pressure on." The Rebels crept forward using

Wilderness cover, trunk, stump, and bramble.
A flight of balls raked the branches above,
causing soldiers to flatten out in a wave.
He rolled behind a pine trunk, braced himself
and waited. He put one eye around the tree.
Before him, shadows moved in shadows. He raised
his rifle and the line fired with him in a splurge
of flame and smoke. He tore a cartridge and loaded,
waiting, his hearing blunted, and just as he
was about to rise and move with others springing
forward, above his head a volley scythed
chest high. He heard men scream and groan. Smoke boiled
through the wood, and musket racket rose and sputtered.
Again they waited. Officers conferred, adjusted
the line and ordered them forward.
                                "Two hundred yards,
men, two hundred yards," a captain cried.
"Go forward, Georgia!" The line surged, his heart
surged, musket fire slackened, receding
ahead of them, thickets and brier patches thinning
out, sunlight shafting between the pine trunks.
Racing through green leaf odor and acrid smoke,
pace and pulse throb gathering momentum, the mind
equating the drive with diminished fire, the ironic,
irrational notion that hurling oneself headlong
into peril was the surest way to neutralize peril,
a crooning Rebel yell spurred his feet,
and despite himself, beyond his reckoning, he caught
the taste and savored it, felt the caress of her hands,
swift brush of her wings, felt he were charging
a precipice, that he would step over that verge into bodiless

air willingly with absolute faith he would rise.
The line of soldiers burst from under a shelf
of branches to an open swale and dazzling light.
On a rise ahead, a house with columned porches
billowed flame, and smoke disgorged from a gaping
hole in the roof. A tumult rose on the left,
at the farthest reach of an hundred acre clearing,
rolling in crests and troughs through the line of infantry.

"What is it," he asked, going from one to another.
A soldier, begrimed, his teeth white as a slave's said,

"The wings of the army has met—Lee's has met
with Jackson's corps! The danger is over now,
my friend, and trouble for Yanks is gwine to commence."
Now the shout like a mighty wind redounded
to a place behind him, swelling jubilant. A horse,
winter gray with storm cloud mane, stepped
a canter up the rise toward Chancellor Mansion.
The rider sat erect and solemn, his frock
plain, his only insignia three inconspicuous
stars high on the collar, his broad brimmed straw hat
level above his eyes, his only weapon
opera glasses slung across his shoulder.
As Traveler came, the crowd of soldiers parted,
hands waving, hats leaping in air, two walls of water
divided and held erect by ancient miracle.
The prostrate wounded gathered strength to prop
an elbow and watch him pass, hoarse with cheers.
He gained the rise of ground and presented himself
in tableau with ruination of the manse and lifted

his hat, the hoarfrost beard cropped close, the face
betraying no exuberance, in spite of victory
and hysterical adoration, which he received as a man
might take the sacrament in uncomprehending awe.
Garland caught the conference of a nearby officer.

"It must have been thus in ancient times that men
by deeds attained to the very dignity of gods,"
the gauntleted hand grasping a saber hilt,
his blouse brand new, no speck of mud on his boots.
He looks the sort who'd like to be a god.
A courier rode up, his horse's shoes gouging
black earth, and passed a note to an aide and only
then did he notice General Lee was attended.
The aide perused the note and handed it over.
Lee's face altered and his gray eyes roved, searching
Wilderness's deciduous shadows. The hand holding
the note hung straight at his side for a moment. He turned,
dictated an answer and began giving orders, no doubt
for a rapid realignment and advance. Hooker was trapped
between the coiling Rappahannock and the Rebels,
and Lee was bearing down, poised for the kill.
Garland longed for the kill to happen, do
the thing and go home, but that night the Federal Army
slipped across the river; the Yankees were safe.
They would fight another day. The Rebels marched back
to Fredericksburg, returning to winter quarters.
Never would he have thought a piss poor, sod lined
hearth would appear so welcome to his weary heart.

May 5, 1863 Fredericksburg

My Dear Duessa—
I write to you, a veteran
of my first engagement, the Battle of Chancellorsville.
Since last December, I've shivered by fires, sustained
by pretty poor fare, and then one morning we're herded
out on the road, marched twenty miles to the thickest
wood you've ever seen. They call it the Wilderness.
The terror of the guns was overwhelming; this action
acquainted me with horrors difficult to drive
from thought, impossible to keep from dreams. Yet here
I shall pass them over, not being proper for the finer
sensibilities of women. I confess I leave
much to be desired as a soldier. In the battle's chaos,
I found myself lost in the dark wood. And once
when occasion arose, I was not able to shoot
an unwitting Yankee. Though guilt oppresses me
for not pursuing an exact fulfillment of duty,
I assuage myself I'm not a natural killer.
But sweet Duessa, know that through the months
of camp life's tedium and battle's horrific hours,
I am sustained, made strong by your sweet memory.
We two have shared the holiest and happiest conjunction
man and woman may know. I would our bed
of pleasure be a bed of union. My greatest wish
is you might wish it also. Ah Duessa,
the loss of love is such a heavy fate,
the wonder is your gentle soul could bear.
If I might give you any hope for the future,
my dear one, trust another love to make

185

your life's path true again. Trust me, Duessa.
After the war, I will return to you.
My happiest day will be to find you waiting.
My hope is yours and all my love,
                                    Garland.

He regarded his scrawls. He was asking a great deal.
Why should she tender him her sacred affection?
For a chance meeting of strangers? The word of a boy?
And why should she wager her heart again with a soldier?
He had written what he had written, declared his intention
to love in an oath lent substance by his uttered word.
He must live what life remained to match her worth.

May 15, 1863

"They having his funeral today."
                                    "Yeah, I reckon."
"T'ain't no good for us."
                                    "No, it ain't."
His face was wreathed in steam, he and Caleb
concocting sassafras tea with root bark he'd shaved
and dried some weeks ago. It was steeping nicely.
Caleb wished he'd been at Chancellorsville
to see the general cheering the conjunction of the corps.
Such envy, in another context, might have made him
feel enlarged and worldly, but glory was far
from his thoughts. "It was awful, seeing Henry killed."

"Dreadful."

   "Didn't you spend some time with him
in camp?"
   "In the worst fatigue duty they is,
retrenching the sinks. What disgusting work,
and Henry stood in shit and whistled. I asked him
if he was afraid to die. You know what he said?"

"What?"
   "'No.' Just that, in a voice that suggested
he thought it an odd question. And when he talked,
it was all about missing Samson, Alabama,
his mother, and the rutabagas she grew in the garden.
I think he missed the rutabagas most."
Caleb was wincing.
      "What unconscionable waste.
When a boy like Henry, of simple heart, dies,
bearing away his integrity, unthinking courage,
a little more soul is firked from the South's heart,
and we lose far into the future. These are the wages
of conflict, the cost we never mind to reckon.
A nation needs its upright more than heroes.
When the war is over, the generous and obedient perished,
the flower of youth which sprang from Southern soil
ploughed under, shirkers, the supervenient, speculators,
the wealthy and the arbiters of wealth remain and spiritual
drought ensues, alike in victory or defeat."
The catastrophe's logic stunned his heart.
        "This great
calamity, it's also true for the North?"
        "Of course,
but even in this they can more afford to lose."

"From whence comes justice then and justice for all?"

"For yet a little while, and the wicked shall not be."
They touched their cups and sipped their sassafras tea.

May 24, 1863

The light was keen, his heart was light, he strolling
through oak shade, the green music of a thousand
tongues. He happened to pass the colonel's tent,
where Regis whistled astride a workbench, relishing
afternoon and repairing some leather harness,
his deft hands wielding the awl with expert skill.

"Mister Regis. How are you, sir," he pulling up
next to his bench.
                    "Fair to middling, massuh.
How is you?"
                    "I'm 'bout two to the hill.
You fixing colonel's harness?"
                                "Sholey I is.
I gots to git Massuh Herbit back on Dolly
and arter dem Yankees."
                        "The colonel's a brave soldier."

"Massuh can whale a dozen Yankees fo' coffee
is hot, fair fight."
                    "Course, you a fine soldier
yourself, Regis."
                    "Awe, go along now, massuh."

"No use truckling. I saw you fight in the Wilderness.
You load and fire quick as any veteran
soldier, north or south, black or white."

"I knows how to handle a rifle, I reckon. Fo' the war,
I used to hunt with massuh all the time.
Quails is some good eating and smother fried squirrel."
Garland perceived those unseen fortifications,
curtain and glacis, the servant's sure defense
and rear guard putting on to put off white folks.

"Regis, you're fighting on the wrong side, fighting
against your own freedom. Why don't you run
away and join the Yankees? There's not a man
with any sense of justice who'd lay you blame."
Regis straightened from his work, put down the awl.
His expression showing, what—alarm, annoyance?

"Massuh Garland, what you say ain't true
cause life get snarled up and a man ain't got
no choice but to sort out a passel of tangled truth
and decide which one he gwine to have to tie to."

"So what's your truth?"
                              "I loves Massuh Herbit."
The idea reamed his brain like a ball. Of all
possible answers, he would—he could have stood
in this shade a hundred years and never guessed
that such a word might issue from Regis's mouth.
"Regis ain't gwine to pass those lines and put
no bullet hole in Massuh Herbit. What kind

189

of man would that be making me? Massuh
treats me well. He kept my wife and chirren
together these many years and never went
to lay a hand on her"—
                    "Well, I can see
respect for humanity and justice, especially in a system
that doesn't require he render either one,
but how can you love the man who robs your freedom?"

"Jesus says to love, and love is his law.
Mister Garland, you a conscript, ain't
that right?"
          "Yes."
                "You didn't want no part
of all this suffering and death?"
                              "No, I didn't."

"But here you is. You didn't want to come,
but here you is, and if'n you take a notion
to turn yo'self around and go back home,
some officer will put a bullet in yo back as sho
as the Devil gots a pitchfork. Now tell me, suh,
is *you* free?"
              "Not in that respect, I reckon,
but after the war"—
                    "After the war, sholey,
you will be freer than Regis is, but other mens
with mo' power than you will always be telling you what
to do when time comes when they need you. I gots
the ankle chain, you gots the chain a command."
This sudden wit sent Regis a fit of mirth.

"That's sholey right."
                "But Jesus say the truth
shall make you free, and his truth make a man free
in the only place he can be free fo sho,
in his spirit. The grace of de Lord can raise a mansion
in the ragged heart of a po slave, and no
white man can tech it, hallelujah and amen."
He resumed his work with the awl, and Garland left him,
strolling through patches of wavering sun and shade.
Did the gleaming porticoes of a heavenly mansion shimmer
in his heart or had Regis merely parried him?
Where had Regis got religion? A white man
no doubt taught him, and scripture placed Master Herbert
in the Master's place and made his slave complacent,
a fact convenient for Herbert, having a slave
serving with goodwill as to the Lord and not to men.
Rebel privates had no less religion than slaves.
They'd been more Jesus preached in the Southern army
than there were whiskey stills in Tennessee.
Generals knew that Christians made good soldiers,
better disciplined, calmer under fire,
and what foul enterprise to fashion Christian killers.
But if God would save a man, why should he care
if salvation were spread by suspect human motives?
Mammon will be Mammon, men will serve it.
Could God have made our weakness his dwelling place
there to prevent our hope unraveling in cosmic
mockery, in the muzzle flash of infinite stars?
Or was this merely slavery's sinister genius
that used a man's good character, his loyalty and love,
to anneal the chains that bound him body and soul?

What is worse, to break a man or dupe him?
Above in a cluster of oak leaves, a cardinal struck
his crimson spark. Was he killing men for slavery?
And just as vexing, were Yankees killing for freedom?
And either way, could love defy such malice?
Here is Regis in thrall to his master's welfare,
which he has made his choice, slaying those
who come to set him free. If there were a cross
of Christ bestowed to men, Regis was bearing it.
Here was the Gospel message on hands and knees,
crawling its desperate way across the earth,
and glory coming behind like morning light,
and here a truth for the ages: men saw it not.
Who was Jackson or Lee compared to Regis?
Above, the oak leaves babbled, confused as flames.

June 1, 1863

May 14, 1863

Dear Garland:
              I take my pen in hand to write
my beloved son. I trust you are well. As usual,
rumors came in the van of news of the battle
at Chancellorsville. Folks on beat fourteen
were glowing with pride and praise of Jackson and Lee
went up to Heaven. Our puny country had thwarted
the great Goliath. But when the Register *came*
and I read the account, the paper fell from my hands.
Twenty five thousand casualties on the Union side

and all those boys with mothers praying fervently
as I. Who can imagine so many dead?
It sickened my heart that I had been so glad
of victory. And who but God can know the days
of happiness scores of young have forfeited from their lives,
except what those poor souls may find in Heaven?
And now, our Christian soldier dead, the people
fear that God has removed his hand from the South.
But win or lose, I wouldn't trade a thousand
Stonewall Jacksons for a single Garland Cain.
I fail in my duty to maintain a Christian patience.
I wake from sleep in breathless anxiety, a bundled
ache where my heart was used to beat so free.
But I pray that God let nations come to pass
or pass away though he spare my only begotten.
May merciful Providence so grant.

Your loving Mother.

June 2, 1863

Dusk shadows covered soldiers till fires revealed them.

"Looks like Little Powell is gonna be giving us
    orders for the time being."

                        "You don't say, Papa."
"Do say."
            "Better Hill than one legged Ewell."

"How come General Ewell don't suit you, Snake?"

"He done been spiled by that woman what he married."

"That rich wider woman?"
                                        "I heared he's so
confounded by his own good luck, he interduces her
sometimes as 'Mrs. Brown.'" Snake winked at Garland
across the fire, his face wavering in the dry
heat whipping up from flames. Beyond their circle,
a whippoorwill's plaintive notes burdened the dark
with sorrow, leading his thoughts away from the talk.
Sparks flew up and mingled revolving stars.

"I'd like to know how a one legged man gets on."

"I reckon like most folks else, Preacher, on the left."

"Awe Snake"—
                        "I heared McLaws pulled out yestiddy,
done marched to Culpepper where Hood and Pickett
                                        is stationed."

"Who toll you that?"
                        "Brutus."
                                        "Hit must be true.
Brutus knows everthing."
                        "Everthing 'cept who killed Caesar."
Lieutenant Mordecai, lost in abstraction, wandered
into fire light, drawing a flat, elastic shadow
from dark's boundary, headed to Herbert's tent
with a sheaf of papers.
                        "Left Tenant, yer gallus is popped."

He stopped and regarded his regulation blouse.
The fire sighed and sniggered.
                            "You're a humorist, Papa."

"Say, Left Tenant, when we moving out?"

"Pap, you know I can't tell."
                                "You're no great shot.
I guess the generals don't talk where you can hear."
His look hardened.
                        "Keep your chitlin holes closed.
I mean it. Little Powell's done told his staff
we headed out tomorrow, going north.
Our corps will stay and cover the army slipping
behind the mountains, then to Ashby's Gap
where we'uns is gonna bung old Hooker's barrel."

"Nabocklish," whistled Patty.
                            "There's your mule."
Mordecai, smiling with satisfaction for stunning
Papa into respectful silence, strode away.
Garland left the fire. A shaving of moon
made rooflines faint in the town straddling the river,
many punctured, burst asunder by guns,
scorched by fires. He thought of the Bateman House,
the slave songs raising sorrows in midday heat,
its pristine whiteness refunding refulgent sun.
Was that house whole? Would it be shivered open,
seared by fires of blue raiders, fractured
by shot, all its finery despoiled, the settees,
piano, china, Brussel's carpeting, slave quarters?

The house could go for all he cared. And what
it stood for could go. That house had brought down judgment
on his head. His only concern was the gorgeous woman
residing there. Yankee bummers were fond
of Negro women. Plenty of time had passed,
why wouldn't she write him? How could she account
his heart of such slight consequence to use him thus,
to take him to bed and send him off to war
with bosom glory perturbed by doubt and hope.
The river flowed through stars, the air smelled green.
Thought of her stirred his heart, and even despairing
desire was sweet to him. He relished the whippoorwill
quelling night with longing, the muted campfire
chat behind him just some neighborly talk
on a creaky stoop, somewhere on beat fourteen.
A wagon rolled off into distance. Tents were struck,
couriers and teamsters came and went in the dark.

June 15, 1863 toward Ashby's Gap

Shadows limned as men, a mule's braying
ricochets off the tree line, flat as a fence,
gape of a bottomless ditch, a row of shadow
batteries, a shed by the road. Again the outraged
braying, a weird herald, inviting earth
to receive the infernal wagon to which it is harnessed
down the sheer dark to the shadow world,
receive the shades waiting in marching order,
the soldier's first job to wait for all things bound
in red tape, pay and rations, orders and bullets

and mail, killing, dying, burial, and entrance
most likely into the Kingdom of Heaven.

Your name, soldier?

Garland Cain, sir.

Unit?

Eighth Alabama,
Co. H., Army of Northern Virginia.

Private, your papers are en route to this post. Fear not,
the average wait is less than a thousand years.

Three times he attempts to strangle the saint, but Peter's
ghostly form disperses like smoke in his hands.
A horse comes drumming distance behind his back,
canters to a stop, a mumbled salutation. Foot scrubbing
ahead. A shove between his shoulder blades.

"Move along, cousin, we'uns taking a walk."

"Giddyup."

"You gwine to march like Moses, boy."
Dawn lays shadows low, and the dust rises,
parching throats amid Elysian verdure
of Virginia country, patchwork of pasture and crops.
When the road bends, the column stretches for miles,
masked by forests and emerging to flow over hills,
through dales, with centipede motion of thousands of legs,
all voices hushed, portent with audacious enterprise.

"We gwine to beard the lion in his own den."
The speaker, a haggard veteran, knows the chilly

odds of victory, and Garland wonders at the tenor
of happiness in his voice, a mark of confidence or madness?
The thought occured that war, just like religion,
requires its faith and soldiers like the saved
believe till they die. *Hast thou an arm like God?*
A clutch of pacing scarecrows began to sing.

Lay bare thine arm,
Stretch forth thy rod.
Amen.
That's Stonewall Jackson's way.

The sun sets fire to crowns and golden boughs,
and the singer heaves the song with rustling breath.

But the battle to the strong
is not given,
while the Judge of right and wrong
sits in Heaven.
And the God of David still
guides the Devil with his will.
There are giants yet to kill.

A halt for rest, and the army crowded way
disperses as soldiers seek the roadside shade.

"Where we headed, Papa?"
                              "North."
                                        "You got
a specific idea?"
                    "I reckon Mars is aiming

to take some pressure off the boys at Vicksburg.
So we gwine to visit the Yankees and seek some trade."
Noon and the sun has set its heel hard
on the road. No one sings, no one speaks.
Men strive with grim exertion. He focuses attention
on hip and thigh, on knees and heat, yet scenes
swarm like blow flies, the man a shell obliterated,
scores of staring corpses, Henry's mangled
face; he'd heard a man named Syphret was shot
in back of the head, the bullet cleaning out all
his teeth but four. He'd lived to be sent home.
The troops loved bartering stories of odd survivals.
But making it home to die, that was something,
to say goodbye to your mother, gum some cornbread,
close your eyes and join the innumerable caravan.
At long last they are halted and ordered to bivouac.
The sun sits down on the land like an empty throne.

June 26 toward Sharpsburg

Blackwood shambled up to Company H.

"Drop yer pizzle sticks and listen up.
Our unit's number two to cross the Potomac,
so shuck it down to the silk hairs, bundle yer kit,
and stay in files. We'll mosey across on my word.
Oh, and scouts are saying to stay alert.
They spotted a picket across the river posted
on our left flank, comprised entirely of *women,*
and some have armed themselves with opera glasses.

Soldiers are ordered to stay in ranks, no matter
how irrepressible they feel the urge to engage."
The regiment halted fifty yards from the bank,
in refreshing, cavernous shade in a copse of oak,
and all the men stripped naked.
                                          "Stuff your step ins
and socks in your boots and wrap 'em in your shirt and pants.
If they get wet, your feet'll blister and your crotch'll
chafe, and you'll be fixed for the Devil's misery."

"I'm obliged, Papa."
                              "T'ain't nothing at all, Garland."
Though routine at crossings, the sight of tens of thousands
of naked soldiers elicited various commentary.

"Cover yer ass, Brute. The Yanks'll think
we've surrendered."
                              "What's Co. B, the Boiled Chickens?"

"All right men, plug yer corn holes and mosey!"
The river refreshed the men after pounding dust
all morning. Mid current they were able to see the girls
on the far bend, crowded around three carriages.

"Looky boys, they waving the white flag!"

"Let's break ranks men and round us up some prisoners."
The Potomac gave his scrotum a cold touch,
tingling hips electric. He bent his knees
and drank, holding above his head the sun warmed
barrel and bundles. The boys kept hallooing the girls.

He gained the bank and used a spare shirt to dry
his feet and groin. They marched through a dense growth
of black oak, pine, and shagbark hickory. The shade
suffused damp skin with cool. Ahead were wagons
and soldiers filing past. Left Tenant walked down
the line.

       "Commissary wagons, fellers. The Old Man
is gonna pour you boys a drink." When they came
to the tailgate, Preacher declined. The soldier behind him
stepped forward.

         "I'll take hisn." A corporal fed him
two ladles full of whiskey, and many men
were taking the drinks of soldiers declining their ration,
singing again with exuberance. Garland was next,
producing a pint sized blue glazed demi-john.

"Here y'are, private, a shot of rifle knock knee."
The files swung out of the copse and back on the road
in full June sun, the soldiers singing *O Maryland,
My Maryland*, but soon the drunks began to sweat
and straggle. The singing died. Laughter swelled
ahead and when they marched up to it, he saw
a soldier at shoulder arms marching with elan
alone in a waist high corn field. A Rebel observed,

"It is not the road's length but its width that troubles him."

June 28, 1863 Fayetteville, Pennsylvania

Consciousness dawned creeping above its horizon,
gathering clarity, men under blankets, stains

of exhausted fires, corn fields and wheat fields, wagons
bringing up rations. Oscar was busy busting
fence rail kindling for the cook fire as Garland sat up,
rubbing sleep from his eyes.

      "Morning, Oscar."

"Morning, Garland. Commissary scared up a passel
of flour and bacon."

      "You going to eat it, Oscar?"

"I can't leg thirty miles a day with only
rice in my belly." He sliced the flitch of bacon,
dropping rashers in the sissing skillet, the hearty
aroma drawing the men and roiling his innards.
Oscar worked some dough, gathered ram rods
from stacked arms and coiled the dough around them,
stuck them around the fire, turning them
to brown. When he served him bacon, ram rod bread,
a dollop of boiled white rice in his steaming mess kit,
Garland caught his wrist.

      "Thank you, Oscar.
Thank you for taking such fatherly care of us."
Oscar was surprised and pleased.

      "You're welcome, Garland.
See here. We Rebels liberated some Federal coffee,
compliments of General Ewell and his lightning strike
into Maryland." This was the first real coffee they'd had
in at least six months, and he sipped the pungent char
roast odor, closing his eyes in abandoned relish
of simple goodness, black coffee, frying bacon,
sucking air to savor searing grease.

Oscar ate last by the fire. A Jew sat chewing
a mouthful of pork, breaking ancient covenants.
Did the violation obliterate the storied blood
that lent the man his nature, bequeathed from patriarchs,
from the moment a boy lay bound, his father's knife
poised to strike him, spill his promised blood,
allowing the wilderness to drink it down, when a voice
interdicted? And was it delusion or conscience blossoming
or even the genuine voice of the wild Almighty,
proclaiming divine holiday, abeyance of sacrifice?
But blood is always required; nothing is woven
tighter in the warp and woof of human life.
The old Jews got that right beyond a doubt.
Cain and Abel, Abraham and Isaac, Jephthah
and his daughter, Absalom and Amnon, and even Christ,
who came to call all men to brotherhood, preaching
from anchored skiff, must have looked at the throng
and imagined their faces contorted in hatred, heard
their voices demanding sacrifice, dreading heartbreak
of the telltale kiss. Oscar ate with meditation,
yet nothing changed of his studied cheer, and his heart
kept going out to him in loving gratitude
and admiration. What earthly government preserves
a human nature? A man can only count
on himself for that. Oscar drained his coffee.
The soldiers rose for the march.

"Thankee, Greasy."

"Better'n a jab in the eye with a sharp stick."

"Best grub I had since last I et at the Spotswood."

The men cleared off.
                    "Oscar, doesn't it bother you,
eating the pork?" Oscar pondered a moment.

"Garland, the words of our scripture tell us this,

For thou desirest not sacrifice; else would I give it: thou delightest
not in burnt offering. The sacrifices of God are a broken spirit, a
contrite heart, O God, thou wilt not despise.

God gave the law so a man might secure his life
on integrity's foundation, pleasing God, but our fathers
knew that rules should not be stumbling blocks,
which is why they said, *If you're going to eat some pork,*
get it all over your beard. Did you see how messy
I was this morning, Garland?" He laughed at Oscar
and admired his freedom of mind while he himself
felt sprawled on a mountain anvil for a cosmic blow.
Oscar rose and scalded the cast iron pots,
heroic Oscar, humbly serving with joy,
stepping forth from history's Goshen into cataclysmic
war, and yet he is cheerful as a man at tasks
he loves, acting in the world with kind intention.

July 2, 1863 toward Cashtown, Pennsylvania

Scuffles marking time in darkness, stretching
away before and behind, the road was dotted
with flop, deposited yesterday by passing trains,
attentive infantry stepping around the gobbets.

"My Gawd, what's Heth and Pender using to fodder
they mules?"
     "The stink is mighty."
           "And will prevail,"
said Patty, striding behind him. The march was morning
somber, slowed by wagons, the soldiers breathing
a dusty fetor; they started and halted, dawn light
thinned the sky, but the rising mountain kept them
buried in nether shadow. The march turned east,
a legendary serpent, winding and undulant, seeking
the Cashtown Pass. Ahead, the regimental trains
of the Ninth Alabama, some twenty wagons, their canvass
taut as sails, followed by a regiment of Negroes
shouldering spades, then medical wagons where surgeons
checked the stragglers, this order replicated for miles.
Knees and breath laboring the peak, he was awed
by the land's majesty, spruce, black oak, tamarack,
and the grand hemlocks ascending the steep's flanks,
and here and there showing through leaf meal, belts
of limestone with dark striations of imbedded slate.
The mountain top was anvil flat; at the edge
the land fell away in a breathless precipice sheer,
but timbers were bearing up in counter rush
sublime and vertiginous, plunging through woven mists
along the eastern prospect, and north and south
terrain was jutting from green expanse, vertebrae
in the land's muscular back.
        "Gettysburg,"
said Buzzard as they watched a distant battle line
erupting in scintillations and puffs of smoke
and heard the guns' attenuated reverberations.

Ecstatic cheers unbidden burst from the Rebels,
and the column moved forward to make the steep descent.

"Hoofing it down's a sight easier than hoofing
it up," said Hog.
                    "The way to Avernus is easy,"
Caleb observed.
                    "I thought we's going to Cashtown?"
The men descended through mists in clothes of lofty
sunlight, and the ranks were swept with another elation,
stepping down from mountain clouds like gods.
The macadamized road reached toward Cashtown, a hamlet
of pasture and plow lands. They passed, loitering on stoops
of neat brick dwellings, young men of military age,
watching blandly as Rebels invaded their state.

"Makes you wonder whom they hired to fight
their war," said Caleb. But other soldiers taunted
the malingerers.
                    "Pluck up yer courage, boy, we'll let
you join us."
                    "How's this for your played out rebellion, Yank?"
The stomping files tromped past an old Dutch farmer,
who had pulled his wagon off the road to let
the Rebels pass, some shouting,
                                    "Och, mine countree!"
They passed a two story house of brick, its fine
American bond shone apple ripe. On the porch,
a girl was posted with hair of jet, the Federal
banner draped across her shoulders and gathered
in her fist at her ample bosom, her eyes flashing

a fierce and impetuous genius. There were some calls
of appreciation regarding her imperious beauty.
The lady was having none of it. A gray back shouted,

"You'd better take that flag off a you, Miss."

"I shan't do it," she retorted. "Why should I?"
                                        "Well Miss,
I'll tell you, these old Rebel's is hell on breastworks."
The woman whirled herself around and slammed
the door as laughter sighed like wind through wheat,
and he was troubled her honor had been insulted
and he one in a long line bearing the insult,
hearing the merriment spark as the tale was recounted
to men who'd been out of ear shot, the way a line
of wagons will drop their wheels in a washed out rut,
pounding rhythm on a long and desolate highway.
They passed through Cashtown, where wagons crowded streets
groaning with wounded. On some uncovered flat beds,
surgeons applied their skills in blood and agony,
but evidence of battle anguish made no one grim,
still treading steeps of mountain top exultations.
The men were halted in forging sun as troops
came up from the rear, a brigade to lead the march
twelve miles to Gettysburg, stepping high, their dignity
burnished by dust, proud they were called to the van.
Snake shouted out,
                    "Hey Papa, who is these fellers?"

"At air's Perry's brigade of Florida boys,"
said Yancy, "The Second, Fifth, and Eighth, I allow."

When the Second regiment passed, Snake called again,

"These Florida boys marched out'n the swamp and ain't
had nary a bite of iron clad possum in a year."
Some soldiers laughed, but most were reluctant to sully
a unit leading a march to a go with the elephant.
The Florida Eighth strode past the Eighth Alabama
and saluted, and boys in his unit saluted back.
A cheer went rolling along the line for Florida.
The heady spirits knuckled down their grim
resolve, but flesh, though willing, was flesh, and sun
bore down, parching throats and sapping strength.
Before them, battle racket loomed; the generals
tried to keep them screened by trees as they crossed
a ridge then beat down dusty roads, canteens
ringing. At last, in battle order, they stepped
into a wood, refreshed by shade and glad for rest.
Men sat silent, jimmied in brush at the foot
of Seminary Ridge careful not to break cover.
A grackle trilled its torquing whistle tighter.
He rifled his kit and swore beneath his breath.
Ainey crouched beside him, threw his arm
around his shoulders and pulled him close, shaking
him and smiling.
                        "Don't chew fret none, Garland.
A brave man's just a coward's what's took off running
in the wrong direction." Caleb chuckled softly,

"Ainey, you ain't got sense God give a goose."

"I reckon not, but I'm sure shitting like a goose."

Only Deke was untroubled, checking his piece
then falling fast asleep. Buzzard's fingers
were white on his rifle stock. Preacher's eyes
were closed. He looked to see if his lips were moving,
allowed his gaze to pass from face to face,
Apple Jack, Hog, Saxon, Brutus, and Patty,
whistling an Irish melody. He longed for a brave
shot of rifle knock knee. The men sat stippled
in light, whispering and chuckling in apprehension.
Their necks were marked with gathered dirt at margins
of dried sweat, their cheeks still scarlet with marching,
eyes intent with fortune's surmises. The colonel
came up and greeted his regiment, walked to the tree line,
pulled down a bough, revealing to Garland the lush,
summer mile, stretching to Cemetery Ridge,
and his heart quailed. The colonel's back was stiff
as stave oak, and he said,
                          "Hillary A. Herbert,
shall you commit to doing your duty this day?"
And then he answered, "As I am a man, I will."
He went to Herbert still eying the swale and troughs
of grasses yellow spiked with orchises, betraying
erratic winds, and farther, gouged in the hill,
parallel trenches of infantry prickling with blades,
the ridge line crowded with rows of squatting guns.
This clear blue day would erupt in violence of earthquake
and volcano, all brought to bear on a suicidal dash
over leaves of grass for a hilltop in beautiful July.

"I've no idea what duty is in this matter
or the reason any man here should die for such,

but I'd like to know before I run this mile."

"Duty is only gratitude for the goodness our fathers
  bequeathed to us; therefore, in recompense we serve
  our parents, country, and God, vouchsafing occasions
  to show ourselves honest and brave a privilege." He grasped
  his shoulder, clasping his warm brown eyes on him.
"And son, I'm afraid to say this run is more
  than a mile. We'll make it together and we'll be men."
He stepped past Garland, offering final instructions
  and speaking encouragements, neat in Rebel gray,
  locks and curved mustaches combed and trimmed.
Gentlemen always appeared as fresh from the barber.
He dropped himself by a storm felled ash tree, jostling
  Caleb, lost in thought. Duty could not
  accommodate a white man's affection for a Negro woman.
But now was the reason he'd taken her to himself
  and carried her in his heart to this crossroads hour,
  so her grace might sweeten his life arrived at its end
  and prove his integrity. Because of her his love
  attained an exquisite fulfillment. He'd serve no law
  that worked against his happiness and purposed to do
  whatever he had to do to be with her.
This resolution evoked her skin, delicate
  as shadow, she waking that morning of their first day,
  slipping from bed unaware that he was watching
  her naked in the window, bracing her palms on the sill,
  the gentle muscular contours of her body igniting
  in rapturous morning, a vision half light, half shade.
She closed her eyes, stretched feline on the balls
  of her arched feet, his eye for beauty's sake,

aching along her body's supple lines,
her witch hazel arms, between which swung her milky
breasts, nipples gold as honeycomb and sweeter,
shoulders flexing their small wings, the arch
of ribs fanning to the gathered waist, the plump
of buttocks, dimpled and savory, to undulating thighs,
sweeping behind the knees into bunched calves,
those thoroughbred legs he craved to touch again.
She was so stunning he forgot his tortured eyes,
then as now. His sense surrendered to longing,
her lissome arms clasped about his neck,
she gasping plaintive *love me, love me, love me.*
Now Caleb was pulling him up to his feet, dispelling
his invention.
     "I hope that was a nice place you were at,
'cause we've got orders to join the Monkey Show."
Garland put his hand on Caleb's shoulder.

"If I have been honest or brave, even in a moment,
I owe it to you. Your friendship has meant a lot"—

"I value our friendship as well, and I look forward
to its long continuance. No goodbyes."
         "All right,
no goodbyes, but I'd like to ask a thing
as a friend."
     "Just speak your mind."
         "If it be possible
given our circumstances, neither of us
will allow the other to be left in Pennsylvania
if he is alive."

"You have my word."

"And you mine."

The command to fall in rattled out. The men
formed up and stood at attention for Captain Blackwood,
who gave their orders.

"All right boys, we gwine
to pull back forty or fifty yards and cook
some victuals." Battle expectancy, broken by prospect
of dinner, the men chortled and doubled back
to shade of Pitzer's Wood and stacked their arms.
Soon skillets were crushing embers and hizzing, the wood
full of delicious odors like a peaceful bivouac.
Oscar knelt by Garland, slicing fat back,
and Count stood opposite, intent on frying a cornpone.

"When we were in line this morning, I know I heard
a goose honking from the farm house north of us.
I'd love to get my hands on that Yankee goose.
We'd have us some eating sho nuff."

"You can eat goose?"

"Sholey."

"I too desire flesh of dis goose."
As if Count's final utterance had been a signal,
the skillet Oscar was minding rang like a bell.
All heads raised like cattle sensing danger,
hesitation portent. A ripping scourge of bullets,
and hands were snatching stocks, he hearing the terrible,
wet slap of lead on flesh, glimpsed a soldier
spin and fall, groaning an eloquent animal
lowing as he threw himself behind the log

where he'd been sitting. Captain Blackwood scrambled,
diving to his left, swearing, and Caleb lay
on his right. Another volley pinned them down,
ricocheting cooking pots and stones in lethal
cacophony.

        "These bastards is damn good shots," said Blackwood.

"An impression I share," said Caleb, pouring a cartridge.
Blackwood shouted,
                "Stay low and watch yore asses.
They probably sharp shooters. Use the trees for cover
and try to work your way to the edge of the wood
for a shot. Watch 'em up high. They's at least a company."
Then to Garland and Caleb, "Bollocks, you'd know
we'd be the only muggins without no cover."
Left and right, a ten foot leap to the nearest
tree, done in a second, but a second was all
a Yankee sniper needed to ream their brains.
The three lay staring at oak leaves. He got an idea.
He handed his rifle to Caleb, dug his feet in,
and heaved against the stodgy log with all
his strength, forcing it out of its crushed trough
and off its mat of wet, black duff. Exposed
to sun, roaches skittered away for dark
of leaf mold, one centipede unwinding mechanical legs.
The bole was barely tall enough for cover,
flattening saplings and cracking sticks, he huffing,
splayed his length. "Hot damn! Garland. Keep us
moving," laughed Blackwood. When they made the wood's edge,
Yankee rifles drilled the front of the log.

They had to stop a couple of times on account
of well directed fire, hunch their knees up
under chins, and wait for volleys to slacken.
Their moving redan drew such fire, the boys
behind were able to work their perilous way
to the wood's edge, providing them cover in turn.
The captain stole a glance around the bole,
which splintered behind his head. "They's a mite bit
of a rise some thirty foot out front. Let's try
and get our log up there to get us some deflection,
but for sake of dear sweet Jesus don't let this log
roll off the farther side of that goddamned hill
or we'll be sucking hind tit in prestigious fashion."

"You mean prodigious."

                   "I reckon y'all know what I mean."
He heaved the trunk, they scrambling elbows and knees,
grunting and huffing, as bullets struck the revolving
log in death melody like a music box cylinder,
zing of trajectories inches above their heads.
He trundled the tree trunk until the hilltop took
the bole's weight. He unearthed a stone and wedged it,
chocking the head log. On the crest, they had good cover
though they were alone and cut off. The sun was stark,
revealing the vivid counterfeit of an afterlife earth,
as if he were recollecting this present moment,
a trough of mortal time from eternity's summit
through dazzled perception, imbuing with ineluctable
clarity blades of grass, beatific oak crowns,
worm rails, and far behind, the tree line's cover,
wistful as a former life. Beside him, in pristine

flower, a patch of ox eye, angel's substance,
and beyond a golden wheat field, swaying spikelets
and bristling awns chevroned by afternoon breezes.
The Federal picket had fallen back a ways,
but there was a sniper up high pinning them down.

"Put your kepi up quick and snatch it back."
Caleb raised his hat on his rifle barrel.
A Minie ball splintered the log. Garland raised
his eyes to a line of trees a hundred yards
in front, counting from the shot, *One, two,*
three and saw a phantom breech smoke drifting
up like the tree's ghost and among the branches
a shadow, man shaped, hugging the high trunk.
He sank back down, laying his hat on top
of the log, and when he counted eleven, a shot
cracked, making his kepi somersault. The Captain
was swearing, but he was counting again. When he got
to twelve, he said to Blackwood,

                              "Draw his fire."
He bobbed his head up and down. A shot rang out,
and he threw his rifle over the log, counting,
looking for the shadow, *where is it now*, moved
to the other side of the trunk, the Enfield's stock
cool on his cheek, his eye holding the crescent
bead, centering the shadow. He squeezed the trigger,
the report stuffing his ears, the stock recoiling.
Breech smoke cleared, the shadow fell and snagged.

"Get him?" asked Blackwood.

                    "I got him." The Captain sprang

away to gather the company and get them in line,
who were coming now on the run, using the rise
of ground for cover. A body fell down beside him.

"Hail Garfish, you could snipe a gallinipper
off a sleeping jackrabbit's ass a mile away
and not even spoil his slumber." Hiram, exulting,
threw an arm around his shoulders and hugged him,
he taken aback, who'd never witnessed the sergeant
proffer affection, but now the stolid soldier
seized his gaze, his eyes like early leaves
burnished in their hour's gold, he stabbed with sudden
gladness Hiram should be so handsome, so young,
whose countenance altered now, as if he'd caught
a glimpse of himself in a mirror. "Good luck," he said,
then hopped the log pursuing Federal sharpshooters
through pasture grass, then wading through the wheat.
Behind him in grim phalanx the Tenth Alabama
swept across the field. Overwhelmed, the skirmish
line of snipers faded. The Federal reconnaissance
thus dispersed, they returned to Pitzer's Wood,
scrounging morsels and orts. But now, their cover
broken, Federal gunners greeted them
with furious missiles whistling around their ranks,
snicking tree limbs and bursting earth eruptions.
He flinched when a solid shot struck an elm trunk,
making a double crack, first striking the tree
and then the two sides clapping back together,
showing no wound at all, but a puckered gnarl
he took for a comforting omen. A spiraling whine
sheared a quick, wet swath and made a fluttering

knock on tree trunks behind. To his right, one man
was cut in two on the ground, behind him a corpse
beheaded, and beside that heap, two arms and a leg
strewn amid their writhing owners crying
out, eyes imploring the sky, and untouched
bystanders painted with crimson stripes. One soldier
went to aid the wounded, but the rest kept attention
fixed on the puffing ridge and gleaming trenches.
He too looked straight ahead, his stomach clenched.
They lay on the ground for an hour, watching the sun
stand still, some muttering prayers to hurry it on.
But finally the officers took their places; he thought
it must be four o'clock, and Herbert called,

"Attention! Eighth Alabama, Battalion of direction!"
Grips on rifles clenched. "Forwa-rrr-d, march!"
They stepped from trees into preternatural sunlight,
taking momentous strides to the plaudits of guns.
Ten yards in front the Rebel Stars and Bars
fluttered in southerly breezes as he watched the gorgeous
suicide march of the color guard. The undulating crest
of Cemetery Ridge spread before them like a house
of austere mansions. Heat bore down on his shoulders.
His thirst rose, but he feared his hands would not
obey to open his canteen for its pitiful swig.
Ainey strode on his right, Deke his left,
grinning, eyes burning with battle hate, the suppressed
violent smoldering he'd seen in Jackson's eyes
two months ago. Yet all the same he was glad
to have him close, crazy, but not afraid.
They covered about a hundred yards a minute,

jingle of kit ticking mortal seconds.
The Yankee picket's desultory fire quickened,
popping a firecracker braid. A battery left
on the ridge began convulsing, and every soldier
knew the closer they got to the hill, closing
the angle, they would be enfiladed. To the right,
concealed by a slope, a Rebel battery fired
across their line of march, its smoke rising
above the hillock and drifting; the roar blocked out
most sound, except for the tangled hornet swarm
of Minie balls, compounding terrors as musketry
rattled and hummed. Their band struck up a jaunty
tune, drumbeats platting through gaps in the racket,
thunderous reverberations of cannon vibrating
his feet inside his boots, his sternum and teeth.
Now the enemy batteries loaded canister,
projectiles stropping air with ductile shrieks,
assaulting the will in piceous smudges, crescendos
of heaving dirt, unnerving screams, winnowing
becrimsoned men in droves, sprawling behind,
some still, some writhing, and yells and groans and curses
were clamped to earth beneath the battle's clamor.
They strode through clouds of smoke, and for long moments,
the battle was only racket of guns and arms,
commands and cries and tortured shrieking voices.
They gained a rise of ground and officers halted them
to pull the line together. Being thus disposed,
they viewed the battle's prospect and saw their regiment
on the far right flank of brigade and corps and army.
To their left the Tenth Alabama was three hundred yards
away if they were an inch. The Eighth was cut off.

A few spontaneous oaths were followed by calm
resignation, it being folly to hope; all soldiers
know the chance of battle may place them here
in the desolate valley of shadows, and they were come.
On the ridge a tiny American flag was waving.

"Hey, who is them boys?" His eyes roved
the field following other men's gazes. Left Tenant
behind them peered through glasses.
                                                            "Well I be dipped
in buttermilk if hit ain't Barksdale's Mississippians!"
The wind pushed past a cast of smoke, revealing
the ridge in panoramic vista, the gray
advance making spectacular sweep of the hill.
The Federal left was being refused in haste.
Like a terrible engine chuffing with glorious banners,
the Mississippians fired and stepped through breech smoke,
close ranked, inexorable. The Union flank was yielding,
but stubborn and deadly determined. This was no route.
Sight of that iron courage shivered his nerves,
gray hammer poised above a steel blue anvil.
But fact dismissed respect evoked by virtue.
The blue line was weak; the sooner they stove it in,
the safer they would be.
                                        "Look here, boys,"
said Papa, "that battery closest us ain't nothing
but three inch ordinance and one ten pounder Parrott.
Let's gobble 'em up." And Blackwood,
                                                            "Y'all heard Papa.
Let's fotch us some Yankee guns!" With crooning avian
shriek, the Rebels surged again toward thunder.

219

The pop and crump of canister was knocking gaps
in their line, strewing blood daubed men in flung,
ecstatic postures or sending the lucky, clutching
a coveted badge of blood, galumphing to the rear.
"Left oblique." As a great submissive animal,
every man in midstride made half face,
closing the gap between the Tenth and the Eighth.
Having come in musket range of the foremost trenches,
they suffered a volley. The racket stuffed his head,
batteries—thunderous, oppressive—and musketry popping
in concatenated runs and the closing hiss of balls.
With harpy purring a canister spindled down,
a deafening blast, Deke was gone, the line
pulled in, a stranger was running crouched beside him.

"This is awful," he said in an even voice,
a deliberate observation. Confederate guns
tore up the Yankee pickets, which melted away
behind the makeshift barricades of stones and fence rails.
In and out of crowded palls of smoke
they ran. An order came from a different officer,
his voice's tenor of backwoods hollows and chitterlings,
drawling commands. The Union fire intensified,
stabbing air, the screaming a steady strain
of agony and bellowed oaths to keep men's courage
at pitch. The Rebel line was a ram's horn, walloping
up the ridge, men ducking under electric
warp and woof of death. The enemy line
increased in definition, a palisade of rifles,
soldiers' faces inclined to sights. A canister
burst, a black smudge stroked on air, its ghastly

Legion voices singing past him, the blast
hurling a shattered body in his path, he tumbling
over, hands spread, his right still clutching his rifle,
canteen digging his ribs. Men charged ahead of him.
He tried to will control of panic, a hare
gripped by a hawk's plunging cry, crimson
and keen. The new officer addressed the flank
of the Tenth Alabama,

                 "Move along, Cousins.
You'uns is drawing the fire our way." He wobbled up,
willed his legs to move, saw Caleb trotting
in and out of scumbled haze, a shot
scarring earth behind him that a second before
would have shorn his friend in two. He surged through smoke,
a soft gray door that closed his vision and opened
on the ridge, implacable slope erupting brimstone.
Caleb entered a house of cloud and vanished.
An officer spurred up behind the advance brandishing
a saber and shouting jubilant,

                 "Forward, boys!
Home is just on the other side of that hill."
The officer's face transformed, thrilled by glory,
then something beyond, otherworldly, the man still smiling
as he tumbled out of the saddle. He quickened pace
to regain the line. The ridge and clamor loomed,
a uniform racket, beneath its vast oppression,
the massed crooning of the Rebel yell, deranging
men for contact, and now the stern set
of Yankee faces. Not one man looked afraid.
And then he caught the head-on shriek of a ball—
a violent blow closed the door of sense

to a crack of light, a kaleidoscope's fracture and spin,
tree line tipping backwards as if he'd slipped
on a roof's high peak, rolled to the eave and plunged
weightless and gasping. His rifle rose above trees,
canteen and cartridge bag rose, and then the impact,
a giant hand striking between his shoulder blades,
racking out breath, discordant battle furor
sweeping over, a glowing poker worming
in his thigh's muscle, seized in a thrilling spasm.
July cumulus trembled with Patmos thunders.
Pain nailed him to earth, and now the flourish
of retreating senses. He tried to cry for help,
but his voice would form no speech, and besides, no one
would stop; soldiers were trained not to stop. He must wait
for stretcher bearers, a long and desperate wait.
He gruffed a voiced noise through teeth, the wound
burned wavering blue, his pant leg stained with black,
his vision a lantern hung outdoors a cold
March night, the rise of breeze building the flame
until it gutters and is quenched, and he lapsed into troubled
unconsciousness, hearing thunder trembling the nation.

He trembled himself awake to aching cold
and thirst raging, like hideous brothers guarding
some vast exhaling subterranean entrance.
Wounded sprawled as if they'd plunged from Heaven.
He had seen it at Fredericksburg. He would be buried
in a shallow ditch, the cold soil hitting his face.
A wisp of thought, her memory brushed him like wings,
astonishing Duessa, that dawn she stretched at the window
in gorgeous morning naked timelessness.

For an hour he had possessed her, and it was glorious.
He let his fancy embrace her compound phantom,
her beauty, her grace suffusing his blood, exulting,
though he lay on an unforgiving bed, recalling
her cheeks' exquisite structure, framing the delicate
setting of her eyes, those sovereign realms, all
a man might ever wish to own, her cleanliness,
her fine perfumes bewitching, he longing once more
for silks and scented downs, feeling their pulses
subside toward blissful sleep, but then an encroachment,
a terrible premonition. She was standing disrobed,
reaching her honey arms and weeping; he would touch
her hands, but his groping stung his body, a matchstick
hiss in kerosene, catching its raging breath
and pain striking, catching his throat, the vision
receding; he saw strange coils swagging her neck,
a breathing mosaic fire, a wedge of head,
waving and nodding, the pupil's crescent, a tongue
testing air. Something evil had happened.

Far off, a murmur, two muttered syllables, a man
was groaning in darkness. They always cried for water.
Pinned in suffering's vice, he wished he would cease.
A presence, shuffle and chink, odor of sweat,
causing his unmoored consciousness to gather sense,
as a gentle hand lifted his head.
                                    "Here's water, poor fellow.
Have a little sup." A canteen was pressed
to his lips. The water shocked him—his body jerked
as if he'd snagged lightning, which action paralyzed
his right side, but pain notwithstanding, he sucked

the water with vigor. "Slow there, take it easy."
The compassionate shadow brought him round. He'd never
seen a kinder face and felt returned
to life, and all his exhausted flesh eased
in sweet relief for being rescued.

                              "With your help
I can stand, and you can tote me off to our lines."
He struggled to elbows.

                    "Friend, I can't take you back."

"Why not?"

              "The Rebs will shoot me." Confusion took him.
He searched the shadow face, the dark uniform,
and there on the soldier's opened haversack
the stenciled *U. S.* letters. He turned his head.
The man said nothing else but busied himself
with Garland's leg. Scissors sheared through cloth.
The man unbuckled Garland's belt, loosened
his pants a bit so he could slide one hand
beneath his torn thigh, which action replaced
despair with agony. He felt a cinch at his groin,
above the burning wound. "This should quell
a further loss of blood. Are you cold, friend?"
Garland nodded, and his nurse produced a blanket.

"Why are you helping me?" The soldier looked perplexed.

"What a funny question." He tucked the blanket
under his arms. "I've filled your canteen. Save
your strength and don't give up. Your people will come."
The soldier touched his arm and then moved off

in the groaning night, dodging corpses.
                              "Thank you,"
he whispered after the Samaritan. Pain and fear
transmogrified perception, marking time inert,
a vacuous eternity, but the blanket kept him warm,
revived his threadbare hope. Raising his head,
he could see down the ridge's slope men milling about,
tending and hefting wounded, but he had no strength
to call, so his head fell back and he fell asleep,
but even in sleep he knew his throbbing wound.

A rousing touch.
                        "Garland. Can you hear me, Garland?"
A familiar voice, and sleep staggered toward waking
like a cripple forcing his legs to essay their walking.
Caleb was kneeling above him, "Garland Cain.
Why'd you go and get your fool self shot?"

"I didn't shoot myself, a Yankee shot me."

"Garfish, you been bleeding like a stuck pig.
I'll swany, it took some scratch to tie a tourniquet
above that wound."
                        "A Yankee did that too."

"You don't mean it."
                        "Yes I do."
                                    "Well shut
my mouth, but I guess the Yankees owed you one.
They's a soldier's truce obtained to clear the wounded,
but first light breaking, the war will be on again."

"All right."
    "This is going to hurt like hell."

"I reckon it has to." Caleb crouched down and gripped
a wrist, pulled him up to standing, not looking
at his face.
        "When I say, get your good leg under you,
then fall across my back." He called on reserves
of all that made him a man, which just sufficed
for pluck to shrug his weight on Caleb's shoulders,
slumped like a sack of corn and feeling he'd been shot
a second time. He swore to himself he would not
cry out and Caleb held his wounded leg
against his body, to keep it still and free
from shocks, yet every footfall fired his nerves
with nauseating heat, sweeping his senses in eddies.
He'd never felt so happy enduring such hurt
as Caleb swerved along through battle trash
and scattered corpses, rifles and kit and yawning
cries of casualties, begging for water or merciful
death, and his heart was rent with joy and guilt.
They passed by Federal soldiers tending wounded,
most not even regarding their awkward transport
as they gathered their comrades. Caleb's heavy treading
squished across a hummocky ground, then splashed
bogging across a run dividing corpses,
Rebel and Union on either side, men
who'd clawed their way to water to drink and die.
They swung around a farm house pocked with shot,
windows like bared teeth, the fences dismantled.
His temples pounded. He fought the urge to vomit.

Caleb shrugged down an incline and huffed them out,
then halted on the prominence opposite, whispering,
                                        "My God."

He craned his head and sighted a row of bodies,
their feet describing a perfect line. Three soldiers
had fallen forward, the rest, at least three score,
had fallen backwards, shouldering arms like upset
toy soldiers. Yankees had stunned them from ambush,
who lay now giving off a ghastly light.

"Who are they?"
                    "North Carolina boys; they're famous
among the ranks. How gallant they must have been."

"It breaks my heart." The moon teetered on the ridge,
full bore and cratered, bleached as bone. He was desperate
to move so he could be set down and make
his throbbing wound easy, but Caleb seemed entranced.

"A curse on the people who forget such sacrifice."
Then Caleb scuffled on with labored breath
through ministering voices among the groans and weeping
and then a breathed and eerie purling, the whinny
of horses around a battery, many guns crippled,
leaning on shattered axles, behind them droves
of broken horses. Some animals raised their heads,
snuffed and whickered as rifles cracked among them,
quelling misery. Survivors were led away
to fodder and rest, and limbers and caissons were pulled
to the rear to rendezvous with ordinance wagons.
They skirted the edge of a ruined orchard, the faint

scent of peaches buried beneath the rancorous
stench of sulfur. A Federal ambulance was parked
nearby and soldiers worked with dispatch to load
their wounded. Caleb shuffled a few more yards
to a stone wall, which he straddled and sat on a moment
to catch his breath. A Rebel soldier emerged
from dark, mounted the wall and began to sing
a mellifluous agony stilling groans of the wretched.

> *Dearest love, do you remember when we last did meet,*
> *How you told me that you loved me, kneeling at my feet?*
> *Oft in dreams I see thee lying on the battle plain,*
> *Lonely, wounded, even dying, calling out in vain.*
> *Weeping, sad and lonely, hopes and fears in vain!*
> *When this cruel war is over, praying to meet again.*

Caleb plied onward, Garland's senses dimming,
a dot of flame consuming a straw of tinder
and puffing a thread of smoke. His last recollection
was Federal soldiers cheering the Rebel singer,
a dream discordant sound among the keening
wails of men and animals, among the battle
waste and orchard corpses in the moon's pure shining.

July 3, 1863 Gettysburg

Like a coin of dawn capping a cavernous passage,
the groans of tortured men lightened his sleep.
He woke in the dooryard of a sturdy rustic cabin,
now a field infirmary, parceled with ordered

ranks of sufferers. Medical staff had tied
together sheets and tent flies to shade the bereft.
A few men wounded in arms and torsos, leaned
on tree trunks, eyes like empty cisterns aimed
at the moaning yard. Stretcher bearers came
and went culling and stacking the dead. He was crowded
cheek and jowl in agony's jamboree,
amidst the undulating throb of the half conscious,
who moaned without ceasing, and when he thought he might
go mad from the dull caterwauling, he heard the plaintive
coo-ah-coo-coo-coo of the mourning dove,
and his mind rallied around that inconsequent pleasure.
But force of will he brought to bear on suffering
could not forestall presentments of his etiolated corpse
heaved in a ditch, and terror threw her cold
arms around him. If he had to die, all right.
Many were dying and he no better than they,
no more deserving of life, but he had a notion,
the anodyne to terror's icy kiss, that his bones
should rest in Wiregrass loam. He made that death
his object. He slept in fits, weakness pushing
him toward sleep, the moaning pulling him back.
The yard sweltered, but to all the bled out patients,
heat was a comfort. A staffer gave him a drink,
hoarfrost stubbling his face, his sweat streaming
from hairline down his cheeks, beading on his nose.
He wiped the drop away, another formed.
He worked with dispatch, daubing Garland's face
with a damp cloth and covering his eyes with a bandage,
and he lay in easy reach of fraternal hurt.
Sometime past noon, he heard the bump of a gun.

A pause. Another gun fired. And then in awful
chorus artillery erupted, suppressed in muted
waves by the interdiction of Seminary Ridge
as if the earth were grumbling against the heavens.
Blind and alone with suffered knowledge of the trial
his friends endured, resurgent affection surprised him,
not only for Caleb and Oscar, boon companions,
or Hiram, Ainey, Papa, men of character
and courage, but also the wayward, Patty and Brutus,
Preacher, Hog, Buzzard, and even the Critter
were redeemed in thought for charging mortal hillsides
through fronts of steel. He felt the impulse to pray—
for knowing friends were making their assignations
with fate was more inciting than personal emergencies,
but he touched the juju bag and called their names,
incanting a charm against the calamitous rumble
of guns like thunderstorms sweeping a neighboring county,
and a sentence came unbidden, *How are men
to call upon him in whom they have not believed?*
And seized with violent rage, he answered the voice
out loud,
   "I do not believe you are not, sir,
but I do not believe you are as others say.
Either you do not care or care from a distance,
and either way what use to men are you?"
The moaning around him abated. He envisioned pitying
expressions. All afternoon tympan undulations,
till evening, by six he guessed, they faded. How terrible
was waiting, not knowing if friends had lived or died.
Medical staff were working at fever pitch,
moving clenching bodies to stretchers, lifting

and bearing them through the surgery door, adding
to the sanguine architecture of unremitting screams.
He tried to put from his mind his turn in that room.
A middle aged man with a grizzled face was lying
next to him, his right arm shattered and bloody,
propped at his side in an odd articulation.
When the stretcher bearers lifted him, his head
lolled toward Garland. They had as yet to speak.
He raised his useful hand, a saluting gesture,
but his face's pallor was an eloquent valediction.
All day and evening, the cries of men whose limbs
were.severed by surgeons' catlings tortured air,
oppressing his mind. Fever lulled him to sleep;
chills shivered him awake. At midnight, braying
of mules and spiral ache of axles conveyed
an influx of wounded in reaper loads, the wailing
a stadium circle, making sleep impossible.
The hours were vagrant with nothing to do but attend
the harrowing choir; that night endured a lifetime.

July 4, 1863

Dawn, a raddled visage smoldering in darkness,
and sleep returned with morphine comfort. He dreamed
of gorgeous Duessa, bold as Circe naked,
her brown sorceress body beguiling his senses,
the baked bread of her skin he craved to break
and taste, baptismal cataract of hair washing
his face, revelation of his body inside her body,
her eyes in his, her Louisiana indolence and ease,

shade of serpentine mosses in the watchful bayou.
In the ivory gate of dream, they were embracing,
locked in love's delightful privacies, his power
flooding out and striking him with Philistine
weakness, who had been strong and whole, but fantastic
pleasure made him shift his body, bayoneting
his thigh; gasping, his eyes shot open to the cabal
of blood, the sun's shock and humiliation,
where now on the second day the incapacitated
lay in the wracking stench of feces and urine.
Two staffers stood at his feet, one sharing a twist
of tobacco with his comrade.

                              "When they gonna start?"

"I don't reckon they gwine to attack today.
Not on the glorious fourth. Round about noon
we'll likely hear they guns," he said, picking
and eating tobacco from his palm, the scraps he used
to slap his hands and scatter, but sun went well
past prime with no reports as summer cumulus
raised its pristine Babel towers grumbling.
All morning details were loading patients for transport.
Rain began to fall in stinging drops,
the wounded covering faces with blanket corners,
tent flies, soiled dressings, all gone silent
as even the effort to moan were being husbanded
to thwart shivering rain. He had to urinate.
Knowing he'd be on the road for hours and loathe
at the prospect of pissing himself and lying in stink
and shame, he gritted teeth, rolled to his side,
unbuttoned trousers. He pulled his blanket back

and purposed to start his stream as far away
as he could. He felt a twinge for the soldier beside him,
but he was dead. He let it go and almost
screamed, the contraction striking a lightning zigzag
of heat from ankle to groin, seizing his stream.
He clutched a handful of mud and strained again,
agony resurgent, blurring vision, which ebbed
and dimmed, his left hand gripping mire, his member
grasped in his right. Another torment, he cupped
his scrotum, vexation seared his flesh in twinging
eruptions. He fumbled his belt, opened his trousers,
discovering a biblical plague of chigger welts.
He twisted his blanket in fists to keep himself
from scratching parasite mansions of burrowing pests.

"Storm and hail in Beulah land," he shivered.
He only lay in the rain a couple of hours
before the stretcher bearers came for him,
the staffers slathered in mud and haggard, weariness
weighing every countenance of the brave and beautiful
servants of the damned. They dropped him in a wagon bed,
adding his shocked cry to the agonized choir.
No straw for comfort, no axle springs, at least
the bows were stretched with canvas, and he lay packed
like a canned oyster, among ten ruined soldiers.
The man above him pissed himself, the stream
coursing bed boards, soaking his hair and blouse.
Beside him a boy with wavy forelocks, no more
than sixteen or seventeen, and Garland's pain abated
for his handsome face, the sturdy cheek bones, angular
sepals of lips, gorgeous though flesh were pallid,

his manly bearing betraying moral goodness.
He lifted the boy's blanket sodden with blood
and water. He'd taken a bayonet in the side.
A domino popping of whips, vehicles surged,
a wave of curses crested toward their ambulance,
their own cries timed to the peak of lamentations,
as the wagon jerked forward, ecstasies tapering
as wagons behind them jostled on cringing axles.
The journey begun, at every tug and hold back,
at wheels pounding in pothole or gully rut
of washed out road, at every braking, there rose
a spasm of tortured wailing as clothing matted
in dried scabs tugged open edges of mended
flesh and rasped infected wounds, putrescent,
oozing, and ends of broken bones were grated.
A man in front repeated,
                              "God let me die,"
and many swore, enjoining their driver to stop,

"God, just put me out and let me die!"

"Stop goddamn it, stop goddamn it, stop."
The teamster only applied more violent curses,
urging the mules into braying, grudging paces,
and Garland felt a pang of pity for him.
Hour after faltering hour, with every carom
and jigger of the wagon bed, pain and wailing
abraded resolve to bear, and he swore to himself,
It's root hog or die, old son, it's root hog or die.
He braced himself and raised on an elbow, looking
over the tailgate at the road scything away

and ambulance wagons far as he could see.
He wondered how many miles the thing stretched out,
how many men to the mile of abject suffering.
He lay back down in stink, shifting on the rough
hewn boards of the bed to make his hurt leg easy
and found the boy's eyes open and felt accused
by the irises' lustrous blue, his vision residing
beyond the ravishing torture in mercy of diluted
consciousness; a faint, ephemeral smile, and his face
relaxed in salvific abandon, dead and divine,
the way a June breeze cools one's face and passes.
He stroked the boy's cheek and closed his eyes.
Then rocking forward, accepting the blade thrust deep
in his groin, he put his hand behind his neck,
drew their faces together and kissed his lips.

July 5, 1863

Endless hours of maddening caterwauling,
chiggers and trauma goring tormented flesh,
bone thrilling jolts of the road igniting nerve
conflagrations, the only respites coming when trains
bunched up and stopped. The ordeal ended, he near
delirium, his senses frayed like unwhipped rope.
That night he woke up yelling. Someone had touched
his wound. The grip of hands tightened on arms
and legs, his vision extirpated by glare,
a lantern swaying, the room pitching seasick.
He lay naked to the waist, crowded by strangers.

"Copious suppuration—a positive sign.
Probe." A bloody hand produced a long,
thin stick and passed it to another bloody hand,
which held it poised like a paintbrush or pencil and plunged
the blunted end in the swollen purple crater
in his thigh. He came up off the table. They pushed him
down. Somewhere beyond himself, he heard himself
moaning, his body fixed by a fiery stake.
Faint and nauseous, he tossed his shoulders, rolling
his eyes around the benighted chamber, he gnashing
his teeth and telling himself, *I will not cry out!*
He grasped the side of the table on which he lay
with the strength he had and found a projection there.
He lay on a door they'd taken off its hinges
and propped upon two chairs. He was gripping the knob.
It looked more like a catafalque than it did
an operating table.
                    "There it is! I feel it!"

"What is the depth?"
                    "At least five inches, sir."

"Make the incision here." He craned his neck
and watched the scalpel open flesh, tracing
fire. Another thrilling cut, he huffed
through gritted teeth, a knock on the floor, the ball
rolling out.
            "Nice cutting, lieutenant."
                              "Thank you, sir."

"Max, bandage the wound. We'll take him next."
They yanked the probe out quickly. Garland fainted.

July 6, 1863 Harper's Ferry, Virginia

He woke to a blade of light exhuming the world.
The medical staffers had staked a piece of canvas,
lean-to style, to shelter him and half
a dozen patients from the sun. Pillars of cloud
swung shadows across the yard, and winged black vortices
drifted above. The sun at prime felt good,
and being settled, they were given rations of hardtack
and rice. The hill fell away in pine tops smothering
the confluence of the Shenandoah and Potomac Rivers.
The man who lay beside him, shot through the chest,
saw him gazing at the town.
                                        "See down yonder,
the engine house with them three tall winders. You know
what that is?"
                    "Nosome."
                                  "That there is John Brown's Fort.
That crazy son of a bitch has cursed us all."
That afternoon a nurse made rounds, distributing
papers, his face dirty with whiskers, his cheeks
wasted from constant labor attending to ordure
and pain. He handed Garland a *Richmond Examiner*,
saying in a hang dog voice,
                                        "Vicksburg's fallen.
Pemberton's done surrendered his army wholesale
to U.S. Grant. Lot of folk's saying hit's treachery.
Now why you reckon the president put a Yankee
in command of a Rebel army? That dog won't hunt."

"They've got the Mississippi. We cut in half."

The nurse furrowed his brow and spoke to the yard.

"Boys, hit's official. The Confed'racy's sucking hind tit."

July 12, 1863 toward Richmond

A dream journey, suffused with rhythmic knock
of wheels on track. He lay in a cattle car
with other invalids in clods of ripe manure,
the reek intensified in the car's close heat.
They stopped in dark; the uncoupled engine chuffed
into distance, then silence till peep of morning birds,
their slight wings whispering in and out of the car,
and rungs of light pinning his body down.
The heat swirled in feculent currents, a desert
wedged in his throat. Then in languishing reverie,
voices moving up and down the ladder.
The slatted door rolled away, the sufferer
lying next to him was crucified in sunlight.

"Oh my God, this car is full of soldiers!
This is an outrage. They should find the men responsible
and hang them all." That afternoon, he woke
in a crowded ward, shadow panes slanting his bed,
the fetid air more pungent than the livestock car.
A woman came with a sweating jorum and poured
a drink for the man beside him. A ragged soldier
stalked across the ward, dragging his steps.
From a bed opposite, a grating voice,
                                        "You walk

like a frost bit chicken." He raised his heavy head,
the patient had one arm and a Texas accent.
Hobbles aimed his vacuous gaze at the boy.

"I'd trade my wound for yourn."

"How come is 'at?"
The soldier regarded the female nurse then moved
his languid eyes back to the Texan.

"When my girl
back home finds out where I been wounded, she won't
be my girl for long."

"Pard, you should a wore you
a Kentucky button."

"To hail from Texas, you talk
like a flannel mouthed Dutchman."

"That's enough of good advice,
Mr. Fleming," the nurse intervened, placing the dripping
pot on a bedside table. She approached the crippled
soldier, placed her hand on his breast, closing
his top blouse button and whispering, "Now you don't know
that's so, Gabe. She'll be kind to her hero, you'll see,"
but proffered compassion made him turn his head.
She came to Garland's bedside.

"Awake at last,"
she pouring water, the cup turning cool in his palm.
"I'm Kate. I'll be in charge of you for a while.
If you need anything, just call. I'm never far."
Garland snorted the well water down, cold
and sweet, and Kate dispensed him another cup,
which she gently pried from his hand when he fell asleep.

July 13, 1863 Fourth Alabama Hospital, Richmond

Bewitching Kate passed the rose hued windows
with basin and rag.
               "A bath will make you feel better.
I'll get you first, then Texas."
                  "Much as I stink,
a bath will make us all feel better." He unbuttoned
his blouse, and Kate rung out the washcloth. She was tall
and handsome and so compassionate every patient
wanted to be her beau. She lathered his hair.
Her fingers massaging his scalp weighed down his eyes.
The Texan was bumping his gums about how his brigade
could have saved the day at Gettysburg, if only. . .
Bathing his face and chest, she asked him questions
about his home and family. A woman's hand
was more restorative and succoring than a man's rough touch.
She went to Texas next, unwrapping his stump.
Fetor from infected flesh oppugned the air.
She gave his wound a look of sad distress,
held his stump and cleansed it, making him wince,
then washed his chest and face. When he was nodding,
she crossed to the man by Garland, Fisher by name,
another loquacious soldier, whose mouth rang
like a clapper, but he succumbed to sleep as well
for enchanting ministrations of the merciful nurse.

July 15, 1863

Most days Kate was on the ward before six,
remaining till well after midnight, feeding patients,

changing dressings, washing and shaving and reading
the Bible or letters from home, and writing replies.
There was no task beneath her dignity if the thing
were done for a soldier. A captain from O'Neal's Brigade
was shot in the jaw, and surgeons removed it. Kate walked
miles before dawn to a farm each day and purchased
milk at her own expense, his only nourishment.
He discovered the captain by accident strolling the ward
with aid of crutches, trading gossip with the boys.
The hall's last bed was cordoned off by a sheet.
That morning, the curtain not pulled closed, he glimpsed
Kate holding in a towel the soldier's rag of jaw,
she pouring swigs of milk in the mouth sack,
a slack irregular hole. He could not even
suck as an infant might. The milk spilled down
his face as his tongue protruded and lolled in vain
attempts to swallow, his head cocked back to drink
like some terrified fowl, his eye rolling to fasten
on Garland transfixed, watching him gargle and weep.
He hobbled off the ward to a bitternut hickory
on a hilltop, beneath him raging tides of wind
in dense Virginia canopies, his mind raging
at the shame and cowardice of hiding that man away.
Afraid he might lose hold of his senses, he goaded
himself again, *Old son, it's root hog or die.*

July 16, 1863

Drowse of dog day's heat was stirred by the strident
voice of Kate, waxing hot and accosting

the Texan, who, of course, was provoking her, allowing
how some folk thought her work was not respectable,
saving smiles for Garland when her back was turned.

"Not respectable! And who has made it so?
Our men are daily exposed to the enemy's deadly
missiles, fatigues of hard marching in scorching
heat and biting frosts, exposure to dangers
and disease. When such brave heroes do so much
for us, what in the name of common sense
are women supposed to do, true women, who love
their country, when there is many a parched lip
to quench and wounds to bind? We face a foe
merciless as Attila, cruel as Tamerlane, resolved
to lay our towns in ashes, lay waste our fields.
If a woman must seize her rights to do her duty,
then duty demands a woman seize her rights!
It will not do to say opinion prevents us.
A cowardice society tolerates remains a cowardice."
Her passionate encomium reached its period, the Texan
beating a drum behind her back with his one
good arm and pumping his legs in marching time.
When she left, he asked,
                              "Who's 'at muggins Tamerlane?"
Garland shrugged,
                        "A nasty fellow, I guess."
Along in the afternoon, he was up on crutches,
restless with boredom and Fisher's plying soliloquies,
so stumped about the ward and explored the yards.
Having made an hour's excursion, he happened on Kate
alone in the window of the darkened washroom, staring

outside.
        "Why, Miss Cumming."
                "Mister Cain."

"You're looking rather pensive." Her smile was troubled.
He guessed she might be brooding on the jawless captain.
"It's not a weakness to share a bit of your burden."
Her eyes clouded.
             "A month ago, we hired
two sisters, Mary and Elsie, to do the laundry.
Their family was poor, the girls were broken with scurvy,
and they were glad for the work, as grateful for meals
as for pay. They worked so hard, with such good cheer.
They told me they were going to save and buy
some earrings. Think what it must have meant to them
to go in a store with money and buy some beautiful,
useless thing to wear like Richmond belles.
A week ago, they pierced each other's ears
with a straight pin, and now they're lying in the ward yonder,"
she faced the window, "dying of erysipelas."
Her voice went hollow, void of all emotion.
"Their lovely, common faces are rotting away.
This war is merciless. No one is spared its cruelty."
She rose, supporting herself with a hand on the chair back,
amid the tubs and washboards and stacks of linens.
"There's work to do. I can hardly afford to indulge
my feelings." But then she looked at him and wailed,
"It's all my fault. It was my idea they should come."
She buried her face in her hands in anguished weeping.
He swung two cumbersome steps toward her and held her
as she trembled and wept, till sorrow began to ebb.

"It's never a fault to try and help a neighbor,"
he stroking her hair and resting her head on his shoulder.
"No man here will forget the good you've done."

July 18, 1863

John Fisher let up talking just enough
to learn that Garland served in Wilcox's Division
and had caught a ball at Gettysburg. These chances
shared in common created in his mind an intimate
bond. But John's ball shattered his knee, and the surgeons
had taken his leg, yet to Fisher mutilation
was fortune's windfall. The army couldn't use him.
He'd be sent home, and all he talked about
was home, seeing his wife, their new born son
he'd yet to meet, tending his acres of corn.
He longed for Troy, Alabama like a saint for paradise,
evidently blind to his incapacity to farm,
and Garland dreaded his rapturous disquisitions,
expecting him at any time to fathom
the cruel twist of his condition. For dwelling on home,
he returned there sure as he'd made the journey by wagon
or rail, a shift in his eye a shift in location,
the world reordered to suit his own affection.
This wild swerving from reality unnerved Garland,
but the more unsettling thing was, hour on hour,
Fisher's lotus memories took him prisoner.
A precise detail would draw him in—grasping
a stiff dry shuck, the grain on fingertips
like shoddy cloth or hearing the oaken groan

of the mill's apparatus and, underneath, the grist
being breathed into meal—and he was an instant guest,
beguiled by sane conditions of seed time and harvest
in another man's life and work. This sultry noon,
lulled by the cadenced rhythm of Fisher's voice,
he attended him to Troy, to the grassy prominence
where stood his dog trot shack of split pine boards,
a preacher's cubby built out on the narrow stoop,
and Lucy, her red hair smoldering, her verdant eyes
teeming with proffered affection, her throat touched
with delicate lace of her best blue Sunday dress,
and she started with a cry, running to embrace him, arms
outstretched, her lips a warm and joyful salutation.
The sky, its fathomless waters, began to moan
and fracture, the way a basin casts a wavering
scintillation against the ceiling. He opened his eyes,
aggrieved to have that rapturous kiss dispelled.
The ward was hot and stinking, patients groaning.
Kate was handing out newspapers. Fisher took one.

"*Richmond Enquirer,* Seven July. The writer,
conveying early reports from Gettysburg,
has Meade skedaddling to Baltimore, pursued by Lee.
Longstreet has bagged, get this Garland, *forty
thousand* prisoners!"

                    "Who could pen such fantasies?"

"I reckon these Southern editors can skin a cat
on a cob web when they're a mind, just like they do
up north." Fisher cast a glance about.
"Say, what went with old *arm and the man*?"

                                    "Huh?"

"The Texan, where did he go?"
                                        "Ask Kate when she comes."
But a pang struck him; he hadn't written Duessa.
Her heart would not be swayed by lack of courtesy.
Tomorrow while Fisher slept, he would write to her.

July 19, 1863

He'd had to importune Kate for writing materials,
for teasing curiosity regarding his correspondent
kept her insisting she write the letter for him.
Then Fisher offered his services, claiming a preternatural
gift for wooing females, offering for proof
his successful capture of Lucy's pristine heart.

"I'm sure with my aid, we can snare you a girl almost
as good."
            "From your own account of Lucy's virtue,
I think she likely considered your suit with pity."
Garland became so abashed at their protestations,
he asked them to drop the matter, but later, in opiate
afternoon heat, Fisher and most of the patients
fast asleep, Kate brought pencil and paper,
coaxing him in a whisper,
                            "Light the sparks!"

My Dear Duessa,
            I have been brought to Richmond,
recovering in the Alabama Hospital with a wound

in my right leg. They're taking good care of me here.
I've all the water I can drink and a ration
of hardtack, two biscuits, each day. I often feel guilty
when I think of friends sleeping on the hard ground
and me on a chafftick mattress with laundered sheets.
But now in the midst of dog days, the ward gets stifling
even though they throw the windows open.
I borrowed pencil and paper and folded an envelope
from a sheet of Richmond Enquirer, *wherein you shall find*
some right fantastic reports on Gettysburg,
which feels like a sword our country has fallen upon.
My best friend Caleb found me on Cemetery Ridge
the night of my wounding and toted me off on his back.
He's one of the finest men in the CSA.
He's like the disciple, I can't recall his name,
who had no malice in him. My dearest one,
as I lay in moonlight torn and bleeding, harboring
desperate thoughts, you came to me in a vision,
your pure affection sustaining my soul's long night.
Without that recollection, I would have perished.
Dearest one, a word from you would touch me
more than you can know. I long for the day
when we shall meet again and walk together.
Though I may hitch a bit.

Yours, Garland.

July 20, 1863

"When did you get to the war, John?"

"I arrived

in time for Second Manassas. We flustered Pope
so good he couldn't tell his headquarters from his hindquarters.
How 'bout you?"
                    "Fredericksburg. I arrived
sick but recovered enough to be detailed
for stretcher duty on the ridge among the batteries.
When I gained Marye's Heights, I saw in broken
glimpses through hanging palls of cannon smoke
the grand, steady lines of Union infantry.
I stood for a spell and watched them make a charge."

"That must have been a sight."
                              "A terrible sight.
I stood on a hillock at Gettysburg and watched
as Barksdale's Mississippians swept the flank
of Cemetery Ridge, and that was superb, but I'll never
see another like the first."
                        "What about it
moved you, Garland?"
                        "I felt I witnessed glorious
carnage, that Union men were laying their bodies
down on fiery altars, taking leave
of life on paths of glory. That moment the war
became a moral drama. But finding myself
in their place at Chancellorsville, I felt no sacred
fervor, only the icy dread of dying.
I wonder am I a coward or did I err
taking the part of my state against my country."

"Ah Garland, how this must have troubled you,
but don't you see, blue and gray mean nothing.

War is not the moral drama, life is.
God's lines cut every way across our lines
and touch the spiritual battle raging in men's hearts,
each an echoing plain of cries and alarms.
We can't see true, for we see through a glass, struggling
for spiritual glimpses by work and revelation."

"Whatever labors Providence requires, I'm willing
to perform, but I find they're not what I've been taught,
and I'm embarrassed."
                              "Christ teaches the life of the spirit.
Do we really think that God adjoins his will
to ours in enterprises of death and devastation,
of cruelty and suffering, of the widow and orphan's sorrow?
What difference Christ or Moloch if God be partisan?"

"You mean it doesn't matter which side we're on?"

"I mean what I think it is that Jesus means
when he exclaims, *The kingdom of God is at hand.*"

"But if all our knowledge is partial, how do we know
we're not just fooling ourselves?"
                              "There's nothing but faith,
and willy-nilly, you'll put your faith in something.
I choose Christ to answer myself this question,
What will I believe about the world?
Did a god of malice create this vast machine,
soulless and cruel, which brings us to sense to terrify
and destroy us? Or did a radiant deity speak us
into being so love might teach us his feats of joy?

It's the meaning I want to find in God's creation.
If I'm made a fool, I'll laugh at God and die."
His heart enlarged with new affection for Fisher.
He was even a little ashamed he'd counted him
as one who could talk the hind leg off a donkey.
A mindful rebellion surged his thought, setting
aside received ideas, redrawing battle
lines in anfractuous fortifications of men's souls,
reordering ranks of enlisted men and officers,
Confederate and Federal, German, Irish, and Jew,
slave and free. As he gazed on Fisher's face
with welling affection, he noticed a spot on his cheek.

July 21, 1863

Dawn and Fisher's face was streaked with rosy
inflammations. When Kate appeared with linens,
she halted, her smile adjusted itself, and saying
nothing, she went and fetched the doctor, who ordered
John removed to the erysipelas ward.
Though Fisher chuckled, allowing the move were a lark,
his cheer was tinny, and the look he cast on Garland
was that of a man ascending gallows steps.
Two nurses came to heft him out of bed.
Garland hobbled over, following as the squad
moved out, turning down darkened hallways on creaking
floors to another wing of assaulting ordure.
And there a familiar, exasperating voice,
                            "Howdy
Pards. I'm glad to share yer company again."

July 23, 1863

"I've got a paper, John. You want to listen?"
John's eyes split open like pods, swam in his head
for a moment and found Garland. A smile caught up
the way a small flame glows when a spark sticks
in a wad of tinder and the fire is a faint stain
before the breath coaxes it to blossom. John nodded
perceptibly, licked his lips. "Here, take
a sup of water." He fed him a drink. "Let's see,
here's an item from the *North Carolina Standard.*

*If it pleases God to build up and perpetuate this new nation of
Confederate States, He will do it; if not, He will not do it—that is
all we know about it.*

Now there it is whole hog. We cannot fathom
divine will, which might suggest humility
concerning our acts, and yet we kill each other
with premeditation, assuring ourselves that God
approves our derelict wisdom." John strained his voice
to whisper,
            "Fear of the Lord is the beginning of wisdom."

"This disregard for fear confirms our pride."
Fisher's eyes were closed, his face contorted.

"I have a favor to ask."
                    "I'll do anything,
quicker than a hog can swallow turnip greens."

"I want you to write my wife."

                      "I'll fetch my paper."

"No, I mean to say I want you to write her
after I'm gone. I want you to cherish her
for me one final time. You alone
of all men know how much she means"— emotion
choked him. He took John's hand,

                          "I'll write to Lucy."
He felt John's grip relax and panic swept him,
but his breast rose and fell. He was just exhausted.
His face was decayed in suppurating ulcers, now spread
to chest and arms. The odor of rotting flesh
from all this human wreckage was exquisitely stifling.
Their suffering illustrated an irrepressible fact.
Divinity never intended a reasoned connection
between a man's deserts and what he gets.
The temporal world was not and would never be just.
The substance of things hoped for? The evidence of things
not seen? This man's corrupted body was the emblem
of faith in risible and stultifying enormity and terror.
Poor John would take up arms with heaven and earth
to get back home, embrace his wife, and touch
her hands, but earth and heaven had flanked him out
of his life, and his own heart sank when he considered
writing to Lucy. How could words assuage her?

July 30, 1863

When dawn was wasting dark, he went to the ward,

and John put out his hand, and he held it for hours.
Garland knew where he was, knew whose winsome
company he relished, desperate to clutch at life
by holding her phantom hand. To pass the hours
and repulse the Texan's conversational bushwhacking,
he stitched together roving, disjointed soliloquies
especially when he thought that John was sleeping.
Today he found himself recounting a spring
plowing time after their mule had died,
and he and his father put on collar and hames
while his mother held the traces and drove them hard,
speaking to them as if they really were mules
and telling neighbors about her two new jasacks,
Patrick and Garland. One, she said, was *the* most
stubborn creature she'd ever lived to see,
but she would never specify husband or son.
His father always said Garland, and Garland his father.

"Sure as shooting yore momma meant you, Pard.
You'll only get more stubborn the day you die."
John had turned his head away to weep.
He tried to think of a story with no implications
of home and recalled this chestnut about a hog.

"There was once a pig of legend. His name was Streak
and his reputation spanned six Georgia counties
for being twice as fat as a four term congressman.
The owner was a free Negro named Gisentanner,
a farmer who never said a word without first
spitting tobacco. A man from Milledgeville
dropped in to see his wondrous piece of pork.

When Gisentanner led him round to the sty,
the man was astonished to find the hog was stumping
around his wallow on a wooden leg!

                        'What happened?'
Streak shot them a worried look. Gisentanner
spat,
   'Massuh, dis hyar hawg done won me
three blue rippins at de county fair dis yar.'

'A most impressive feat,' said the city gentleman,
'but what about his leg?' Gisentanner
spat,
   'Massuh, last fall dis hawg a mine
done won me two gold scallions at de state fair.
Dis hawg is something special.'

                    'Yes, I see but'—
Gisentanner spat,
        'Massuh, dis hawg
can still jump a sow's back even wid he stick,
and every time he do, I fotches three dollar.
Dis hawg'—
       'Confound it'—the city man erupted.
'I can see he's one fat pig, but what in hell
has happened to the critter's leg?' Gisentanner
spat,
   'Now massuh, what kind of durned fool
would dis ol' nigra be what God done give
the bestest hawg in de state a Georgy, if'n he
commenced to eat him all at once?'" John smiled
and heaved in whispers,

              "They have made me the pig."

The effort caused a fit of coughing in croupy,
anguished spasms, Garland catching the phlegm
in a cloth. His eyes rolled back, for an hour he lay,
his body laboring to take in breath while Garland
held his hand. In his forehead, a ball peen hammer
beat a rhythm on account of the putrefying odor
though he didn't know for sure if it were stink
or anger causing his head to rage. John's face
was ruined, streaked with rivulets of oozing pus,
like a Christmas ham squirming full of skippers.
The pain had been excruciating. How the agony
of hours must have seemed like arduous seasons.
He hadn't spoken of home in many days.
His breathing altered rhythm in shallow rattles.
His body seized, he tried to murmur, said "Luh"—
and after that syllable, that broken word, the storm
of suffering ceased, his body descended in calm.
He put his hand to his lips, then closed his eyes.
The Texan, who'd broken a record for silence, observed,

"Sure as the world, Garland, that story kilt him."
Garland held the limp hand growing clammy
as if in death he still might sense her presence.
"You really ain't seen no hogs till you come to Texas."
He sat for hours as hospital staffers came
and went, understanding and letting him be, his mind
grappling loss and sorrow, but he was recalled
to the ward by a surgeon and several attendants crowded
around the Texan, the stink of his wound savaging
air like a bark knife, the boy gasping his breaths,
"Hit's all right, Pard. You gone and do what you can."

255

Kate approached.
                    "What are they doing to Texas?"
Her visage betrayed a quick contortion of dismay.

"The surgeons are debriding his wound."
                                        "What does that mean?"

"The gangrenous flesh is treated with hydrochloric
acid, to burn it away so its injurious effects
will cease."
                    "You mean they're pouring acid in his wound?"

"Yes." The Texan's legs were marching in place.
The doctor's voice,
                        "Retract that mass. Treat there.
That's good for today. We'll apply some more tomorrow."
Kate sat on the edge of the bed and touched his shoulder,
allowing his eyes to rest in hers a moment.

"We have to move him, Garland, before it's dark."
He clomped off the ward, a steel toothed saw biting
the thigh's large muscle and sought his bitternut hickory.
Here was proof, if any more proof were needed,
man was prince of this world. What use to think
he'd understand it someday? That night in bed,
his spirit convulsing, he considered John's last utterance.
What was he trying to say? Love? Lucy?
He thought of the letter he'd promised to write and swore.
What could he say? What could anyone say?
He nodded off, water coursed in his dream,
a river, an ocean, waves transmogrifying

to reaching flames. In the conflagration's midst
Duessa was seated, gorgeous and grave, pristine
beyond possession in the stern of a burning ship,
rigged with fire though unconsumed and rocking
backward across the water. The deck was crowded
with Negroes shackled and chained, singing and burning.
The tugging wake was noisome, the heavens crying
heart break lamentations. Another change,
she stood on a lea, small waves washing her feet,
naked with golden bracelets, cowry necklaces.
Behind her, verdant dark of jungle continent,
but her face, a white woman's face, her countenance striking
his heart desolate. He woke, his brow streaming,
and mopped it off with the top sheet. He felt he would never
possess her now and wrestled desperate thoughts
as a patient groaned a lonely song in the dark.

July 31, 1863

My Dear Mrs. Fisher:
I write to you
on this sorrowful occasion to say your husband John
has passed away. I cannot know the sadness
your grieving heart will bear, but having known
John well, I know if ever a man had hope
of new life raised in incorruption, John Fisher
lives that life and now enjoys its ease.
He and I were wounded on the second day
at Gettysburg, he more severely. The surgeons
were forced to amputate his right leg

at the knee. The operation appeared to be
successful. John was recovering well, his spirits
high, a boon to me and all the patients
and staff, animated by his love and faith in Christ
and desire for home. Then erysipelas set in
and quickly took the light of life from his eyes.
He passed on yesterday about 3 P.M.,
bearing with manly courage and Christian patience.

Mrs. Fisher, I am a stranger to you,
but you to me are like a long acquaintance,
for the theme of John's conversation was ever his dearest
Lucy. He introduced his lovely wife
to all whom he encountered, and the case was plain
his reminiscence was calling forth your shared
affection, sustaining your loving devotion and ruth
to him, despite your absence, despite his trouble,
giving him peace. The final word he uttered
in this life was Lucy. I wish as much for you.
If ever love might break the tomb's cold bonds
and heal a heart it purposed once to cherish,
your husband's love will find its way back home.
May the blessing of God be with you and help you bear.

I am your obedient servant,
                    Garland Cain.

He scanned his cursive's looped and windowed raggedness,
his fingertips stained with ink, his conscience tossed
with guilt. Yet this is what loved ones want to hear,
lies about Heaven and salvation because the truth

just makes us wretched. The world's truth is hell,
and the self's truth a hell of invalid hopes.
He sat in shade of his bitternut hickory. His ward
was built on one of Richmond's seven hills.
South of the James, a summer storm raised tumult
in treetops, describing empires of spirit chaos.
He cleaned his nib and went to sit with Texas.

August 7, 1863

Dawn roseate in windows trapping stenches, Garland
sitting with Texas, pocket Testament in hand.

"Want me to read some more from the Book of Matthew?"

"Naw, Pard, I reckon not just now."

"Does the Gospel not give you comfort, Texas?"
                                        "I believe
the Bible, Pard. I just don't understand it."
Texas had once been comely before his youth
was wasted, suffering's exertions everyday blasting it
weaker, the way that May green fades by summer.

"How'd you make your way to the war, Texas?"

"I begged my daddy to let me jine. He said
I was a fool, but I begged till he give in."

"Why'd you fight so hard to join the fighting?"

"I'd never left home before. I reckon I wanted
to see some things. I'd never done too much
'sides watch the Brazus scrape along and footle
away the peck of time what warn't spent working."

"How old are you?"
                    "Eighteen come September."
The boy began to weep a little.
                              "You hurting?"

"Hit's always hurting, but I just want to tell you thanks,
Pard, for keeping me company like you done.
Dying would've been lonely, except fer you."
He offered a lady-like hand and Garland shook it.

"I bet you Heaven will be a lot like Texas."

"Only God Almighty could make it better."
He closed his eyes. They never opened again.

August 21, 1863

A corporal he didn't know with pox on his face
came through the ward with mail.
                              "Garland Cain?"
"Here."
        "You have a letter." In flowing hand,
the name *Duessa Fontaine*. His heart swelled.

July 29, 1863

Dear Garland:

   I wish I might come to you, for even
a little while, so I could say what I need
to say and make you comprehend the world
as I comprehend the world. The saying is hard
because the world is hard. Perhaps it is better
then to write, let reason step in graceful
time with feeling for my soldier far away.
I cannot know the sufferance you bear in Virginia,
but I have cherished each of your letters and feel
I have come to know you well, confirmed in my first
opinion of your noble character. Garland, you are
a good boy and an honest boy. I have believed
your promises, every one, knowing that you
would move the earth and heavens to prove your word.
As I never doubted, I ask a favor of you
and pray you will grant it. Believe what I write you here.
My life is tainted with the living of it; you want
a woman coming to you clean, Garland, clean
with a past not compromised by fate and sorrow.
In the months since my husband fell on the muddy banks
of the Atchafalaya, my heart has only once
been light and those were moments spent in your arms.
Even your fear, your fear of dying unloved
was sweet to me. If I were the last gift of God
to you, I count it an honor to be so conferred.
As I am thankful for you, you be thankful.
But Garland, please understand. The outcome of the war
is inconsequential, what difference North or South?
Fate incomprehensible settled me

in the only place where I could live with liberty
and pleasures strewn at my feet, where I, being black,
could live a white life, and although the city
survive, the life lived there is passed away
forever. And then I came to this house, placed
in the charge of a man who was not the friend my husband
thought him to be. What promise or hope for me?
As you live a day or a grand extent of years,
remember I belonged to you for a season.

She wrote as if she had foreseen his death.
These were not the words he wanted from her.
She'd penned her thoughts in sorrow's season, burdened
by loss of her husband and the city where she was free,
but time would pass, another season turn.
She had been happy in his arms, and her heart held room
enough to house a lover and a lover's memory.
Her double nature caused him no alarm.
Once he returned to Bateman House, it may be
all he would need to do were take possession
of a heart reconciled to love by time and youth.
If he could get back, her soldier near to hand
would persuade her love can vanquish obstacles to love.
He buttoned up her letter next to his breast.

October 11, 1863

The train delayed, he paced the platform for hours,
bored and fretted by sparking Leyden jar twinges
underneath his thigh's wide scar, cursing himself

as if he had by some neglect of power
failed to mend his flesh and now must suffer
gnawing consequences. Would he finish service
a wagon dog, falling behind on marches,
sleeping in fence corners alone? The sun had leveled
shadow pines across the tracks, when a faint,
encroaching gruff approached the station and shrieked
to a halt. Some soldiers debouched.

                                  "Where y'all been?"
he asked a middle aged private in filthy butternut,
soggy with sweat.

                            "Engine exploded five miles
out of Danville. Killed the crew and wounded
almost everybody in the car behind the tender.
We had to clear the refuse away and wait
for another train to be brought up. Say,
you know whereabouts I might scare up a game
a poker? I got a twenty-four-hour pass,
and whatever I can't spend on whores and Hooseletter,
I want to give some lucky bastard at cards."

"Can't help you, friend. I spent the last eight weeks
flat of my back in the Alabama hospital."

"Where'd you catch a ball?"
                             "Gettysburg."

"I should of died ten times at Gettysburg.
It was after that I decided I's gonna have
a drink and a hand of cards and ride a Dutch gal
ever chance I get till the Devil gets me."

"They's a bordello across from the State House. Sorry I can't
help with the poker game." The soldier laughed,

"Count on the whores to follow the politicians.
Cut of the same cloth, sholey. I thank you. I'm sure
I'll get on fine." Garland boarded, the engine
seething steam. The whistle loosed its keening.
A bevy of women swerved around the corner
of the platform, laughing and gadding, twenty-five
or so, some young, most ancient, dressed in homespun
and flour sacks, squawking at the conductor to hold
the train, still resting, and filling the car with chatter.

"Gals, look—a sojer!"
                              "A handsome sojer!"

"Out of my way."
                              "I saw him first, he's mine!"
A pretty young woman rushed to the seat beside him,
gazing with mock adoration,
                              "My name's Annie,"
squaring her shoulders like a belle and offering her hand.

"Don't talk to Annie, her whole family's Yankee."

"Alas, it's true. I am a daughter of the Philistines,"
and the girl kept pressing her sleepy eyes into his.

"I'm Garland Cain, private, Eighth Alabama."

"I wager you been in the hospital near two month."

Garland was taken aback.
                    "How'd you know?"

"Because yore hair's so long. Won't you come home
with me and let me cut yore hair?"
                              "You're kind
to offer, but I got orders to make a straight line
back to camp."
              "Look at Annie working."

"Working him like a blind dog under a gut wagon!"
A gammer front of the car said,
                          "Who can blame her?
I'd let him park his brogans under my bed."
The women shrieked, their rantipole causing his face
to burn. Annie was not disposed to mind
such comments. She plied her charms, two whistle blasts,
and the chuffing engine rolled the groaning cars.
The women produced their snuff cans, dipping and offering
pinches to those without. The dust diffused
and fired his nose, and soon they began to spit,
hanging their heads so the viscid strings thinned
and broke.
          "You sure you cain't sneak away for a while?"

"I'd really like to, Annie, but orders are orders."
Now the flock of women had eaten their snuff,
they grew complacent. "Do y'all have work in the city?"

"Yessum, we sew uniforms for Rebel sojers."
The car had begun to sway. His eyes grew heavy,

heat was heavy, wrapping his limbs in bolts
of wool he couldn't shrug off. Rushing air
transmogrified whistle shrieks into long, low moans.
An old crone turned to him with a muddy smile.

"Care for a dip," offering her tin.
                                        "No thank you,
ma'am." The woman's face was wizened. From each
corner of her mouth, creases dropped straight down
and framed a mechanical chin, one crease flowing
with snuff spittle. The old crone winked at Annie.
Annie smiled and fanned her hair from her shoulders,
revealing a bosom of autumn apple ripeness,
but this risible, histrionic parody of desire
bemused and troubled him, their innuendo
and gadding making sensual prospects repugnant,
as inhale and exhale of steam, side rods knocking
like a monstrous clock's escapement, even his piston
heart thumping like valve gear, counted down
his destination to battle's horrific appetency.

"How come the army gets you and not me?"

"Just my bad luck, I reckon."
                                    "Well, I'll tell you
what," she said rummaging a small purse,
"I got me a pencil, I'll write you my address,
and later. . ." and then her eyes fell on his breast
pocket, an envelope protruding, which with a fleet
whisk of her hand she snatched away triumphant.
"This here's why we'uns cain't turn this sojer's head.

He already got him a gal. In Troy, Alabama!
Her name is Lucy Fisher!" The crones were awake,
hooting as Garland froze, following the letter
as one hag plucked it from Annie's hand and passed it
to another who sniffed it for perfumes, another whisking
it away, pressing it to saddlebag bosoms, all
laughing, singing the name, "Lucy! Lucy!
I bet she is a sight!"
                              "Sweet to be sweet on."

"Got him a home town gal." The letter rose
and fell as if the wind were toying with a scrap.

"Lucy is John Fisher's wife. He died of wounds
in hospital two weeks ago. She doesn't know."
The letter halted in air and all went silent,
the way wind giving voice to a field of corn
dies, and the clerestory of silks and tassels is rapt,
and day is held for a moment in perfect calm.
Now the envelope traveled in reverse, hand
to hand, returning to Annie, who looked at it hard.

"Why ain't you mailed it yet?" He slipped it out
of her fingers, stuffed it back with his other missive.

"This letter will leave her a widow, her son an orphan.
Why not a few more days when they should hope?"
The women were facing forward or watching trees
and scrub brush flashing past, rising and falling,
and all was silence except for a steady hot wind
in windows, the tapping pats of spittle hitting

the floor, and the engine's rhythmic labor, and thus
they remained until the train pulled in at Orange.
Then all the women rose and left the car,
but Annie turned, her visage tracked with wet.

"Sorrow is sorrow, Garland, but hope is cruel.
You should mail that letter now." She kissed her fingers
and touched his cheek, and moved by the gesture, he bowed
his head. The car was vacant, engine hissing.
He rose and saw the floor riddled with piceous
stains, the stink of it rising on the car's heat.

Autumn flamed above the sutler's wagons
leading into camp, the hickory's noble bronze,
the sunny beech, the dogwoods robed in purple
wounds. He found his mess this glorious evening,
surrounding a canvass, raising clamors of cheers
and cries of despair. Caleb saw him first,
and rose and went to him and they embraced.

"What are all these no counts up to now?"

"The latest gambling rage, ridiculous and pediculous."

"Gone louse bug, git gone!" Along the periphery
of canvas were mounds of Confederate notes opposing
slighter stacks of greenbacks. At the canvas's center,
each on a plate, two louse bugs scuttled and ceased,
their masters tapping fingers behind to drive them
or correct their errant plunges right or left.

"The long odds is on Lincoln, cause Davis's king!"
Caleb explained that Davis was Patty's vermin
and Lincoln Snake's. Davis, the swift of feet,
was already legend for winning races and wagers.
The heated race had come to homestretch inches.
Lincoln drove forth but persisted in veering right
while Davis scurried a line as drawn by a rule
as if he read by dent of strict construction
his vermin guide in the Morse information Patty
was tapping behind, and all who favored the long odds
chanted "Abe! Abe! Abe!" But Davis,
quick in his get along, crossed the victory rim,
and anguish seized the losers, who ripped apart
their covering notes and swore as Patty, smiling,
herded his bug in a vial and stoppered the glass
with cotton before he swept his earnings from the mat.

"I'll give you twenty dollars for that there critter—
U. S. dollars."
     "Here's your mule, now, Buzzard.
I'd be a muggins to sell me wee champion."

"I wouldn't take a dead Negro for that varmint."
The contest over the boys took note of him.

"Garland Wilburn Cain! You come on out
at hair. I know you's in thar, boy, I see
yore ears a waggling!"
     "Hello Garland Cain!"
Yancy shouted, loud enough to ensure
he could be heard by all the men in bivouac.

"Awe, Yance, no." But it was too late.
The greeting was swept along, echoing and rebounding
from group to group in camp until the call
was taken up by the regiment in a cannonade
of salutation, tapering away in the shouts
of the corps. Yancy grinned,
                              "Welcome back."
Oscar sat him on a box of forty dead men
and boiled a towel to steam and moisten his beard.
He stropped his razor, shaved his face, and trimmed
his hair, and Garland stood up much refreshed.
Tonight they were having grits and dodger pone,
and Oscar gave him the fat back he fried as a welcome
home and means to help him gain back strength.
The men were hungry and ate their meager portions
fast and in silence. Deke came shambling up,
holding a Dominicker hen by her rung neck.

"Deke, that's a pretty bird what's been in the corncrib."

"Critter, colonel catch you poaching chickens,
he'll clap you in at guardhouse faster'n grass can get
through a goose."
                "H'yar now, Snake, this hyere hen
done swoopt down off'n the roost and commenced to pecking
my noggin. I only kilt her in self-defense."

"We allow the plea of self-defense," said Patty,
"and the court considers an enemy of Deke an enemy
of ours." Deke plucked the fowl, tossing feathers
in the fire, hissing and smoking.
                              "My God, Critter,

you savage as a meat cleaver." Smiling snaggle toothed,
he produced his camp knife, severed feet and head,
sliced the carcass breastbone to tail and reached
in the cavity, extracting, with noise of liquid suction,
the innards, which tangled and sagged between his fingers.
He held them up, glistening in shifting fire light,
looked at Garland.
            "At's all you air, boy,
a passel uh guts." With that he hurled them off
a ways, behind the adjacent mess's tent.
He hung the carcass and a canteen's worth of creek water
over the fire, and soon the hen was simmering.
Deke sat down close to his pot and Garland said,

"Deke, I saw you fall on Cemetery Ridge,
and I was afraid you'd answered the last tattoo."
Everyone laughed, already in on the joke.
Deke scowled as if he'd bitten green persimmon.

"The Critter thought he'd been kilt too," said Patty,
pulling a loving stare away from the pot.
"But it was me and not the Yanks what got him.
See now, on such a hike as Rebels were making
into Dutch country, I allowed t'would be a powerful
chance to do some retail, so I called on the sutlers
and loaded me pack with every sheet iron cracker
in camp, which I had to keep close about me as I'd melted
a pretty sum. Now there I was moseying
along up Cemetery Ridge with naught in my heart
against me neighbor, when a spherical case burst
behind and a ball, which could have nicked me spine

like a matchstick, ripped through me pack instead and sent
a galling fire of hardtack into rear of the advancing
Rebel line, the brunt of it raking the Critter
in savage fashion. He commenced to carry on
like he was swatting yellow jackets and screaming,
'I'm deader'n a beeve, you Yankee sons a bitches!'
By the time I reached his side, his case was grim.
And boys, I knelt and kissed the Critter for his mother."

"Shut up you goddamned Irish potato bastard."
But laughter drowned the insult, and Deke, incensed,
carried his hen to the woods and ate alone.
After dinner, Garland said to Caleb,

"Thank you for taking the trouble to tote my kit
while I recovered. It would have been peeled away
for sure if you hadn't."
                                   "Yes, the thieving's rife."

"Looks to me like our ranks are somewhat thinner."

"Yes. Wait till you see the regiment at roll call.
You and Titus were wounded. He got shot
across the front of his belly, the bullet lodged
by the hip. The surgeons removed it and he's doing well.
He's lucky. We reckon Blackwood is dead; he's reported
as missing. Hiram, Count, and Guide Post were killed.
Poor Count was shot while trying to bake a pawn
of cornbread for lunch in Pitzer's Wood." This last
affected Caleb, and he paused. "Gettysburg.
The Yankees beat us Rebs like a rented mule."

October 14, 1863 toward Bristoe Station

Anderson's corps astride the Orange and Alexandria,
two files double timing toward Bristoe Station,
boot heel and barefoot friction scuffing cross ties.
They were hustled out of bivouac yesterday dawn
and marched all day. Last night, it had rained pitchforks.
He'd bedded down by a hickory, pulling its fall
of leaves around his body, but already soaked,
he shivered, a hacked ice dropped in hot tea.
The country around Bull Run had seen two battles,
and armies had bivouacked here, stripping hardwood
and pine for fuel and shanties. They approached a row
of abandoned Federal shacks, the pine boards planed,
the roofs split shingled. The Yankees had even brought
their saw mills with them. Waist high pine trees covered
the rolling hills. Families had long since skedaddled,
and fields lay fallow. In that landscape nothing moved.
As they made a rise of ground, the soldiers ahead
of him pointed, excitement stirring.

                              "There they are!"
When he made the crest, minute blue figures were gathered
in the watershed below, lounging and washing their feet.

"Is that Bull Run?"
                    "Broad Run."
                                        "Who are they, Papa?"

"Yankees, tired and straggling."
                              "I mean which corps."

"I hear we been chasing Third Corps' tail."
                                        "You reckon
we mought just give 'em a surprise?"
                                        "Not likely, Buzzard.
Hill's ahead of us, Heth's division leading.
They'll get first swat at the Yanks." A ten minute rest
was called. They'd hoofed three miles in fifty minutes,
and Garland's leg was throbbing hip to heel.
The barefoot were given the option to stay behind.
Not one remained. A distant firing made
for a short ten minutes. They pressed the road, he thinking
how every step was now a trial of endurance,
the shuffle of feet recalling the huzzing of saws.

"Little Powell's making them Yanks turn tail."

"Bull Run's a good place to fight."
                                        "It air a fact."
Retreating soldiers passed them, whole and unbloodied.

"Looky them North Carolina parlor sojers.
What on earth you running from blue bellies fer?"
Now wounded came drifting down the road, torn
and dazed, the two files parting in silence around them.
A soldier pressed a hand to his wounded head,
blood pouring between his fingers, his uncovered eye
wide, expectant, as if he stared through a key hole.
Another hobbled, using a friend for support,
a pant leg black and wet, the boot squelching.
And then a group of three, the middle one struggling
against the help of comrades, writhing and calling,

"Where is the light? Brothers, where is the light?"
A ball had struck his temples, firking out
his eyes, gouts of blood issuing from ruined
orbits, the nose jutting like a shop shingle, the bridge
sheared away, and he came on railing at darkness,
"I can't be a blind man, friends. I can't be blind."
An eerie silence obtained, the guns had ceased,
and soon they approached a line of naked trees,
shielding an old encampment along the run,
the cut intersecting the stream on the perpendicular.
Approaching the run from the south, they found on the swale
men in butternut strewn in the slains' shocked postures.
The spread of corpses told the story, forming
an acute angle drawn inside the angle
of the run and railway cut, the thickest cast
of dead at the vertex. Heth's men had charged the run,
ignorant Federals were massed in the cut, an embankment
concealing them. When they stood and fired, the Rebels
swung back like a gate to get head on to the ambush,
hinged on the pile of corpses and pivoting round
and up an incline. They were stopped half way in a mortal
instant by a massed volley that ushered a thousand
men to their long home. Confederates gathered,
the Yankees already vanished across the river.
The order came to bury the dead, but he
by then was searching among the sprawling chaos,
where a sudden tide had washed ashore a haul
of corpses. He noticed a face, its pristine suppleness,
no trace of beard and rungs of curls, a boy,
just a little taller than the rifle he'd carried.
He knelt and heard the shuck scratch of his breath.

"Please God, don't let me die."
                              "How old are you?"
The boy heard, but the eyes roved, unmoored.

"Fourteen yare this June." Through a rent in his blouse,
  one of his wounds inside a cratered bruise
  pushed out blood, the way well water gushes
  from a pump's spout each time the handle draws down.
"I want my momma," his fingers clutched the earth.
"I run away. She don't know where I am."
His head was turned to the railway cut, the way
  his march had taken, burning oak and poplar.
By a sympathetic ache, he felt what the boy desired,
  to roll back time, to charge this run again,
  prescient of tragedy.
                        "You've got some serious wounds—
tell me your name and where you're from. I can write"—

"Buncombe," he said, and then the pale green irises
  turned opaque to light as an apothecary's jar.
He caressed his feminine cheek and closed his eyes.
The clean October horizon stretched forever,
  obdurate and silent. His company fashioned stretchers
  with poles and blankets and loaded the wounded for transport.
As he hefted a stretcher, a stab electrified his thigh,
  a black stain blossomed on his trouser leg, his wound
  reopening. He cursed and put aside his work,
  hitched a ride with a teamster back to Orange.
He arrived ahead of his mess and went to sleep,
  dreaming a vitreous green October sky.

October 21, 1863 Orange County Courthouse

The tooth and claw of winter came at last,
rattling down the Rapidan, stripping branches.
All week, he'd sat by the fire, wrapped in a blanket,
saying nothing, his leg stove up with stiff,
aching cold like an oak branch covered in hoarfrost.
Caleb and Oscar pestered him onto a pallet.
All night the wind leaned against the fire,
brushing away its heat and making him shiver.
At supper, Oscar slopped his kit with gruel,
and he would eat with quiet inadvertency,
and night and day, the mess maintained their irksome
contentions. Another verse to prove the Bible
condoned slavery. Another subtle token
of God's favor. Their yammer wearied him to death.
In the beginning man made God in his image, hacking
his agonized faces on the grotesque totem of faith.

October 31, 1863

Afternoon, a chill breeze feathered the camp fire.

"A blind man sees you've got the mulligrubs, laddie,
and Patty's got just the thing—the Irish cure.
This here is bona fide rifle knock knee; hidden
away, I've had it, in a hollow tree, what I've been
mellowing with the carcass of a cock I borrowed. Sacrificed
a pretty repast for this whiskey, I did." He winked,
opened his canteen, and Garland made a pull,

tasting the fiery plunge from gullet to gut.
"Aye, it's fine, ain't it? 'Tis why we Irish
call it *the water of life.* Come now, laddie,
we've got to get you up and exercise these legs
a yourn." Patty stood and pulled him up,
he rising stiffly and staring straight ahead.
"Do you need to throw an arm about me neck?"
He shook his head and hobbled beside Malone,
keeping his blanket wrapped around his shoulders,
stumping along by the Irishman swigging whiskey
and exuding oblivious cheer in speech and manner.
They made their way down a cow path out of camp
to a field with two dozen sutlers' wagons in park.
Clusters of soldiers milled or picked through wares
or haggled with merchants. He tried to remember the last time
they'd been paid. "This way, Garland, lad,"
called Patty, gracious as a monk, leading him on
by a field of brittle yarrow to a section where women
were standing about, unkempt and girdle slimmed,
some smoking pipes, and all of their faces painted.
At the last wagon, three women stood by side boards.
Black headed, busty, they could have been cousins or sisters.
The tallest girl, probably oldest, wore a keen
appraising look, her features worn and threadbare
as her clothes, the middle one's hazel eyes were wide
with destitution, and the shortest girl had eyes
of black patience to wait out the end of the world.
As the soldiers approached, the women began to sing,
and he was soothed and drawn by their beautiful harmony.

O brother beware how you seek us again,
  Lest you brand on your forehead the signet of Cain;

That blood and that crime on your conscience must sit,
  We may fall—we may perish—but never submit!

The pathway that leads to the Pharisee's door,
  We remember, indeed, but we tread it no more;
Preferring to turn, with the Publican's faith,
  To the path through the valley and shadow of death!

Patty hugged him close. "Nothing like a ride
on a Dutch gal to get a fellow's spirits back
in order, aye?" The tall one captured his gaze,
and he could not look away. She pulled a string
in her bodice till it slipped its knot. Running her hand
inside the threadbare fabric, she lifted out
her breast, its porcelain flesh, the nipple black
as a coon dog's nose. "See there! She's taken a shine
to you, she has." Patty slapped his palm
with a wad of Confederate notes, and he recoiled
as if a canister exploded behind him. "Be Jazus,
lad, but you do require some letting off steam."
Seeing the money, the woman glided forward,
the bead of her eyes on his, slipping the bills
from his hand and raising the hand to her breast, he noting
it was cold and finding this odd. In a graceful step,
she swung him round to the tail gate, hiking her skirts,
climbing inside, then helping him tumble over
with his bum leg. When he fell on top of her,
she laughed riotously. The wagon bed was full
of rugs and pillows, exuding a sour tang
of dampness. She sat and tugged her loosened bodice
beneath her breasts, which swayed like fleshy pendulums,

unbuttoned his trousers, handling him like a milk cow.
She closed her eyes, making exaggerated moans.
Her crinolines were frowzy, odor of trunks, sweat,
and powder perfumes. His engine gaze drove forward,
observing spidery jags in powdered skin,
fracturing corners of her mouth and eyes. Her face
was crumbling, poised to fall away. Her hair
thinned out at the crown, a tiny forest where communities
of lice were holding fast. He didn't realize
she'd made him ready until she hiked her crinolines
and guided him in. She gripped his buttocks, moving him
back and forth with a farmer's strength, her hot
breath reeking fermented heat of sauerkraut and mustard.
He felt he'd dipped his wick in a greasy puddle.
Her body began to vibrate, she lisping words
he didn't catch at first, for she lacked front teeth,
the pinch of rosy gum like a cooter's snout.

"Goot tholdier boy, oh, goot tholdier boy."
She relaxed her grip, sinking back on the rug,
he pulling up his pants as quick as he might.
"Vee ave goot pots of iron if you needs zem," indicating
a gallimaufry of cast iron hanging from the bows.
He clambered over the tailgate, catching his blanket
before it fell in the mud. Patty had vanished.
He hobbled back to camp, a headache pain
blinding hammer strikes against his temples.
He felt he had lain down in evil's bosom
and stars in their courses had leveled their sights on him.

November 23, 1863

He made himself scarce, strolling along the Rapidan.
Though still a little stiff, his leg had improved.
Exercise loosened the muscles, and he relished sight
of the muddy river screened by skeletal trees.
The river was gratifying, noble, patient, intent
on destinations, whispering its winter airs.
The sun stooped low through a barren gray cathedral.
In the frozen choir, no bird sang, and unawares
he found himself happy with woodland loneliness. His appetite
stirred. He followed the river back to camp.
The colonel was there, the conversation intense.
His mess kit warmed by the fire, two dodger pones
wrapped in cloth beside it. The metal delighted
his hands. Inside, a dollop of field peas simmered
with fat back. Compassionate, thoughtful Oscar, the master
of scant rations, on his cook table cloth, the faded,
clay footprints of the drunk celebrant.
                                        —"Each one of us
from Lee to the meanest private knows we've roused
a giant. Lincoln wields leviathan powers,
not only in armies, but also in opinion's theatre.
The proclamation shows him determined to fix
the contest's meaning on the image of shackled Negroes.
State's rights, strict construction will never fare
when pitted against that history of sorrows. As it captured
England, that image will seize the popular mind,
captivate hearts and conquer rhetoric and religion."
Garland bit a dodger pone. It was light
and crisp in the crust, the peas sweet with grease.

"Caleb, you mean if we lose, what folks'll remember
is the proclamation—that we's fighting for slaves?"

"Great civilizations are always built by slaves.
We must not forget the north created the slave trade
and relied on slaves until they found them inutile.
Their admonishing the South is entirely hypocritical."
Garland had a tin of salt in his sack.
He seasoned his peas with a pinch; they were delicious.
He closed his eyes for a fleeting vision of home
and opened them to tiresome, blowing windbags.

"Pardon me, colonel, but the right or wrong seems moot."

"The South is fighting for the Word of God," said Preacher.
"I allow it's dreadful to pull the trigger on a man,
to kill a neighbor and send his soul to judgment,
but all through the Bible God uses his chosen people
to smite his enemies." Snake was smiling at him.

"Preacher, seems to me religion ain't giving you
much in the way of consolation. In fact,
it's got you confused. And you can keep up quoting
Bible verses till they's enough frost in hell
to kill snap beans, but here's a fact as big
as all outdoors and part of the house, the God
you worship doesn't approve of slavery or war.
If God is one to abuse his creation or approve
of others' abusing his creation, then he is evil.
And you can't make up your mind if he's evil or good."

"Well that's just flat out contrary to the Word of God."

"What you say's contrary to the teachings of Jesus Christ,
your boss man, general, president. He tells you to love,
and you refuse."
                              "Snake, that's just not so.
I love as I am able."
                              "Pardon my boldness,"
said Herbert. "Perhaps our exchange evinces the ease
with which religious reasoning is brought to bear
on either side of the argument. I'm inclined to regret
so many soldiers yearn for religious sanction
to justify the decisive action combat requires
when all we need to do is attend to history.
Men have to fight, have always had to fight
for any civilization worth preserving.
What if Leonidas had abandoned the pass at Thermopylae
or General Wellington refused to fight at Waterloo?
I consider it honor to follow such men in duty."

"Don't you think the question of slavery matters?"
asked Snake.
                              "It misses the point. There remains the greater
contention—whether we will read and revere
the words of the Constitution even if the words
be offensive to some. I do not believe that Southern
success is dubious; but history will show our children
if our present calamity served to correct the wayward
course of our national polity and return us once
and for all to the Constitution, recalling the spirit
of our righteous fathers and the sacred trust bequeathed

to us in the words of our immortal documents. The struggle
itself may serve to set America to rights."

"What do you mean, colonel?"
                                    "I mean, if the South
wins independence, the Constitution survives,
the guiding star of our new Republic. If we lose,
the Constitution becomes in our minds a new
ideal, one bought in blood, cleansed in the holy
sacrifice of slaughter. The nature of man is violent,
from the beginning willing to shed his brother's blood,
and yet he considers killing serious business
and must strike through horror's mask to find a meaning.
That higher meaning is heroism, virtue, honor.
Honor demands we nobly engage our foes
though our foes in this tragic case should be our brothers.
We must take heart and do as our betters say.
That is our way, and I know God approves."
The colonel knew they were going to lose. His betters
had wagered his life on a foolish gamble, a wild
adventure. His stomach roiled, he tasted an acid
plunge and felt like he were burning at the stake
and hated Herbert's handsome face, his certainty,
his money, manners, and waxed moustache, who was rising,
noting the hour, bidding his men good night.

"I find myself agreeing with the colonel," said Ainey,
stretching, "I got no truck with fighting for religion.
They's a sight more honor fighting civil war."
And now Mordecai's voice, no longer able
to contain repressed opinion's smoldering violence.

"Only *those people* call it Civil War.
We do not fight to possess the Federal government.
Ape Lincoln and his Black Republicans can have it.
We fight to escape it, backed by our own government,
army, president, congress and constitution,
having withdrawn for the same principle our forefathers
embraced, the right to shed a foul tyranny.
And what if we lose? Men in ages hence
will know our cause was just, our courage real.
And fellows, let me tell you something else.
If the Confederate Congress freed the slaves tomorrow,
you really think the gorilla would stop this war?"

"I reckon not, not now."
                            "You bunch of muggins
need to do some serious cogitating about why
this war's engaged and why you're fighting. *Freedom*
won't mean squat when the Federal government's looking
over your shoulder telling you what all's right.
On that day, America's idea of democracy vanishes,
and it won't come round again for the Southern man,
nor black nor white nor horse nor cow nor mule."
Wearing a disgusted expression, the lieutenant rose
and sought the privacy of tent and right opinions.
Oscar banked the fire, and everyone slept,
and unbound winds of anger tossed him till dawn.

November 29, 1863

They strolled a dappled wood, through warm and chill,
Caleb having pestered him off his pallet

and out to take the air.
                    "What is this?"

"A soft elm."
                    "Beautiful. Does it have any uses?"

"Momma used to boil the inside bark
for a cough elixir. The smell is stronger than the taste,
which is slightly sweet, but maybe she added sugar,
I don't know." Caleb circled the trunk,
running his fingers along the bark. "Sometimes
when forage is scarce in winter, you'll see where deer
have stripped their bark. I don't know if the medicine
really worked."
                    "Must work fine, I've never
heard a coughing deer." Garland shivered,
pulled his blanket tighter around his shoulders.
The day was fine and clear, the woods were peaceful.
Caleb had brought his rifle along on pretense
of bagging a squirrel but nothing stirred as far
as they could see or hear, their footfalls padding
the soggy leaf fall, converting to loam. "It's inspiring
often to witness the fortitude of animals and see
the things they do to survive a season of dearth."
A cathedral silence obtained. A shaft of sun
struck warm on his face. He regarded Caleb with suspicion.

"What about this one?"
                    "Damnation. You city boys
ever go outside? That's a persimmon."

"I'll be. We sell them a nickel a bushel in the store.
When I's a kid some wiseacre led me to bite
a green one once and"—

                    "It turned your mouth to chalk."

"Yep. How can you tell when they ripen up?"

"After the season's first frost the bitterness leaves."

"The same way rigorous trial hardens a man?"

"My God, Caleb. Are you reading Sunday School primers?"

"No, I'm just catching as catch can."

                        "Well,
have mercy on me and stop it."

                          "All right, I will.
But I'm worried about you. I know this war is vicious
and terrible, and every man must seek the means
to see his soul survive if his body will.
But Garland, I hope you find some other way
than visiting bats. Aside from a sullied spirit,
you can introduce yourself to odious suffering."

"Patty got me drunk. I didn't enjoy it.
I won't be returning." But he was stung that news
about his transgression was known by men in the mess.
"And besides, why don't you leave me alone, Caleb?"

"I'm just concerned about you, friend."

                          "I don't

need your concern," he shoving Caleb, who staggered
back, regaining balance and returning the gesture,
and Garland, released by rage's freedom, struck him
two quick blows, Caleb recoiling, absorbing
the right's brunt, but ducking to make the left
a glancing blow and landing a punch to the eye,
dazzling Garland's vision. This strike provoked
a hail of blows, tattooing face and chest.
Reeling under the onslaught, Caleb delivered
a ferocious kick above the other's knee.
With an anguished cry, Garland collapsed, and Caleb
sprung upon him, gnashing his teeth, fists
poised, Garland seizing his throat, their eyes
meeting, and each man came to himself in shame.
Caleb rolled off exhausted, and Garland lay,
fixed by a throbbing bolt from hip to thigh,
turning his face away from his friend to weep.
And once he started, he couldn't hold it in,
but wept and groaned, too hurt to be ashamed,
and Caleb gathered him up in his arms and held him
for a long time until his passion was spent.

"I don't know when it happened to you. I reckon
it happened at Bristoe; with me, it was Gettysburg.
Cemetery Ridge defeated me as a man;
the violence cut something vital out of me.
I witnessed a solid shot hit Hiram's chest,
and during the long seconds it took him to fall
I looked through his body at grass. The fact of my own death
imminent, my valor fled, and I lay stupefied
by dangers, paralyzed by fear, crying like a girl."

"You've nothing to be ashamed of, Caleb."

                                          "Garland,
it isn't shame. I never flaunted my courage
as others do, never purposed to measure
my worth as a man by execution of deeds.
I came with the sole object of doing my duty.
But I've been torn apart, humiliated by war.
Other men had no right to do that to me,
and I'm overcome with anger. What shall I do?"

"Here they's no such thing as good advice.
A man of courage would fight his Cannae, survive
if he's lucky, and return to home and family, but we face
Cannae after Cannae, none decisive
or settling anything. Gettysburg was a great
action. We didn't win, we didn't lose.
And what's our prospect now? Come this spring,
another Gettysburg and then another.
There's only this for a soldier, *It's root hog or die.*
But know it's not just you you're fighting for,
it's you and me. I can't survive without you."
They lay in the quiet wood hearing a stream
purling unbroken sound and far away
in a distant field the tumbling gabble of crows.
"Caleb, attacking you was the sorriest thing
I've ever done. I hope you'll see your way
to forgive me."

                        "This act reflected well on neither
of us. We should never speak about it again."

December 25, 1863

In cold assaulting flesh like a cursed robe,
he stoked a blaze and glanced across the Rapidan.
Now branches tinder thin were flamed with sun,
revealing river currents and venerable chestnuts
along the banks. He'd already harvested split
pods, used his camp knife to pry their compact
glossy kernels, the rich brown streaked with ochre,
and set them on to roasting. Caleb drew out
a package from his sack.

                    "Merry Christmas, friend."
Garland brought the parcel to his nose and breathed.

"I swany, Caleb. Where did you scare up coffee?"

"Waded the river on picket about a week
  ago and bought it off a Yankee."
                          "Caleb,
you suffered the blue bollocks to get me a gift.
Got your cup along? We'll boil it now."
Keeping an eye out, he went to the bank and filled
their cups, then rummaged his sack for Caleb's gift.

"Merry Christmas." Caleb smelled the pouch,

"A strange aroma. What is it?"
                          "Soft elm bark
I dried. It's really more of a thank you than a present."

"It means a lot both ways. After our coffee,
we'll drink our elixir and be as quiet and croupless

as winter deer." A chortling voice shattered
morning's frozen peace.

            "Happy Christmas
to you, Johnnies!" Two blue clad soldiers supported
each other's unsteady gait, one raising a bottle.

"Merry Christmas to you boys," Caleb answered.

"Say, Sesech, you don't have orders to move?"

"I reckon not. Quiet as church over here."

"Topping. We're having a little Christmas cheer.
Wanna come have a *reunion*, Secesh? Come over
under the white hanky?"

            "Thank you kindly, boys,
but the river's too cold to wade. You'uns go
and celebrate. We'll keep to ourselves by the fire."

                    "All right
then, Johnnies, we'll be seeing you soon."

                  "Yes,
you will."

      "Happy Christmas."

           "Merry Christmas."
They slipped and laughed, their feet skidding the bank.

"Wouldn't mind having a snort myself 'bout now."

"Coffee's better than nothing. Here's to the blessed
day of Nativity."

       "Christ is come to the world.

Hallelujah." They sipped their brew, the freezing
air turning breath into breech smoke. After months
of Jeff Davis coffee, he savored the genuine roast.

"It's nice of those boys to wish us Merry Christmas,
even if they are a little tight.
They show an Advent spirit."
                              "Do they really?
Or is our amity only a salve for conscience,
for Christians killing Christians for a claim on God."

"It's true the bolder we are to hold God fast,
the more he slips our grasp. Like trying to shimmy
the greased pole at the fair, the more we struggle
to rise, the harder our boot soles clap the ground."

"Or more like this. Our clawed toes grasp a branch,
and our clawed hands clutch at Heaven. Human nature
is another consoling falsehood; there is only nature.
I've proved a creature not a Christian."
                                        "Wait—
you, barren of the nature of Christ?"
                                      "I kill
in a place where Christ would have never come."
                                        "He would have,
with lint and stretchers, and gone about as you do,
ministering to the wounded and bereft. I admire your rigorous
thought and manly honesty, but you set yourself
to compare to the son of God. If your bosom Gospel
be true, who can be saved?"
                           "But Christianity

is precisely that, our living up to Christ,
and how are men saved? Because they say they are?
We defy Christ, create a world of wrath,
then comfort ourselves we'll escape the wrath to come
on account of his favor!"

                            "Our Puritan fathers conceived
an angry God in ambush with doomsday abacus
and thunderbolt. It's just not so. God's love is all,
and only he can lift us up through grace,
and if God is love, then evil cannot be."

"Caleb, what you say—it's beyond belief."
He pondered the sluggish river where it bent out of sight,
hemmed in by crowded trunks like gutted mansions.
Pendant on jutting rock and exposed roots
along the banks, the season bared its teeth.

February 10, 1864

Cold revealed his ragged breath aghast
before him and bit his flesh at cuff and collar.
His socks were threadbare tubes which rode up ankles,
exposing feet and toes to burning chilblains.
He entered the tent and dropped some soggy fuel
on the fire, making more smoke than heat, and lay down
by embers, pulling his blanket over his head.
When dusk encroached on ink stroked branches, aroma
of frying meat drew men to the cook fire.

                                   "Steaks!
My God, Greasy, who'd you have to murder?"

"The critter committed suicide. Drowned in the river.
And Company C dressed it."
                              "What sort of critter?"

"Hit were a brevet horse."
                    "Rebel blue beef.
I knew it," said Ainey, regarding the hissing skillet.
"I'll have a rasher." And not a single man
refused his windfall portion though most preferred it
cooked well done. Oscar whistled to himself,
frying prime cuts two at a time in a large
cast iron spider, adding wild onions by handfuls.

"I haven't been this full in a month of Sundays,"
he said to Caleb.
                    "Never saw this meal coming,
that's for sure."
                    "S'way it lays in Davisdom."

"Patty, I hear this mule had luck of the Irish."

"And how's that, Papa?"
                              "Drowned in a river six inches
deep."
          "And how did he manage such an extinction?"

"He found the hole."
                    "Lads," Patty chortled,
"we all got luck of the Irish. We've found the hole."

"He's pulling a Jeff Davis music box full of crackers."

Deke looked up and grumbled,

                         "You mean at's mule hair

all over 'em crackers?"

                    "Sorry to say, Critter."

"Nobody axed me to swaller the whole damn varmint."

"Yeah, but you done did."

                      "Critter, I'll swany,

I believe yore ears is growing longer."

                          "Hog,

you go ahead on and pound some slats up yore ass."

The night was complete. The cook fire rendered faces

in haunting chiaroscuro.

                    "Well," said Papa,

"Hit looks like another campaign season is on us."

"Another year of sucking our paws," said Ainey.

"Another year of bottom rail on top,"

said Hog.

              "Papa, tell me one good thing

you've learned in the war." Yancy scowled at Preacher,

"A good thing here? I reckon yer senses is addled."

"Now Papa, I know you well. I know you're a better

man than when I met you. Tell us a reason."

He thought a moment. His hardened aspect softened,

"I love my wife and boy with a clearer mind."

"I love my home," said Ainey.
                              "Once the war
is done, I'll be a better Christian," said Saxon.

"I'm going to marry a beautiful woman," said Oscar.

"Hit's taught me how to kill without'n no bother."

"I've seen the truth of our Savior's grace," said Patty.

"What is the truth?"
                              "That he loves and provides our way
to love in spite our mean ways of doing. And Orator,
what of you?"
                              "Like you, I've learned that grace
is the highest reality and God's fulfillment for man."
Garland was silent. All eyes turned to him.

"I think Christ's grace is harder than chopping cotton."

"But easy too," laughed Caleb, smudging a finger
with ash and touching his forehead once and twice,
"Garland Cain, you are marked as Christ's own forever."
They sat, each man with his thoughts till the drum beat taps.
"Well, I'm turning in."
                              "I reckon hit's time
to piss on the fire and call in the dogs," said Yancy.

"G'night Caleb, Papa."
                              "Night Garfish."
                                             "Night Cain."

March 27, 1864

He deserted camp in darkness, picking steps
through wastes of stumps and mud almost a mile
to mount a wooded hill. He longed to grapple
a contentious angel's battering wings, suffer
resurrection in his heart's dry sticks. At last
a sanguine pool dislodged from earth's edge,
a blinding hole, a dazzling clockwork fire.
The stone on his heart would not be rolled away.
After a Rebel lunch of sweet potato
and corn pone, Caleb and Garland followed other
soldiers to a pine brush arbor, the scent redolent,
mingled with campfire smoke and the rain smell
of spring time air redounding from winter dearth.
The soldiers were singing the final verse of a hymn.

Plenteous grace with Thee is found,
Grace to cover all my sin;
Let the healing streams abound,
Make and keep me pure within.
Thou of life the fountain art,
Freely let me take of thee;
Spring Thou up within my heart,
Rise to all eternity.

And now the regimental chaplain read:

"And they entered in, and found not the body of the Lord Jesus.
And it came to pass, as they were much perplexed thereabout, be-
hold, two men stood by them in shining garments: And as they

were afraid, and bowed down their faces to the earth, they said
unto them, Why seek ye the living among the dead? He is not
here, but is risen.

Soldiers, you know this story of the first Easter,
how Mary Magdalene finds the empty tomb
and meets the men in shining garments proclaiming,
Why seek ye the living among the dead? He is
not here, but is risen! Brothers in arms, have you been
to the Lord's tomb? Have you yourself experienced
the Resurrection? That empty tomb is the simple
Easter message and the end of knowledge for man.
The tomb is empty. He is not here but is risen!
Brothers, we gather today swept along
in a great historical moment, each of you
having left your hearth and home, the comfort of loved ones,
to offer your very life for defense of our country.
As long as men regard our common past
and bow their heads revering noble deeds,
your flawless paths of glory, your sacrifice,
will be a chastening model for generations.
Divinity manifests in human virtues, and thus
ideals become our godly possessions. It is written,
Greater love hath no man than this, that a man
will lay down his life for his friends. Southern warrior,
having come so far with God, won't you secure
your soul by acknowledging the sacrifice of Christ?
When mortal man directs his step to that empty
sepulcher, he begins his march toward life eternal.
Soldiers in Christ, let me invite you to come
and experience the Resurrection, to know first hand

the tomb is empty. He is not here but is risen."
They declined the altar call and took a walk
to a nearby farm, where they paid a soldier's widow
a dollar a piece for four boiled eggs. She was chopping
ruined stalks of corn and okra, raising
chickens and two little girls. Her eyes were chestnut,
full of autumnal eloquence. She ground them pepper,
and he relished the acrid savor, pasty texture.

"Where did your husband die, Clara?" he asked.

"Right here. Come on and see." She led them back
of the house, a sturdy cabin of close fitting logs,
evidence of skill with sweep gouge and gutter adze.
Chickens, scratching yellow dust and swiping
beaks sidewise, squawked and waddled out of their path,
some flapping wings in flightless agitation.
Clara's hair was tied in a brunette loaf,
swinging time between her shoulders, her skin
smooth as flour. They walked to a shady elm
and stood by the heaped earth where her husband rested.
"The day he left for muster, he stood at the door
and he said, 'Clara, I'll never see you again.'
And he would not look at me. I touched his face,
but despair had closed his heart. That's how he left,
and I knew of a sudden the evil of what had come
to make my Jeremy offer indifference for love."

"But the prophecy didn't come true. He returned," said Caleb.

"And when he did, I'll bet he looked at you."

She smiled,
        "He wouldn't take his eyes off me.
Whenever I looked up from any task
I was about, his poor weak eyes beheld me,
sure as the world. And he would try to smile.
On his sixth day back, he struggled to get his breath.
It hurt me so to watch him breathe for naught.
He reached for me, I took his hand, he whispered,
'When I was hurt, I prayed I'd see you again.'
He closed his eyes and his hand let go in mine,
and I knew my husband cherished me. I know it."
Her daughters' laughter floated from the cabin dooryard.
She turned away to regard the grave and Garland
watched a bead of light caress its way
along her cheek. He quelled an impulse to touch her,
fearing a moment's support might topple her
as she was used to bearing her burden alone.
The two men touched their caps and crossed the swale.

"Garland, do you ever think how many women
you and I have made like her?"
                         "Yes.
But I'd like not to think about it today."

April 1, 1864

"Where're we going Caleb?"
                        "Going to kill
a man."
          "What! We're going to kill a man?

Why?"

"Because he means to kill us and a host
of our friends if you and I can't stop him."

"We don't
have rifles."

"We going to kill him with words, hoist him
on his own petard." They walked the muddy cow path
to the sutler's wagons and milled with soldiers crowding
tailgates and haggling, moving in and out
of voices hawking housewives and sausages and tooth powders.
They stopped at a grog-shop wagon, ribbed like a great
leviathan, a barrel lashed to the tail gate, a dipper
perched on its rim. The sutler sat on a stool
in the wagon's maw, his voice booming, his one eye
roving. A soldier straddled a cracker box drinking.
He laughed as he spoke, rubbing his hands on his knees.

"Word is we moving east round the Union left
to take another poke at Meade. I have
to allow I ain't looking forward to meeting the Yanks
again. They fites like devils, makes me feel
a mite bit spotted."

"Come now, Yanks ain't nothing
to worry 'bout none. Have another horn
of this here rifle knock knee. No, son. On the house.
Pleasure for Skeeter to treat a southron lad."

"I thank you, but then I got to mosey back
to camp. I got to go on picket."

"Sholey."
Caleb stepped forward, nodding toward the barrel.

"Two shots for me and my buddy."

                        "Two bucks a pour."

"Mighty cheap for the times."

                    "It's lousy whiskey,"

Skeeter chortled ladling, "but she bites like a badger."

They sat on crates, the sutler looming above them.

His left profile showed his one good eye,

but turned opposite, the visage was wild and monstrous,

the hollow orbit lumped with scars, the eye lid

sagging. The good eye busied itself in the path

leading south to Richmond, perusing milling

soldiers, impelled by hunger for things to see.

"Fellers, have another red eye gratis.

Here's for whatever grief the Lord hath given thee."

"That's mighty white of you, Skeeter."

                        "We're obliged."

"Now gentlemen, what name do your friends know you by?"

"I'm Caleb and this here's Joshua."

                  "Glad to know

you boys. You're fine men, giving the Yankees hell?"

"Hell on a stick."

          "We give 'em goss without sweeten."

"That's the spirit, fine young men. The South

has nothing to fear as long as she can rely

on courage like yours."

             "Our lives are hers."

                      "Amen."

Two soldiers staggering arm in arm passed singing,

But the battle to the strong
is not given,
while the Judge of right
and wrong sits in Heaven.
And the God of David still
guides the Devil with his will.
There are giants yet to kill.

"Forgive my boldness, son, but I notice you got
a hitch in yer get-along. Injured in battle?"

"I caught a ball in the leg on Cemetery Ridge.
Hurt like hell. I nearly peed like a puppy."

"I got my eye shot out in the woods of Shiloh,
like a swat upside the head with a cross peen hammer.
Never been hit so hard, not even by my daddy.
But it were a curious thing. I turned around
to look behind me, and I figured later, the ball
coming the way it was would have reamed out both
my eyes had I not moved the very instant
I did. Pretty damn good for piss poor luck.
Allow me to join you boys in a toast." He topped
their cups. "To men who beat death."
$\qquad\qquad\qquad\qquad\qquad$ "Cheers."

"Three days later, I opened my eye. I was staring
through a hospital window, and I saw our flag waving
on the breezes," his voice choked up.
$\qquad\qquad\qquad\qquad\qquad$ "I was saved

by a Yankee sojer. He come up during the night
and gave me water and tied my leg with a tourniquet."

"You're telling tales?"
                              "No sir. I owe that man
my life and this man too—this no count scoured
the ridge line half the night until he found me
and toted me off on his back."
                              "Another toast.
To good Samaritans. God bless them all, both blue
and gray, and bless you boys in the coming fight.
The young man here before you was telling me
you boys are marching back to Chancellorsville
to show old Meade some southron manhood"—
                                          "No,
that feller's a muggins—we ain't headed back
to no Chancellorsville."
                              "Well friend, I don't know.
Skeeter's just a poor old retailer, following
Rebel armies, but Chancellorsville is some
good ground for a fight, and the feller seemed to know
what he was about. . ."
                              "I say he's a clabber head
and a dunder puss. The feller's got saw dust for brains,
I say, ha, ha."
                              "Well I don't know, my friend,
but he seemed awfully sure."
                              "And did he say
where he got his information?" asked Caleb,
sloshing his drink and his words.
                              "No, he didn't.

Probably just camp scuttlebutt. But I recall
from my days as a sojer after the boys get wind
of what the officers are about. . ."
                                   "I got more'n wind,"
Caleb's eyes widened. "More'n wind!" he hooted,
then flourished a folded paper from his blouse pocket.
"We'uns is striking out towards Gordonsville
and surprising Mr. Meade on his right. This paper
is an order from our colonel to cook us three days' rations
and be prepared to march like Moses on the seventh.
I found it in the weeds outside his tent, wrapping
three cigars." Skeeter slipped the sheet
from his hand. Caleb's chin had fallen on his chest,
but Garland held the sutler in a sidelong glance,
his face stropped like a razor, the voracious eye
devouring script in rapid, right wise jerks.
He folded the sheet.
                      "Here's your paper, son.
What about another kick in the head?"

"Don't mind if'n we do. But let me pay
for this one. My friend and I have interposed
much too much on your hospitality, Skeeter,"
the syllables of *hospitality* snarling together.
They knocked the whiskey back and took their leave.
Caleb's speech at once began to mend.
He shook his head. "That was deadly corn juice,
sure as I live."
                "So what was that about?
And why in the name of Saint Peter did you show
that man an official order?"
                      "It's a phony order.

Herbert give it to me to wave in front
of Skeeter's eye. He thinks he might be passing
information along to Yankees concerning
our movements and numbers, whatever sort of stuff
he can pry from unwary soldiers after his bust head
loosens their tongues. You see his eyeball bulge
when he saw that paper?"

                            "Come crawling out of his head."

"I'll say if the Yankees post a brigade between us
and Gordonsville next Thursday, he's a dead man."
They put their arms around each other's shoulders
to help negotiate the tilting road.
Thus steadied, feeling triumphant, they started singing,

But the battle to the strong
is not given. . .

April 8, 1864

"Well I'll be hanged if that mackerel snapper Patty
ain't done turned out and found him a Catholic priest."

"Look at him sitting right on the gum stump, smiling
like a fat pig rooting in a dead horse."

                           "I reckon
he jess might pass fer a Christian fer the next hour."

"Patty's gone be the bride at every wedding
and the corpse at every funeral if'n he can be."

Father Sheeran approached the altar, on loan
from a Methodist church in town and borne on the backs
of volunteer soldiers to this field, now tarnished green.
Rosaceous of complexion, he wore a snow white stole,
his manner somber, his voice intoning,

                              "Let us pray,"

and men of the Eighth removed their hats and rose
on ground expansive with puddles breeding lilacs of frost.
"May the God of Battles grant our humble access
to his mercy and the grace of his son's redemption, Amen.
Greetings, Christian soldiers, in Eastertide.
We who have the confidence of the Resurrection
can rejoice, rejoice alike in adversity or prosperity,
in chastisement or reward. For we can say with our beloved
St. Paul, 'In all these things we are more than conquerors
through him that loved us.' Indeed, we are conquerors,
even though this war grows long and tries
us sorely, even though we meet reverses,
for reverses come directly from the hand of God.
Now some of you may ask, Why must we suffer?
We suffer that we should know by whose hand we are saved,
that we should understand on account of dire
tribulation the value and the price of nationhood.
A just God requires it for we are irresponsible,
and the law is written before the world's foundation:
there is no atonement without the shedding of blood.
This blood which is shed on these fields by true Americans
is sacrificial blood and will supply from age
to age to all Americans, as long as we
remember, an atonement, a sign to the world that we
have heard the call to the vocation of nationhood.
There is no atonement without the shedding of blood,

and so when our brothers pour out their lives in battle,
when limbs are shorn from our bodies, when we are pierced
by balls as Christ was pierced in his side, rejoice;
yea, rejoice, and should it happen you lie,
torn and bleeding amidst the battle's chaos,
lifting your eyes to Heaven, bless the Almighty
that you were called to Christian sacrifice
and righteous suffering, the likes to which the Father
before the world's foundation called his son.
If we count it honor to follow the life of Christ,
can we know a greater honor to follow him
in death? The blood we shed will cause this nation
and this nation's destiny to spring from resurrection.
Brothers, be ever mindful of our sacred mission,
we who follow not the opinion of men
or nations, but the eternal glory of the cross of Christ.
Trust our Lord's might and may his power
make our hearts keener and our courage more."
Caleb and Garland wandered back to the mess.

"Another day without any grub and another
sermon on the God of Battles. If this ain't fodder
on green peaches, I don't know what," said Ainey.
"Fighting for Christian honor on an empty stomach."

"A feller sucks his paw awhile," said Garland,
"he gets a hankering for more Confederate blue beef."

April 21, 1864, Orange

Oscar had invited him to a Seder meal

at the home of Jewish friends of his named Freeman,
and today was the day they agreed to run the blockade.
He'd laundered and patched his uniform and scrubbed his person,
using his cake of soap for this special occasion,
Oscar having alerted him to the presence
of the Freeman daughters. They headed out of camp
and found a friend on guard.

                 "Howdy Oscar."

"Hello Merz. Captain give me leave
to pick some herbs for *Pesach*."

                 "S'why yer all
got up like a dude, to go and grub for herbs?
I'm not a *schmuck*, Oscar. See yer pass?"

"He told me I could go—just to the field
beyond camp or to Orange if I need to."

                 "Awe Oscar.
You gonna git in trouble. We'uns done sent
our surplus baggage to the rear four days ago.
What if the army moves?"

                 "An army won't
be hard to discover. Be a *mensch*, Merz,
and give me the countersign."

                 "It's *Old Allegheny*.
Oscar, don't git caught and bring me some *motzah?*"

"Sure, Merz. And thanks." So the two soldiers
set out walking along a wagon track
dividing stretches of woods and fields, he reveling

in sumptuous evening, numinous light of dusk,
naming slash pine, white ash, Jacob's ladder,
and Helen's flower. Oscar's attention came
and went. Garland supposed he was nervous for leaving
camp without a pass as he was never
one for breaking rules. They arrived at the Freeman's,
a neat two story, wood frame pile on Main Street.
Noting two rifles leaning beside the door,
they leaned their own by the other post and knocked.
Oscar presented Alcinous and Leah Freeman,
their daughters Rachel and Phoebe. Mr. Freeman
presented his nephews, Zeke and Isaac Levy,
of Co. A 46th Virginia.
"Oh yes, the Richmond Light Infantry Blues," said Oscar.
"We know you boys." Zeke had a fine full shovel
beard, a bushy mustache that curved to hide
his lips, except for a bit of the bottom lip
about the width of one's thumb. His profound black eyes
leveled a penetrating, eloquent gaze,
suggesting he had seen a lot of the war.
The dining room was small but bright with lamplight.
The wind gusting through opened windows stuttered
the wicks, bending all the shadows of the room
in séance unreality, yet deliciously cool.
There was silver service, the mahogany table in such
high polish, he could see his face in stark detail
as if it were mirrored in blood. The table's centerpiece
was a serving plate with hard boiled eggs, greens,
a chicken neck, a sliced root vegetable, and unknown
sundries. The meal began with lighting of candles
and prayers, Mr. Freeman leading the ritual.

He blessed the wine and then directed Mary,
the servant waiting table, to fill their glasses.
She made a circuit pouring, filling two crystal
goblets beside his place. Oscar whispered,
"The other glass belongs to the prophet Elijah.
Don't drink it." The Negress was middle aged, her skin
a luminous midnight hue, her face handsome,
and she wore a gorgeous, red silk dress, no doubt
a gift from Mrs. Freeman, elucidating
with beguiling force her womanly contours and whispering
as she moved about the room. When he returned
his appreciative gaze to the company, Phoebe's eyes,
fierce as the yellow silk she wore, fixed him
a withering glare. He was chastened, though for what
he could not imagine, so looked away, conscious
of her stare and becoming more discomfited. Her intensity
did not abate, but now seemed less accusatory,
seemed in fact to be searching something out.
Phoebe and Rachel were two distinct personalities.
Rachel, the oldest, was full of fun, given
entirely to the ritual's solemnity and, he suddenly noticed,
bestowing her loving smiles solely on Oscar,
and he returning her adoration in specie.
But even as Phoebe conversed and spoke the rites,
one could glance at her and see her mind
aloof and working. As others at table could not
help hearing the stage aside about Elijah,
they began directing explanatory remarks
to him regarding the meal's symbolic meanings.
Now everyone dipped his fingers in a bowl of water,
upon which floated broken petals like tiny

paradise boats, and he was pierced with horror,
recalling himself spooning several mouthfuls
of such bland soup down his gullet at Bateman House.
Clancy must have thought him a great buckra,
and Lord, he was thankful Duessa had not seen it.
His face grew hot as his fingers cooled in the bowl,
and when he revived from private humiliations,
Phoebe's arrowed glance was nocked dead on him,
her keen suspicion leavened by quizzical interest.
Zeke took a sprig of parsley, dipped it in another
dish of liquid.
        "This is *karpas*. It stands
for spring renewal, the water the tears the Israelites
shed in slavery." He dipped his sprig and tasted
salty water. Mr. Freeman rose
and took the *karpas* and the bowl of tears, offering
them to Mary, in silence. Her eyes hardened
to obsidian, and though she did not speak, her countenance
gathered itself in regal proportions, proud,
defiant. Mrs. Freeman appeared incognizant.
Oscar was flummoxed, Isaac looked ready to bolt.
Zeke turned away his sorrowful gaze, and Rachel
looked askance until her eyes found Oscar's,
and she forgot whatever the trouble was.
He knew of one thing only on earth that might
transpire between a man and woman with force
to plant a look like that in Mary's eyes—
though the feeling there, that was an education,
deadly and quick and crushing with nuanced torment.
Then Phoebe, her vision bearing down again,
making it clear she knew what Garland knew.

My God, this girl was terrifying. He'd rather charge
a Union battery than sit with her at table.
He drained his wine. Mary must have taken
the *karpas,* for Mr. Freeman seated himself,
his mien possessing an air of satisfaction,
which look he focused on several *matzoh* crackers,
breaking them in two. He opened the *Torah*
and read a passage aloud on the Hebrew Exodus,
and when he uttered,

             "Ye shall take a bunch of hyssop,
dip in the basin of blood and strike the lintel". . .
He thought of his rifle leaning beside the door.
Phoebe asked the four traditional questions,
and Mr. Freeman answered, and then they ate
a slice of radish on a morsel of *motzah* and drank
at intervals directed by the rite more cups of wine,
he sipping a distillation of earth and rain,
savoring essence of a dark fruit whose bruising
gave forth light. He longed to be having wine
and having Duessa, her body Heaven's vintage.
Now Phoebe's eyes were clapped on his again,
this possessed Jewess, Cassandra and Deborah combined.
Now Zeke asked Mr. Freeman,

                   "What is the meaning
of the statutes of God?"

                   "One may not eat dessert
after the paschal sacrifice." Oscar began
but Isaac cut him off with the question,

                   "What is
this service to you?"

               "It is because God acted

for my sake, when I left Egypt." The women chuckled
and Rachel said,
                    "Isaac is the rebellious son."

"Always a Rebel," he smiled, and Oscar,
                                    "What is this?"

"With a strong hand the Almighty led us out
from Egypt, out of the house of bondage." He turned
to Garland last, his eyes full of affection
and placed a hand on his shoulder, "My son, it is
because of what the Almighty did for me
when I left Egypt." A quiet ensued. The meal
was ended. Mrs. Freeman announced she would
retire, and Mr. Freeman went to his study
to smoke. Isaac and Zeke departed with warm
wishes to their co-religionists and fellow soldiers.
Garland noticed no one closed the door.
Rachel and Oscar seated themselves on the porch,
and Phoebe took Garland's arm.
                                "Let's take a walk,"
her distaste blasting him like canister. She strode
around the house and through their luxurious garden,
his intoxication intensified by ecstatic odors
of gardenias, a feminine sweetness. They mounted a knoll.
The cleansed moon dodged in and out of cloud
like cannon smoke. She shook him off and crossed
her arms. He despaired at fathoming her disdain but savored
delicious pathos of standing upon this promontory,
in tableau with a robust moon beating like his heart
in company of this Jewess, fetching, if somewhat discontented,

and he having given his heart to another woman.
How the setting sparked his longing for Duessa,
her arms of bronze, her hair pouring like a cataract.
He ceased his pining to be polite and grasped
for words that might be soothing.

                                "The moon is beautiful."

"The moon is distant and barren."

                                "The moon is changeable,
like a woman's heart."

                   "Ha! More like a man's."

"So young and you've forsaken men already?"

"So old and you've already forsaken women?"

"I haven't forsaken women."

                          "Really now?"
She spun around. He took a short step backward.
"Then you'll be kind to answer me a question?"

"Whatever you'd care to ask."

                          "Why is it so many
Southern men cannot be satisfied with their wives?"

"I don't, I mean, I didn't know they weren't."
She huffed and sputtered, refusing to look at him
as if he might contaminate her eyes.

"Are you become such a tower of moral resolve
that offered a slave girl, you will refuse to bed her?"

Garland blanched, amusing Phoebe. How could she
know? She couldn't—he was her stalking horse,
by which she accused her father, whom she could not
otherwise accuse.
                    "Phoebe, I hope that love
may change the brute to the angel, yet I know how man
who would act the angel often acts the brute,
his greatest virtues becoming most splendid vices."

"Splendid for him. A husband should keep his word."

"I agree. Without honesty, love cannot thrive."

"Are *you* honest, Garland?"
                              "I strive to be."
"Are *you* honest, Garland?"
                              "I hope I am."
She stepped forward, pouring her eyes into his.

"Are *you* honest, Garland?"
                              "Yes, I am honest."
He had no idea if he were honest or not,
and the fact unsettled his mind and set it working,
thrashing about intoxication's slough; annoyed
at Phoebe's aggressive fustigation, he didn't notice
how his answer changed her, her face reflecting moonlight,
dim but distinct as earthshine, until her sweet
perfumes pierced his sense like a saint's torture.
He wanted to pull her close, but doing so
would be dishonest.
                    "What would you ask of a woman?"

"I'd ask that she be honest, loyal, and wise."

"And you—would you return those virtues in kind?"

"I'll make it my sole endeavor." She hugged herself.
But Garland had no coat to offer her.

"The moon seems not so distant as it was before."
But the moon was sailing gusts across the sky,
and Garland wondered what she meant. When she spoke
again, her voice was resigned and weary. "You really
are the son who does not know how to ask.
Please take me back." They descended under the hill.

Garland and Oscar sauntered the dark forest
beneath its new blown leaves, breezes heaving
spring redolence, invigorating as fallen manna.

"Oscar, the Jews have taught me a lesson."
                                        "Yes?"

"How God desires to transport every man
from the state of slavery to freedom. Oscar, you're not even
hearing a thing I say. Why this moon-calfing?"

"Rachel has condescended to give me her hand."

"Oscar, I'll swany, you robbing the Devil blind.
Congratulations! Rachel is a fine woman,
a powerful sight more tame than her little sister."

"Thanks, Garfish, but we got to hush. We getting
close to our picket." But luck returned them to Merz.
Oscar delivered the promised *motzah,* and the two men
sought their tent, which huffed like homeward sails.

May 4, 1864 Verdiersville

Buoyant clouds made effortless headway as men
reclined at roadside, blown from a ten-mile march,
and easy breezes shunted dust away.

"What they call this pretty place?"
                                    "My Dears-ville."

"I wish I might could say hello to *my* dear."

"Wish't that I could too—I hear she's a dear."
A soldier threw a haversack, and the other soldier
tossed it back.
                "Hot damn, skillet wagons,"
and down the Plank Road they rolled, drawn
by spavined mules. Oscar drew their rations,
and soon the fire was popping, his pot simmering.
Garland stood to stretch his stiffened leg
and smell the bubbling food. Across the road
at the headquarters' tent Traveler and another mount
were tied. He stamped and shook his stormy mane.
A staffer brought them fodder. Oscar ladled
dollops of steaming rice and peas, with golden

floating drops of fat back glistening in the pot
liquor.
   "Sorry boys, two worm castle crackers
is all the old man can do for us today."
He passed their hardtack rations. No one spoke
as each attacked his portion. Caleb had splashed
his face in a run they'd crossed while hunting wood,
a darkened band of wet dirt shown at his throat.
Ainey wiped his mouth on his sleeve. Yancy
caught a belch, puffing his cheeks and expelling,
Yancy, always the same in bivouac or battle.
Danger to him was incidental as weather.
When others praised his courage, he shrugged it off.
But he sat these days with his rifle across his lap,
not stacking arms like he was supposed to do.
Something was changed about him. He couldn't say what.
Marches went harder. Buzzard and Ainey were blown.
Even Critter looked whipped, and for all his protests
of having a lark in battle, he wore a permanent
scowl that made his underbite more severe,
lending the fierce appearance of a prehistoric fish.
During the march that morning, soldiers had slowed
their pace on a knoll of Plank Road and gazed
once more at the Wilderness's nebulous verdure, miles
of brier and vine tangle, portentous shadow.
Night crept over. He lay on a folded blanket.
The Milky Way scattered its shining path like a passel
of cosmic seed flung out from the hand of God.
The dipper's bowl tipped out eternal darkness,
beguiling and mysterious, its cold indifference offering
a kind of freedom. Why be a slave to fear?

A life well lived is lived in kinship with death.
The handle arched to the plowman beside the virgin.
He always imagined the lusty farmer giving
her chase, but now it struck him how many millennia
the pursuit had gone without consummation, an ancient
light forever young. At least he'd had
the fortune of seizing his maiden, Duessa's skin,
casting celestial light, their bodies moving
to that lovely culmination and sweet release.
He considered his reasons for soldiering, his new found freedom,
and knew Duessa's love had made him honest.

May 5, 1864 The Wilderness

Dawn light nervous in elm leaves, the Eighth in line
astride the Plank Road and surging forward,
passing clusters of elderberry's star burst blossoms,
and Garland breathing the dewy air, cool
in the lungs, counter sensation to stomach fire,
cramping his heart and bathing his throat in acid.
They traversed a fallow field, the grasses nesting
corpses, a valley of dry bones, still clothed
in blue serge uniforms, rot stiffened, discomposed,
the skulls rolled away by rooting hogs
or snipping buzzards. Striding over a dire
threshold of bleached bones, he entered the breathing
Wilderness, its awful presence, tense expectancies,
every shadow putting a bead on his chest.
To the left, a clatter of muskets, rising and falling,

then a long sheet tearing. He knew from its scaling
tenor the engagement was fierce and braced himself,
the dread in other soldiers' guts gripping
his own like sisal's twisting in laid rope.
The Rebel advance slogged through brier snag.
He gripped his rifle hard, but still the fidgety
muscles of his hands trembled like snared birds.
Sunlight fell through crowns like marble pillars.
They passed another cemetery of uniformed skeletons
in tatters of gray. A blast above snicking
and hustling branches, raining twigs, they diving
for cover, and Caleb, Garland, and Oscar went down
around a shallow grave, Oscar staring
at a skull's hollow face.

      "Was there ever a more
severe rebuke to human pride than the mocking
smile all men assume and wear forever?"

"All flesh is grass and all the glory of man,"
said Caleb.

    "But the Word of the Lord endureth forever."

"Feel better?" Oscar asked. The bone just grinned.

"By these presents we see that your whoreson dead Yankee
will rot inside a year." Oscar laughed,

"Unless he be a tanner for then he will hide
like an officer."

     "I swany, you boys are swell philosophers,"
said Garland. Nall came dodging along the line.

"Orders slap from General Lee. They's a gap
between the roads we got to fill in a hurry.
Oblique left now. Let's go like a house on fire."
The soldiers rose and scrambled an arduous mile
through Wilderness bramble and thorn. They halted rear
of the position, were shoveled in line between Ewell and Hill.
The firing slack, most men scratched shallow pits,
gouging earth with rifle butts and camp knives,
lifting loosened soil with hands or mess tins,
grubbing their animal burrows. He'd seen them gnashing
rancid fatback, unbolted cornmeal, flicking out
dirt or weevils from filthy tins, or not,
lean hunger driving some to swallow all
with no more thought than a dog or an ape might have.
And what was their famous yell but a savage animal
keening? He sat against a post oak bole,
watching Caleb dig with a limb he'd beveled
to fashion a crude shovel, dabbing his brow
with a kerchief. He wore his toothbrush pulled through his top
blouse buttonhole. Looking around the trench, he counted
at least a dozen soldiers so equipped.
A tearing swell of musketry erupted on their left.
Hill had gone to the well, a grinding, stand up
fracas, rabid and all out. Nall appeared,

"Hug the ground like the gal yore missing, boys,
and step up yore fire. We'uns got to drive
a nail in them thar Yanks and tack 'em down."
The firing rose to a pitch and sputtered, rose
and fell, then seesawed back and forth till dark.
Caleb, Garland, and Oscar huddled together,

sleeping on arms and rolling their blankets for pillows.
He stared at the black canopy, smothering stars,
and succumbed to a burrowing animal's mindless slumber.

May 6, 1864

Dawn, a boy racing along a fence,
pine stick pressed to white washed palings, mocking
contented houses, making clatter music
for summer joy. The tatterdemalion sprints faster,
and faster rattles the stick, and men are shouting
after the rascal now, the racket filling
lane and sky, and the boy has vanished, replaced
by attenuated light in a claustral wood, and battle
under way. He rolled himself over on the cool
damp, saw nothing but hanging boughs and smoke,
so began firing massed volleys at encroaching
Wilderness shadows. Buzzard shouted at Nall,

"I ain't seen Herbert."
                           "Got hisself shot yestiddy.
He's bunged up good. Lt. Col. Royston's
taking his place fer now. Now boys, let's work
together and shake a rug in front of these Yanks.
Keep your muzzles low—Aim, Fire!"
Another racket of musketry and rolling smoke,
but Yankees were coming on, the blue line massing.
When the front rank fell before a Rebel volley,
twice their number surged ahead, stepping
intrepid through palls of rifle smoke and shelves

of leaves, the nightmare wood having raised up corpses,
crowding for cover, firing over each other's shoulders,
their return volleys scathing the Rebels and raking
their line in flesh slaps and screams of wounded.
The massing congress of blue emerging through smoke,
he made out faces, grim, determined, powder
blackened. A small white feather tickled his neck.
A volley struck like a reaping blast, shredding
twigs and leaf meal, blinding him a moment,
Rebel soldiers peeling from the line, dodging
away through thickets. The feather was high in his chest,
half his company leaping briers rearward.

"Oscar! Time to mosey!" Garland pushed him
backwards, grabbed the collar of Caleb's blouse,
hauled him up and pushed him along in front,
as they broke at a run through root trip and bramble,
the terrible wall ramming past again,
rending bough and branch in splintering showers,
one ball nicking his pants leg. Federals hurrahed
and careened forward. He kept pushing Caleb ahead,
dodging behind trees. Twice as they swerved, a clatter
of balls rattled the trunk behind them and zipped
the air on either side in mortal proximity,
stoking fear and making them swift of foot.
Approaching a pine, they saw, on either side
of the trunk, two arms waving, legs raising,
a soldier exposing his limbs to enemy fire.
He yelled, passing, "What the hell are you doing?"
A skinny, terrified private, his brown hair socked
on his head like a bowl, yelled back,

                              "I'm waving fer a furlough."

Flabbergasted, they kept their mosey on.
Another volley broke but not as crowded.

"Stay low," he shouted, hoicking Caleb back
behind a white oak through brier thicket, tearing
ankles, panic the blood's ramrod, they crashing
through bramble and hanging branches. A fleet half mile
and sunlight of intensity blinded both of them bursting
into a clearing, with several hundred other fugitives
from Hill's retreating corps. He was grateful to swell
a crowd of troops, caring more for censure than shame.
Ahead, a curving row of batteries, arranged
behind them, caissons, wagons, a slew of horses
and supply. Lee's headquarter's tent was there and the general
himself, sitting his horse, watching the rout.
Abashed, the soldiers trudged across the field
like malefactors, sat by the limber wheels,
rattled and blown. General Lee walked Traveler
up and down the line before the batteries.

"Now don't you worry, boys. It's all my fault,"
the delicate crows' feet pinching his shining eyes.
"It's all my fault. You needed reinforcements,
and I had none. But don't you worry, boys.
We're not whipped. General Longstreet is coming.
He'll save the day, and we will help him do it!"
He sighted the line of infantry, faces smudged
with breech smoke, many bloodied, uniforms shredded
by brier and shot. Some had discarded rifles
for unencumbered flight. Some were weeping.
On the general's orders cannoneers got busy

shotting Napoleons with grape and canister. The routed
crawled behind the guns and caissons, watching
the gunners, cheerful at having a role at last.
The signal to fire, and limbers bucked backwards,
the grape shot shrieking over heads of Rebels
still pouring out of the woods, they hugging earth
or scattering, a flock of robins when the hawk's plunging
shriek rifts through them, the gunners raising a peel
of laughter. Beyond Plank Road, Federals were massing
at the end of their mile-long drive, winded now
and out of line. A battery opened upon them
with terrible effect, gashing the huddle of troops,
fragments of kit and arms and legs flying
into air, milling soldiers now bolting for cover
on either side of the road in fear and confusion.
He stopped his ears with his fingers, explosions drumming
his skull like ball peen hammers wrapped in burlap.
Napoleons had rumbled an hour when Longstreet's column
appeared. "Who are you, my boys?" exulted
General Lee, saluting with his hat, his forehead
shining in sun.

     "Texas boys!" they cried
at sight of him, elated they'd arrived
in time to save his battle and he to watch them.

"Hurrah for Texas!" he shouted waving his hat,
"Hurrah for Texas!" The brigadiers halted their troops.

"Attention Texans! The eyes of General Lee
are upon us! Forward. . .march!"
        "Texans always

drive those people," Lee shouted, churning his hat
like a windmill. The brigade parted around the guns,
striding in smoke as if they walked on clouds,
and Lee, his eyes betraying a strange transport,
spurred his horse and followed. He and Caleb
exchanged incredulous looks, a spectacular roll
of the dice to break the Federals in a decisive charge.
But then an odd group mind engaged as it dawned
on the Texans what the old man was about to do.
Without an order given, the brigade halted,
stacking men in the front ranks, forming
a grumbling mob.

           "Lee to the rear," a soldier
shouted, now others joining,

                "Lee to the rear!"
But his mesmerized countenance was forged determination.
He followed the general's steel gray gaze to the Wilderness,
smoke in infernal columns pouring from canopies.
Longstreet sat his horse. His face was stone.

"Go back, General Lee, you go back."
A sergeant pushed through the crowd, took Traveler's reins
and led the general back to the line of guns.
He seemed to come around when he saw a regiment
formed behind the batteries.

              "What troops are these?"

"General Laws' Alabama brigade, sir!"

"God Bless the Alabamans!" His words were bellows
to a raging forge, and the Alabama and Texas

soldiers whooped and strode across the champaign
meadow, stepping forth in fated elation,
and entered the claustral wood. Now Kershaw's troops,
men from South Carolina, Mississippi,
and Georgia came up, hooting and mocking the soldiers
sitting begrimed among the caisson wheels.

"You-uns in Lee's army?"
                                        "Y'all shore ain't
the men we left behind."
                                        "Worse than Bragg's men."
Their line formed and advanced, their battle flags
rippling with *Gettysburg* and *Chickamauga,*
and now the tattered, uncalced soldiers raised
their trilling cry and buoyed the routed spirits
of retreated soldiers. One picked up his rifle,
strode to the field and stood at trail arms,
squinting an eye the side of his blood slathered face,
evoking the lonely air of a concrete monument
in silent watch above an unkempt graveyard.
The other men of the Eighth reformed the regiment
around him, and Garland, torn between despair
and pride, stood and joined the ranks. It was no
use thinking about it. This war, whatever men
might say now or later was a contest regarding
Southern manhood. Poor whites and yeomen preempted
the cause. Who was fighting for his interests? The idea
was absurd. They fought because the world that formed
their notions measured a man by how he fights.
The regiment surged, crossing the road and striking
into woods palled with smoke, acrid in nostrils,

trapped by dense canopies. They formed their line,
and since the firing was light, they scuffed entrenchments.

"We cowards got to lick our calf over."

"I reckon so, but I thought we's running right bravely."

"Thank you for giving me cover."
                              "It warn't nothing."
Deke and Ainey came over.
                    "Y'all mind if we hornswaggle
your holes?"
              "Sign in. I'll ring the concierge."
But Deke stayed put. He never dug a ditch,
the dictates of laziness stricter than Holy Gospel.
Garland picked a nit off his shirt. His belly
rumbled. Off to their right they heard the clash
of battle erupting. Yancy stood in his hole
to listen.
            "You know, that there was the only time
I ever flat out run. At Gettysburg,
bloody as it was, the Eighth fell back in order."

"Now see here, Pap, the wisdom of the Bard what says,
Cowards die many times before their death;
the valiant never taste of death but once."

"What of that saying, Patty?"
                          "Hit's good advice,
Pap. The valiant stay dead the rest of their lives."

329

"Awe what of running nohow? This here's war,"
Deke spat. "And war ain't got aught to do with honor
and all yer finefied shit. War's about killing—
killing them sonabitches across the way—
which is hard to do if them sonabitches kill you.
Hell, I's running so fast I might of flown
if'n I had a feather in my hat. But here's ole Critter
again, commencing to shoot more Yankee bastards."

"I never thought about it that away, Critter."

"Ainey, old Critter's telling you bald headed.
Don't think. Just shoot them sonabitches fornenst us."
That afternoon, a Yankee corps was hot
in front, entrenching and firing, the scruff of shovels,
the scatter and pluff of spoil, masked by frequent
runs of musketry. Snipers crept close, exploiting
Wilderness shadows. Firing intensified, and Nall came
hopping hole to hole, a frightened hedgehog,
and two shots nicked a pile of earth behind him.

"You damned officers is always drawing fire,"
Buzzard groaned.
                           "I reckon it's cause we're essential,"
said Nall. "Garland, old buddy. How's that leg
a yourn?" He threw an arm round Garland's shoulder.

"A sight better, I allow."
                           "You got our orders
to move?" asked Caleb. All the men were expectant.

"Nome. That's Burnsey across the way. Mars says
we gots to nail him down. We'uns can't budge
or let old Burnsey shuck out reinforcements."
He raised his eyes just over the edge of the ditch.
"We thought he was sitting on the right all day. Don't know
where he's been. But boys, all hell is gonna break
loose on your left quicker than a fat hog
can wreck a turnip patch. Now when you hear it,
step up your fire and make things hot for Burnsey.
I've got some cartridge boxes coming up."
He slapped Garland's back. "Y'all watch yer asses, hear?"
An hour later, a faint growl, building
to a pitch, the Rebel left was up and over,
driving Federals. A wave of racket broke
above their heads and swept away all sound.
Garland's nerves were brought to a precipice edge,
hearing the rising tide of Federal *huzzahs*
growing behind the racket of arms, trepidation
of thicket and branches, as if the inanimate wood
were preparing a charge, then blue infantry crashing
through brush, close enough to read insignia,
and Rebel officers forcing them to hold
fire till the final lunatic moment when a mass
volley sent Yankees reeling whiplashed backward,
and tension eased, a screw loosed out of its bushing.
The work was exhausting, and darkness halted the fighting,
the preternatural dark of the Wilderness. He slumped
in his hole, shoulder to shoulder with spent friends.
The cool soil felt good. He stretched the seized
muscle of his leg. No skillet wagons tonight.

From the mind's blankness, a rising agonized lowing,
then, his hearing clarified a screaming choir.
He woke coughing, his lungs seared with smoke.
He sat up, hearing the noise of a conflagration
breathing. Smoke lay close to the ground, flowing
in eerie currents.
         "A Stygian murk," said Caleb.
A breeze had picked up while they slept, setting
blazes, spreading faster than wounded were able
to crawl away, their cries disembodied
and pitiable, the wood so vast the suffering wailed
from every quarter. He moved to leave the trench.
"You reckon it's wise, tonight?"
                    "It's never wise."
A silence.
        "Meet me here at dawn?"
                       "All right."
He sought a landmark, here three shagbark hickories
on the cusp of a shallow ravine, a stingy streamlet
dribbling a horse track below. He hustled down
a fulgent nave dividing towering fires.
He didn't want to get cut off or herded
into enemy lines. He did not want to burn
to death. He sprinted forward, finding scattered
dead in a copse of ignited pine pulsing
like signal fires, scented with turpentine,
the smoke reflecting halation of false dawn.
The conflagration hissed in locust swarms,
radiated scathing waves. By a raging wall,
a man was lying, both feet splayed in flames,
reaching out his hands in supplication.

He threw an arm across his eyes and charged,
plunging headlong in air like boiling syrup.
He grabbed him under the arms and dragged him away,
a needle prick tingling his thigh electric.
At fifty yards he splashed across the run
he realized he could use as a fire break.

"I'm mighty obliged," was all the man could say.

"Sholey," he said and returned to glowing murk.
Masses of tree crowns tossed with flame, ethereal
around their skeletal limbs, in suspiring rage.
Lashing fire cracked at his face like a bull whip.
He tried to hew to the conflagration's boundary,
close to heat radiating breathtaking waves,
for here the agony of suffering men was most
exquisite in clamor's hysterical architecture.
A gun's report, but not, a trunk's fracture,
a scorching oven blast on counter rolling
waves of churning sparks, a roaring pine tree
crashing before him, voicing a prolonged exhale,
the heat an agony as if his mother's iron
were taken straight from embers and held near his face.
He spun and retreated, covering eyes and coughing
and passed a smoking carpet of dead, a cast
of Union soldiers stretching from dark, to light,
to dark, roasting in ghast char of flesh.
His stomach knotted, his mind recoiled, and he swallowed
hot gorge. Flaming walls communicated
branch to branch in groined vaults and arches,
the forest floor venting slag and brimstone.

Strange, the wood was issuing so many screams,
and he couldn't find a living man. A rifle
crack, another pine fell, its branches pulling
a comet tail to the forest floor, the impact
pluming air in rioting currents, describing
curlicue paths of backward churning sparks,
inside the flames a chorus of anguished cries.
He shielded his eyes and squinted against the heat.
The falling boughs had doused a huddle of men.
By a corpse he found a blanket, beat at fires,
yelling "Come to me!" Were there three or four?
His body boiled like a kettle frying cracklings.
He reeled backward from blazes. Three were there,
one with his arm casual around his comrade
as if they lounged on a stoop on Sunday evening
instead of this fiery godless furnace. He choked
and coughed, and bursting reports stunned his vision
with ruddled blots, floating behind closed eyes,
as cartridge pouches touched off fulgurant blossomings.
Fearing he might be blinded, he scuttled off
down labyrinth paths of treacherous shifting holocausts.
Hearing a proximate scream, he altered his course.
A man was pulling himself along on elbows,
his trouser legs alight. He smothered the flames
with his smoking blanket. "You able to walk?"

                                        "No,
I'm shot through both my legs." He gripped the man
beneath his arms, raised him to his waist and dragged him,
bumping his heels on roots and smoldering limbs,
for heat had sapped his strength and his thirst raged.

"I'm sorry. I know this hurts like hell."

"Go on!
I've just been sprung from hell and glad to leave it,"
he gasped his words, clasping his savior's arms
tight as he could, both for security and help
for pain jolting and wracking his useless legs.

"I know. I caught a ball at Gettysburg."
He propped the man against a trunk.

"Thanks,"
he uttered in a pained gruff, and just as Garland
started away, he added, "Johnny." He regarded
the benighted face, a hunkered, suffering shade.
"I'll have to hate you come tomorrow, friend."

"I understand you have to. I hope you may."
Vertigo swirled his senses, and he swayed a little,
picking his way through flames. A roiling smoke
engulfed him. He went to ground and breathed. Close by,
a scream of writhing nerve contortions, a rising
scale of ghastly notes and weeping, contending
in bitter cacophony of words and heaves,

"No,
God!" He on all fours like a casting hound
loped away amid the noisome breath
of burning brush and flesh, ethereal piffs
and flash of cartridges and crack of arms discharging,
the malefic threnody guiding him to a man
prostrate on a pile of Federal dead, swathes
of blouse and trousers charred away, exposing
black cauliflowers of ruined flesh. He was slight,

and being dragged away, began to moan,

"Oh thank you, Jesus. Thank you, thank you, Jesus,"
his speech grown faint, head lolling on Garland's breast.
Stumbling under his burden, his mind seething,
he picked his way through raging lines, skirting
burning brambles. Judging them safe, he set
the man beneath a sweet gum tree and eased
himself down beside him, spent in stick and sinew.

"What regiment you in?" No answer. He jostled his shoulder
and the man slumped in his lap. He put two fingers
to his throat. Nothing. "Well, at least you died
believing God answered your prayers. I reckon he's making
excuses by now. I'd love to know what they are."
He put a comforting hand on the soldier's back.
"It ain't a wonder Southerners love to pray.
What folk delight more in hearing themselves talk,
especially to God, the greatest listener in the universe."
In his forehead's center, a rhythmic hammer strike
beat a throbbing shank. Breathing the swart
char seared jowl and throat, filled lungs with fire,
his senses swimming in dizziness, coming and going.
His throat was a parched stalk in seven year drought,
bathed in dyspeptic acid eruptions. He waved
the cottony air and thought he heard in the raging
Wilderness house his father call his name.
Three times he heard the beckoning and shook his head
to clear the hallucination, driving vision
through opaque air and scrutinizing burning vaults
and buttresses pendant and threatening. He glimpsed a soldier

wandering a hazy aisle, close to flames,
strolling with casual deliberation, untroubled
by danger and vanishing in smoke. He set out after him,
plunging headlong into nightmare wailing light
down rows of apocalyptic oak trees, searing
radiant against his face like a smithy forge,
hissing like myriad slack tubs. The man appeared
in air scudding ashes. He called to him to no
avail, pursued until he reemerged
in ghost translucence and close enough to lay
his hands on him. "Where are you going?" he shouted
above the devouring clamor, but his eyes were vacant,
staring. Behind, a groined arch of limbs
collapsed beneath a raging clerestory and rooftree.
He grasped his hand and sprinted from blazing ruins,
an aching cautery piercing his clothes, till a pine
cascaded in fans of needle shingles glowing
and curling, blinding tearing eyes and choking.
The man's visage contorted in idiotic terror,
he screamed and made to bolt, but Garland seized
his blouse, he ranting in circles like a mule on a sweep.
"Get hold of yourself," but driven by mad panic,
he broke away and plunged into furnace swelter,
his clothes burgeoning in Heaven's ecstatic light.
Surrounded by conflagration, his flesh was baking.
By creature instinct, he seized his chance and sprinted
to the burning pine, timed his step and closed
his eyes and leapt into flames, planting a foot
on the trunk and pushing off in a high jump,
taking two strides on bodiless air, the searing
gust fading behind, the ground sudden under him,

his body tumbling breathless and sprawling on leaf meal,
he beating smoldering sparks from breeches and blouse.
He lay some moments, panting, keeping his nose
low in untainted air, then struggled onward,
till fires pulsed behind him, returned to visible
darkness, still laden with vilest odors, weary
with weight of his limbs, his mouth a clogged, dry hole.
He wandered the forest, seeking the stingy run,
and finally the stand of trees, which seemed the ones
where he had parted from Caleb. Sure enough,
he found the shallow ravine and stumbled in
on hands and knees, cupping water to mouth
until he had gulped an entire puddle, then crawled
through cool mire for deeper pools, the draughts
sweeter than Horeb's waters sloshing his belly.
In all the months of battle, of marches and trenching,
he'd never felt till now a mortal exhaustion.
He crawled on slackened limbs out of the stream bed,
and there a curled shadow, Caleb, sleeping.
He lay down next to his friend and stretched his leg,
and sense gave way to profound and vacant slumber.

May 7, 1864

Dawn came rolling away the stone of sleep.
He woke in the Wilderness's grotesque curing shed
to odors of broiled flesh. He winced at the stink,
sat up, stretched. Jostling Caleb's shoulder,

"Arise and walk, friend, it's"—but the sleeper wore blue

and nothing save the final trump would return
a human vision to his vacant eyes. A gash
furrowed the skull. From the fissure, brain matter leaked
frothing, and blood had trailed away. He followed
the black path where it ran and gathered and poured
down to the streamlet, impressions of his hands and knees,
muddy cups, dirty and wine dark.
He spun on all fours, retching hard, heaving
with nothing to vomit. He caught a second retch
at the bottom of his throat, forced it down by will.
He rolled the dead man over on the burst skull,
his face handsome, except for the staring orbits.
Caleb appeared,

     "There you are. You look
like you been dragged to hell and back."

          "I can't say
if I've harrowed hell or hell has harrowed me.
I thought I'd bedded down with you last night,
and when I woke up, you'd turned to a dead Yankee."
Caleb glanced away from the oozing heap,

"God forbid I make a repentant Rebel
or a young corpse. This stench is giving me
the collywobbles."

      "Let's mosey." Embers hissed,
the outraged *yearrr, yearrr* of a blue jay faded.
Keeping the doused sun to the left, they paced
through fuliginous Wilderness and came to gouged trenches,
Deke asleep on the edge, his fish mouth slack
and drooling. Ainey was picking hardtack crumbs
from his haversack and sucking dirty fingers.

"Heard the news?"
                    "I reckon not," said Caleb.

"Gordon's boys rolled up the Yankee right
like a rug—all the way to Germanna Plank Road."

"But the other news what ain't so hot," said Yancy,
propping feet on a box of forty dead men
and caressing his Enfield barrel with an oiled rag,
"is Longstreet caught him a ball in the throat."
                                        "Is he dead?"

"He lived to git in an ambulance. At's all I know."

"I hope Old Pete comes back," said Ainey. "When he
shows up to a fight, more Yankees start dying than Rebels."

"I hope to hail they chopping wood for cook fires,"
said Deke, the mention of rations putting a twist
in all the soldiers' guts.
                    "Sorry Critter,
but I moseyed over to see who's chopping this morning.
They cutting a road."
                    "A road?" said Garland, "Where to?"

"Don't know," said Yancy.
                    "Who's in Old Pete's saddle?"

"I asked Nall," said Snake, "Anderson will take
command of First Corps. Looks like we get Early."

"Old Jubilee."

        "He's a goober grabber,"
said Ainey.

        "Quiet as a church. Thank God," said Brutus.

"Oh yeah," said Yancy, "they'll be no fighting today.
Grant is whipped. Tonight he'll do a Hooker
scoot across the Rapidan, you wait and see."
Snake, Caleb, and Garland traded perplexed,
concerned expressions as Yancy stroked his rifle.
They fell in at nine; at three a.m. they moved.
The Wilderness kept on burning in revenant, pokerish
glowing, pulsing will o' the wisps, as troops
went dodging bonfires, bent under smoke and hacking.
They turned on what the army was pleased to call
a road. Approaching wayside fires, a man
would appear, taking form in crepuscular light
then vanishing back into dark, the next man coming
and going, in files of a ghastly shadow army,
clambering stumps and debris. Another patch
of attenuated light, and he was astonished at hints
of darkness stepping forward, shaped like men
and lining the road, thousands of Negroes, armed
with axes and shovels, watching the march, their plat-eyes
thrusting out of the night like queer lanterns.

"Hit's darker than a sack of black cats," said Caleb.
Then something stirred his sense. He found the ecliptic.

"Caleb, I do believe we're marching south."

"I reckon we are."

        "Caleb, Ulysses is retreating
in the wrong direction."

          "Garland, if you ain't right."
They swung onto Catharpin Road, he breathing acrid
waft from soldiers' clothes, recalling edifice
fires, myriad corpses smoking and swart,
and back of his throat the taste of abhorrent wine.

May 8, 1864

Dawn an exhausted blaze in oak leaves, he stooped
along in a picket line, muzzy from hunger,
penetrating farther the country of inanition,
primitive gorilla man, his flesh revived
by some insane Ezekiel, intent on survival,
cornered in creature instinct. He pulled a dandelion,
bit and spat out flower heads and ate
the bitter greens off roots and dirt, broom sage
whispering, hunger whispering, her warm breath close,
scent of perfumed skin pristine, dew-beaded
on honeysuckle vine, knuckle-shaken on his grasping
hand, reaching to possess her twilight skin,
fathomless eyes, their pure desire, those sturdy
hips the gods could not foreswear, vacating
thundering peaks, forsaking ambrosia and nectar,
omnipotent but mortal in the lovely thigh cradle,
that makes a god a man, a man a god,
transient conviction of eternity harbored in a fleet
hour, his pulse and her pulse beating voracious

time, he humbled by her generosity, giving world
without end, craving her virtue with leviathan need,
historical hungers of all the quick and the dead.
Slap in the face, not his, but the beast's, startled
awake by the rataplan of muskets. A stand
of buttermilk pine resolved, knee high sage,
a hillock the picket had climbed while he was in reverie.
The men had hit one knee for cover, most
having fired, but he, still standing, laughed out loud,
discharged his piece then dropped the butt to the ground
and began reloading, Caleb yanking him down.

"You want to get your ass shot off?" He grinned,
tearing a cartridge, gunpowder's gritty tang
on lips and tongue, rammed it home as two balls
sizzled above their heads. Federals were masked
in the tree line. His picket raised and fired. A shout,
a kerchief fluttered on a rifle's waving barrel,
drawing attention to a man between the lines
plowing a mule. The Yankee went to him
instead of coming to the Rebel line. "Truce,"
Caleb yelled to the men on either side.
"Pass it on." Garland looked around.
Where was Captain Nall? A pang of curiosity
urging his mind, he decided to go and meet
the parley. Coming on, he heard the whicker
of horses. The brigadier's uniform was dusted dull,
no rents or tatters, brass buttons and braids still shiny.
He was neatly barbered, eyes intense but strangely
vacant as if he weren't the sharpest blade
in the drawer, and, ah, somewhere about his person,

aroma of sorghum and fried bread. His mouth
poured, his sow's eyes narrowed rife with lust.
The farmer was speaking in tones too low for him
to catch. He was wretched, stripped to the waist, his neck
suntanned plum, barefoot, breeches ragged,
almost plowing naked. The Yankee's hair
was flowing blond, his mustache bushy, who saw him
approaching, saw the lean and wolfish look.
The general took a slight step backward. He laughed,
a throaty wheeze. *Me and my butternut brothers,*
all clad alike, a pant leg missing from my knee,
cartridge pouch tied by strings of rag and rawhide,
we of this grand army of beaten scarecrows,
who charge full tilt against the flailing arms
of a windmill God, and he turning inexorable
from before original chaos to quash us with blows,
who thought we were his sons. And you provisioned
with every arm and eatable, whom God has chosen
to give us death at the end of some famished march,
what portent for you has hunger made of me?

"Are you an officer?" He put his wolf's eye
on the general and let the question drift away.
The Yankee shifted ground, said to the plowman,
"This is a field of battle, sir. You must
clear off."
             "Field a battle, squat. This hyar's
my gotdamn farm. What right do you have hyar?
You'cn clear off." The words were angry but carried
no heat, the voice gentle as a whispering lover's.

"We could shift our battle west and fight over there."

"And leave my flank dangling beyond the hill
where I've artillery and so be forced to refuse
my line? I'm not susceptible to Rebel tricks."

"You mean that hill yonder where you got artillery?"
He did not smile at the general's reddening face.
"Well hell, you choose. You Yanks already got
between our hog and hominy. You won't stay north,
then take whatever you want. It's what you're doing."

"I have established my lines, and I shall hold them."

"You-uns make a brace of gotdamned fools.
I aims to plow. I got mouths to feed
if you'uns don't kill us off wholesale, man, woman,
and chit. What air I done to you up north?
Take my slaves if'n you find one anywheres.
I'm the only nigger in this here field,
and you can go to hell or send me there,
but I aims to plow this ground. Hit's all I got."
The general threw up his hands.
                              "He's your people.
I'll give you fifteen minutes for humanity's sake
to get him evacuated. In twenty minutes I shall commence
to move against you. Good day." The Yankee strode
across the swale, wafting delicious aromas.

"You gonna die if you don't leave."
                              "I reckon."
The plowman's watery eyes remained transfixed
on the coulter's polished iron. "I got three girls

at home what's starving. Hit's hard for a daddy to watch."
To the left a clatter of musketry sparked and ceased,
hushing peeps of birdcall. He lifted his pouch.

"This ain't much—some bits of rancid bacon,
a handful of cornmeal. It'll feed your girls today,
and tomorrow, well, if God provides for sparrows,
maybe he'll give to your daughters."
                                    "I ain't figured
on God none, but I don't aim to take what's yourn."
But he didn't resist when he hung the strap on his neck,
pellagra or scurvy in scalloped evidence there,
his awesome despair weighing blades of grass.
He wondered if shot and canister might not be
confounded by its density, its rock-like impassivity.
The mule stamped, twitched its rump's taut hide
dislodging flies, its wet black eyes weary
as a martyr's. The farmer's hands had never let go
the plow handles, seasoned with sweat, the coulter wedged
in the furrow, swingletree resting on earth. He rocked it
free to give the mule an easier start.

"You boys take cair. They's 'bout two dozen, dismounted,
with carbines. They pulled two guns by the house and left
a guard. Heya," the quiet voice urged, his glacial
patience scouring the world's valley. He descended
the gentle slope, and Caleb and other soldiers
gathered round him.
                    "What's the news, Garland?"

"The blue general's in high feather on account

of the Rebel plowman bungling his tactics. I offered
to shift our lines of battle west or east,
but the general wouldn't hear it."

                    "Ha, haw!"

"Commander Garland treating with Yankee officers."

"You oughta wire Lincoln right away
  and make your complaint official on this upstart gener'l."

"I'll see to that later, Snake, but the Rebel farmer
won't leave off his plowing, hail or storm.
Try not to shoot the poor son of a bitch is all."
The scarecrows watched the farmer pace in tableau
with rifles and sky, traces draped over shoulder,
could see just barely top of the rise the coulter
changing grass to cool earth clods, transforming
promiscuous weeds to a garden's bare prospect,
he trudging the row, world weary, implacable will
dismissing hope, eradicating certain death
arrayed in carnival around him, his mad volition
inexorable for the raging, ordained, violent act
of plowing, escape from horror of watching the revolting
corpse assume the likeness of his dear ones' faces,
steering his swayback mule to the throne of God,
to rest his hollow eyes in infinite ones
and tempt the Almighty with a single slack-jawed question.
"They's a couple dozen cavalry toting carbines,
two guns on that hill yonder, and they left a guard
stationed at the farmer's shack. I say we bully
around our right, ask the guard to dance,

get on their flank, and when the music starts,
we cross their T and push 'em back on their guns.
Five or six on top of this rise would mask
our movement. General's give us twenty minutes
to get around him. We got the numbers."

                                        "You reckon?"
It was Captain Nall, intent on Garland's outpouring
of martial strategy.
                    "The plowman allows we do."

"All right, old son, I'm with you. What do you say?"
All the men nodded. "All right. Garland, you lead
the platoon. You pick up the guard and get us in place.
But when I give word to charge, we go to it
like a calf licking yeller jackets. We might have numbers
but the Yanks got carbines, so we'uns got to make
the goose honk high, I mean we got to go
all the way to the well with it. You'uns follow me?"
Again, each man nodded. "All right, Garland,
go ahead on, and I'll put five or six
in position here and come along behind."
They charged the farm house, greeted the dismayed guard,
then raced on the double-quick through wood and field
headlong toward battle racket and rattling smoke
of carbine fire oblique to the Federal line
arranged along the piney crest of hill,
below which five outnumbered Rebels worked
like tumbleweed in spring tornado. He realized
Oscar was one of the five and sprinted ahead,
raising his voice in the eerie demon glee
of their battle cry. Three blue troops swung round,

awed and wide eyed as he crashed through boughs
and leapt atop a limestone rock and vaulted
in air still shouting, a bullet snicking the stone
where his feet had touched. Hitting the ground in stride,
he fired, the shot dinging a Yankee's canteen,
who turned and fled, others churning, then catching
the current and flowing. A shout went up,

                           "Flanked!
Flanked!" The Rebels loosed a volley to hasten
their flight. Nall was whooping,

                         "Bell to the trace,
boys, bell to the trace! These Yanks have swallowed
the Devil red hot from home! Let's give 'em hell!"
But the Yankee cavalry was disciplined, forming quick
positions, returning fire and husbanding ammunition.
Hungry and blown, the Rebels were soon outrun.
But they swept the guns, pausing to exult and tried
to touch off a twelve pounder to hasten the Yankee
exodus, but all they managed to do was splinter
a sycamore tree, so they brought up the captured mounts,
limbered the guns and returned to their unit triumphant.
Nall was beside himself with fruits of their victory,
two guns, two dozen horses, and a sour corporal.
"Goldamn Garland, I never seen a Rebel
sojer fly, but you shore took to the wing!
You give them Yankees goss a gracious plenty,
put the scare in the lot of 'em all by yerself,
had them Yankees hopping like graveyard rabbits!"
But exultation was short-lived. They formed
once more on Catharpin Road, slogging south,
exhausted. A quarter mile from the Brock Road,

they could see the intersection cut in the trees,
splendid with sunlight and down the lane, an officer
leaning over his galloping horse's withers,
the creature lathered, hagridden. The soldier reined up
close in a spree of dust cloud and flecked foam.

"You've got to run! Take cover behind our logs.
If you don't run, the Yankees will have us all!"
The unit started phalanx-square, then bulged
to a ram's horn. He looked back once to see men trailing
behind the comet nucleus of careering troops.
They swerved as a body left into Brock Road,
reaching for the disputed barricade, a gallimaufry
of tree trunks, fence rails and rubble, and coming on
at the double quick, blue troopers, faces grim.
He hated seeing their faces.
                                        "Hold fire," Royston
drawled, he feeling bodies piling on the breastwork,
"Ready," a rolling wave of rifle barrels
coming level. "Fire!" At twenty yards,
the Federals struck a mortal wall, spinning
and sheering bodies back from the knees. They returned
fire, breech smoke covering their break for safety.
Too far away to lend the needed force,
a full brigade came stepping smartly toward them,
clear in sunlight, company banners snapping.
The pines along the road were slim and stately.
This time, a hundred yards away, they charged.
Royston held their fire till forty yards,
the flaming wall reaping front rank soldiers,
small explosions in their clothes, astonished agonies.

The Confederate defensive line was massing all
along the makeshift breast work, across the lane,
spreading to woods on either side of the road.
In front, the Federals gathered whatever was near
for cover, fence rails, corpses, some were digging.
A lull ensued and then sporadic firing.
Caleb tried to sleep and nodded off
for a while. Garland lay against the works,
observing in fathomless blue the evening swifts
swerving and circling, making glamorous patterns.
Before the sun set, Federals massed again
and charged, running hard and crying *huzzah*.
He sighted a soldier and fired on command, watched
in bizarre, retarded motion the man fling up
his arms in mortal surrender, his bodily momentum
scythed backwards, he mindful how falling wounded
took such a long time, the man enveloped by a mass
of running troops. The brigade bulled forward, but courage
availed them nothing, a Rebel volley leaving
milling soldiers naked to scathing fire.
They dropped, stacked corpses for cover. One soldier lit out,
leaping bodies and debris like a startled deer.
Someone laughed, another voice countered,

                                   "Shut up."
The dusk deepened. There'd be no time for another
charge before dark. Sighing relief, he fell
on arms into the arms of sleep. Then someone's foot
prodded him till he woke, a man thrusting
a shovel unceremoniously into his hand.

                              "What's this?"
The engineer was tall with wavy hair, weariness

sagging beneath his eyes.
                              "An efficient implement
for the redistribution of earth," yet the eye glinted,
his giggle dodged like a mouse. "Dig on this line,
depth in proportion to how much you value your skin."

"I'll need a bigger *implement*," he yawned, considering
how deep exhaustion's tap root must have delved
that he had slept while men plied picks and shovels.
The Yanks had fallen back just out of range,
and far as he could see, gray backs were chopping
trees, rolling abatis, and dragging the stripped
trunks to front their trenches, chocking them inches
above the ground, creating rifle embrasures.
Behind him on a promontory gunners were dropping trail
of artillery, positioning pieces for the deadliest fields
of fire. Caleb looked up and dabbed his brow
with his dirty kerchief.
                              "Skillet wagons. Thank God."
Nall made sure they drew their rations first.
He kept on digging, exhaustion accruing like snowfall,
stiffening muscles, every shovelful heavier
than the last. Oscar served his supper, a dollop
of field peas, a sickly rasher of pork. His stomach
seized like a caged animal. He grasped the tin,
spoke his thanks to Oscar, and poured the food
in his mouth, gnashing peas in gulping swallows,
sucking the pillowy fat back for sweet savor
of grease, then bolting both his hard crackers.
Caleb received his proffered rations, a stooped
shadow, seated on a log of the breastwork, thrown

into faint definition by a deep traverse behind him.
He crossed himself, spread his dirty hanky,
arranged his kit on his lap and hung his head.

"Papa, where we at?"
                    "Spotsylvania."

May 10, 1864 Spotsylvania Court House

Dawn light bleeding across the groggy sky,
a shovel handle lay across his lap.
He didn't remember sitting down to rest
or deciding to go to sleep. Men huddled in the works,
snoring and clutching picks and shovels like brides.
A few had fetched out blankets, and these lay humped
like graves. He rubbed his face and started to the rear,
dodging sleeping soldiers, mounted a rise
where batteries tilted stoppered barrels, the gunners
propped asleep against the carriage wheels,
one boy awake telling a rosary and staring.
A horse among the beasts standing asleep
whickered a greeting. He stroked her elegant muzzle.
For a good half mile from side to side, they'd spaded
a bulging mule shoe, the toe of which subsumed
a hill, crowded with batteries. The extent of traverses
would shield whole regiments from enfilade. Breastworks, slopes,
and redans were formidable. Chevaux-de-frise like hunkered
porcupines and rolls of abatis cordoned
every rise and fall of ground to halt
a Federal charge in fields of withering fire.

For hundreds of yards in front the trees were felled,
the salient's vast skirt of stumps and leaves.
Men would cross that terrible space, crying
in waves and lay down their deeds among green bays.
The sun entangled itself in a net of tree limbs.
A pot boiled on the fire.
                            "Sup of coffee?"
Oscar asked.
                    "By Geoffrey, where did you get
coffee?"
            "Hit's coffee boiled from green corn
and dried peas."
                    "Ah, Jeff Davis coffee."
I'll have a horn." Oscar poured the steaming,
amber liquid, odor of hominy. He blew
and sipped, regarding soldiers nursing cups.
Here and there a man was plying his shovel
though most, spent from the night's toil, slept
on cool turned soil, crowding the ditches. He thought
of the plowman, his starving girls, wondered if their sparrow
eyes were liquid and thriving. Caleb stirred
beneath his blanket, so he took him some coffee.
                                        "What's this?"

"It's what we're calling coffee." A thought unbidden,
like a bird swerving into vision, Caleb's goodness,
his devotion, had not just rescued him from death,
it had saved his life. His wholesome virtue stirred,
if not a prayer, a Heaven-directed utterance,
Father, let me die before he dies.
Foreboding silence pervaded the afternoon.

His regiment manning the fire step, he nodded off.
The first report, muted by distance, failed
to wake him, but when the fused shot struck the ground
scant yards behind the ditch, blowing a crater
like a violent pillar out of the earth, he flinched
awake. He and Caleb fumbled cartridges
and stacked a convenient pile. Across the wide
clearing no enemy stirred. Shelling increased,
worming courage with twisting shrieks, tension
screwing them tight in the works, for they knew from long
experience Federal artillerists were dangerous as snipers.
The hours hobbled; at four, the firing ceased,
and thousands of eyes emerged above the breastworks.
Away on the right, ordered rows of blue.

"Who is it?"
                    "Looks like Warren's corps," said Papa.
"They gave us pure old hell at Gettysburg."
They began to advance. The landscape held its breath.
First a scratchy noise, the rhythmic sound
of steps and faint music. When they came in range,
artillery opened, gouging their ranks, an avulsion
of arms and legs churned up, the way the blade
of an up and down saw mill sends the sawdust spouting.
The regiment snagged the abatis. The first rank formed
behind the rolls, drove in bayonets and bulled them
forward, men behind them pouring through the gaps.
The Rebels concentrated fire on head gates of streaming
infantry, wreaking destruction, but Federal courage
was dauntless as soldiers clambered over the dead
and pressed to point blank range of the roaring breastwork,

thinned to a suicide line too weak to matter.
Ainey chortled,
                    "Them Irish sons a bitches,
they can fight sho 'nough." Company I,
an Irish unit in the Eighth Alabama, was in line
to the left of Company H.
                    "Sholey," said Snake,
"I ain't ever seen such intrepid musket fire."
Their company flag was satin in emerald green,
billowing *Erin Go Bragh* on an Irish harp.
Rebels were bringing cartridge boxes up
and the walking wounded stooped behind the lines,
many from the Irish ranks who had borne the brunt.
A cannon barked, the roar of guns rushed forward.
For four miles and more the Rebels hunkered
down in burrowed earth. The air was black
with layered racket and hellish melody, the bass
report of guns below and high above
the treble fugue of turning shrieks ascending
the arched sky and toppling over in nerve fraying
wails, one plummeting shurr untangling from the wide
cacophony and falling near, the burst heaving
and raining sheets of dirt. He steeled himself.
Smoke roiled across the rise of ground behind them.
Up on the hill, a caisson had exploded, and gunners
left alive were shoveling dirt on tar buckets
aflame and beating them with shovel blades.
Around six thirty, the firing ceased again.
He unclenched and stretched, trying to work tension
from sinews. Caleb stared through a stripe of sunlight.

"Ladies, hike your skirts up, here they come."
Only a few more men than they comprised
the salient point where legs of an angle joined.
He squinted under the head log, confidence withering.
A Federal brigade was coming at full gallop,
four rows deep, not stopping to fire. Cheering
grimly, they pressed, a hammer to pound a wedge.
As Rebels conceived the Yankee plan, its genius,
musketry erupted, and men came sidling in
from the flanks, filling in rows behind Company H,
trying to make the wedge an anvil, lending
a sense of safety and dismay of close constraint,
rifle barrels extending beyond both shoulders.
Captain Nall,

        "Patience a Job, boys.
We'uns got to wait till the possum climbs
the gum stump, then we'll give 'em a howdy do."
Yankee guidons snapped above their ranks.
A hundred yards, they sprinted straight into sunlight,
the first fleet row outpacing the three behind.
"Ready," the captain drawled, "and fire!" Half the row
dropped. They knew it was not enough and fired
at will, culling the hustling Federal onslaught.
Soldiers of the last two rows saw they would make it.
Discerning success and survival, they raised a deep voiced
huzzah and put on speed. The Rebels only
got off one more volley, blue troops bounding
the fallen and belly flopping the breastwork's glacis.
A Federal gained the earthwork's lip, discharged
his piece point blank in a Rebel's face, the head

bursting like a watermelon. This was courage ennobled
suicide. The hour was late, and Yankees only
had numbers for stalemate fighting. Rebels kept coming
to fill the ditch, ducking fire and getting
more guns in line. Sometime after dark,
a shout.

   "They heading back!" And Federals rose
and dashed away, Confederate volleys urging
swift retreat. The firing sputtered out.
He and Caleb rummaged sacks for food.
He heard two voices from the Irish company.

             "Ira?"

"Aye Galvin."

   "I wisht that ever Yankee they is
was in hell."

    "Don't you be saying such blarney, Galvin.
Hit's a terrible thought and a Christian's swift undoing."

"How's that?"

   "If ever Yankee they is was in hell,
Mars would have us digging trenches outside
and going in come the morrow. And Galvin"—

             "Yeah Ira?"

"It's hot enough where we are."

      "By St. John's bones,
you're a dreadful knowing critter, Ira. Hit ain't
a wonder you got to be First Shirt ahead o' me."

May 11, 1864

Dawn, a bead of silence, trigger pressured,
he lay in the ditch, hour after languishing hour,
expectant for action to distract from fiery insides.
By afternoon, he could stand it no more and declaring
his intention to visit the sinks, wandered a ways
behind the lines and tried to get his mind
in his botany book, searching nodding blossoms
to distinguish Squirrel Corn from Dutchman's Breeches,
when a shadow encroached on petal and page, Yancy
looming above him, cradling his Enfield close.
He sat on his heels.
                          "Howdy, Papa."
                                          "Howdy.
Bend yer ear a minute, Garland?"
                                          "Sholey.
Got all the time they is till the war starts up."
Yancey's eyes roved across the tree line.

"Garfish, joining the army was the worst mistake
I ever made in my life. It was moral error."

"Why do you say that, Yancy? Your people called,
you're fighting for home and country."
                                          "Who are my people?
The morning I left, I stood by my son's crib,
watching him sleep, and I began to see him
like for the first time, how beautiful he was.
And you know what I was thinking?"
                                          "No Yance, what?"

"About them verses in Genesis, the Lord God making
everything, the light, the moon, the sun and stars,
and none of that compared with what I'd done made.
Think about it, Garland. In all of time
he was not, and then he was born. I gave him his name,
and there he lay, my son, beautiful and helpless.
He was counting on me, and I walked out on him."

"Awe Yance, you just can't do this. None of us knows
if he's gonna live or die, and even if you do die,
your boy will always know you gave your life
for a greater good."
      "Sons need fathers, not heroes.
My daddy walked out on me and my momma for liquor
and women, and that was the lack, Garland, what kept me
from seeing things the way they are—the truth
about fathers and sons—until I made my mistake."

"Yancy, your son—what is his name?"
         "Edward."
"You'll get back home and Edward won't even remember
you ever left. And you and Sally will pick up
right where you both left off."
       "She never said
a word against me going, but it was plain
in her eyes. She was so disappointed in me. I promised
to cleave to her and then I left. Ah Garland,
never again will I know my beautiful wife."

"Yance. My God. You got to stop this now."
He stripped pigweed, distracted, dropping the flowers.

"Every bullet has its billet, and the bullets
are coming more and more. And even if
I live, they's some mistakes what can't be mended.
I hurt her, Garland. I hurt her bosom heart.
She trusted me to be the man to love her.
I promised to do it. It's all a marriage is,
that promise, and I let her down. I'm so ashamed."

"Yancy, you're looking at things the worst way.
Sally will forgive. And Papa, you're a great man.
I know it, and the hearts of great men can be healed.
You got to fall back and dig in. It's root hog or die."
He closed the book and gave it to him, reaching
for his musket, which Yancy clutched but then relinquished.
"Read about the flowers. Settle your mind
in a lovely, guileless thing. Fall back, dig in.
I'll have your rifle when you come back to the line."
Yancy had always been the sturdiest man.
What bitter dregs he'd drunk from the cup of war,
and now he sat, broken, the botany book closed
beside him, mechanic fingers reaping blossoms.
If Yancey couldn't survive, how would he?

May 12, 1864

One rose-hued shard in dark and attack coming,
he lay on the trench's lip socked in a stinking
row of soldiers, intent on scuffling boot soles
in front and high above that shuffle, music,
jaunty and blithe. Three hundred yards in snaggled

fog, formless attackers emerged as men.

"Cold, steel patience, boys, cold as a whore's heart.
Let's let these courageous sons a biscuit eaters
come ahead on." Captain Nall was standing
on a cartridge box, a pair of specs to his eyes,
"We gwine to let 'em get close and give 'em the old
sockdolager, show 'em who's tall hog at the trough."
The Federals closed and a wave of barrels leveled.
Why did their guns not open? Silence kept stretching
out, the sky's fabric unscathed. A repercussive
bump convulsed the distance, and Federal shells
rained shrieking, explosions groping along the trench,
and Rebel musketry running in troughs and crests
of racket up and down the line, and billows
of breech smoke rolling illumined by candescent flashes.
The gray pall lifting, Yankees had gone to ground,
strewn blue forms on the vast green winding sheet,
while some had made the long haul back into mists
as if they entered their eerie uncreation.
Three hundred yards to the forest and no brigade
was visible. The men slunk down on arms, and Nall
got up on his box, "Well shit fire and save
matches! If that warn't a feint." He cocked his head
to battle hum on their left a mile away.

"Where's our damn artillery?"
                                "They limbered up
and rolled away in morning dark," said Ainey.
He shook his head. "Mars was guessing Grant
might steal a march around him, so he pulled 'em back

to get 'em out quick."
                    "But this time Mars guessed wrong."

"Yeah, but Mars don't often guess it wrong."
A general's aide came trotting down the line.

"Orders from Wilcox. The Yanks have used overwhelming
numbers to break our line at a salient. He needs
two companies to help us on the double quick." The captians
of H and I stepped forward to volunteer.
Company H moved out behind the Irish
swearing with magnificence. Near the fracas, they were met
by an officer, directing the captains to their point of entry,
but once the Irish soldiers discerned their place
in line, they whooped and careened ahead, screaming
above the battle's clamor,
                    "Hub-bob-boo!
Bag 'em, drive 'em back for General Lee!"
They sprinted over a strewn and bleeding unit,
flat out for the fight's most vicious point of contact.
At most they were fifty men, half a company,
but charging full tilt and screaming like a division,
they burst on the salient. Compressed inside the curving
outer trench, twenty thousand Federals
rammed a half-mile cut, facing backward
over the rear revetment, many crammed
so tight they could not raise their arms to fire.
The Irish rushed the trench, screaming hysterical
mad and firing, volley smoke swallowing them,
he dashing through to watch the Irish vanish,
tumbling headlong in the ditch, falling on top

of Yankees and each other, wailing like banshees, thrusting
bayonets, swinging stocks, fisticuffs and cudgels.
His company belly flopped on the trench's edge,
musket fire a web of death above them.
Inspired by Irish zeal, the brigade they'd passed
now rushed the trench in a wave, holding their volley
for point-blank range, then clubbing with rifle stocks
as they poured in the ditch, firming the Irish foothold.
He dragged himself along under hizzing fire,
sliding down in the trench, Caleb and Oscar
falling on top of him, they throwing their weight
behind the rabid Irish. But Federals, having lost
all semblance of order, owing to their quick success
at breaking the line, began to surge from the trench
and over the parapet in a great blue breaking wave;
the last men tied to the point of contact, trying
to follow the sudden retreat, were shot in droves,
like the last in a covey of quail to rise from grasses,
the hunter holding the gun's bead dead in his eye.
The trench was corduroyed with corpses, he thinking
We'll never be able to kill them fast enough.
A cry went up from Rebels supposing for an instant
the Yankees were on the run. They didn't run far.
Hurling over the parapet, they sprawled for cover
on the work's glacis. Now the armies squared off,
scant feet of unobstructed ground between them.
A Rebel soldier raised his head to peer
above the earthwork, his face erupting in a shower
of scarlet spray, a rifle barrel discharging
inches from his nose, cleaving forehead in an axe
gouge, leaving clotted hair and shreds

of flesh, gray matter bulging in ooze, and nostrils
runneling blood. The fire was rampant and wild
across the parapet, shouting and cursing roiled
around him. Interspersed among the Rebel faces,
begrimed, wide eyed, were Negro faces smutched
with the same grime, the same expressions of fear
or concentration. Here one, loading a musket
and passing it up, and here another, sprawled
beside his owner, firing steady into masses
of Yankee infantry. The fire raged as targets
presented themselves. The dugouts back of head logs
chinked for rifle embrasures were deadly as soldiers
on either side were ramming barrels through,
impaling enemies or shooting them point blank.
Two hours, and dint of fighting was gaining momentum,
the racket dinning his ears. A Rebel climbed
the breastwork's edge to get off a shot, and a Yankee
thrust his bayonet in his yelling mouth,
he dropping his rifle, his arms swimming in air.
He recalled the first time his father took him fishing
for crappie, he marveling how their tilting eyes,
empty, scintillating, repelled the light
like isinglass. So this man's eyes as he swallowed
the blade's shank, and just as he exulting
had hooked his fish and hauled it from the river, the Yankee
hauled the corpse across the parapet with a cry
of glory. He shuddered, tore a cartridge, and tried
to force his mind grim. By midafternoon,
he thought he must have fired a hundred rounds.
Breech smoke hung above them as if they fought
in a burning house, rifle fire crackling

around them and every time its roaring slackened,
it surged again, redoubling its former racket,
till he thought his head might rattle off his shoulders.
The men engaged with crazed endurance, fought
by willed strength and ruthless delight of slaughter,
urging all to sanity's precipice, for often
some lunatic in blue or butternut would mount
the parapet to fire down on opposing ranks,
his comrades tossing him loaded rifles, so he
could get off one or two shots, sometimes three,
before an enemy picked him off the barricade,
clean as shooting a bottle off a fencepost.
His Enfield got so hot, he couldn't touch
the barrel or bands; as he poured a cartridge, the powder
flashed, searing nose and eyes. He coughed
and sputtered.
            "You all right?" asked Oscar. He nodded,
retching burn from his throat, rubbing his eyes
and bringing in focus a Union soldier, visage
swart and shiny, mounting the earthwork shouting.
A gray back hurled his rifle like a spear, piercing
his belly just below the sternum, freezing
his motion in agonized rack, his gaze rolling
downward aghast at the loathsome wound, his arms
flailing to reach for help that was not there
as he tumbled backwards off the parapet, his eyes
assuming the sky's vacancy. A hot revulsion
choked him with dread, stubborn refusal to act.
He climbed the revetment out of the trench and shut
his eyes, willing the calm of self-possession,
like hunting a familiar object in a midnight room.

He forced his hands to tear another cartridge.
Clamor piled above him, a uniform noise,
a bedlam weather. A bedraggled soldier came out
of line, scrutinizing heaps of trash and bodies,
knelt by a corpse, unbuckled the dead man's knapsack,
and rifled out handfuls of freshly laundered clothes,
he using old tatters to daub the perspiration
from face and underarms, the tops of shoulders,
baring down to the nubbin, buttocks white
as cotton and comic; then hiking up his step ins,
he pulled on breeches, buttoned a blouse of homespun,
and regarding him with a look of complete refreshment,
smiled, tipped his slouch hat, and returned to the fight,
treading a bundle of letters tied with a ribbon.
"I reckon we just seen it all," said Oscar.
The Rebels lying behind the trench were whirling
like windmills loading and firing. Soldiers piled
behind them sighted with deliberation, distinguishing
friend from foe. He stretched out by Caleb, leveling
his rifle, scanning the parapet edge for blue
through shifting smoke. A man to his right shook him,
a Negro, an implausible giant, his face plump
as an infant's, holding a rifle like a toy in his meaty
hand, his face glistening, countenance bereft.

"Massuh is hurt. What I gwine to do?"
He looked beyond the Negro's massive shoulders.
Master lay on his back in regulation gray,
once clean and pressed, now coated in dust, drenched
with blood at the collar. He held a hand to the wound
at his throat, the other gripped a sabre, his body

straight as a tombstone effigy, his eyes fixed pillars.
A spray of bullets churned the earth around them,
and Nall shouting,

        "We running out of cartridges."

"I'll fetch us a box. What's your name?"
           "Moses."

"Moses, hitch your master up on your back
and follow me." He expected the Yankees to solve
this problem by shooting them all as soon as they rose,
he crawling to a stack of empty cartridge boxes,
the last with only twenty or thirty rounds.
Behind the crates, a heat-sick man was vomiting,
another sitting beside him, clasping knees
in his arms, rocking and rocking, his eyes disjoint,
shaking his head and moving speechless lips.
He leaned his rifle on a crate, turned, and Moses
was there, his master limp on his back, small
as a boy. They set off dodging soldiers and plummeting
shells cratering earth and raining soil.
They shrugged through a grove of boles eight inches round,
pollarded shoulder height by musket fire.
A hundred yards ahead was a conference of officers.
He made for them and shouted, "We need cartridges."
An aide pointed to a park of guns and caissons
still harnessed to mounts, and he turned his sprint toward these,
another hundred yards away, praying
some hawk eyed Federal cannoneer would not
mistake the guns for an active battery. The ground
heaved open before him, bowling him ass over mess kit,

sprawling, ears ringing and raining dirt come pelting.
Before he could gather his senses, he was lifted up,
his feet not touching the ground, like a girl's doll.
Moses was holding him under his arm with one hand,
now setting him gently down. "Jesus, Moses,"
he muttered, spitting and blinking.

> "Is massuh all rat?"

"My name is Garland. Let's go." They made the row
of caissons and Napoleons parked on the road's berm.
They went to the other side of the guns for shelter,
and Moses lay his master's slackened body
in the shade. Garland felt his pulse. Nothing.
"I'm sorry Moses."

> "Oh massuh cain't be det.
He cain't be det. Oh po Miss Caroline.
What she do now? Her sweet heart's gwine to break."

"I'm sorry, Moses, but I've got to get some cartridges
back to the line or the Yankees will gobble us up.
You can stay here with your master." Moses' aspect
clouded in consternation.

> "Massuh be det.
I got's to have me a white man. You is mine."
Danger, urging haste, postponed dismay
sparked by this declaration. They heaved a crate
of ammunition from a caisson, rummaged a tow hook,
and wedged the crate's cover till the nail heads showed.
Birling shriek of a fused shot keened above,
they ducking as it struck earth and burst; a fragment
slashed an artillery horse's belly, the creature

rearing, eye racked wild, bowels disgorging,
slapping the ground, glistening and dirt-caked. It was odd
how much their screams resembled human screams.
A shell exploded before her, she rearing once more
and trying to bolt, restrained by harness, jostling
the other animals in the team, her back legs tangling
in unspooled guts. She shrieked, tumbled down hard
on a shoulder, the concussion winding the great lungs
as she struggled and pawed the earth. Arcing shrills
crowded air, catching the precise pitch
of the mare's wailing, tensed and extended the pealing
as if her cries of outraged, uncomprehending
animal pain were filling up the landscape.
Lying on her side, she raised her head, found him
with her ravaged eye. He sprinted three steps forward,
crying outrage, swung the tow hook a savage
blow to her skull, its violence rippling her body,
dousing her wild misery. Then with a wild
cry, he swung at the cartridge box, unhinging
the lid and knocking it off. He did not look
at Moses, but felt his regard lingering, troubled
with pity. Grasping the crate's rope handles, they heaved
along the trembling road through the churning field
to the mule shoe trench, he dropping the box and collapsing
breathless beside it, where men were already waiting.

"Thanks," said Oscar. "You saved our Rebel asses.
And thank you too for your help."

                                  "Sholey massuh."

He nodded, gathered a handful of cartridges, and joined

his company. Oscar and Moses lay behind him,
loading rifles, and Caleb sprawled on his left,
firing by turns so one would always have
a loaded piece, each man covering the other.

"Look there," said Oscar. At the mule shoe's apex, where the fight
raged with unbridled savagery, one man stood,
pouring a steady fire in the Union line
or parrying Federals threatening to cross the trench
with feint of his bayonet. He cut a slight
figure, but he fought like a wildcat. As far away
as he was, Garland could see his eyes roving,
watching for Federal incursions and raised barrels.
"That's Max Frauenthall, a fellow Jew."

"He ain't gonna live long there," muttered Caleb.
But an hour later, the diminutive Jew still stood
at the closest point of contact, gallantly mustachioed,
a Lion of Judah if there had ever been one.
A storm blew in, obscured by battle smoke,
the guns' cacophony masking far off rumblings.
At once a rain came sluicing from gray batting,
continuous with battle haze, drenching and cooling them,
rinsing air of cannon smoke and breech smoke,
and pinnacle thunders extended the noise of guns
high in the heavens. Fewer vomited from heat,
barrels steamed. He wondered how long they'd been at it.
They were closer now to the foremost point of battle,
having taken the places of other fought out men.
He dared not raise his head above the earthwork,
but keeping low, he'd watch for a barrel or kepi,

then hold his rifle up and pull the trigger.
Yankees lay on the glacis twenty deep.
A wild shot couldn't miss. He passed his rifle,
was handed another by Moses. A sudden freak
threw him back on his haunches, scourge of blue
bolting across the parapet, bursting through a door
of rain on a suicide rampage, gripping his fixed
bayonet at waist level. Unthinking, reacting
by instinct as he tumbled back, his right hand caught
the shank, guiding the thrust between his chest
and arm, the long blade spading harmless in earth.
The soldier hung on the rifle butt, teeth bared
and growling, eyes deranged, his face black
as a Negro's, streaming sweat and filth, the mouth
twisted, filled with taste of a bitter cud.
Counterpoised, locked like rolling stock, they grappled
and throttled each other, he gripping the throat, and the side
of the Yankee's head was scythed away, spraying
gobbets of blood mussed hair and pulverized skull
into Garland's face and mouth. The frenzy evanesced
from the soldier's eyes, becoming a man's again,
his grip relinquishing, his body easing down
the rifle stock, to lie on top of him gentle
as a lover, he tasting between his teeth and lips
unconscionable grit. To his right, Moses was kneeling,
still sighting a rifle. Sogged with muck, he shrugged
the body off, spitting and gagging, stood
in splashing rain and bullets, seized the feet
and dragged it, the chin a coulter cutting a muddy,
blood streaked swath, the dirty water closing
it up like a wound. At the reserve trench, he felt

his palms caressing leather uppers. He flung
the body over, sat on a stump and swapped
his boots. On his shoulder, Moses' great black hand.

"Dem Yankee's gwine to kill you if'n they kin,
but anger will kill yo soul. Then where you be?"
An ecstatic pain rived his head in two.
He thought he had been shot, and crimson tulle
fell across his vision. He trembled, fearing
he'd burst like a boiler. He lifted a leg, kicked
the corpse in the trench, muddy waters splashing
and angry stares raising above the lip.
He rose, not looking at Moses, snatched his rifle,
and led him back to the line, ducking into frenzy.
He fought for another hour, and a ball cut his sleeve
at the elbow. Oscar crawled up.
                                   "That's two close calls.
"Come on—let's get to the rear ditch and sit
a spell." Ainey slapped his back, crawling
forward to take his place, intent on the earthwork.
Pulling him up in a crouch, Oscar led
him away, Moses tagging along. He slid
feet first in the trench, squelching muck, surprised
to find so many men. Moses grabbed
two empty cartridge boxes tall enough
to keep their backsides dry. The soldier next
to him was rocking to and fro, his eyes
a wall of rain. Some were holding wounds
in quiet suffering. One wept, his hands working
around his hat brim. Others, to his disbelief,
were passed out sleeping from fatigue. Oscar produced

three crackers. "Let's have ourselves a worm castle."
Garland nodded and bit one, steeling himself
against a fused rage. He shivered in rain
splashing soundless, creating the bizarre apprehension
of dripping rainfall noising rataplan of muskets.
Solid shots kept bouncing over the trench,
spinning rooster tails of filthy water.
He leaned on the muddy wall and closed his eyes.
He couldn't let himself become like Yancy,
couldn't sit here and weep like a woman. He must follow
his own advice. Fall back, dig in. The sun
was close to setting, but the battle's pandemonium
raged above them ubiquitous thunder and lightning.
Oscar regarded the trench's lip with mild
concern. Moses held his feet out of water.
A shape in the ditch's effluvium caught his eye,
an oddly familiar pattern, too incomplete
to trigger recognition, then resolving to a face,
or the muddy sculpture of one. It was the mad
soldier he'd kicked in the trench, tamped and treaded
into muck, now almost buried except for the nose,
the slight depression of orbits, a bit of brow.
He perused the watery slop a little ways off,
and there the toes jutting upward. Flowering guilt
blew open inside him. The soldier twisting his hat
squealed and vaulted the trench's lip, his brow
drilled by a ball, his body toppling in muck,
his head submerged, his last exhale of breath
bubbling ditch water and blood spreading like wine
on a table cloth. No one stirred.

                                    "Come on," he shouted.

"I'm fixing to get a chill. Let's join the line."

"All right," said Oscar. Moses boosted the two men
out of the ditch, flat of their bellies to keep
beneath the fire. When they gained the trenches, they lay
with drenched and filthy comrades and baffled corpses
filling blood puddles, and began the ritual loading
and passing of rifles. They slogged away in gore,
killed and maimed the enemy till darkness settled,
which showed ignescent projectiles illumine clouds
like falling angels, and dropping through, the fuses
plummeted like hurled spears, and along the trench
muzzles burst like stars. At last the firing
relented, the noise of battle replaced by groans
of wounded, pleas and weeping, a young boy begging
for his mother. In all the fights so far, distance
had separated survivors from casualties. Not tonight.

"Oscar, how long you think we were at it?" He removed
his pocket watch.
                      "I'd say near sixteen hours."
Caleb appeared, toting the top of a cartridge
box and a rubber quilt.
                          "Here, we can lie
on these." Oscar, ensconced in mire, was already
sleeping. Moses declared he was going to hunt
his master's kit. Caleb and Garland made
a pallet and covered their faces from drizzling rain,
the groans fading to comprehension's periphery
when Caleb shifted and sat up, clutching his sleeve.

"I can't abide these cries. I will go mad."

"Hold it there, old boy. Hold what you got."
He dug his sack and produced the remaining plug
of blue mass Carl had given him long ago.
He massaged the ball in his hands to make it pliable,
then broke it in two and stopped up Caleb's ears,
who nodded relief and soon was snoring with Oscar.
In dark and waste he watched these men he loved,
thinking it good to love those deserving of love
as an army of maimed and dying cried around him.

May 13, 1864

At 4 A.M. they were roused by Captain Nall,
locating men in his company, shaking their feet,
and whispering,
              "Fellers, they got us another ditch
prepared, five hundred yards to the rear. Move out."
Garland put his arm around Caleb's shoulders,
sloshing through dark, the walk the shortest, hardest
march he'd made, his sinews loose as shucks,
struggling through branch and trunk debris, past knee high
stumps. Reaching the trench, he made no pallet,
just lay himself down in cool, soft muck and slept.
A jangle of kit. He squinted against the light.
He sat up and rubbed his eyes with filthy hands
in a waste of mud and trash and shining puddles.
Oscar was burning the cartridge box he'd slept on.
He joined the group gathered around the fire.

"Morning," said Oscar. "Have a cup of coffee."
Caleb winked. It tasted like boiled socks.
He drank it down, then noticed the old cook table,
the cartridge box, sunk askew in mud,
covered with the laundered cloth, the cutlery washed,
ordered in rows, and affection welled in his throat.
Oscar maintained a Rebel outpost of manliness.
Amid the death throes of the United States,
destruction of lives and livings, houses, stock,
and crops, he rose before others and set his table.
Compared to this, Bateman's table was monstrous.
Oscar forbade the world to taint his character
and made himself a servant of the most wretched,
exhausted, barefoot, filthy, tatterdemalion.
High and low, angel and devil, he served.
The man was a burning bush, a pillar of cloud.

"Boys, I done had me a snoot full of fighting."

"I'm with you now," said Brutus.
                              "Got almighty,
another fight like that, I'll shoot myself,
save the Yankees the trouble." Oscar smiled,

"Snake, I'm like the Presbyterian what fell
down the stairs."
                "How's that?"
                              "He got up, brushed hisself off
and said, *Thank God that's over with.*" Caleb
chuckled a little.
                "I want me a furlough,"

said Buzzard, a stricken alarm loosed in his face.
Patty put his arm around his shoulders.

"Lad, you can want in one hand and spit in the other,
and see which one is liable to fill up first."

"Fellows, did you hear? Stuart was kilt yestiddy."
Several dirty faces scowled, heads shook.

"Who's gone tell General Lee where the Yankees are?"

"I think from here on out, we all gone know."

May 15, 1864

Caleb read to the mess from Garland's testament
in the Book of Acts. He inclined his body aching
from a night of digging, a blessed breeze sighing
in a towering white ash, breathing gentle fire,
gold leaves beat to airy thinness, waving
lazy, a sheet let down from Heaven, he drifting
to slumber, lulled by Caleb's voice and spirit
winds. His name was called. His eyes shot open.
A man was approaching. Garland noticed first
his dangling sleeve and then the horse he led,
then recognized Esau Diggins, a minister's son
from home. Esau offered his left hand in greeting,
pinning the reins against his palm with his thumb.

"Howdy Garland, you dang old cuss. Hit's good

to see you're doing well."

"Good to see you,
Esau. Looks like you've had a run of bad luck."

"Well I's commencing to capture the Yankee army
all by myself up yonder at Stones River,
working for old man Bragg, and I's making out
just like a bob tailed bull in fly time when a dang
old Yankee gunner shot my arm clean off."

"Esau, this is Caleb."

"Glad to know you."

"And this here's Ainey, Snake, Patty, and Moses."

"How're you boys?" Each of them nodded to Esau.

"How's yore momma?"

"She's fat enough to kill.
How's yourn?"

"She's doing fine, the last I heard."

"Well Garland, I brung some news from her. I rode
up here to see my brother Jacob. He's a corporal
in the 26th, and fore I left, I moseyed
out to yore place to see if I could fetch
you anything along from your mom. She give me a couple
a letters and some sundries." He loosened saddlebag straps
and rummaged, producing epistles, socks, dried beef,
muscadine jelly, and a box of Lucifer Matches.

"I'm obliged, Esau."
                    "Warn't nothing to it, and if you boys
let me join your mess tonight, I'll share
a pound of bacon and a jar of rifle knock knee."

"Hog and hooseletter will make you welcome." After mess,
the men were eager to fill their cups, having had
no whiskey ration since last June crossing
the Potomac into Maryland.
                    "Esau, this red eye kicks
like a mule. We're obliged," said Ainey.
                        "You boys are a sight
welcome. I done been sojering in Bragg's army,
and I know what a drink of whiskey means to a feller
living on creek water and worm castle crackers."

"S'at whar you lost yore wing?"
                    "It air a fact.
We'd marched through Murfreesborough and crossed the river,
and I's in Hardee's corps, out on the left.
McCook was entrenched agin us, and come that night,
they built a passel of untended fires, extending
their right, to make us think that we's outnumbered
and scare us back across the river. I don't know
why in hell they thought that plan would work.
We'uns outnumbered every time we fight.
So we spent all blessed night extending our own line,
and come the dawn, up we gets and charged
and not a Yankee soul in front of us,
so we wheeled hard right and crossed old Rosy's T,
chased him near three mile all the way

to the Nashville Turnpike. We's going hark from the tomb,
screaming like devils when I got hit so hard
I's birled around like a bobbin. When I stopped spinning,
I's facing the Rebel charge, my left hand holding
my rifle, my right arm lying on the ground at my feet,
and I'm the damnedest liar what ever straddled
a fence rail if a Yankee didn't shoot me in the ass."
A wave of laughter coursed around the fire.
"I's riled all the way down to my pasted shuts."

"The Yankees, they ain't got no sense a fairness."

"I can't believe that Bragg let Rosy back
into Chattanooga without even knocking his hat off."

"General Bragg had lost the confidence of his men.
If a general ain't got that, he ain't got spit.
Davis let him stay in there too long."
Caleb passed to Garland, who took a pull.
His head revolved with stars. He loved this feeling,
as if the mind, with all its apparatus of worry
and bedevilment, had come unmoored and set to drift
on peaceful currents.
                    "Esau, what sort a rat killing
you up to these days down in the Wiregrass?"

"Well sir, I'm back to farming."
                              "And how's that?"

"Well sir, when I come home all took apart,
I set myself down on a cushion and did some thinking.

Time was I didn't have to think at all,
but now I knew what with all the peas in my cornfield
done spiled on the floor, I's gwine to have to have
a plan. So I took a little army cash
I'd done set by and bought me a brace of Negroes."

"Esau, God forbid this war don't go
yore way, you've melted a considerable sum."

                                            "Well sir,

I've planned fer *contingencies*. I'd had these fellers a week,
and neither one would hit a lick at a snake
without'n I had a peeper clapped right on him.
So I set 'em down and I says, You'uns see here.
You plant my cotton and gather it up and whatever
I make in profit, I'll give each of you five
per cent. And you can use the money however
you want or buy your freedom back—I'll only
charge what you cost me. And after harvest is done,
you can take what work you find and the wages are yours
to employ for comfort or freedom after you pay me
a little for room and board. I ciphered it out
if the South could last two years, then I'd break even,
but Lord have mercy in the past six months, the way
them fellers are going, like blind dogs under a gut wagon,
they'll be free in a year to eighteen months."

"So after a year, you lose yore hired hands."

"Maybe I will. It's a part of the deal I'll take 'em
north if that's what they decide they want.
Charlie might go, but Jim has got him a wife

he wants to buy, and I'm thinking seven per cent
might keep him here. But even if they leave,
I'll recover my investment, and if we lose the war,
these fellers are gwine to still need work to do.
Why shouldn't they stay with me? I treat 'em good."

"Esau, soon you'll have a big white house."

"Nome, never a big house, but that don't matter
none. The house what I got suits me fine,
and I'm easy in my mind with how I'm getting by
in the world. When I was coming along, I always
worked with my daddy, and me and him, we managed.
And I'd a never considered buying no slave
if he hadn't up and died and me lost an arm.
But I found out what people say about slaves
is just a load of bunkum. I've gotten to like
them fellers. All they want to do is look out
for they selves. They ain't a man alive who ain't
like that. And them two is smart. I didn't have
to explain what five per cent was, I'll tell you now.
The whole time we was talking I could see
the numbers flying behind they eyes. Them two
can figure the dollar of cotton per acre in a heartbeat.
Jim is a fine carpenter, and Charlie can read
the Bible good as me. And I'll tell you what,
I admire a feller what can improve hisself,
you think how hard it was for them to learn
anything with obstacles a slave has got in his way.
I'll say it here and now, them people's got smarts
just like any other lot of folks,

and when they got a interest, they can be
industrious as any other man. And come
to human feelings, shoot, they ain't no different
than me or you. Hell, it's true as anything.
Why Garland, yore momma wouldn't have growed the cotton
to weave a hanky if hit warn't for Levi. That feller
has shown a right fit sense of obligation,
good as any white man I could name."
His mind adrift on the pop skull's easy current,
Garland felt his unfettered spirit wafting
ahead of the wind's gusting, breathing forest
music. But his sluggish brain catching up
to the talk, snagged on the one word *obligation*.
That was a strange idea. He was pleased to know
that Levi was being kind to his mother, but that word,
obligation, what an unusual way
to convey his meaning. He thought the obligation
passed from Mr. Pinkerton to his father. What other
obligation could there be? From Levi?

"What sort of obligation might Levi have?"
He didn't hear a challenge in his voice, had not
intended one. He could barely make out Esau,
a shadow limned by a scatter of wind-burnished embers.

"I just meant—don't you—I didn't mean to imply
anything irregular, Garland. I mean to say
that Levi was showing some honor to be a slave
is all. I'm a little whiskey tickled, shoveling
my words like a field hand slinging marl."
                                        "But you said

384

obligation. I just"—
                    "Come along, Garland.
Esau meant no harm. He says he didn't.
Let's we'uns let"—
                    "Absolutely no harm, Garland.
I got nothing at all but respect for you and yours."
Esau was standing. He could tell from his voice's height.

"Better get going anyhow."
                    "Esau, it's late"—

"I ain't seen Jacob yet. Gentlemen, my thanks
for a pleasant evening and thanks especially for what
you men are doing for our country. God Bless you all."
He made to rise, but his sense of balance staggered off
three different ways, and he fell on his ass.
                                    "Esau"—
But Esau was already mounted and spurring his horse,
judging from violent oaths, beseeching the almighty
to damn in exquisite fashions the horse and rider
treading bedded Rebels. Caleb was wrestling
fits of laughter.
              "Well, old Garfish, I reckon
Esau sold you back your birthright for some porridge."

"Damnation Caleb, what the hell do you mean?"

"I reckon I mean Esau knows something he thought
you knew. But you don't." Another snorting convulsion.
"What he knows is the porridge. What you don't
is the birthright. Or maybe it's the other way around."

385

Garland looked up at the twinkling plowman's outline,
plodding his row through vast, unfathomed darkness.

"Caleb, you too smart for your own damn good.
Or anybody's else's." But Caleb was passed out snoring.
Levi's obligation flummoxed him.
He decided first chance he got, he'd write to Carl.

May 19, 1864

"Master Garland, you've acquired your first slave.
Scrape up nineteen more, you can quit this war."

"I didn't acquire him. He acquired me.
When his master died, I tried to part ways, and he said,
I gots to have me a white man. You is mine."

"So what's your servant going to do with you?"

"Can't say what his plans are, but I know mine."

"What's that?"
                "To act before his master's mistress
sends for him." The prospect sobered Caleb.
"I always regarded slavery in a casual way,
as other people's indulgence in a system of greed
and cruelty. That's all it is, and everybody knows it.
And now a servant's acquired me, I am confirmed
in my first opinion. Everything he does for my comfort,

discomfits me."
        "I was just now thinking how sad
I would be to see him leave. Since Moses came,
our camp is clean, our clothes are laundered fresh,
and Lord that man can forage. If there's a yard bird
on a farm for fifty miles what scratches her way
to an inch of the property line, Moses' hand
reaches out of the bushes and seizes her neck.
During all the war, we've never eaten so well.
How quickly comfort opens the door to wrong."

"But there's another thing that weighs my conscience."

"And what is that?"
        "That under my care he should die
for the privilege of having lived a slave is repugnant.
I can't stomach it."
        "What are you going to do?"

"I'm yet to talk to Moses, and nothing can be done
without his cooperation." Caleb lowered
his voice.
        "Are you going to try and set him free?"

"It's only a matter of getting him through the lines.
The question is will he go? There's a peck of slave
in every man that chains him to familiar woes."

"Please be careful. You're breaking the law of man
the money making animal, and laws involving
money are ones most strictly observed and executed."

"We both know there are laws and there are laws."

"Don't get me wrong. God in Heaven is with you,
but men on earth are not, and they're to hand."
Moses sauntered up with an armload of fuel.

"Hello gentlemens."
             "Hello Moses."
                  "Say,
Moses, you've rustled a lovely chord of wood,
where'd you go to find it?"
            "Never mind, Moses,
don't tell us where you got it." Garland rummaged
his sack. "Here Moses, have a cracker."
               "Thankee,
massuh." Garland shot him a look. "I means suh."
Moses looked around to ensure their privacy
and reached in his pocket, producing two brown eggs,
smiling. "They is biled." Caleb was transported.

"I'll swany, Moses, if you're not an angel of light—
I love boiled eggs."
        "Have you had yourself one, Moses?"

"Yassuh. When I wents"—
        "No, Moses, don't tell us
where you got them."
        "Now Mister Garland, all's
I did was stumble on a guinea hen nest in de woods.
De Lord is goot to Moses. At's all hit is."

"Moses is good to Moses. These eggs are too big
for a guinea fowl. They was laid by a Dominicker hen."

"I swany, Mistuh Garland, what a man say
when a silly yart birt leaves her farm to lay
in dee woods? You can't most always sometimes tell."

May 21, 1864 to the North Anna

Spindled fog, a ghost river's flowing, frozen
above the Po, the way a housewife shakes
a bed sheet above a mattress, rippling and hovering.
The regiment was stripping down. He stuffed his sack
with neatly folded tatters. The men milled
like a flock of geese, their necks burned plum, sexes
wiry, buttocks pale.
      "Heyar now fellers,
I done shucked down to the bare nubbin." The speaker
was James Allen, a fresh fish, conscripted
after Spotsylvania, his forehead a polished awl handle,
and he talked a lot. The veterans found him intolerable,
who thought it proper a new galoot should go
full chisel a while before he started holding
forth on the war's prosecution. He'd had some trouble
in his first mess and was reassigned to Garland's.
He'd told a veteran grousing about the weevils
in his sop, that the government, after all, was beset
as the rest of the country and was doing its best. The soldier
stood and shucked his blouse off, revealing a row
of knarred white scars, speckling chest and shoulders.

"Now listen to me you gotdamned cotton valley
shit kicker. Ater *you* git shot the *first* time,
then you can tell me to shut my chittlin hole up.
But till then shut your own and keep it shut."
It delighted him to imagine that rebuke.
James was the only man speaking, squinting at fog.

"Naked I came, naked I cross the river.
Blessed be the name of the Lord."
                                        "I'm glad you ain't
a man what charges God foolishly."
                                        "No, Preacher,
I only charge Yankees foolishly. Who'd a thunk
a man would find himself in the public way
amidst a thousand men in a state of nature?"

"A difficult thing to see coming, sholey," said Preacher.

"Sholey a difficult thing to see," said Snake.
The order forward, a thousand bare feet shuffled.
The fog obfuscated the farther bank; the ranks,
two abreast, broke the skin of the river.
Wading waist deep in cloud, holding their kit
above their heads, they vanished. He stepped from the bank,
gasped as the water shocked his groin, tip toeing
at the depth to keep his head above the water,
feeling colder currents swirl his legs
and tug his body down river, were it not for the silty
bottom, receiving his feet and holding, he shifting
forward to break the suction in bogging progress.
Mid-river his vision cast off in a depthless plane,

an exquisitely lovely emptiness, a heavenly ambush.

"Move along, cousin. This here river is cold."
After a headlong drive down a railway cut,
they were put in line. He joined a passel of soldiers
gathered round Yancy.
                              ". . .Mars has got us in two
long lines open like a hinge, frame wing and door wing."
He touched his fingertips in a V. "The hinge knuckle
rests on the bank of the North Anna River at the only
spot where that bank's higher than the other, and Mars
has placed our guns there. If Grant should have to move
to reinforce one corps with another, he'll have
to cross the river, hike a long way round
to stay out of range of our guns, and cross the river
again. While we'uns got interior lines
and can reinforce from line to line in a spate,
like a feller tossing an apple hand to hand."

"Folks in this hyer army's always thinking,"
said Buzzard. "We'uns may march like Moses, barefoot,
hongry, and nekkid, but by God, when the fight comes on,
we're sitting pretty with a box of forty dead men."

"We always lacking ever'thin, but shots and powder,
but If'n I'm a gonna do without,
I'll sholey takes the bullets."
                              "Hog," said Saxon,
"you can wire Josiah Gorgas your sincere gratitude,
and when you do, ask him to send some rations."

May 23, 1864 North Anna River

Mordecai ordered the men to pile their sacks.
He filed past throwing his own on top of the others.

"We need to post a guard," said Mordecai. He spoke up,

"Moses can do it. It's work more suitable to him."

"Very good. Stand here, boy. Do you know how to shoot
this rifle?"
    "Yassuh, I's sholey kin."
            "If anyone
disturbs this kit while we're away, you defend it
on *my* authority."
      "Massuh can count on Moses."
Mordecai said,
     "Now men, we've got a Yankee
feint across the river, a few companies
at most. We gonna thrash 'em back the way
they come. Light work for the Eighth. He nodded to Papa.

"All right boys, git yer dance cards," said Yancy.
What a relief that Yancy had come to himself
and resumed his place as the highest ranking private,
always keeping them one step ahead of orders.
He called to Garland and coming on he was dogged
by a new recruit, a boy too young for whiskers,
loping like a blue tick pup and Yancy showing
a rare irritation, "Son, don't bust a gut.
You gwine to get your chance to be a big bug."

The boy, chastened, hung his head.

        "Don't want
to be no big bug, Pap. I want to be
like you." He put a hand on the boy's shoulder.

"Do something for me, son."

       "Yes sir. You name it."

"Choose a better man to be your measure."
The boy began a protest, but Yancey stopped him.
"Josh, go stand by Buzzard. You and me
are gwine to go in together." The boy was elated
and hurried off. "He ain't no more than a chit."

"Seems like some sons do need heroes, Papa."
Yancy smiled wistful, offered his hand.

"You a good man, Garland. It's been a honor to know you."

"I owe you a lot, Papa; you've taught me well."

"I got a note here. Hit's sealed and addressed. If aught
should happen to me, you'll see it gets to Sally?"

"I don't believe in premonitions, Yance,
but I'll take care of your letter, you have my word."
Yancy shrugged,

     "War's a dangerous business."
Garland took his place in line near Caleb.

"Look, there's Mars." Behind them atop a knoll

the general sat his horse, surrounded by staff.
Next to Lee was Hill, his bodily posture,
even from such a distance, conveying morbidity.
In the brunt of sunlight, Lee's gray mount looked pale.
The general peered through glasses across the river.
The men were grim but confident. All they had
to do was brush away a Yankee detachment.
Nall drawled out *Forward march!* and they were off.
The colors surged ahead of the line, carried
by a fellow—he knew his name—Canavan, an Irishman,
he toting the heavy pole unarmed, the rippling
banner snapping, making straight for the trees.
They were covering rapid ground, his feet whisking
the grasses, stems of cardinal flower thrashing
his knees, the tree line looming, the Yankees holding
fire, letting them come. The longer the silence,
the greater his apprehension. Now there were swatches
of blue behind the stones and trunks, and a bloom
of smoke rolled out, the instant sizzle of balls,
and crackle of discharges scoring the racked air.
Canavan spins and falls, a soldier running
behind him drops his rifle and gathers the flag.
Garland grabs his musket as he passes, kneels
and fires, tossing it away and resuming the charge,
labored breath, jarring footfall, and knock
of pulse, all jacking up his blood. The Rebel
banner unfurls once more in the van. He looks
to the left and right. The Eighth is rushing disaster.
What lies ahead is not a few mere companies
making a feint, but at least a brigade. A boiling
of breech smoke, bullets stinging and swarming, one

ball striking his elbow, thrilling the bone, the volley
gleaning so many, the soldier nearest him
is thirty yards away. The remaining men
begin to drop. He goes to earth and glances
around, a ways in front, a convenient corpse.
Knees and elbows, he clambers up and hunkers
for cover, rolling the body over. It's Snake,
not dead but hurt, his eyes shining, tracking
cheeks through a layer of powder burn, one filthy
hand pressing his belly, staunching blood
and agony. With the other he places his rifle barrel
inside his mouth, locking his eyes in Garland's
to ask the question and force the answer, lest pity
intercede, prolonging torment. On the lonely field
Garland braces his shoulder against the stock,
trigger pressure firm against his finger
and cannot face the next transmogrifying instant
so closes his eyes.
                        "I'm sorry Eugene." He pulls
the trigger. Transfixing horror so crowded out
the battle noise, his hearing recorded only
the hammer clap the dud percussion cap.
Again Snake's eyes are driving forward, to firm
Garland's resolve by declaring his own. He unbuttons
his pocket, shakes out a handful of caps, and the other
upsets them in the trembling act of taking one,
placing it, cocking the hammer. Again he closes
his eyes, seized by tremors as if he were led
to his own execution and crying in indignation,
the rifle's report swallowing up his clamor
outward in reverberations and tapering echoes

beyond the trees, the enemy line, the river.
The tear of musketry rushes over him,
the sight of Snake's slack face, his vacant eyes.
He sprawls a terrapin half circle, starts
the arduous belly crawl in retreat, dragging
his rifle by the muzzle, inching the hard scrabble earth,
zing and hizz of fire pressing him down.
He craned to see the tree line. Leaves were still.
The breeze had died away—a lucky stroke
as rifle smoke would hang in settling swells,
obscuring the enemies' vision. Two men were up
and running. He raised a little, saw them gain
the wood but quelled the impulse to follow suit,
committing himself to eating dust, to his slithering
struggle. Fifty more yards, beneath the mortal
warp and woof stretched tight as a winding sheet,
he entered a ravine, covering him to the tree line,
his skin registering the change of air, from sun
to luxuriant shade. A limestone boulder rose
from brush, the stone's face pocked with white depressions
of pulverized dust. He crawled behind it, exhaustion
dulling terror's receding tremors, bleeding
out of his limbs. A body fell down beside him,
Caleb sat bowing his head, a stream of blood
fantastically bright coursing his face from his hair line.
Joyfulness flooded his heart like mighty waters,
but all he was able to do was grip Caleb's sleeve.
Moses left his post and knelt between them.

"Let's look at yo hurt, massuh." His hands were beefy,
his touch delicate as a midwife's, dabbing the blood

and winding Caleb's head with lint and bandage,
he wincing nonetheless.

     "My head. Dear God."

"Massuh lucky he still gots a head."
Musket racket died away behind them.
"I's could use mo lint to hep these other mens."

"Wait here," he said and went to the pile of sacks,
 returning with Caleb's, his own, and Snake's, which he opened
first. He handed Moses all the lint
and bandages, who went away to bind more wounds.
He rummaged a demijohn of whiskey. Snake didn't drink.
He must have kept the stimulant for medicinal use.
There were books, a pocket Testament and a small volume,
titled in gold, *The Sayings of George Washington.*
"Hit by a ball?"

    "The first volley."

      "You're lucky.
If you'd been on your feet for the second volley,
you'd done gone up the chimbley for sure."

        "How many
you think we lost?"

    "I don't know, but we sho
got cut up bad." As they spoke the underbrush rustled
as men came crawling back underneath the fire,
tearing their way through vine tangle and panting.
"Have a snort of the good creature, compliments
of Snake."

   "Why'd you raid his sack?"

       "Snake

don't need a sack anymore."
                    "Oh, I see."
Caleb took the demijohn, "Smells like pine top."
He proposed a toast to Snake when Josh appeared,
holding his musket high like a shield and weeping.

"Them Yankee sonsabitches done kilt Papa."

May 24, 1864 North Anna

A drowsy rataplan jarring nerves and dawn
caressing soldiers like a young wife's blushing fingers.
The men in companies assembled before their tents,
an ordered cornfield in chill November gloaming
when a winter storm has bent the hollow stalks.

"Good morning men. I'm Lt. Col. Emrich,
standing for Col. Royston, who was killed yesterday.
Boys, that charge was plain bad luck for the Eighth.
We run through pure hell fire and lost a bunch
of our friends. But the dead will not have died in vain
who live in our admiration, the hearts of family,
and the Master's love. I'm not too good with words,
I think that's about as close as I can come
to saying my respects for all the heroes we lost."
Captain Nall stepped out before his company.

"Fellers, yestiddy we was pissing nails.
But today we're back, standing up here like men.
The Yankees give us a drubbing sure as hell's

got brimstone, but we got grit to hide 'em again.
If they'd been less than a corps, we'd gotten a rise
out'en them bastards, give 'em the old sockdollager
right in the puss. Put dollar signs in they eyes.
But a bear is just too big for a badger to swaller.
But don't you fret. We gwine to put on a patch
and buckle up; we're better men, fip for fip.
They gwine to lick they calves over next tight scratch.
They gwine to grab that Rebel badger by the lip
and howl. Them Yankee dogs'll have their day.
We'll put a twist in 'em. At's all I got to say."
Now Rice, the new Lieutenant, stepped forward to read
the names of dead and wounded from Co. H.

"Cobini, Eugene, killed.
Dunn, D. W., wounded, discharged.
Goodman, J. Yancey, killed.
Harwell, Caleb, wounded.
Mordecai, Enoch, killed
Pearce, William, wounded, discharged.
Stroud, E. D., wounded, discharged.
Titus, Benjamin, killed.

Now men, General Lee has set a trap
for Grant, and he needs the Eighth to help him spring it.
A decisive victory here might end our struggle.
Men of the Eighth, we've suffered a vicious blow.
We've suffered blows before and still our courage
is undaunted. Yesterday our noble fellows relinquished
life and limb for all that we hold dear;
now Heaven bequeaths to us their glorious sacrifice

to see their deaths will mean their highest honor."
Come to his climax, Rice looked over his shoulder
to see if the colonel were showing signs of approval,
only to find his attention directed elsewhere.
A shadow darkened his face. They marched to the line.

"Top of the morning to you, Mister Garland."

"Patty, don't you ever get the blues?"

"And why should I be pulling a long face now?
I've survived the japes of the Devil and the angry looks
of Yankees, and here is Patty, bless me, to do
more mischief yet till the day me bullet finds
its billet."
                    "Have any word about Brutus or Critter?"

"Aye, I have. The surgeons had to divest
the Critter of his right wing, the bone being shattered.
And our friend the Brute got four of his fingers shorn
from his left hand. Seeing as how they survive
the erysipelas and the gangrenous, each will mend
to be a greater no count than he ever was,
and so the army perfects the work of our Lord."

"Patty, how old was Snake?"
                              "Nineteen, I allow."

"And Brutus?"
                    "The Brute was twenty-one, and don't even
ask of Critter's age, for I can't say."

Patty crossed his arms and closed his eyes,
"Rouse me, lads, if the war should start again?"

"All right, Patty." Ainey and Oscar leaned
on the parapet.
                "It's a right gorgeous day," said Oscar.
"I can't remember when last the birds were chirruping."

"Did you see us at roll call?" asked Ainey. "I bet we've lost
near half the blessed regiment."
                        "Half at least."

May 31, 1864

Evening after mess and Garland headed
to the creek to do some laundry. He'd made a show
of ordering Moses along with pail and soap.
When they got to the stream, Garland started the washing.

"If Mistuh Garland gone to do the work,
what he bring Moses fer?"
                  "I want to talk."
He was working one of Moses's shirts in the bucket.
Moses looked wistful at the suds. Garland stared
at him, but the Negro would not meet his eye.

"'Bout whut?"
            "What do you think of the war, Moses?"

"He thank you can't most always sometimes tell."

"What do you think the outcome will be?"

                                        "Lord knows,
but Moses don't. Don't concern him no how."

"You know the South is losing, don't you."

                                        "Don't know
no such."

                "You're shoveling horse shit, Moses. Tell me
what you think."

                        "He thinks you white folks done
scared up a passel of trouble—on account of us niggers."

"Goddamnit. Stop insulting me, Moses."

                                        "Whut,
Mistuh Cain?" He rose, stepped over the bucket,
shoved the hulking Negro backwards to put him
in range and threw a right to his midriff— "Hey,
whut chew"—then landed a harder left, his punches
recoiling from Moses' muscled belly like striking
a sack full of grain, and then he brought his right fist
back to land a blow on his big darky face,
and Moses struck him, he seeing only a blur
of motion, a stunned blindness, felt his back
hit the ground, his limbs sprawling, and a dull throb
above his eye. "Oh my dear sweet Lawd."
A pure joy broke in his heart and he laughed out loud.

"Moses, I knew you were a man I could rile.
Would you help me up, please?"

                                "Mistuh Cain, is you trying
to get Moses in trouble?"

                        "Yes, in more trouble

than you've ever known. Any day Miss Caroline
will get a letter with news of her husband's death,
and then she'll write a letter back, inquiring
about her property. You'll have to return to her."

"When Missus sends fo me then I gits home."

"But you've got a choice."
                                        "I gots a choice?"
                                                          "Yes.
Mister Lincoln's proclamation makes
you free. All you have to do is pass
the lines. It's the easiest Jordan to cross they is."

"Then I be free?"
                  "Yes."
                                    "Free to do whut?
Go hongry? Be conscripted?"
                                        "Well, I guess.
It's the same damn freedom everybody else has."
Now Moses was looking at him, his eyes severe.

"How you get me over dar?"
                                        "You know,
about once a week, I go on picket? Well sometimes
the Yanks and Rebs are standing close, and we chatter
back and forth. And once in a while, we visit
each other. We would raise a white flag and call
a truce, then go across."
                                    "Mistuh Cain,
Moses don't wants to be no nigger or contraband,

I wants to be a man. You reckon dem Yankees
gone let me be a man?"
                              "The only person
who can make you a man is you. The Yankees have
their interest, ain't no doubt. You're useful to them,
a part of how they plan to win this war.
But they'll give you a little freedom, and freedom is such
that a man can do a lot with just a little.
The choice is yours. You think about it and let
me know what you decide. Here," he kicked
the bucket toward him, "wash your own damn clothes."

June 1, 1864

"Dig and dodge, dig and dodge, my God,
I've had a snoot full of digging and a craw full of marching."
Oscar chuckled,
                    "Well, you gwine to love this,
Garland. Orders are to move out—tonight."
He spaded his shovel in earth. A murderous volition
seized his will, a hawk's talons gripping
a hare's spine. He quelled the impulse to swear,
fearing he wouldn't stop once he started.
Rice cocked an eye on him.
                              "Col. Kershaw
will begin the march at two o'clock in the morning.
Remaining brigades will come out of line in order.
We're going to join with Hoke and fill the line
between the Old Church Road and Gaines Mill.
We going to bull into little Phil and give him

a big push. Let's get our kit together."
Just after midnight, to Garland's surprise and delight,
Caleb returned. Tents were struck, and men
lay about on blankets. He could just make out the bandage
around his head.
        "How was Company Q?"

"Exquisite." Caleb sat beside his blanket,
began unloading his sack.
        "What chew got?"

"Walking back, I stopped by an old man's farm
at Gaines' Mill and bought some buttered biscuits,
milk, and some nice strained honey." He'd poured the milk
in a spare canteen. "Have a biscuit and honey,
Moses."
        "I thank you massuh."
                "Thanks, Caleb.
This is grand. We got no rations today."

"Here you go, Oscar, have a biscuit."
        "Thanks."
The biscuits' centers were spongy and sweet with butter.
They spooned the honey on and savored tingling
sweetness of transformed clover blossoms and washed
all down with gulps of fresh milk clotted with cream,
enjoying the pleasure of taking pleasure with friends.

"How's yer noggin? Did you manage to get any rest?"

"Hospital's not the greatest place for rest.

For so many boys, dying is noisy business.
The cries assault one's nerves." The silence filled
with rhythms of hooves and wheels and teamsters' curses.
"Did you ever see a man with erysipelas?"

"There's an erysipelas ward at the Richmond hospital.
We'uns are moving out at two a.m.
You need to sleep." But Caleb was wooden as a cigar store
Indian, so Garland unrolled his blanket, stowed
the victuals, lay next to his friends and drifted off
while Moses rested against a stump, watching.

June 2, 1864

Dawn, damnation, courtesy of being kicked
awake, a drum beat, Rice growling,
                                        "Boots
and saddles," and soon he stood in a long column
of ragged shadows flowing down the road,
emerging from darkness behind and vanishing ahead
into dark, green scent of spring rain redolent on air,
and heat lightning battle flashes across the heavens.
Kershaw's division was leading. They approached their new
lines in a couple of hours, the engineers
and gangs of slaves busy gouging trenches.
He reckoned they must have marched past three or four miles
of Negroes throwing spoil. When the march came close
to the trench, he saw their white eyes, disembodied,
weird. One man, plying a shovel, sang,
A rock-uh muh soul in the bosom of Abraham,

the darkness replying, *Oh rock-uh mah soul,*
the strike of pick ax marking laboring time.
Company H stepped down in the dank trench,
files of crepuscular soldiers floating past them.
One spoke to a Negro,

                "Dig at hole deep, boy.
I don't be wanting to git my ass shot off."

"Yassuh, massuh, we don't want that be happenin'."
Garland and Caleb exchanged subdued amusement.
Then a commotion, a pair of voices, each raising
the other's ante. With nothing else to do,
they walked to the knot of slouching shadows and gestures
of weak gray light to see what the chafe was about.
He saw Col. Kershaw, had seen him first in the Wilderness,
speaking heated words to a man sumptuous
in silk accoutrements and holding what appeared
to be a giant plume in his hand. He supposed
a hat was under it somewhere.

                    "Sir, I've served
two terms in Congress. I'm accustomed to leading fights
on and off the floor."

                "Colonel, making
speeches and making war are enterprises so"—
He noticed the Congressman looking around to find
men gathered to swell the crowd to sufficient size.

"I must remind you, Colonel Kershaw, that I
outrank you by six months." Kershaw's eyes
flashed the way a knife edge, after slow,
slicing strokes on oil stone and the swarf wiped clean,

deflects a keen, thin light.
> "Very well.
The offensive is yours, *sir*." Kershaw's teeth
were gritted so tight, his words might have burst them to flinders.
As he stalked away, the other raised his voice.

"I think true men from the state of South Carolina
can whip a rabble of Yankees any time."
Peeling cheers and hats rose over the brigade.
The colonel made his hat to roost on his head.
"Captain, place five companies in battle order.
Lieutenant, bring me Sweetheart." He strode away
to form his line, junior officers in tow.

"'Ho in bloody 'ell is that?" Malone
snorted.
> "I heared his name was Kite."
>> "Could be—
'at a mighty long tail, even tied to a colonel."

"Excuse me, sir; his name is Colonel Keitt,
the Congressman-soldier from the state of South Carolina.
He'll show you a thing or two 'bout handling Yankees."
Malone turned and, seeing the boy, the gray
overcast of war's boredom was pierced with rays
of opportunity.
> "Colonel Keitt, indeed!
An impetuous Palmetto man, first in secession!
Now laddies, there being no doubt of the colonel's bravery,
I 'ave to say I find him a *wee* bit wanting
in martial acumen." He reached in his pocket, his voice

all lush and meadowy, as if he were wooing a virgin.
"Patty has fifty crisp shin plasters what says
    your colonel won't live to ride past those two bushes,
    there on the right." The young men looked aghast,
    their gumption thwarted. "Laddies, no caviling now,
    it's the hallowed honor of South Carolina in question."
One among them, with eyes of blue stained glass,
    a thin beard framing a delicate cleft of jaw,
    jammed his hand in his pocket up to his elbow.

"Here's five—hit's all I got—on Colonel Keitt."
With that first impulse, all the other boys
    were full in, producing bills or coin,
    and handing them over to Patty, a mercatorial
    joy in his eyes. One boy unfolded a wallet,
    his thumb fanning some bills, chose one, and offered
    it up, turning from the group green with sickness.

"There's for honor—the rest I'm sending home.
My wife and boy is hungry." When he walked past,
    Garland grabbed him above the elbow and whispered,

"If you survive the first volley, fall down,
    and stay down, you got me?" The boy nodded, entranced.
Malone announced the bet to other takers,
    and a few veterans guffawed, causing the raw
    troops consternation. Other veterans who had kept
    themselves mum, allowing Patty's machinations
    full scope, began to revile that thing the veteran
    could not abide, the posture of empty courage,
    those survivors of hard lessons, whose only value

was the hard lesson, arbiter of men and boys.
One came up and slapped a private's back.

"Hit's mighty white uh you to see that this here
worthy Irishman is gonna be drunk when you're gone."
Another veteran sang out,
                              "Sold to the Dutch,
and now the dumb shits's giving away they screw!"
Keitt arranged his line and took his place
in the van. The boy he had warned looked back and caught
his eye, fear wild in his visage. The colonel saluted
with avian flourish, called out encouragements, gilded
snatches on women's honor, Southern soil,
settled his plumage and pointed the way with his saber.
The one word *charge* carried a little ways,
and he found himself regarding the general's mind,
drunk with command's power, the portent sky,
coveting the guns' historical thunder, that glory,
that thrill of staking one's all on a single act.
But Garland's eyes had had their education.
The ground declined for several hundred yards
against a tree line thick with undergrowth,
not bushes, however, but cut boughs concealing infantry.
The perpendicular where creek growth met this line,
sunny as a fence corner, no doubt disguised an ambush.
With guidons fluttering above their ordered heads—
he'd never seen the light of day so stark
in spite of lowering clouds smothering sun—
the line surged, Keitt impeccably dressed,
Sweetheart, a sorrel, picking her forelegs high.
He didn't even come close to a hundred yards

of the two bushes. Sheridan's cavalry opened
with their carbines, a precipitate, scathing fire, striking
the colonel too many times to count, raising him
out of the saddle, the slack corpse poised, then coming
down on the mare's haunches, which bounced it up
in the air, whirling a sprawling cartwheel and landing
in a loosened heap as Sweetheart, dragging her reins,
cantered back to the lines. A covey of laughter
flushed from the Rebel ditch. Malone now stood
by Garland, having risen to watch the charge. He clucked
his tongue.
       "Poor South Carolina; too small
to be a country, too large to be an insane
asylum." The veterans now were calling out,

"White bread and buttermilk."
            "Got to get me
one of 'em purdy hats."
      "Parlor sojers!"
The green troops, seeing their colonel thus dispatched,
stopped and milled, presenting convenient targets.
Some boys screamed when they were shot, some cringed
and dug bare handed for cover, the Federals dropping
them with withering fire; but the quarry's mass,
swift of foot, came surging back, striking
through a wall of hoots and jeers, veterans ducking
as they leapt the trench and kept on running.
          "God awfullest
display of Confederate manhood I ever did see."

"On to Richmond, fellers, on to Richmond!"

The boys who had their money riding on honor
of colonel and state, were abashed to see their fellows,
having just run forward for glory, run back for their lives.
The soldier whose wife and boy were hungry now lay
a sprawling corpse. The rout just happened to gather
around Malone, cutting a rasher of tobacco.
Not looking up, he addressed the blown and bloodied.

"Them Spencer carbines have got a pretty range
at two hundred blessed yards. A decent Yank
can load on a Sunday and fire the rest of the week.
And for marksmanship? Well, I suppose our friends
in blue have proved themselves. Consider it lads,
before you let as warm a patriot as Kite
work you up for another tight scratch with the Yanks."
Garland looked at the boy with the blue john eyes,
wide with defeat and fear, words for *knowledge*.
He hoped he'd learned a lesson. Patty spat.
Rain began to fall in dangling sheets.

June 3, 1864 Cold Harbor

Infantry stirring in the dawn's early light,
he raised his eyes up over the head log slow
and saw the line was shallow, less imposing
than the one at Spotsylvania, and began to divine
its deadly genius. Lee wanted the Yankees to come.
Traverses and ditches emerged from the landscape's features,
each spur and knoll and slope bristling with rifles.
A distant scrubbing footfall, the deep chested *huzzah*,

his gut wound like a watch spring, in rolling waves
along the trenches their muskets leveled. He sighted
a column of blue, knowing the order to fire
was long in coming, breezes parting grasses
in gusty chevrons, the sky milky with summer.
Nall was behind them.
                              "All right boys, we gone
beat the Devil and carry a rail, I swany.
Aim. . .fire!" The earthworks erupted flames.
"Now souse right into 'em, fellas, go full chisel!"
He put his bead on a Federal raising his rifle,
but before he pulled the trigger, dust fogged out
in three quick puffs from his bobtailed jacket, his kepi
spun from his head. He sighted another Yankee,
and watched as two puffs steamed like winter breath
from blue fabric and the man dropped. They kept on
coming at the double quick with icy courage.
Artillery coughed, projecting gargantuan voices.
A coarse and rolling pall of murk was churning
toward the field, and sometimes moments passed
before a man emerged. A breeze shunted
smoke aside. Soldiers were milling about,
using stumps for cover or stacks of dead.
Federal fire slackened and so did Confederate,
but still they tensed in the ditch, regarding droves
of corpses in drawn triangles, at the apex of each
a man of unquestioned courage. On a ten acre swath
every corpse was touching another corpse.

"Good God in Heaven. How long could that have lasted?"
Oscar produced his watch.
                              "The fight commenced

413

about four thirty. I'd say we's shooting eight minutes."
From under the head log they stared at the broken charge,
hillocks crawling with wounded. Two hundred yards,
Union infantry hunkered, an officer occasionally
scampering amidst their ranks like a terrified muskrat,
and the Federals stepping up fire, a dense hedgerow
of cloud obscuring the field.
                              "Appears the Yanks
has got a belly full of assault," said Ainey.

"Hell, who can blame 'em," Garland said.

"Not me."
            "Not me neither."
                                "Sweet Lord, look at 'em."
That night the Yankee troops pulled back, dug in,
staying in musket range. He made to go
give aid to the wounded when Caleb and Oscar, sticking
close, put in to go and slipped the trench.
They found their way by groans of wounded men,
he gathering spare canteens to offer the living.
The others followed suit, then Caleb whispered,

"Garland, Oscar, get on over here!"
He stood above a face down corpse, pointing
to his back between his shoulder blades, then knelt,
unfastened something from the blouse, handed a note
to Garland, who turned his shoulder to the moon, unfolded
the slip of paper and read aloud,
                                    "My name
is George Burgess. I lived in Upton, Vermont."

"Look. Every Yankee pinned a note
like that to his blouse. Every blessed one."

"Jesus, Mary, and Joseph," muttered Oscar.

"They knew what they were facing. They knew our defenses
better than their officers."
                              "You think them arrogant
sons a bitches even rode our lines?"

"I just can't see it, Oscar, and order such
a lunatic charge?" The three men squatted by a corpse.
Caleb pilfered his sack, producing a diary.
Oscar shook his head.
                         "They had forsaken
the vainest hope. What brave fellows they are."

"God bless the Yankee dead. God bless their souls.
And shame on their country if they forget these men."

"Shame on them indeed. The truly dead
are those who have been forgotten," Oscar said.
Caleb offered the soldier's diary, opened
to the final scribbled entry. Garland read,
June 3rd. Cold Harbor. I was killed.

June 4, 1864

Next night the three went out again.
                              "Behold,

angels of Yankee mercy in the east," said James.
Ignoring him, they climbed from the trench.

                                "It's strange
they've made no truce for the wounded," said Oscar.

                                       "I reckon
that means they'll be a passel of men to help."
They dropped their voices. The fact there was no truce
meant the field was dangerous even at night.
He followed throbbing murmurs to a man and poured
some water in his mouth. He drank a long while,
and when he had to stop to catch his breath,
Garland saw he was weeping.

                         "This is the end
of me."

        "Not at all, my friend. What it is
is root hog or die. Determine you're going to live.
We'll have a truce tomorrow; your people will come."
As he spoke, the invalid's eyes roved over his uniform.

"I feel it somehow. This is the end of me,"
slipping his hand into Garland's and holding it. "I thank you
for bringing me water. I don't hate you."

                            "I don't
hate you. I hate this war and want it over."

"May you live to see it end."

                  "And so may you.
Your people will come tomorrow. You will see."
He grabbed a handful of canteen straps and moved
away, and saw on the verge where his eyes were just
able to penetrate the dark Oscar standing

transfixed. Caleb approached, and he went to join them.
A husky Union soldier was stretched on the ground.
His well soled boots were splayed outward, his rifle
lay across his lap, his arms drawn up
before him, his hands poised, fingers closed
against his palms as if he'd just performed
some delicate task like shaking a dinner cloth out
to cover a table. Almost imperceptibly, the chest
rose up and down, a faint gargle in the breath,
which cast forth white coagulated strings, piling
a sticky beard about his face. A hole
had augered his temples, gray matter oozing and bubbling
in gouts on either side of the sufferer's head.

"How could a man with a head wound live so long?"
asked Oscar.
      "Christ have mercy."
            "I don't know,"
said Caleb. "Someone ought to end his misery."
Caleb's face was cast in dark astonishment
as if he'd heard another person utter
the words he'd spoken. He too was shocked but thought,
It's done for mules and horses, why not men?
In the thin moonlight, Oscar's face was also
pallid.
      "I'm sorry, friends. I can't do it."

"No need to explain anything, Oscar. I'll do it."

"No," said Caleb, interposing himself between him

and the ruined man.
                    "But Caleb, I have" —
                                        "Now listen.
Ever since you came to the war, you've carried
a great burden for humanity's sake, for the wounded
you aid, for me and Oscar and all of us,
North and South."
                    "Your view of me is generous but"—

"Garfish, this is no flattery. All the men
in our unit know what you do, and even though some
despise you for it, they do so because your example
accuses conscience." He put his hand on his shoulder.
"It's just not right to add to your truck. I'll do it.
Y'all return to camp. I'll join you soon."
They left the groaning hillside. He looked back once,
a shadow was kneeling, his hand on the breathing corpse.
He and Oscar had gained the Rebel lines
when the report came. They did not look at each other.

June 6, 1864

Oscar conducted the mess behind the line
as far as Rice would allow and kept a handful
of green pine branches burning for perfumed smoke.
He reclined with a day-old copy of the *Richmond Whig*.

"Feller here writes that Grant intends to stink
Lee out of his position."
                    "Who says that?" asked Caleb.

"Some Yankee deserter. Allows how Grant is a butcher
and a mule headed Suvarov."

"If a stink can beat us, this one
sholey will."

"I don't smell nothing," said Hog.

"The offense is so oppressive, Garland can't bring
himself to render aid to the Yankee wounded,"
said James.

"You'll be glad to know that all the wounded
are dead."

"How could Ulyss let his boys
die whimpering?" asked Oscar.

"Too damn proud to ax
for a truce."

"Or ambitious. If Grant had requested a truce,
the headlines would've declared that Lee had gotten
the best of the fight," said Caleb. "Of course, I'm sure
the general equates ambition with military necessity."

"But how could the most ambitious man in the world
not be moved by the cries and groans of those boys?
How could he be so"—

"Cruel"—suggested Caleb.
He knew what Oscar was thinking, called to mind
the human wreckage stretched on the ground and burbling,
but studied Caleb, who seemed to have achieved
a new found equanimity, arising, he supposed,
from conviction he had performed a proper act,
terrible, but proper. Oscar folded the paper.

"If I am ever discovered in such a state,
I hope someone will muster the courage I lacked
and show me mercy."

                "What are you talking about,"
asked James.

           "It's not your tow on the rock," said Oscar.

June 18, 1864 toward Petersburg

A treadmill dawn, the army pushing down
the Petersburg-Richmond Pike, shuffling dust
above their heads. Intensity of noonday sun
was close as smithy fires bellows fierce,
beating a sour breath from lungs, pulling
stragglers far in the march's wake, the officers
letting them go to arrive when they may. They knew
the meaning. Yankees were on their hooves, and the brass
was herding Rebels to the Petersburg ditches fast,
weary souls trickling down the watershed
of battles. The cloud they raised was cast in shade,
a coursing flow of vultures, a river raised out
of nether regions, sluicing between a bank
of sun and one of dust, the current running
backward to its noisome source at Cold Harbor
in riverine, oxbowed counter motions, swirling
whirlpools wobbling along the flow, then peeling
away, component of the river's ancient malignity.
The thought of human bones picked clean by fowl
birling his mind toward anger, he raised his rifle,
fired at coasting rapine. A nearby officer

shouted,

    "Shoulder arms!" A few swart feathers
floated down, but no bird dropped, the aperture
closed, the river flowed.

               "Somebody want him
a brevet eagle for supper." A few men chuckled.
They crossed a brand new span on the Appomattox,
footing cross ties behind the afternoon train,
crossing from dust to the engine's hanging combustion,
then flowed down main street, where crowds were gathered
                                   cheering
their saviors. But the women were middle aged or old,
no adoration in their looks but matronly care
and worn anxiety. A woman gave him a biscuit.
Her pagoda sleeves and engageantes were fresh
and clean as were her shoes and tatted collar,
the style that ladies had worn two years ago.
He thanked her, broke it, offered Caleb half.
The bread was warm, its center soft with butter
and long sweetenings, and his eyes welled with gratitude
and shame. They marched beyond the cheers and passed
a quaint white church, partially covered in ivy,
its sober fenced-in plot with ranks of stones.
Now the brigades were dispatched down several roads
to take them to assigned positions. Wilcox's men
filed through a copse cool with shade then swung
by a dog trot shanty. On the porch a dirty urchin
in nothing but tattered breeches was churning butter.
When the Rebels emerged from the woods, the handle ceased
its motion. A few hens scattered. A wag called out,

"Tell yer Maw we'll all be back fer supper."
At this the boy sank down behind the churn,
only his knuckles showing and wondering eyes.
The march drew parallel to the trenches stretching
thirty miles and more, connecting Richmond
and Petersburg, protecting vital avenues of supply
and communication. They passed ten thousand Negroes
throwing spoil and engineers directing
their labor, gouging ditches and traverses, heaping
forts and redans. At their place in line, they discovered
Beauregard's defenders five and ten yards apart.
Fear of a Yankee charge had wasted them
to trembling sticks and wraiths with staring eyes.
They tried to raise a cheer as Company H
filled the trench, but jubilation caught in their throats.
The pressure and grinning threat of the Federal corps,
a hundred thousand or more, had stayed its hand.
Their generals' lack of competence always astonished.
They could have ended the war at a stroke, but then
again, he imagined Cold Harbor's looming ghost,
which made an empty line of ditches breathe
a wicked doom. The soldier beside him sank
to his haunches in mud and began to weep, holding
his head in his hands. In the part of his oily hair,
battalions of lice were arrayed. He turned his back
and sighted his rifle. A thousand yards of muddy
wallow and waste of stumps, no stick for cover,
and out of range, Federal troops were forming.
They marched and counter marched in neat phalanxes.
At noon they came in three divisions running,
a great blue swell that struck an invisible coast,

thinned and retreated. All afternoon the Federals
lay on the verge of musket range, hugging earth.
At four o'clock the Yankee bomb proofs rode
their lines. They strained their eyes beyond the scattered
cast of chaff-blown corpses at the distant movements.
There seemed to be confusion; men in the rear
were standing up and lying back down again.

"The vet'runs is telling them boys to get back down,"
said Oscar.
            "They got some sense."
                      "At's why they vet'runs!"
Then several hundred blue clad men stood up
and stepped over comrades, forming a meager line.
"Them what's coming is goddamned green," sighed Ainey.
All the ditch went silent. Caleb whispered,

"Into a valley of pointless death, strode
the six hundred." The Federals' backs were straight as staves.
They marched like men who'd never been afraid.

"Hold fire. Let the brave bastards get up close,"
Emrich shouted. When breech smoke cleared, they lay
in a perfect row, far in advance of their line.
The Rebels hunkered in the foul, infested ditch,
stench in the air, disgust in soldiers' faces.

June 20, 1864 Petersburg

"Drill and more drill. I swany, if I

ain't learned to march by now, I never will."
He plopped himself in shade, Caleb entering
the tent. In a moment, he called. Garland ducked
beneath the fly, Caleb gesturing at the tent pole.
A dead hen hung by her feet, the beak open,
the thin translucent lid covering the eye.
Beneath, a half dozen eggs lay buried in straw
and scratched in earth the words, *I's off acrost
dat Jordin.* Caleb grinned,

     "I bet they biled,"

caressing an egg.

    "I reckon you know what this means?"

"Moses has flown the coop," he tapping the egg
on the pole. "You smuggle him over?"

       "I told him how
I'd help him run away, and he ran away
without me."

    "He didn't want you to share the risk.
He's protecting you."

     "And this was his first act
of freedom, a gesture of generosity."

       "The second.
His first act of generosity was to leave you and me
with a chicken supper. Our last manna from Moses.
So fair and fowl a day I have not seen."

July 2, 1864

The soldiers gathered in a clear cut space. In front,

a brush arbor constructed of felled pines, green
and scenting delicious air, sheltering seats
for the chaplains, a row of benches for soldiers singing
in a makeshift choir, who rose and sang a hymn.

What a friend we have in Jesus
    All our sins and grief to bear.
What a privilege to carry
    Everything to God in prayer.

Then Reverend Broadus came forward, took his post
at the pulpit.
                "Hear with me, friends, the Word of God.

And Jesus said unto them, I am the bread of life: he that cometh
to me shall never hunger; and he that believeth on me shall never
thirst. But I said unto you, That ye also have seen me, and believe
not. All that the Father giveth me shall come to me; and him that
cometh to me I will in no wise cast out.

My brothers, Jesus offers the bread of life
and living waters. He who eats this bread
will never hunger, and he who drinks this water
will never thirst. And he who eats this bread
and drinks this water will seat himself at the table
of the marriage supper of the lamb. Do you own that life
tonight? The free gift of Christ's salvation?
Does he live and reign in your heart, your one Lord
and Master? My brothers, the day comes even now
when the Son of God reveals himself in glory.
His invitation stands. Jesus is calling you.

All of us have seen our friends laid low
in battle; some of you no doubt have held
the hands of the dying. Where are they now? Tomorrow
when the battle rages anew, perhaps a ball
will pierce your breast, and you will lie down and sleep
with heroes. But friend, where will your soul be then?
Where will you spend eternity? Will Jesus raise
you up on the last day or will your soul
inhabit the place of torments, of darkness visible,
where there is wailing and gnashing of teeth? Friends,
it's no choice at all. Jesus casts no one out.
His yoke is easy, his burden light. Our Savior,
Jesus Christ is calling you now. He wants
to give you life and more abundantly. Soldier,
won't you accept him into your heart tonight?
Some weeks ago, I visited the Richmond hospitals,
and there I came to the bedside of a good physician,
Dr. John H. Cowin, of Birmingham,
who left his practice to enlist as a private soldier
in the Fifth Alabama. He was an orderly sergeant
in his company and fell on the field at Gettysburg.
As I held his hand, he said,
                                        'I am sinking fast.
Tell my father I fell near the colors, in the discharge
of my duty, and I die with the Christian's full assurance.'
And then as I bent low, I heard him whisper,
'Even now I see the Savior's face,'
and his hand relaxed in mine and he was gone.
Think, friends, what peace he gained, what toil
and suffering he is spared. Dr. Cowin
will be raised up on that day. Will you be there,

in that city where sorrow shall be no more? Is *your* name
recorded in Heaven in the Lamb's Book of Life?
If you don't make it home, won't you choose
that home where loved ones all one day will gather?
Won't you accept the Lord as your Savior now?"

James was among the last to join the mess,
having stayed the longest at the altar call. The talk
subsided when he arrived and stood in the circle
of men, sprawling about on logs and stumps,
Oscar boiling a bit of rice and field peas.

"Fellows, I feel like the spirit is moving me
to encourage each and every one of you
to heed the words of Reverend Broadus's sermon.
If any should fall in the strife or end our days
in a dismal Yankee prison or a Yankee scaffold,
I'd like to meet you again across that Jordan.
Accept the Savior, that's all you need to do."

"That's all, James? Are you sure?"
                                        "Yes, Caleb,
and I know we've had our differences in camp, but I hold
no grudges. Won't you accept the Lord and be saved?"
He stood and rounded on James, his face in a swelter,

"James, you toss pot, you arrogant ignoramus.
What the devil do *you* know of the state of my soul?
Are you God? Should we all fall down and worship you?"

"That's blasphemy." James wore a look of smug satisfaction

for having provoked Caleb, and Caleb must have
noticed too. He chuckled and sat back down.

"James, you peddle God's grace like magic snake oil.
One sip of this salvific concoction is guaranteed
to save the soul so a fellow need bestir
himself no further. Your grace only fosters complaisance."
Several fresh fish were present, Coon and Sprowl,
both eighteen, and Palmer, almost fifty.
The boys were trading shocked, appraising looks.

"Fellows, don't let yourself be led astray
by new ideas contrary to the Word of God.
You must believe on the Lord Jesus Christ and be saved.
And this is the only way to avoid perdition,
wailing and gnashing of teeth as St. Paul says."

"Matthew chapter thirteen, not St. Paul."
James turned red-faced and spoke a parting shot.

"I would not that ye have fellowship with devils."

"The Orator hath the Son of Man in a swivet,"
said Saxon.
          "He would foist a rutterkin's widdershins brain
upon us," said Patty. When Oscar made to scald
the vessels, Palmer offered help.
                              "I'm weary
of men being scared to the cross for a ticket to Heaven.
Government makes them fight, then herds them to church
and turns salvation against them."
                              "By urging them on

to works the Devil loves."
                    "That's right, Garland.
Men knit their tribal ties professing Christ,
but their malice shows that deep in their hearts they hate him."
The talk went on this way till the drum beat taps.

July 19, 1864

Scuttlebutt had it the Yankees were digging a tunnel.
Caleb lay sprawled on the ground, pressing his ear
to the bottom of a tin cup.
                    "I can't hear anything.
What did it sound like, Buzzard?"
                        "A kind er scratching."
Garland lounged in shade from dog day's heat
while others squatted and listened. James came up.

"You boys is wasting your time. We done some mining
for coal along the Warrior River when I was
coming up, and hit's a fact you can't
dig a tunnel more'n four hundred feet with no
ventilation shaft unless you aiming to suffocate
to death. Pegram just wasted his boys' time digging
them ditches behind their position."
                    "I'm slow to doubt
the Yankee penchant for finding solutions to problems."

"You seem to have a fondness for Yankees, Caleb."

"I'd call it respect. Which has served to keep me alive."

"I'll leave you men to this important work."

"Please do,"
said Buzzard. "We'll let you know if we hear a Yankee."

"Yankee moles and earthworms likely as not."

July 30, 1864

Standing guard on darkness, dawn a fancy,
he kept his station, brooding under the stars,
found Antares, pulsing scarlet heart
of Scorpius, writhing low on the southern horizon.
A peaceful morning, no firing, no voices, alone
by the empty ditch. The war would have to end soon,
and he could have Duessa, her slender arms,
her milk and honey skin, her breasts like revelation,
private and divine. He knew how Adam must
have felt when first he saw her stepping through the fern,
dew sprinkled and perfect, scented with honeysuckle.
He took out her letter, held it a moment, still folded.
Dawn was coming by earth's inexorable turning.
How often he and his father had watched it burn,
after the milking, slopping, harnessing the mule
for plowing before the heat of day. A flash,
as if the sun had bulled up out of the trenches,
balled its fist and struck him a blow in the back,
hurling him forward. The explosion's shock rippled
his body, a bed sheet whipping taut on a clothes line.
A whining gnat squiggled inside his head.
He rolled over. In apocalyptic tableau,

smothering dawn, standing so tall it gathered
the feeble light, a massive column of smoke
and dirt, its top churning inward underneath and billowing
outward above like cumulus. He watched the monolith
poised like a fantastic mushroom, till its fact sobered him,
he seized his chance, grabbed his rifle and sprinted
for a caisson, rolled on his back, cringing underneath,
as a hail of soil and stones and body parts
came rattling down. Coughing, he scrabbled out
on hands and knees in murk. Men were calling.
He pulled his blouse up over his nose. The Yankees
had dug their tunnel and must have packed in tons
of powder for such a blast. He strained to listen.
Why were troops not bursting through the salient?
A breeze began to build, shunting the dust
aside. The ground was covered in loosened soil
and rubble, wagon wheels, rifle stocks,
a human arm, and lodged in the earthwork's embankment,
muzzle first, a Napoleon sunk to its trunnions.
Angelic whining twinned the gnat in his ear,
and earth began to tremble in monstrous footfalls
stomping toward him. Federals were surely coming.
He trotted north through perdition of Yankee shells
raking the blast site, the line abandoned, Rebels
having fled in doomsday panic. Light gained strength
in rutilant haze. An officer on horseback shouted,

"Make for the breach and form a line!" He quickened
his step, fell in with two other soldiers, one
who kept repeating,
                              "Gol damn them clever Yankee

sons a bitches. Gol damn!" They stopped astonished
on the lip of an excavation that swallowed two hundred
feet of the Rebel line. Federals milled
in the smoky pit, crossed by intersecting rifts
and crumbling valleys, some strolling about like tourists
in amaze; a line of Union soldiers formed
on the opposite rim, gawking, then surged in the crater,
packing the floor toe-to-heel with soldiers.
A withering sickness pierced him. Perhaps it was instinct
to congregate for safety, to dive in a hole,
but Yankees were taking bait of the trap they'd laid.
Officers moved them to Pegram's trench not fifty
yards behind the fresh raw wound in earth.
The enemy shifted to counter battery fire
as Rebel cannon barked out flame, raining
shells on soldiers inside the crater, churning
dirt and kit, arms and heads and screams.
And now a hush like snowfall settled the trench.
Wheeling around in smart formation, skirting
the precipice edge and coming straight for their ditch,
where men stood stupefied, aghast in unbelief,
till the world of what they witnessed burst in their minds.

"Well I'm goddamned, if at ain't a regiment a niggers!"
They broke in a sprint, in perfect order, black faces
sheened with sweat. He sighted and heard them crying,

"No quarter!" And hunkering Rebels shouted,

                                        "None given!"
They pounded dust, disciplined and fierce as war horses
charging, and glory was theirs; they poured on the glacis

toward lowered muskets, and not one face he could see
was marred by fear. These were men who knew
what they were fighting for. A jolt of thought—
beyond his understanding—they were coming to take
her back, and his heart thrilled with a bayonet thrust.
The order to fire, the Rebel curtain erupting.
The front ranked Negroes reeled and many dropped.
He watched their colors lean then straighten, capturing
breezes once more as the second rank stepped over
fallen comrades. Another volley thinned them,
causing the last ranks to mill or flow in the crater.
Garland was jostled by soldiers filling the ditch
behind him. A man slid down the parapet wall
square on buttocks, the fall's force launching him forward,
gangly, bug-eyed and one cheek bulging with chaw,
a shiny brown freshet running from the mouth crease.
He caught his shoulders, saw nits around his hat band
and stood him up. He must have been fifty. At no time
during his slide did he stop chewing.

                                    "I'm right
obliged fer you ketching me that a way."

                                          "Sholey."
The man removed his cap, extended his hand.

"The name's William Howard, Fourteenth Georgia."

"Nice to know you, Howard. Garland Cain.
Who you fellers with?"

                              "We'uns Mahone's.
We come a fur piece down the way with two
brigades to help you fellers heal the breach."

He kept on chewing, his hand caressing up
and down his rifle barrel, "They be saying
a troop of niggers done rushed us?"
                                        "They be right."
The man squinted his placid eyes at the crater,
dirty blue, a puddle reflecting sky.

"I ain't never tried to kill no Yankee sojer
between engagements. I reckoned they was doing
that what they got to do, jess like as me,
but here on in I'm killing ever Yankee
what I can get my sights on. I ain't having
no nigger equality, no sir. I ain't having
no goddamn niggers lording over me."
Emrich was behind them now, drawling orders.

"Let's mosey over there quick, but take the periphery
of the abyss with care. Our gunners have give 'em goss—
they's probably not much left of the Yanks. Their fire,
owing to their location, will more than likely be high.
However, let us test that proposition with care."
He looked down the line a ways to get his cue
from other officers, "Let's go, men! Up and over!"
A precipitate scramble out of the ditch, pairs
of feet chaffing and crumbling the trench's high
revetment, a stumbling surge and then the mass
of men upright and running, a surging pack,
swagged and ram's horn crooked. Hitting the ground
at the crater's edge, they pulled themselves on elbows
to the sheer ledge. He aimed in the reeking valley
at one or two clots of Yankees before the breech smoke

stole his vision. The last gun's bump and whinny
of shell marked the cessation of robustious cannonading,
Emrich shouting, "Forward! Take the breach!"
A leap down, his body's momentum surging
along the steep declivity toward sheer towering
hunks and earth dolmens angled precarious.
Yankee infantry took cover behind them though hundreds
were coming forward to meet the rush, hands raised.
Some at the pit's far end were clambering the sheer
wall and sprinting the terrible cross fire to safety.
Fires from canister shot were burning on bare
ground, filling the pit with smoke, sulfurous
and caustic. As artillery noise abated, shouts
and screams grew audible and musketry in rickety notes.
As he bounded down the soft soiled wall, the earth
beneath him jerked away, his body plowed under
by a fluid, crushing wave, seizing vision
and breath. He lay sprawled in claustrophobic
terror, aware of spark and twitch where nerve
commanded muscle in vain. He wanted to cry,
but his jaw was clamped; he tried to breathe but his chest
was cinched, and he knew his posture mimicked droves
of dead, his bones poised like a falling man's,
awaiting the plunge into darkness. The final registers
of sense were the maddening itch of chigger welts
on his scrotum, a damp dirt winding sheet, then nothing,
no pain or dread, only his pulse evanescing,
but a noise tipped back, teasing insensate awareness,
familiar in the rise and fall of pitch, the length
of sounds. The immobilizing crush began to lighten.
Graspings under his arms, at his cartridge belt,

hauled him up into daylight, washing out vision.
His legs wobbled, his back pounded, bursting
open the gates of his lungs. The world's own shapes
resolved in his eyes, a blur of voices, shelves
of smoke, a Negro in blue with both hands raised,
and a Rebel soldier thrusting a bayonet, working it
back and forth in the gut, the Negro's hands
not grasping for the blade's shank, but reaching high
to pull down mercy out of the vacuous sky.
The Rebel extricated the blood-smeared pike,
the heap falling over, turned to another Negro,
his hands held high, and thrust him above the navel.
This man grabbed the barrel, rising on his feet
to mount the agony, the Rebel leaning his weight
in a second thrust, the blade going home with a wild
anguished catch of breath and throat gurgle.

"Here now, Lazarus, what did it feel like to die?"
inquired Patty, swatting dust from his blouse.
Caleb and Oscar turned to watch what he
was watching. A brigadier with staff had come
on the run.
          "Desist, and that's an order, soldier."
He stood with arms over Caleb's and Oscar's shoulders
restoring himself with draughts of breath and recognized
the murderer's muddy eyes, the slack mouth working
the chaw, William Howard, and men of his company
gathering behind him, arms and ire repudiating
embroidered thread. Their rifle locks were matted
with hair and blood. "Return to your unit, men."
Not one man moved. The general stood his ground

another moment. "Lieutenant Jones, muster
company B for a firing squad."

                              "Yes sir,
General Mahone." The lieutenant departed. Mahone
took two steps forward, nose to nose with Howard,
his voice's timbre cocked and taken its bead.

"I'm going to shoot each one of you sons of bitches.
I'm going to shoot you first." When Howard felt
himself alone, he stalked off hang dog and hateful,
throwing a canine stare back over his shoulder.
The general cast an appraising look on their group.
"You four—take these men behind the lines
to Blanford Church. Do you know its location?"

                                        "Yes sir,"
Caleb responded.

                  "Put them inside and make
a deadline around the place and post yourselves guard.
If anyone tries to get out—or in—shoot him.
I'm General Mahone. Do you understand my orders?"

"Yes sir." The general hurried off, grousing,

"Goddamned crackers, they'll convert the entire goddamned
Union army into goddamned abolitionists."
Caleb led them around the western reach
of Poor Creek to a road that led to the church.
Garland and Oscar guarded the rear of the files.
The Negroes marched in silence, heads down, till one
of the company began to sing a martial air,
and the rest joined in. He didn't know the tune,

but it was no field song, and this was no exaggerated
darkie happiness, but an air of pride's conviction.
If they'd been ordered forward half an hour
earlier, they'd be offering Petersburg to Lincoln,
not marching toward a fate he couldn't guess.
He figured they'd be sold, but a thought cheered him,
Let some crooked quartermaster deal them
under the table to a friend with cotton or tobacco.
Some master is fixing to buy expensive trouble.
Having risked their lives on the battlefield for freedom,
they'll surely risk it again in the cotton field.
Once a soldier, never a slave again.
He shook his head. Yankee ingenuity was boundless.
The church's clapboard stabbed his eyes with sunlight,
the steeple cross constantly tipping over
beneath immobile clouds, the air tangled
with wisteria. The column halted outside the dooryard,
the Negroes filing out of ranks in a line,
up steps, across the porch, inside the narthex.

"Won't I be dipped in buttermilk," Patty sighed.

"D'you give that order, Garland?" chuckled Oscar.

"I don't even know what it's called."
                                    "Those fellows sure do
know their drill." The church house occupied a promontory,
and Federal gunners had observed the blue files enter
the building. Shells stopped falling, rumbling out
to the edge of hearing, a summer storm receding.
The lot was bound by a little paling fence

they made their deadline. He'd had no sleep for two nights
running, his eyes heavy as shot. He longed
for a cup of coffee. Mid-morning, an officer assigned
to the quartermaster happened by. He requested
rations for the guard detail and fifty prisoners.
He did not bother to mention they were Negroes.
He was more than a little surprised when around one
a detail brought rations. Oscar scrounged about
for a fire, and he, eager to speak to the Negroes,
leaned his rifle by the door, removed his cap,
and entered the church's cool and tenebrous vestibule,
swallowing vision, perfusing him with odors
of dusty hymnals, carpets, robes, and scapulars.
In a moment, his eyes made way, revealing two rows
of narrow benches astride the nave, oak rafters
arching above his head like leviathan ribs.
He advanced toward soldiers's musk, crowding the floor
at the altar. Every eye was on him. Above them,
fixed in the apse, a sword depending on a thread.
Their new serge uniforms were soiled with battle grime,
some were dark with blood while he stood before them
in layered filth, ragged, tatterdemalion.

"Will the officer of rank present himself." A shifting,
a tall Negro rose, the floorboards creaked.
He pulled up in front of him and came to attention,
staring over his head at some fixed point.
"Private Garland Cain, Confederate States."

"Lieutenant Lionel Sharp, U.S.A."

"Lieutenant Sharp, there are two boxes of crackers

in the dooryard. They are your rations. Detail two men
to bring them inside and you may distribute them.
The dooryard fence is your deadline. Don't go near it.
If a man approaches the deadline, he will be shot."
Sharp said nothing, but nodded at two men behind him,
who stood and vanished in the blinding door of light,
and resumed his former attitude. This man was born
an officer.
                    "Private Cain. My men are thirsty."

"After the charge that you men made, I suppose
they are. I'll see what I can do, lieutenant."
In a small outbuilding, he found a number three washtub,
behind the house next door, a cistern pump.
Another Yankee detail carried the water
inside. When they sat the washtub down, a man
with a blood-soaked sleeve reached a trembling hand,
dipped the ladle and poured a long drink down
his gullet. Garland remembered many such drinks.
The dark eyes took him in.
                    "Thank you, massuh."

"Private Cain. I'm your enemy, not your master."

August 7, 1864

Dog days August, blood run dry in its bed,
tongue a harness leather buckled in the mouth,
and stick and sinew spent from morning drill.
The mess had built a shebang and lounged in its shade.

"Here's casualties for our blow out on the Plank Road last May.
Three thousand Yankees down, five hundred Rebels."
Ainey sat with his shirt off, sewing a rent
in a pair of breeches.
                    "Boys, it's commencing to show
how a feller could fight for Bobby Lee and lose
and live to tell his grandchits about his big
doings in the rebellion as opposed to fighting for Grant
and dying to win."
                    "Lee ain't gwine to lose,"
said Josh. Ainey kept his eyes on his seam
and his needle.
                    "Josh, two months ago, old Abe
put out the call for another half million men."

"We just can't kill that many, Josh. Ulyss
is gwine to drown us in a river of Yankee blood,"
said Saxon. Josh's eyes were unrelenting.

"Who is Grant compared to the Lord a Hosts?
We in the right. I done heard it preached,
straight from the pulpit. Hit's been read to me
chapter and verse in scripture what can't lie."
He produced a copy of *The Soldier's Friend* to chuckles,
but the boy's flashing eyes scotched the mirth.

"Come on, Josh, who is it among us can grasp
the will of God?" His face began to alter,
the way September light assumes familiar
objects, the house, the barn, a stand of oak,
in autumn reality, more vivid than in months

of summer glare, not at permutations
of incomprehensible will, with which his mind
was unfit to grapple, but at veterans' faces, whose flag
was stitched with place names spoken around his home
of Clio, Alabama with reverence and glory,
stirring his heart with grandiose dreams of valor.

"Things is different now. At's all we saying."

"It ain't nobody's fault."
                    "Hit ain't a lack.
Rebel army's good as any army
what's ever been."
                    "I'll die right sure of that."

"What is it—how's it differ'nt?" Caleb answered,

"Providence always sides with the heaviest battalions."

"Why you telling me this?"
                    "Because we respect you,"
said Oscar. "Each man here has earned the right
to tell the truth, and each man here respects
your courage enough to give it to you straight
from the teat."
                    "Don't pay no mind to these gloomy fellers,"
said Sprowl. "The dawn is coming for our glorious cause."
Ainey, Oscar, and Patty laughed out loud,
but attention shifted back to Josh's voice,
like the stern of a boat crossing the wind.
                                        "But I ain't

a man of courage."
                    "Stuff and nonsense, lad.
You and me was hip and thigh in the ditch
at Spotsylvania, all day and half the night.
You ponied up the grit for a brace of veterans."

"Not at North Anna. When hit was clear we was bushwhacked,
Papa made me promise to run behind him
and promise to turn around if'n he was kilt.
And he was kilt all right. Shot in the face.
I shouldn't of run. I should of died for Papa."
He began to weep. Everyone looked away.
Saxon got up and left, but Garland went
to him and threw an arm around his heaving
shoulders. What heroic dreams, and all
he got was pain of losing a man he loved.

August 9, 1864

James had equipped himself with an extra pouch,
in which he lugged a full sized King James Bible.
Garland chuckled at how he resembled a pack ass.

"Jesus says the truth will make you free."

"You tend to philosophy, Caleb, not religion.
A man cannot accomplish his own salvation."

"You ever read that Bible you tote around?
Jesus lived in relentless pursuit of truth

while there was a Pharisee praying on every corner
ready to tell him exactly what God required,
but Jesus refused to take God second hand."

"We're here, we're fighting, there's your mule," said Joshua.

"I have accepted Christ as my Lord and Savior,
and I am saved by the precious blood of the Lamb.
Either I will die on the field of battle
or Yankees will hang me after the war is done.
But I have this confidence: I know that Jesus Christ
the Righteous will raise me up on the last day."

"Your faith is for dying only, not for living.
If you survive the war and retributions,
your heart and mind are mired in a slough of platitudes."

"Death is a fact your cleverness cannot subdue,
and when I die and cross that Jordan, I'll walk
those streets of gold."
                              "There you go again,
dismissing the living Christ for the Christ who died.
You miss the point."
                              "I presume you know the point?"

"Belief is not the end of spiritual striving,
some fatuous moral commerce by which a man
barters his wayward urges for fire insurance
and hope of seeing his dear old ma in Heaven.
It's Christ's intent we put his truth into practice,
living by constant reorientations of heart."

"I am not embarrassed by patriotism and honored
to be a child of God. I'm going to preaching."

"James is a gombeen man in the temple door,"
said Patty.
   "Christ would"—
      "Whoa!"
         "What was that?"
A boom and gentle repercussion shuddering
tent flies, followed by several concurrent explosions.
They stood looking east across the desolate lines,
a pillar of smoke smudging the midday sky.

"Whatever hit was, hit was sholey a hell of a bang."

"Looks like hit's over yonder at City Point."

"Maybe that old cuss Grant's gone up the flue
and we'll go home," said Ainey.
      "Yankees got lots
of everything, even more Grants, especially Grants,"
said Caleb. Garland remembered lying in chill
and black suffocation; he found death hard to wish
on other men, but he understood that wish,
how he longed to leave the dirt and destruction,
the terror and tedium.
      "Ullys blown to smithers,"
mused Saxon. The men regarded the mysterious cloud,
a pillar guiding where they could not guess.

445

August 21, 1864

Dark on the fire step, he and Josh, elbow
to elbow in line, some cannon grumbling and musketry
exchanging across the line, two armies risen
early in a bad mood, the boy, eyes cold
and fierce, arms pumping like side rods as he worked his rifle.

"If the Yanks decide to make a rush, you gonna
need them cartridges you spending." The boy squeezed off
another shot and dropped his rifle butt,
staring at desolate ruin between the lines,
haggard pine and cracked clay patches stretching
toward humped forts and contoured rows of palisades,
chevaux-de-frise, stacks of abatis, and spoil.

"Do you believe what all them fellers is saying
about the war?" He gave the boy a sidelong
glance. The young man's beauty made him shudder,
thinking how much virtuous blood the earth
had swallowed up from Bull Run to Petersburg.
Even if they kept surviving battles,
the price was just too high. It insulted conscience.

"Josh, I've made myself a promise I aim
to keep, and that is, I refuse to live my life
lying to myself about the way things are.
We Rebels are outnumbered ten to one, we got
no shoes, no clothes, no fodder, and Yankees, they got
everything, boots and clothes and victuals and arms,
and now they got us tamped in a muddy shit hole

and time is theirs. Every day they shave some
bark off and soon we'll be stripped and ready for the mill."

"What do we do?"
                    "Well Josh, the plan I've made
is to go back home, work hard, marry a good
woman and try to live an upright life."

"That's it?"
                "It's not heroic, but what else is there?"

"Not much if'n you got to go back to Clio."

"You don't think any good thing can come out of Clio?"

"I reckon not."
                    "I can name one thing, Josh."
At the prospect of his personal goodness, the boy smirked.
"Want to know why Papa saved your life?"
The boy was taken aback. "Do you?" He nodded.
"Papa felt guilty for leaving his wife and son.
He told me all about it, how he stood
at his boy's bedside the morning he left home.
Seeing what a grand thing he was, thinking
his wife was pretty grand. But Papa believed
the lies that every fool was telling. The Yankee
is no fighter. The war won't last a month. We'll dab
the blood we spill with a lady's hanky. Well damn
if we don't have an ocean of blood, and Papa,
his struggle is over. But Sally and Edward, their struggles
have only begun and will last their lifetimes." An expression

of fear widened in his face. "And now we come
to you and Papa. He knew he was going to die.
Oh yes. He wrote to his wife and child and gave me
the letter to mail. He knew he was going to die,
and since he couldn't save his own son"—
                                             "Stop it.

You stop it!"
                      "He saved another son instead."
He turned to retreat but Garland seized his arm,
pinning the boy with his body against the revetment.
"The least you can do is try to be worthy of him."
But Josh shrugged his embrace and ran from the trench.
The dawn light came on grumbling discontent.

August 25, 1864 Ream's Station

He was dead tired, his ears still ringing from battle,
sitting by the fire while Oscar boiled some peas.
Hancock had gotten astride the Weldon Railroad
and A.P. Hill was sent to knock his hat off,
Anderson's division anchoring the Rebel right.
The Yanks were stubborn, but the Rebels pinned them down
till Mahone and Heth came up and broke their line,
sending the vaunted Second Corps skedaddling.
When Oscar ladled peas in his mess kit, he swallowed them
down in a gulp and stretched himself out on the ground
with other men of the mess in a corpse sprawl.
Poor Saxon looked like he'd had his nose mashed flat
by the Yankees. He sat in firelight reading the *Examiner*.

"The news is bad from our neck of the woods, I'll swany.

Fort Morgan has fallen to the Yankees, Admiral Farragut with four monitors and seven sloops of war. Rebel torpedoes brought down the Tecumseh. The Admiral directed the action from a high perch, lashed to the mainmast rigging at the futtock shrouds, from whence he declared "D—n the torpedoes. Four bells!" Buchanan surrendered the Tennessee once the ram was stackless, rudderless, and stove in. R. L. Page, Old Ramrod to his men, surrendered the Fort on August twenty third."

He turned the page. "Well, at least we won
our battle."
        "We didn't win. Not altogether.
The Yankees tore up fifteen miles of the Weldon
that we can't get to. We'll have to move supplies
from Stony Creek through Dinwiddie, thirty miles
about," said Ainey.
                "The noose is getting tighter,"
said Patty.
        "Pretty soon we gonna choke."

September 19, 1864

He approached the roistering mess, their shouts and laughter,
chords grown unfamiliar, the levity rising,
he half expecting a unit of new recruits,
but here was Patty, singing and stepping a jig.

Where are them eyes what looked so mild
When my poor heart you first beguiled
Why did ye skedaddle from me and the child
O Johnny, I hardly knew ye.

The Irishman was swifting down the tracks, rapturous
in his favorite mode of transport. Patty was young,
and yet his face was changed; in a glimpse, a passing
shadow, Garland saw the old man he would be
wearing his face of youth like a gauzy mask.
He shuddered a little as he put his lips to the bottle.

"The Yankees surrender?"
                              "Even better," said Oscar,
holding his wooden spoon like a scepter and gesturing
to a pile of steaks on the cook table, freshly butchered.

"My God, Oscar, where did those come from?"

"A deserter told Wade Hampton where the Yankees
kept their beeves, close to Centerpoint, and the general
gathered up some Texas boys, old hands
at moving other people's cattle, I reckon,
and put their deplorable skills to blessed employment.
He broke through the Yankee lines, rounded up
three thousand head of beef, and drove 'em back."

"Tonight we eat like kings!"
                              "Hampton for President!"
His gulp of knock knee set the tiny gears
in his head freewheeling. Oscar was frying the steaks,

center cut, sizzling, two at the time in the spider.
The fry of sputtering fat beguiled his senses
even more than the whiskey and his mouth poured.
As Patty had sung for his supper, he was served first,
bowing to Oscar. The mess was full chisel,
and the meat being served, each man grew quiet, rapt
in serious contentment. He ate his steak to the bone
and chewed the gristle, then set his mess tin down
and closed his eyes. He wanted to lapse into dreams
of his woman, her sultry voice, immaculate skin,
but the drunks around the fire thwarted his reverie,
farting and laughing, singing ribald songs.

October 12, 1864

"Hit ain't no wonder they call it fatigue duty,"
he easing tired muscles. "Six hours digging
traverses keeps a fellow in practice at being
wore slap out."
     "But when the shelling starts,
I fancy traverses."
     "Ainey, a shell is just
as liable to kill you where you wasn't as where
you was."
    "Oh Garland, while you was excavating
your mine, you got a letter. I stuck it in your sack."

"I'm obliged, Oscar." As the mess turned in before taps,
he fished out the letter, was astonished to find a long
missive in his father's flowing hand and a cover note

penned by Carl: *Garland, I couldn't tell*
you all this before, because I'd made a promise
to your father only to send this letter if you
found out. I hoped you would not, yet I am relieved
you have. A man should always know the truth,
even when the truth is inconvenient.
Take it in stride, forgiving the faults of others
the same as you would wish your faults forgiven.
I am as always, your obedient servant, Carl.
He sat alone by the fire; his scalp tingled.

Dear Son,
        If you are reading this, you have
discovered that thing which I endeavored all
the course of my manhood to keep close and secret.
First, son, you must set aside your mother
in your mind. This story begins before I met her
(and I told her all, I never lied to her),
and while her affection overshadowed all
and while her forgiveness overshadowed all,
that sweetness could not recompense my debt
as I had hoped or half hoped, for a man's heart
labors by a strange accretion, so one love could not
cancel out the other, that trespass of my youth.
It is written, Be sure your sins will find you out.
As I lived, I knew no other truth profounder
than that: for in the day's quiet and offhand moments
I was vexed by sin's sweetness. I bore transgression
in a manly way, I hope, mindful of the wrong
I'd done to her, for there was a degree of shame,
consigned, that shows the Negroes no better than we

are willing to believe they are, a flattering hypocrisy,
for we, the whites, impose upon them constraints
unsuitable, from which they lived in glorious freedom
before they wore the raiment of captivity. She was
my mountaintop whose prospect showed the sprawling
kingdoms of American prosperity's rotten glory.
A man will sin and therefore suffer, and we
are taught he must repent and sue for grace,
make restitution when he can, yet often collective
depravity stands in the way and evil's pinnacle,
depravity crowned as virtue. You know that Satan
holds the powers and authorities of earth, bestowed
to him for a season, so he may deceive the nations.
How could Satan damn the earth, garnering
one soul at the time? A consummate politician, he has
his system in the parlors, offices, and halls of justice.
Government is Satan's most formidable engine.
By this you will understand why I worked to keep
you out of the army, beyond those grand designs
that may already, beyond my knowing, be working
your virtue's destruction. I made my choice, I cursed
myself, yet the curse was one part sweetness, which challenged
the edicts of God. The world says she is a nigger—
while men of the world covet her in their hearts.
I say she had dove's eyes. She was a spring
shut up, a fountain sealed. I say she was merely
a woman, merely a beautiful woman. I say
that fact was sufficient. Yet all of this says little,
and herein lies the struggle, to say to you
my beloved son, what my life and trespass meant,
and why I could not make atonement for it.

Sinning with a woman is hardly new in the annals
of wrong doing. But this sin nurtured in my heart
a secret quarrel with God regarding his nature
and the world he made. Among life's seasons, the spirit
of man must find content in nature, companionship,
and work, these the three great gifts which Adam
received from God. When you were seven or eight,
I walked out late one evening searching for you,
having strayed too far to hear your mother's call
to fetch you in for supper. You were ankle deep
in the creek bed, turning stones and grabbling crawdads.
I watched you a while in the premature forest dark,
hearing the constant murmurous waters, the screech owl
purring, the look of concentration on your face,
and I thought, right now, this afternoon, his happiness
must be complete. My heart went out to you there
and there it struck me—if God so loved his son,
how could he make him to die—even for the world?
Love is either what we say it is
or nothing. Do you recall that afternoon?
I carried you home on my shoulders, parading you
through woods like a prince of the waters. I never pestered
God, the way so many men do, imploring
for this thing or that, but I beseeched Him, demanded
in my pride that He should not require you,
on account of my sins or sins of all the South,
for making available she who could never be mine,
and if He require reparation, that He
take recompense from me, in this life or after,
and He not punish the children and the children's children.
Say I could count on his justice, for that at least?

But now with my hand on the door, looking back
on the life I leave behind, I see the scourge
of darkness sweeping our country, touching everyone.
What sort of justice devours the land like a plague?
I pass in great disquiet, nothing is certain.
Satan, not Christ, I feel is standing near.
In the mirth of his cold regard, all seems lost,
my life, my loves, my labor, all that I would.
What shall my soul be bereft of these?
Say she loved me, she told me many times
she loved me, but the fact remains that institutions
robbed her power to choose, rendering her
to the state of a thing possessed and also as I realized
in the endless bitter winter tide of memory
because she could not choose, my choice meant nothing.
If only I could have seen how pecuniary evil
would magnify our pain when she was sold away,
I would have fled, for what man having reason
would choose to attempt surviving such a fall
from joy's prominence? And fall I did, through years
and anguish and ruin. But son, this is the nature
of life: we grope in vast dark for happiness,
and when we step over the putative threshold of joy,
we enter a world of pain. When pain becomes
too much to bear, men call it wisdom. It is pain.
Say I have regrets. I have regrets,
yet had my will the power, I could not will
a single one of them undone; were they
undone, vanity's black shroud would cover all,
and thus I'm bound upon a wheel of fire.
Son, it comes to this. I speak to you

from beyond my life, knowing one thing only,
wherever I am I would I might embrace you,
Garland, my son. From beyond my life, I ask
you to do this thing, that my soul should find a late
repose: this my first union was productive.
How telling I have a black son and a white; they are
indicative of the known and unknown struggling in my life.
But he has his claim on my heart, your half brother.
His name is Levi. I commend him to you and your keeping.
Accept him however you may, but show him mercy.
The letter hung limp in his hand; far off a band
was playing. So neither of them had had a choice.
The fire billowed his shadow against the tent fly.
A braying led away an axle shriek.
His mind felt chained to a world of flattering images.
One thing might salvage love. That thing was freedom.
The pages blossomed yellow and black and ash.

October 14, 1864

Lieutenant Rice came pacing toward the camp
with Colonel Herbert in tow, an embarrassed strain
on his face, Rice's hued with fury, who hurried
ahead and halted, constrained by the colonel's gait.
Reaching the circle of men, he paused, then gestured
to Caleb.
            "Here is the man I spoke of, sir."
The colonel's face took on a natural pleasance.

"Private Harwell. Good to see you, sir.

We haven't spoken since"—

                "The sutler spy.
I've wanted to know what happened to him."

                        "His suspicions
must have been aroused. I'm told he closed
his tail gate, rolled away and hasn't returned."
The colonel took his hand and shook it warmly.

"I'm sorry he gave us the slip."

                "Oh, I'm not.
As long as he stays away, then all is well.
I hate to hang a man—it's grisly business."

"It's good to have you back, colonel."

                  "Thank you.
It's good to be out of hospital." Herbert regarded
the men, who had all stood at attention. "Please men,
make yourselves easy. It appears that y'all are foddering
your lieutenant on green peaches." A couple of chuckles.
Rice quelled the mirth with an outraged stare.

                    "Sir,
this man allows within my hearing and all
the mess that God is not supportive of our cause."

"I'm also a witness, colonel," James threw in,
his concurrence garnering him some murderous looks,
but Herbert pretended not to hear, his face
assuming an air of mock astonishment.

                  "Lieutenant,
are you telling me you've had a message from God?
But why would he speak to you and not a colonel?"

457

He smiled at Caleb, who countered,

> "I said we cannot
know for certain we're in the right as far
as God's concerned."

> "Rice is thoroughly convinced."

"Rice is a man like me and unless he's favored,
as you suggest, by some divine revelation,
he knows no more than I." Herbert turned
to Rice.

> "Lieutenant, surely you understand
the struggle Southern men have dutifully engaged
is a contest for civil liberties? Mr. Lincoln
has jailed his citizens by tens of thousands, no charges
preferred, no recourse to counsel; when his judges send him
writs of *habeas corpus*, he tosses them in the trash!"

"Which shows in time of war opinion must
be curbed, for the army's sake and freedom's sake."
Herbert shook his head.

> "Never will I see
how freedom, the safeguard of liberty, becomes a liability
in time of war when the body politic is called
to deliberate great decisions touching justice."

"Colonel, you mean our fireside chats are a right
and responsibility?" Caleb was taking Rice
to ground and hog tying him.

> "Men, I would urge
a patient respect for each other and our chartered rights."
Herbert sat on a stump and produced his pipe.

Off a ways, a band was playing *Lorena*.
A breeze stirred the ash embers to pulsing,
molten scarlet. The evening air was delicious.
The colonel's eyes were closed as he puffed his tobacco.
Garland had spied the colonel earlier that day,
so noticed Herbert had donned a clean uniform
to visit with ragamuffin Company H.
"I was never much for religion before the war.
My wife represented our family at church, carried
our tithe, kept us thereby in touch with works
of charity the church performed which were our duty
to support, and all this suited me well. Are you
a churchgoer, sir?"
                              "St. John's Episcopal, Perry
Street, Montgomery."
                              "Ah yes, Father Mitchell,
a fine gentleman. Didn't the bishops hold
their own session convention at St. John's?"
                                                          "Yes sir."

"Private Harwell, I see you're a Rebel Christian,"
he beamed, savoring the joke, "but I never thought much
of religion until secession when statesmen began
employing professions of faith in public. It troubled me
Christ is not a warrior, unlike his Father,
who took his people's part against great empires."

"That's right. The Lord God went before the Children
of Israel, smiting the heathen and Philistine multitudes,"
said James, looking like he might jump out
of his skin and Rice beside him sulled up like a toad.

"Christ is not a warrior and never can be.
In the Southern body politic, the largest part
persuaded the better, and we followed the world, not God."

"If that's your view, why didn't you follow Christ?"

"Never could I have imagined so much carnage."
The colonel touched his shoulder.
                              "And killing accuses
your conscience?"
                    "Of course. Yes sir."
                                  "Son, you possess
a manly sensibility, but take my advice. It's better
to follow the Greeks. You know what courage is.
Live by courage, and all will be well with your soul."

"I've tried that course, but it led my soul to despair."

"Life is one straight line from birth to death.
Being men, what see we but our station here?
All we have is faith in what we reason."

"The Greeks pursued their moral virtue by assent
of mind. Christ makes faith a living proposition
that changes a man's countenance he sees in the glass."

"If Christians be so changed, how can you account
for their actions? We Spartans have come obeying the severe
strictures of our laws. But Christians say one thing
and do another."
                    "And there you score against me.

I could not imagine the freedom I had in Christ,
and this is the treasure that earthen vessels hold
that the excellency of power is God's alone, not ours."
Herbert puffed his pipe and shook his head.

"A lovely dream possesses the Christian mind,
but what he believes is at odds with what he knows.
Yet when each of us in his own heart looks,
he finds the God there far unlike his books."

"Colonel," said Garland, "did the ancient Greeks have a Bible?"

"Yes, and devoutly regarded. It's called the *Iliad*."
The colonel puffed his pipe and looked around.
James thumbed his Bible pointing out verses, and Rice
had one eye open, his chin propped in his hands.
Ainey and Patty were snoring, bored to sleep.
"The cook is somewhat reticent." Oscar chuckled,

"I don't have a dog in this fight, Colonel Herbert."

October 25, 1864

The trees being felled for miles, the mess erected
a tent fly lean-to, taut on pine poles, corduroyed
the floor, and he was drowsing in Indian summer,
shirtless, picking clinging nits, crushing
each rice grain body, watching the tiny daubs
of vermin fluid spread beneath his nails.
Oscar scrounged an old straw hat and pushing

461

a leather punch through the crown's weave had fashioned
a sieve. They walked behind a gun emplacement
two hundred yards or so behind the lines
where a dozen horses were tied in a grove sheltered
by the battery's hill. They approached their liquid eyes
and wickers, kneeling amidst their sturdy legs,
he noting many had thrown their shoes, and sifted
the trampled dirt, retrieving two handfuls of corn
and digging another dabble from mud caked
in the hooves' soles. Now Oscar was using this windfall
to make some cush with a bit of rancid bacon.
Black saddle bags depended under his eyes,
still kind for the wear as he stirred the bubbling sop,
seeming content with the whole afflicted world.

"Why did you come to this fight, Oscar?"
                                        "I didn't
think I had a choice."
                    "Remember those boys
in Pennsylvania, watching us march by their houses?
I guess they must have paid their three hundred bucks?
Not all our men are here and they're not coming."
Oscar poured their mush into battered tins.

"Garland, my mother and father came from Bavaria,
where the government forced them to live in a filthy ghetto.
The Jews have borne diaspora since ancient times,
wearing out generations in wilderness cities,
where we and our ways are strange. Now God has led us
to the South and acceptance. If we fight well, are loyal
to the end, then we confirm our worth as citizens.

If I am called to make a present sacrifice
for the future home of a son of Abraham, I will."

"I just hope we are able to survive it."

                              "Garland,
you already have survived it."

                              "What do you mean?"

"I mean you figured out what survival is,
not living, but living intact. After all,
nobody lives, but while we live we are tasked
to be genuine men. As the prophet Hosea writes,

Sow to yourselves in righteousness, reap in mercy; break up your
fallow ground: for it is time to seek the Lord, till he come and rain
righteousness upon you.

You've broken fallow ground aplenty, Garland.
You're going to be all right. No matter what happens."
He regarded the dollop of sop in his tin, floating
with stiff weevils, insipid Confederate soldier
fodder, and he so hungry he could swallow countless
mouthfuls. To the east, the Dictator pounded pulse
of the day, its dull tempo rumbling, the lazy
feelers bouncing through camps. Bent over kits,
they supped their cush, he hearing as far away
the hopping projectiles sploshing mud and hissing
as they spun their rooster tails of dirty slosh,
and then a beating of wings, his hat flew off,
a hollow concussion, something splashed his mess tin,
spattering crimson gruel. A weight lurched

into mud. Oscar sprawled face down in muck,
the top of his head sheared off, a grayish tissue
fouling the sop in his tin, which he set down rattling,
catching a sob and hearing the sound of laughter.
He turned in dream daze. Buzzard, slack-jawed,
chortling a stream of tobacco juice.

                        "Ol' Gar,

another inch and *yore* head would a been knocked
clean off." Buzzard, hard eyed, standing there
tiny and pointless like a wooden marionette.
He turned Oscar over, wiping mud from his face
and closing his staring eyes, then took his hand,
a crimson gloriole spreading behind his head.
The guns' dull thunder stalked beyond the field.
Squeezing Oscar's hand a little tighter,
he looked at the mess tin, saw the excised matter
oozing blood in capillary pathways. He watched
his hand reach out and pick it up, loosened
his grip when the greasy sliver threatened to spurt
away, so it balanced lightly on his fingertips,
feeling as if he were recollecting his action,
something he'd done in a war a long time ago,
recalling how it felt to grasp a flitch
of brain, seeping blood and vital heat.
He fumbled Oscar's shirt pocket, removing the contents,
slipped the tissue inside and buttoned it down
and remained crouching in mud beside his corpse,
sitting his heels and gazing out at the mazed
streets, alley ways, and residences of Petersburg,
seeing a wagon rolling along the outskirts,
regarding the fractured houses, a water wheel turning

on the Appomattox, handing a stream, gentle
as a lover's hand, down to the river, and on
to the James and Atlantic. He couldn't make himself
stop weeping and whispering,

"Oscar, my friend, my friend."

October 26, 1864

A Jewish friend of Oscar's, Jacob Hauersberger,
of Co. G, read the Kaddish in Hebrew,
and he stood by the gashed trench, hearing the glottal
notes, beautiful and incomprehensible, beating
like a timbrel, transporting him far away to the desert
wastes of imagined Palestine. He had remained
with Oscar yesterday and through the night, Caleb
being informed and coming, neither eating
nor drinking. Now Jacob produced a vial and sprinkled
some earth in the grave. The first shovelfuls of spoil
pluffed on the tent fly they'd wrapped his body in.
When the grave was filled, the mourners trailed away.
The day's pulse resumed, the headache throb
of mortars. Caleb had hammered a makeshift marker
and carved in Oscar's name, regiment, and company.
When the two returned to their mess, the men were standing
around the day's rations someone had retrieved.

"I cooked some hoe cakes oncet," Buzzard frowned.

"My momma did all my cooking," said James.

"I'll do it,"

said Garland and covered the crate with the laundered cloth.
The allowance of meal was down to a half pint per man.
The fat back was almost clear and smelled like urine.
"Now Little Phil has burned the Shenandoah,
you boys had better thank God you've got a backbone."

"Why's at?"
              "Hit's something for your stomach to lean against."
That evening, Garland went alone to preaching.

"What a fine hymn that was, brothers and soldiers
in Christ. There is a fountain filled with blood
and sinners plunging into that fountain do indeed
lose all their guilty stain. I hope each of you
has made that plunge and has tasted the sweet savor
of living waters that quench the soul's thirst.
Brothers and soldiers, I come this night to tell you
all a man can do to steel himself
for any wile of the Devil, for any stroke
of fate, for today and tomorrow, for life or death."
The soldiers, bare headed, were rapt, nodding assent.
"My brothers, you must put on the whole armor
of God, for our struggle is against rulers, authorities,
and spiritual forces of evil in heavenly realms.
So gird yourself with truth and wear the breastplate
of righteousness. Tie upon your feet the readiness
that comes from the Gospel of peace. Take up the shield
of faith, fashioned by God and handed down
from Heaven. What scene embosses that seven fold layer
that breaks all points hurled at us by Satan?
No cities in peace or war, bucolic scenes,

no Catiline, Actium, Caesar or Egyptian Queen.
We find a portrait there, a handsome face,
a face I imagine as many of these I see
before me, gathered around salvation's altar,
a visage of youth, a jaw unstained by beard.
Around his head is shining the white nimbus
of a yearling lamb, riding across his shoulders,
who left the ninety nine to save the one.
The love of Christ is the very love of God,
God's yearning for you from before the world's foundation,
to save your soul and shelter your soul and keep you
safe from harm. Brothers, many of us
will never see home again, will never, with earthly
touch, embrace our wives and mothers, never
again reach out to a brother's or a father's hand.
But soldiers wearing the helmet of salvation will find
their loved ones on that shore, where God will wipe
away every tear and sorrow shall be no more.
Soldiers, this cruel war can reap us from life
so suddenly, we may not have occasion for a last
word, a loving thought for those whom we
hold dear. Therefore, we must treat our deaths
as a thing accomplished, and conscious of fate, embrace
a patient nobility, accepting God's will, and leave
with a chaplain or bosom comrade exhortations
to those back home to follow us to Heaven,
assuring them that we have Christ's assurance.
Brothers and soldiers, won't you come right now,
ask his pardon and give your life to Christ?"
The music began and the men began to sing,

Just as I am without one plea
But that thy blood was shed for me.

About the crude brush arbor, the soldiers' faces
softened in firelight, the beautiful faces of Christ,
eyes like sun on gabbling waters, a sculpted
mouth or chin, a nose refined and noble,
such dignity of purpose in their mien; his gaze intent
on them, rising and joining the altar call,
faces streaked with tears, he glimpsed in every
visage, of the haggard, humble and proud, the handsome,
plain, misshapen, officer, yeoman, Negro,
the ennobling divinity in man. The vision tightened
his chest with sympathy for the soldiers' lot, for trials
they must endure, bearing the hopes of a nation,
charging the gates of hell on green corn and courage,
raising the Rebel yell like a wild Laburnum.
The South may be wrong about everything after all,
yet Garland could not deny his profound esteem
for soldiers' indefatigable spirit of sacrifice.
The epiphany dealt him heart ache, thinking of Oscar.

October 27, 1864 Burgess Mill

He hunkered rear of a hastily thrown up work
of stones and spoil. A rising swale of grass
stretched out behind him, a curiously unburnt fence
(he noted a bottom rail gone; he'd go under there),
a crest of hill, beyond that, Hatcher's Run
they'd splashed across earlier that afternoon.

He checked his rifle, charge, cap, and hammer.

"I hate being posted on flank," Ainey moaned.

"Why's that?"
    "'Cause when you on the flank, hit's only
a matter of time before some enterprising bastard
comes along to try and knock yer hat off."
Battle racket rose and lulled on their right.
Nall came shambling up.
     "Howdy boys.
Hampton and Hancock have locked horns just west
of Boydton Plank Road, and Warren's coming our way.
And we'uns gwine to make him pay in specie
for ever inch of Petersburg real estate
he wants to buy. Sojers, we got to dig in
like gophers in a hole. We got to bow up like badgers.
We got to—hey Caleb, what's that word you learned me
just yestiddy?"
    "Tenacious."
      "Hot damn! We gwine
to be tenacious sons a biscuit eaters.
I 'spect ever one a you boys to whale a dozen
Yankees before we mosey. We gwine to go in
hot and raising hell and hold our line
behind the run. Mahone will be on our right,
and we gwine to hook up with him, tongue and groove.
We got to stay in charge of this railroad, fellers.
The chow we git is shit, but hit's better than nothing,
and nothing is what we'll be suppin' if the Yankees take it.
So hunker down fellers. Let's go whole hog."

"Here come the peddlers," said Ainey. Three hundred yards
from behind a screen of trees, Warren's corps
advanced to musket range and the fracas was on.
He chose a target from the line, sighted till the man
went down on a knee, then squeezed the trigger, breech smoke
screening vision. He slid behind the works,
turned on his back and reloaded, pausing to gaze
at the heaven's blue, nothing, nowhere, and endless.
He rolled back over, a bullet skipped from a stone
in front, domed like a skull, carving a dusty
groove. He leveled his rifle upon it and fired.
It occurred to him how boring war had become,
the rote actions of advance, repulse, retreat.
He didn't even fear for his life anymore.
He'd worried about dying so long he was tired of that.
The mindless blue absorbed his useless thoughts
the way it absorbed the pointless noise of war.
He tamped a charge and fired.
                              "They coming on,"
yelled Josh, smiling. He must have fired thirty
rounds already. The boy was always pissing
away ammunition, which used to annoy him, but today
he wasn't vexed and gave him a handful of cartridges.
The boy smiled grim, leveled his rifle, screaming,
"Get up here close, you Yankee sonna bitches!"
Nall grabbed him and Josh by their collars, pulling
their heads together so they could hear.
                              "You boys
is tossing hot bricks in hell. You picking crows
with the Yankees. But now it's time to get our line
in order. Fall back slow as quick as you kin

and crab to the right. We gwine to find Mahone."
They moved in haste for being exposed on the rise,
running in hunkered crouches, turning to fire,
then falling back another stretch. He scampered
straight for the gap in the fence, dove under, moved left,
taking cover behind a post. From here he could fire
over his comrades' heads, and he watched the blue
brigade grinding along behind them in a swarm.
In no time, Federals were huffing against the opposite
side of the abandoned works, some forty yards off
the spilt rail fence, as the last Rebels covered
ground to safety, Patty among them, who stepped
on a bottom rail to clear the fence, but his canteen
caught the top rail, and the strap slung round his neck
yanked him back. Affrighted, he sprung again,
again the canteen snagged the rail, and Patty
stood stretched on the fence like a fly in a web. A Yankee
got a bead on him, the bullet cutting
the strap on his shoulder, Patty tumbling over
on his face. He bound two rabbit strides then turned,
panicked, leaped back to the fence, grabbed the strap
and cradled the canteen close. The Rebels, guessing
the receptacle's contents, erupted in laughter. But the Yankee
shouted,
          "That's right. Run away you Rebel traitor."
Patty, hearing him, halted and straightened, his hands
on his hips.
          "You damned fool. Can't you see
me doing the best as I can?" He spun and bolted.
Again the Rebels hooted. If Patty would risk
his life for panther sweat or throw it away

for a gibe, so what? The man who perished for the great
ideal was just as dead, and dead was dead.
Caleb was laughing with Ainey and Saxon.

                                        "Now there's
luck of the Irish." Nall came up.

                               "Three down,
other side of the fence. I'll fetch one,
but I need two other men." He looked at Garland,
who stared blankly.

                   "I'll go," said Caleb.

                             "I'm in,"
said Ainey, and he and Nall moved out at once.

"Don't go, Caleb."

                "*You're* telling *me* not to go?"
Caleb smiled, touched his shoulder and followed.
They sprinted from cover, jouncing shade tail ricochets
across the open ground beneath a hail
of small arms fire. He watched in calm as the three
crouched by a sprawling form, shouldered his man,
and staggered back to the fence. The firing quelled;
the Union line broke out in cheers, clapping
and whistling, and he brought his barrel up and sighted,
but someone gripped his wrist as he fingered the trigger.
Saxon, looking incredulous.

                     "Garland, this ain't
the sort of thing you want to be thinking back on.
Wait till the other man picks up his rifle."
He shrugged. He saw no reason not to shoot.

October 31, 1864 Boydton Plank Road

Captain Nall stuck his head in their bunker.

"A washer woman's set up shop if'n any
you fellers want to git yer step ins fresh.
She's behind the colonel's tent." He stirred on his mat
of leaves. He was tired of stinking. One of his sacks
was stuffed with damp and soured clothes. "That gal
is enterprising, a laundress, peddler, itinerant farmer,
got pigs and chickens, though how she keeps them critters
away from pilfering soldiers, I cain't say."
His boot prints traced circuitous paths by puddles
and pocked holes of mortars full of water,
reflecting the sky in mud colors. Some stumps
were sprouting twigs. Outside her tent the Negress
worked her hands in a number two washtub. A tripod
supported a boiling kettle. She saw him coming
and put a hieratic gaze on him and did not
speak till he had stood some disquieting moments.

"What troubling massuh today?"
                                        "I have some soiled
clothes. They could use a laundering, please."
                                        "Uh-huh.
And you got troubles, I know, I can see.
You tell Miss Hester. Hester cares about you."
Her knuckles padded by cloth made bleating stutters
back and forth, and she stood in a haze of steam.

"I love a woman who doesn't love me." Her scrutiny

intensified in gaze sibylline and mysterious. Her hands
ceased, severed by water bleeding away
into air.
        "Now you tell Hester and say the truth,
men always know the truth and just don't want
to say it. If yo woman don't love you, what can you do
to make that woman love you?"
                        "Well that's the thing.
Our relations are grown so complicated in my apprehension.
Duessa is a Negro." The woman raised her head,
and she laughed a full throated laugh, deep and free.

"You thank a awful lot o' that, massuh.
White mens sparking up wit black wimmen
ain't no new thang. Hit's because the world says no.
And when the world says no, they's bound to be
some men who gwine to find a way to do
that thang or a pig don't eat no watermelons."
She regarded him again with a serious appraisal,
"Black wimmen wants the same as white wimmen wants."

"They ain't no end to what white women want."
                             "You right."
She gave him a wink and started scrubbing again.
"Massuh, you listen to me. They is only one way
to keep yoself young in dis world. You never take mo
in yo heart than what you can kick off at the end
of yo toes." She shook her head and smiled at him,
a party to his secret, then dried her hands on a rag,
took in the sky with her eyes, "Hit sho be looking
like rain. Massuh, can I ax you to tote that box

a kindling in the tent fo Hester?" He bent down and hefted
the crate of sticks, not really heavy, and she followed
in the tent's cavernous shadow. He set it down
in a spot she indicated, between a stack of rags
and garden tools, and when he turned, she was standing
close, and she touched his face with warm, clean hands,
drawing her own face near and keeping the searching
spell of her eyes on his. He thought that this
was hardly fair, but when her lips touched his
in a heart beat he was back in Union Springs,
wrestling her dark phantom, his saving angel,
he on top of her, trying to push his body
inside her body, inside her soul, to abide there
in fancy's dark. Outside the guns thundered,
and again he strode on the high steeps of that first
euphoric union. When the storm of wanting settled
to calm, and the dull world reeled forward, he held her
close to his body, feeling her chest throbbing
against his own. She kissed him and began to laugh,
"Hester put her magic on you, honey.
And only cost five dollars."

                         "But you didn't say"—

"No, I didn't say, you supposed to know,"
she said and smiled, her black eyes warm, inscrutable,
as she kissed him slow and languorous, disgust opening
yellow petals—but then a counter thought.
Whatever she was, he was obliged to respect her.
Her lips were billowy, better than wine. A patter
of rain, a musical seclusion. "Honey, don't get
yoself blue. I needs money mo than I needs

a man," her fingers smoothing his cheeks, "but hit's nice
to have a man." He fished out a bundle of bills,
fanning them over her bare breasts, she giddy,
looking into his eyes with sincere regard. Who cared
what form redemption took if it were redemption?
This time he forgot Duessa, but kept his mind
keen on this robust, honest washer woman,
as he tupped her again, crushing money between them,
holding her gaze and whispering the name of *Hester*,
who was unashamed to add sweet moans to his
in a soft duet of pleasure, hearing from outside
the grunts of guns and hogs and clucks of chickens.

November 15, 1864

The moon was a shaving dropped on the sky's floor.
He and Ainey had struck out far from their line
to Fort Steadman, the two staying low and trotting
at a crouch, keeping to the path winding through stumps,
abandoned redans, a wrecked and half charred wagon,
until they were challenged.
                    "Who goes there, friend or foe?"
It seemed the night had spoken and his eyes made out
a soldier, his rifle not raised but held in the crook
of his arm, the way a hunter carries it returning
home.
        "Foes, I reckon," Ainey chuckled.

"Evening, Johnnies," replied the Federal guard.
"Poker and Kino in the ditch to your right; in the fort

to your left is the Trading Post."

"Thanks."

"We're obliged,"
said Garland, touching his cap. They entered the fort,
the bunker damp and cold but bright with lamplight
and dug in a circle, on one side guns, trained
on Rebel works, on the other powder kegs
and crates of ammunition. The fort was stocked
like a small town general store. The retailer stood
shivering in the center, ringed by several boxes.
A few disheveled Confederates browsed, one working
a trade with three cob pipes he'd fashioned for a can
of pickled oysters.

"All right, Johnnie, deal."
He took his purchase, his hands caressing the can,
delighted with its heft, sat himself in a corner,
unsheathed his camp knife, plunged it hissing through tin
and worked it back and forth. His own face burned
watching the starving soldier saw the can top.

"We got a passel of chaw we'd fancy to swap
for a gill of coffee if you're a mind," said Ainey.
The man was bending back the jagged lid
between his thumb and knife blade, then jabbing his filthy
index and middle finger in brine, extracting
one lobed, dripping sack, lipped with a fine,
black line, minutely crenellated, dropping it whole
in his mouth and chewing, slow and savoring, transported
in ecstasy. He swallowed, took note of him and Ainey,
held the can out, the salt spray, ocean odor
casting towards him.

"Jew fellers care for a hoyster?"

he drawled. His eyes were wet and rimmed with blood
as if they were being carved from his face in stages.

"No," he cut Ainey off, "No thank you, sir."
The courteous gesture performed, he gnashed the rest,
sucking muddy brine from dripping fingers.

"Gentlemen, I've got a good supply of strong,
northern coffee. The going rate is a shirttail
for three twists of tobacco."
                          "Two shirttails, please."
He stacked the braids on a box of forty dead men
and took in exchange two sacks of coffee.
                                    "Don't think
I've seen you fellers before. Where do you hail from?"

"Company H, Eighth Alabama."
                          "For certain,
you're Beauregard's men?"
                    "That's right," he said, stepping
on Ainey's foot.
              "Well, I thank you for your custom,
and I'm pleased to say that first time traders receive
a lagniappe."
            "I don't got one of those," said Ainey.
The corporal produced a jug and two shot glasses.

"On the house, I mean. This here's scotch,
like nipping a peat fire."
                      "That's mighty white a you, sir,"
said Ainey, smiling at Garland and downing the shot.

"Now that's a wallop. I never had nothing like it.
What you call it, what is peat?"
                                   "I guess
   it's something like dried grass. The Scotsmen roast
their barley with it to give their whiskey its flavor."
Garland raised his glass and poured it down
and felt the spirits getting the run of his innards.
If there warn't no bourbon, Scotch would surely serve.
"I hope you men will come to trade with us
again and soon. As the war grinds on, it's good
for a soldier to make his life a little easier
by seeking out amenities for himself and his friends.
My only hope is the damn thing ends and soon.
We've fought so long, I can't remember why
we started. I only speak for myself, but I say
it's time to mend fences and be friends again."

"Hit's out of our hands, sholey. Hit's them what are
   the tall hogs at the trough that calls the tune."

"Surely the private soldier once in a while
   can call a jig he'd like to put his steps to."
He watched a small light blossom in Ainey's eyes.

"I thank you for the drink. Been nigh three month since last
   I swallered some tanglefoot, and I'm fond of whiskey."
Ainey offered his hand and the Yankee shook it.
They took the path through chevaux-de-frise pulled back
to allow the Rebels passage. "The Yankees think
we all a bunch of traders." Ainey cast
an appraising glance at Garland. "But they's some truth

in what he says. This whole damn war's for shit."

"You gwine to absquatulate, Ainey?" He blew his cheeks.

"Hell, I reckon not. I promised to stay,
so hit's out of my hands, but Garland, the war is over.
They tell us to die for honor, to kill for honor,
a crazy circle that makes no Christian sense.
A can of oysters for three sorry corn cobs, shoot.
And I know what they about in there, but still,
the Yankees is men just as good as we are.
Hit's only our pride what's keeping us here; they's just
no cause for us to go on killing each other."

November 16, 1864

"Another proclamation."
                              "We fasting again?"

" 'Cepting today it's official."
                              "I'm so hongry
my stomach thinks my throat's been cut," said Ainey.

Coon was sullen, "And all our Congress can do
is eat peanuts and chew tobacco and tell us,
Hey fellows as long as you're starving, why don't you pray?"

"This here is just damn cruel, using religion
to put a proper face on speculation

and red tape," said Saxon.
                    "Sholey," said Ainey.
I demand my husks and weevils. Inform Jeff Davis."

"You'uns hear Capt. Nall was wounded?" asked Josh.
"Shot in the breast."
                    "Who took his place?" asked Ainey.

"A feller named Fagan."
                    "Ain't never heared a him."

"Me neither." Palmer came up, his arms loaded
with fuel. "A fine man," said Garland. "I'm freezing.
Where did you find wood?"
                         "I moseyed into town
and tore it out'n a bombed out house." He threw
on smaller pieces to grow the flames.
                              "I think hell
has done froze over."
                    "We'll have to fight the Yankees
on the ice," said Sprowl.
                    "Say," said Caleb, "this morning
at roll call, I didn't hear Buzzard answer or James."

"They done absquatulated and took French leave,"
said Ainey, "repented their Rebeldom and jined the Yankees."

"They prob'ly over there digging they graves with they teeth,"
said Josh.
            "Deserters is piss poor," said Saxon.

"It's none but a stepmother to blame 'em, lads," said Patty.

"I have to say, I'm right surprised at Buzzard,"
said Caleb.
                    "How come?"
                                    "I thought he'd found his place
in our mess. James is no surprise. I can tell you
exactly the way that conversation went."

"How?"
            "The Yankees promised not to hang him,
and that was it. He swore his oath."
                                        "You mean
he unswore one and swore another'n," said Ainey.
"Men like that is better off with Yankees."

"I'm sorry for Jimmy, lads. We'll never know
how hanging might have improved him."
                                        "Many a good
hanging has prevented a bad marriage," said Caleb.

"And lads, I'll miss the Buzzard. He was content
in a regular fashion to share his pay with me
though he was pleased to call his charity gambling."

"What chew gonna do for income now?"

"An Irish broom knows all the dusty corners."

"They's probably sitting by a Yankee fire," said Josh,
"golloping their dried beef and coffee, and 'splaining
how God Almighty led 'em back to the Union."
He spat, "This biscuit's hard as a minster's root."

"Yes," laughed Caleb, "faith should foster character.
An honest man's the noblest work of God."
He regarded Josh, who wasn't listening and cared
not a whit for honesty. He wanted respect from veterans,
wanted to join that army within the army.
Garland put fuel on the fire. The dusk had coalesced,
mortar shell's burning fuses streaking arcs
and dragging the Dictator's subterranean rumble
across the heavens, gorgeous gossamer threads,
catching nowhere. He heard the rising whine,
the shrieking plunge and muffled detonations
and watched each flash, the daylight gasping out.

November 27, 1864

The soldiers gathered for preaching and then the dusk
gathered, hollowed by fires around the brush arbor,
shielded by pine trees far behind the trenches.
Caleb produced a piece of hardtack, broke it,
gave half to Garland.

      "Have a sheet iron cracker."

"Thanks be to God." Caleb smiled then frowned,
willing away the sour reek of the bread.

"Christian Soldiers, the Book of Judges tells us
the story of a concubine, given to sons of Belial,
a sacrifice to spare her Lord, in much the way
that Lot the Patriarch offered his daughters to men
of Sodom that they might spare the angels in his house.

The men of Belial, the scripture tells us, *use her*
unto death. Come morning, her Lord opens the door
to find her subdued, her hands stretched to the threshold.
Her owner takes her body and hews it to pieces,
and sends a portion to every tribe of Israel.
The scripture says that all who saw the sight
said *Never had such a deed been seen since the day*
the children of Israel came up out of Egypt.
For three years now the comity that blessed our house
with ministrations as of a good and comely wife
has been taxed unto death. Reasonable men did not
desire secession. The vote of Virginia showed
she died with hands stretched to the threshold. You've read
this story, how the Lord God commands the Israelites
into bloody conflict with the errant tribe, how each
time they are defeated, the Lord God sends them back
to battle and how on the third day's fight, Israel
cuts off Benjamin's supply line and sacks Gibeah,
routing their army and banishing them to the Wilderness.
And there they abide until that day when Israel
restores their tribe and blesses them with wives.
Brothers, the fight is come to the third day.
The concubine is our ordained institution, our way
of life, assaulted by the North, and we are Israel,
commanded by the Lord of Hosts to bitter war,
to be the arm of God and wreak his justice.
The Lord has pitted us against a foe
that is Legion, terrible in battle, but what are legions,
what are stores and manufactures, when the Lord
puts forth his hand and if he so commands us?
For thy sake we are accounted as sheep to the slaughter.

What then? Are we not servants of the Living God,
and the servant will stand or fall before his Lord.
To be a servant is to obey, to accept the will
of the Master instead of our own will. Years ago,
my earthy father died and bequeathed me slaves.
Yet he also left some debt, so it was incumbent
upon me to keep his slaves and land together
to discharge my obligation. One slave was Charles,
a body servant, I chose to assist me in my work,
attending me in my travels and visits, acting
sometimes as factotum, sometimes as personal secretary,
for he could read and write in a good hand.
One day our business required us to go
on separate errands, him to purchase food
and me to visit a church of my charge, a ways
in the country. We arranged to meet that afternoon
at a familiar place in the road. As I set out,
however, my horse threw a shoe. There being no smith
at my destination and the ride long, I was
compelled to walk my mare back into town
and wait for her to be shod. The night was falling
and it had begun to rain when I finally caught up
with Charles at our designated place. There he stood,
holding the reins of his horse, his hat brim pouring
sheets of water down his back and shoulders,
and behind him in a lovely swale, a dry barn.
'Charles,' I said, 'Why did you not take shelter
in the barn? You could have seen me pass on the road.'
But Charles smiled his benevolent smile and said,
'If Master gets on by, what Charley do then?'
Charles' faith was great, his diligence great,

for he understood how the Master is all things
to the servant, the servant without the Master is nothing.
If a servant can show such love to an earthly master,
how much more should we love our Heavenly Father?
If a servant can render such duty to an earthly master,
how much more should we render duty to God?
Are you a servant of the Living God? Have you knelt
before his throne and offered your life to him?
In every battle we see the scattered dead,
their bodies torn asunder, yet these are vessels
only, emptied of the souls that gave them life
for a season on earth. Those souls are living still
in eternal joy and bliss or pain and suffering.
Have you accepted Jesus Christ in your heart?
If you haven't, friend, won't you do so tonight?
Call to mind the faith of Charley the servant.
If the Master passes on by—what will you do?"
The men as if on cue began to sing,

Just as I am without one plea
but that thy blood was shed for me.

The darkness fallen, Caleb and Garland sauntered
back to their stinking bunker, Caleb musing,

"I fear the murdered concubine is not slavery."

"What is she then?"
                        "An emblem."
                                    "She is what she is?"

"Yes, and North and South are Israel and Benjamin.

Northerners sold her South and *we* are the ones
who took possession of her and used her unto death."

"Can't say I follow."
                "This war is fought for her."
The moon was a solid shot buried in dark.

"You mean it's not slavery, that wealthy men
could set slaves free and use them with greater economy,
foregoing their pitiful maintenance, their shacks and rags,
but what it is, the thing that everyone knows,
but no one will speak because of its ghastly impropriety,
it is not the field hand, but the field hand's wife they want?"

"We fight for the rich man's right to bed his Negroes."
His mind plunging, he glanced up at Perseus striding
across the dark. For weeks his conscience had chided
on account of Hester, on account of betraying Duessa,
and now this added anguish, his heart writhing
in sorrow for what the world had made of Hester.

"A white man's heart is darker than a Negro's pocket."

December 21, 1864

Herbert sat in a laundered uniform, stained
and patched. Garland couldn't believe he'd come back
after his wounding. He could have stayed away.
Why return for the bitter end, and the end
was shaping up to be bitter. And here was Regis,

close as his master's shadow, steady and cheerful.
The least among these has surely become the greatest.
Caleb was speaking.
     "A week ago the Yankees
destroyed our western army outside Nashville
and yesterday Sherman's army arrived at Savannah.
We're alone against the world. What do we do?"
The colonel's face was cut from stone, a calm
that mastered passion.
     "We follow our own ideals
and bear oppression's yoke in manly fashion.
It was not our want of courage but Yankee numbers
undid us."
   "See it through?"
       "What else is honorable?
We must accept our fate though fate be harsh."

"But colonel, who can foresee his fate for good
or ill? You can't most always sometimes tell."

"True sir, but for now, duty and sleep are calling."
The men rose and shook hands, and Garland shook
the colonel's hand, then master and slave traversed
the desolate ground.
     "What do you think?" asked Caleb.

"I think he wants to die. I think his ideals
are censured by failure, and honor, which drove him to glory,
now drives him to perish." Caleb pushed a stick
into embers.
    "Perhaps death is the truest devotion

to the high ideal."
        "It's well and good for the master
to choose an honorable death, but when he does
he likely chooses his servant's death, an innocent
who may not wish to be an immortal footnote,
if that. This deprivation of the servant's will
knows no honor." The brand floated between them.

"Garland, you never fail to wrench my mind
from bequeathed ideas. We must purge all by fire."

December 25, 1864

His eyes eased open in bombproof dark, he breathing
a subterranean dank and masculine staleness
and oppressive fecal stink. Someone had used
the slop jar during the night and hadn't emptied it.
A blanket corner nailed across the door
had fallen, cold flowing in. The fire was smothered
with ash. There was no fuel. They had to walk
for miles for sticks of kindling, and most no longer
bothered, acceding to shiver in wet holes,
under damp blankets. He and Caleb slept
on a mat of candleberry leaves and catkins he'd fashioned
to mask their bodily stink, but the piquant scents
had long worn off, leaving them exposed
to vertiginous assault of stenches. Sharing their burrow,
Ainey and Josh were bedded down. It astonished
how those two, eating so little, could fart so much.
A high, thin shear and muffled *humpf*—the ceiling

creaked, and a cast of fine soil dusted his face.
No explosion followed—a solid shot,
the Dictator working early. His stomach grumbled.
Today his company had to serve its turn
on the firing line. An hour before dawn and one
before dusk, they manned the trenches, vigilant for assault.
Josh loaded his rifle then crouched on the fire step
and fell asleep. Saxon was gazing east,
watching till dawn bayoneted the flat horizon
then stomped his feet on the step.
                                        "Today is Christmas."
He looked neither happy nor grateful, did not convey
by any expression of tone or gesture evidence
that he gave much of a damn, but it was certain
Garland had forgotten today was Christmas day.
The building light revealed the Federal Forts,
gun emplacements, zigzagging curtain, videttes,
redans, chevaux-de-frise, pattern of stumps
like a map of a forest, now waste patches of ice
and mud—for miles, mud and more mud.
In town, a Christmas bell swelled out and failed,
a cheerless wind ushering the peal away.
He thought of Advent, God in a baby's body,
love having entered the world. Tits on a boar hog.
God it was cold. He'd grown to hate the cold.
Saxon's profile was pitiable, the long nose smashed
against his face, eyes squeezed shut as a suckling
shoat's, and all his flesh slack with hunger,
filth, exhaustion, and the wages of killing. Handsome
he wasn't, but he reached in his blouse, produced a twist
of tobacco.

"Here y'are Garland. Merry Christmas."
Saxon turned his attention back to dumb show
shadows, the risible rising of the light. He stared
at the woven rope in his palm and gripped it tight
for a second, took his camp knife, snicked it in two.

"Be more pleasure if you'd see to share it with me."
The two men chewed and spat, watching the works
where Yankees slumbered. Icicles in tapered rows
like shepherd's pipes adorned the trench. He broke
them idly with his boot toe. Face to face with dawn,
Saxon's visage burned with preternatural dignity.
He smiled and thought how much he hated tobacco.

December 29, 1864

The boys had found a tree stump Negroes unearthed
digging a westward line of fortifications.
They bound it with ropes and drug it back to camp,
and all morning long, his mess had taken turns
busting it up with an axe. And now a middling
fire was burning, the wet roots hissing and popping,
sending oozings of sap boiling into flames.
He and Caleb shivered, shoulder to shoulder.

"What are you thinking, Garland."
                              "Thinking how cold
and hungry I am."
                    "Come on. I know that look
of yours. What's on your mind besides your misery?"

"More misery. I can't stop thinking about the concubine.
What a betrayal we've suffered. We've given our bodies
to be broken, staked our honor for salacious luxury,
and the sins of the South will be inscribed and recounted."

"No one can say how history will deal with us.
Our memory may discover other avenues
to the hearts of men who inherit our words and deeds."

"History pays no mind to the poor man's deeds,
except as they are shaped by the rich man's words;
history is his bastard child and wears his features."

"Don't despair on account of history, friend.
A hundred years from now a poet may rise
and sing of the nation's arms at Chancellorsville
and Cold Harbor, of men like us who struggled
to bear a modest light in the darkest times."
Josh was spending his fury on the splintered stump.

January 19, 1865

Soldiers formed three sides of a box and shivered
an hour. Wind explored the threadbare spots
of his blouse. Officers rode back and forth in frock coats.
Three posts were sunk at the box's open end.
At the center, six soldiers tensed at arms rest.
The Dictator and other mortars beat morning's pulse.
At last three soldiers were fetched out under guard
and tied to the stakes. A rataplan call to attention,

an officer strode forward and read the charges of desertion.
The left hand soldier backed himself to his post,
his eyes ignited with terror; he was only a boy.
He began a loud and anguished weeping. A chaplain
appeared to admonish him and offer consolation.
The boy said something, but he could only hear
a cadenced murmur measured between his heaving
sobs. A run of laughter flushed through the men
close enough to hear the conversation.
The chaplain touched the boy, who hung his head.
The six presented arms at the drum's rattle.
The boy wailed, the middle convict smiled,
and the other leveled his gaze upon his killers,
his eye cold, his lip in a curling sneer.
Shots cracked out, three bodies slumped at the stakes,
a murder of crows froze the air with laughter,
casting no shadow, arcing high over charred
and shivered roofs in the town where no bell tolled.

January 21, 1865

Names at roll call ragged and dispersing.
                                        "Great gawd,"
said Ainey, "would jew looky there." A pack of strays,
two hundred if there was one, churned and swept
by the city's outskirts, near pens of the army's abattoir,
a few skinny kine stirring panicked circles.
He'd never seen anything like it, the ranks following
two or three leaders, erupting in fierce ear biting
and flank biting squabbles, going their snuffling way.

A squad began pursuing something, a rabbit
perhaps, and once it was apprehended, the beasts
clumped like magnetized filings, tearing prey
and predator alike. He imagined the cacophony of bare toothed
growls and bitten shrieks. Soldiers emerged
from the slaughter house and fired, driving the pack
away. "I bet they shit a passel," said Ainey.
At Pocahontas Station an engine blasted
its whistle, expelled an enfolding belch from its stack.
Federal mortars thudded their dull obsession,
shells arching repellent trenches, sloughs of mud,
and crumping houses in town or splashing the river.
Later, he sat in bombproof dark, reviving
a fire with pitiful chips, set his cup
beside the wavering flames, water and chunks
of roasted sweet potato, Oscar's concoction.
Ainey and Caleb lay huddled under blankets.
He squatted close to the hearth, his mind huddled,
sensible only to frozen clothes, a stabbing,
open chilblain on his heel. Some days ago,
washing his hands, he noticed deep in his palms,
a blight of stains. His mind was ill. That morning,
he'd dreamed he carried a bushel box of seed corn
in a tent and set it down between a stack
of rags and garden tools and recognized the place
as Hester's. Elated, he turned to her cot and horror
seized him. Her body was jointed, wrapped in paper,
and tied with string as if she'd come from the butcher's,
grotesque puzzle pieces of a woman's shape.
He sprung from the canvass shambles, yet the instant he bolted
outside the tent, he found himself in Petersburg,

clamor of provosts shouting for him to stop,
he fleeing dream retarded past the court house,
capitals and cupola and clock, turned left away
from its gate and dashed by the church, past signs for shoes,
stoves, tin ware, dry goods, wholesale and retail,
and tripped on a window shutter in the ally, the dream fall
jerking his body awake. He lay in the midnight
thinking, *It was not fair.*

                    "Hey now Garland,"
Saxon ducked in the bombproof, he annoyed
to have his troubled thoughts dispelled so kept
his gaze on the fire. Saxon sat and was quiet
for a long while till Garland relented and shared
some sweet potato coffee in a spare cup.
"Thanks," he nodded, sipping. "You know them fellers
they shot the other day for deserting?"

                            "Yeah."

"A feller in company B done told me what
it was the boy was saying, when a passel of sojers
was laughing? You recollect?" He nodded yes.
"The preacher asked if he was sorry for his sins,
but the boy said no, he was sorry because he never
got to know what tail was like. The feller
what told me that, he thought it was real funny.
He laughed and laughed. I stood there watching him,
thinking I don't know what, thinking this war
has changed me so I don't know who I am.
Nothing is what it used to be. I notice
stuff about folk I never noticed before,
and it usually makes me think how mean they are.

I just don't know if I will ever get back
to my life like it was. You ever have that feeling?"

"Saxon, you can't most always sometimes tell."

February 25, 1865

Dear Mother:
   Winter was coy till mid December,
then came with tooth and claw. I've never been
so cold in all my life. Everything is wet,
firewood, bedrolls, even the air we breathe.
I'm sorry it's been so long since my last letter.
I had a friend in the mess to die, Oscar
by name. He was our cook and a good man.
He and I were together the day he died.
It was quick. There was no time for parting words,
but it was painless for him, and I'm glad of that.
The siege wears on and for certain wears us out.
How I miss you, mother. How I miss home.

Captain Fagan, our line officer, dropped in
for surprise inspection one night near a week ago
to find our ditch abandoned for two hundred yards.
He was riled. 'Where in h-ll are the men?' he stammered
when he could finally speak. Caleb told him
they were off in the Yankee ditches playing poker.
He was sulled up like a old toad. But what
can he do to 75 men? They'd have to do shifts

in the guardhouse. Some never return from these excursions.
Their wives are writing them letters urging them home.
Strange to charge a man for deserting to his family.
Ah mother, everyone hates this war. On the last
of January, a carriage left our lines under flag
of truce and entered the Yankee lines. The rumors
went out quicker than a dose of salts, and soldiers
blue and gray clambered out of their ditches
as far as I could see back toward the west
all the way to the Forts the soldiers call
(beg pardon) Fort H-ll and Fort D-mnation, both sides
shouting with one voice, Peace! Peace! Peace!
But peace didn't come, of course; we were cast down.
This month we learn Columbia and Charleston are fallen.
Life will go hard on the people of South Carolina,
but the collar tightens on us all. We are tied to the traces.
Somehow, mother, I hope to see you soon.
I must go and fix our pitiful rations. I've taken
Oscar's place. Can you imagine me cooking?
I know you are laughing.

Affectionately, your son,

Garland.

March 1, 1865

"Got any grub Garland?"

                          "Not nary a bite.
But plenty of ash on the fire if you want to eat that."

"All's I got is news. Regis give me

an old *Whig.*"
        "Can we eat him, Saxon?"
                        "Nome,
he thin as a general's patience, but the Yankees is planning
to inaugurate Lincoln, and Sherman's headed our way."

"I got a cousin wrote me from Columbia," said Sprowl.
"He says the Yankees burned the city down
to the ground, put women and chits with nothing on the road."
Ainey said,
        "Them South Carolina folk
better run up under the hen. The blue tailed hawk
is here and he's flying low."
                        "I swany, the Yanks
will give those people hell."
                        "I swany they's gone
be hell enough and to spare," Caleb observed.
Garland leaned his body over embers.
Every few hundred yards or so were rough
cut shacks the soldiers built for meeting houses.
He hadn't been to a service since last November,
yet he realized he kept up a constant chatter aimed
at God, an argumentative, one sided diatribe.
He recalled his father's contempt for those who pester
God, but what else was there to do but protest,
like Jacob at Bethel, grapple and not let go
until you received, what, forgiveness, blessing,
a hurt that shows you're marked as one of his own?
Now there the Jews had scored again with a truth.
Men know themelves by scars of the suffered world.

"Coon warn't at role call this morning. Anybody seen
that slinking varmint?"
                              "I saw him go over the top
with his full kit. I reckon he done deserted,"
said Ainey. "I commenced to shoot him, but then I thought,
worst I could do to the Yanks is give 'em Coon."
Joshua said,
                "Boys I decided to desert
myself, but then I considered I'd be over yunder
with James and Sprowl and Coon and then I thought,
I'd rather a Yankee shoot me than billet me
with that passel of turd knockers, and then I thought
if a Yankee shoots me, mebbe I go to Heaven
ahead of James and warn the saints he's coming."

"What could they do?"
                        "Clear out if they know what's good."

"You want to go to Heaven?"
                            "Well, I reckon.
Who wants to be in hell with all them Yankees
I shot? I reckon my reception in the hot place would be
rat cool."
            "What if they's Yankees in Heaven?" asked Caleb.

"I'm going to Rebel Heaven."
                              "You mean a part
has seceded?" Now Patty looking stern, intervened,

"You're funning too much, laddies. Our Lord and Savior
will cure us our mean ways of doing in the by and by."

His words quelled the mirth, made all thoughts sober
until he produced from his sack a glass tickler.

"For love of sweet Aunt Sally, where'd you"—
                                                     "Ainey,
never you mind the where, just have a bumper,
and lads, as you taste the good creature, recall
for dust thou art, to dust thou shalt return,
and let us therefore respect our Savior's love."

March 14, 1865

Ainey set his flap soles close to embers.

"If Christians get to Heaven fasting and praying,
we Rebels is gwine to get there on fasts alone."
Caleb chuckled, pulling a threadbare blanket
tighter around his shoulders.
                                      "No rations today,"
said Garland, staring forlorn at the empty spider.
"One of you boys should shoot us a slow bear."

"Have you seen the papers fellers?" Ainey asked.
"The Confed'rit Congress done got up a law to conscript
the Negroes for army service. They say they gwine
to raise two hundred thousand to fight the Yankees."

"Bless ever sole what's charging in front of me,"
said Patty.
                            "Two hundred thousand," Saxon scoffed,

"I know the Negro, the Negro is not a fool."

"The whole *raison d'etre* of the war is fighting
for our property," Rice exclaimed in weary irritation.
"This act is the first step to homemade abolition."

"If Negroes are going to be freed, I'd rather we freed them
than Yankees," said Caleb.
                              "War is white man's business,
and politics is white man's business. Once the Negro
enters those realms, he vies for equality, and he,
though virtuous in many respects, is yet to achieve
the full capacity to engage those roles."
                              "Lieutenant,
with all due respect, I'd rather work things out
with the Negroes than have a bunch of Yankees lording
over us, and if they want to take up a rifle,
I say let 'em come."
                     "God knows they gone
to have to front load and go in hot,"
said Ainey. Patty, who appeared to be musing, said,

"Fear not, lads, the help is on the way."

March 25, 1865

The air jittery as their guns were roaring in
the dawn light, spreading like a freshly opened wound.
For a moment or two, the pop of small arms fire,
and then to his left inside the palls of gray,

scuffle and clank obtaining the rhythm of footfalls,
and Gordon's corps was out of the earthworks, surging
toward the Federal line, raising their wild halloo,
and Rebels entrenched behind them echoed the yell,
as men advanced on the double quick, a hammer
strike; the nail's head was Fort Stedman.
He thought of captured cans of potted meat.
Federals buried in the mound were now awakened
to this fact; the fort's guns coughed to life, wreaking
dreadful ruin, churning flesh into air.
Now counter battery fire rained on the line
as Rebel attackers met the chevaux-de-frise.
Their momentum bled away, but just for a trice,
then the attackers poured through barriers, surging
forward again, and then, another hundred
yards, they breached the Yankee defenses, funneling
inside the redoubt. An exulting cry went up.
He wondered whether they might be ordered forward.
Rebels in the ditch stepped up fire, to make it
hot for Yankees coming to heal the breach.
For an hour and more they kept up tremendous fire,
he wondering, why don't they send us forward now?
But Yankee guns farther behind the lines
were converging fire on Stedman, and reserve troops
came forward, at least a division. By seven thirty,
Gordon's troops were stark in morning light,
hustling the mortal course back to their ditches,
savaged by Federal cross fire; they knew what this failure
meant. If the Rebel Army was grown so weak
it could not move the Yankees by surprise and force,
could not consolidate their audacious gains,

then they were doomed, and now more than ever he knew
he was not a soldier fighting in an army, but a man
fighting for life. He thought, *It's root hog or die.*

April 1, 1865

A hubbub clattered on their right late afternoon
toward Five Forks crossroads. Warren's corps was out front,
pinning them down with musketry. Fagan appeared,

"Fellers, the Devil's grist mill dam's done broke,
we gwine to take to our canoes. Fall back slow
but stay rumgumptious with the Yanks. We gone to git
astride the Boydton Plank Road and hunker down."
The troops moved out at once in a staggered, shifting
line, straightening to fire, then crouching to cover
ground fast and reload. As he trotted away, he noted
two or three veterans walking backwards. As they moved,
the hizzing trajectory of balls angled higher
above their heads, and musket fire slackened
as Federals began to press the Rebel retreat.
Fagan put them in line behind the plank road
facing south and Heth's men filling in
on the right. By midnight, they'd piled stones and spoil,
his chest and elbows compressing the cool earth,
his muscles tensed for an all-out Yankee assault.
He raised his eyes a little above the works,
watching the band of winks and sparks, ethereal
and oddly gorgeous, disjoint from buzzing trajectories.

"Me lads," said Patty, "did you hear of General Pickett?"

"Is he dead?" asked Garland.

"Hardly. When Little Phil
come knocking on our door, he was two miles up the road
enjoying a shad bake."

"And why wasn't I invited?"
asked Caleb.

"But Patty, the shad, was it plain or seasoned?"

April 2, 1865

The fight ground on relentless past midnight, eddied
and surged in crescendos and lulls of catastrophic
racket. His neck had seized to shoulders in agonized
torsion from apprehension and night long labor,
drawing beads on flashes and sparks in blackness.
At last the dawn light hammered darkness thin,
redoubled tumult sweeping them in surging currents.
The Yankees were hitting them all along the line,
the guns' clamor a deluge scouring earth,
and blue divisions driving forward with inexorable
force, but Rebels dug in, slugging it out
for the last ditch, knowing if the line gave way,
then all was lost. Hour after hour, the assault
persisted, the Federal onslaught stubborn and stiff,
the labor exhausting and certainty of so many positions
in the line dubious, nerves were thin as blue john.
They retreated and turned, knocking the Yankees back
mile after weary mile, withdrawing all

the way to Sutherland's Station.
                                        "We must be pert near
twenty miles from Petersburg."
                                        "I'd say sholey,"
said Ainey. "Them Yankees pushed us around pretty good.
They give us goss." Fagan appeared to keep them
in order.
            "Captain, when's A.P. Hill coming up?"

"Hill won't come up again till the Resurrection.
Far as I know, Heth is the senior at division."
Patty and Ainey frowned at each other in silence.
Night time, the ghostly regiments formed on the road.

"Where we headed, Ainey?"
                                    "Captain says
we headed to Amelia to pick up the Richmond & Danville
and get some rations rolling down from the capital."
Venus tripped along in the dark, the shuffle
and odors of men, and night still clung to earth
when files veered right past Fitz Lee's troopers, horses
starved to rack rib and winged pelvis.
Behind them a twin sunrise split the ecliptic.
The farther, fainter glowing troubled them most.
Robert Lee could defend her gates no longer.
Later in morning's fulsome light, the country
was verdurous, pasture grasses jeweled with dew fall,
houses safe and whole, men at their plowing.
But weighing heat of midday turned his mind
to his rags of pressed muck, inundated with stink.
Driven, desperate, they skirted the south bank

of the Appomattox. He swayed as he marched, a reed
in the wind, insensate to all but his belly's gnawing.

April 3, 1865 Amelia Courthouse

Ravenous darkness taunted the army with mile
on weary mile, but he brought Duessa to mind,
and thought of marching toward her conjured hope,
for reason told him losing he would win.
But losing must be survived, so he strove to endure
for her and glorious reunion. Exhausted dawn light
found them poised on a high bend leading down
to a ford of the Appomattox. Longstreet's corps
was snaking over. His column didn't cross
but hugged the southern bank to Amelia Courthouse
and halted in sight of uncoupled rolling stock.
The thought of food sighed relief through the troops,
but then to their consternation, they overheard
an officer reporting,
                          ". . .ordnance equipment, fifty,
crates of ammunition, one hundred twenty;
boxes of artillery harness, ninety six;
caissons, ten, and not *one* goddamned ration."
So down the Danville Road to Burkeville for vittles.
The sun no longer warmed him but passed right through,
his flesh become as air. His vision swam
in vertiginous currents. My God, my God, it was finished.
An absurd volition stirred their feet, and a few
in his mess, afraid of ambush, outpaced their regiment,

passing byways strewn with kit and arms
and broken soldiers, each aware of the goal,
to join the rear of Longstreet's corps for safety.
An army was not a mass of men, but men
under organization, and order had come undone.
Abandoned wagons clogged the way, in front
of one a mule was lying, collapsed, spavined,
struggling shallow breaths, his teamster fled.
He nudged the distended belly. Caleb said,

"What have I done unto thee that thou hast smitten me?"
His foot went out, nudged the belly again.
One lid cracked open, the eye not even revolving
in its socket to regard him, but waiting for the lash to fall.
Emotion welled in kinship and compassion, and he muttered,

"The whole creation groaneth in pain until now."
Regarding Caleb's face, he tried to remember
if he'd ever heard him swear. He was a beautiful
soul, and he was exhausted as a lazy Susan,
when a coulter nicks its stem, the rays slant down,
and the flower withers, a bright cloth tossed to the ground.
They pressed on, agonized miles and a shambling corp
behind them, the world a blur through starvation haze.
The march en route to Amelia Springs, a cold rain
fell, and stragglers emerged from underworld mists.

"Storm and hail."
                    "Lee's Miserables are miserable now."

April 4, 1865 Amelia Springs

"Bad news, men. Little Phil and a corps
of infantry have cut us off at Jetersville.
They gwine to send some rations from stores at Lynchburg
by the Southside Line to Farmville. Let's giddy-up."
Fagan was a marching corpse, his face filthy,
uniform ruinous, breeches torn at the knees.
The fall in sounded.
                              "This is gotdamned cruel."

"Double distance, double time, no rations."

"And you kin bet whatever's waiting at Farmville's
no better than a pussy full of warm piss,"
Saxon scowled, a dangerous cast in his eyes.
The road consumed the hope that inspires complaint,
pointless curses become the march's argot,
raging incredulity that years of hardship had led
to such a retreat, that a once magnificent army
was now a famished gang hemmed in by swales
and railway cuts, being run to ground by Yankees.
He paced his scrubbing head-on dance with hunger,
and always pursuing, the grumble of enemy guns.
That afternoon, they were headed towards a junction
five miles distant, a certain landmark. The friends
parted company, Caleb walking off
the road to the right, he to the left, searching
for something to eat. Come dark, they'd meet at the crossing.
He walked at least a mile through copse and meadow,
to the circular buzz of flies and a jay's scolding,

turning shadows angry in a country undiscovered
by armies. Revived by shade, he shed his clothes
and waded a waist deep river, his body wavering,
confusing golden boughs and buried in cloud.
Downstream, a black woman poled a gimcrack flat boat,
dressed in crimson sun. She ceased exertion
and raised her hand. He saluted, gained the bank
and emerged pouring and trembling with piercing chills.
His shadow stretching behind him, he strayed after chirrup
of sparrows retreating ahead like leaves fluttering.
At a meadow's edge, he discovered a scarce dirt path
and decided to follow its lead, then caught a whicker,
muted voices, so leapt from the way and hunkered
behind a stand of grasses and leafy sumac.
The sounds drew nearer, talk and laughter, hooves
muffled by dust.
                    . . . "and then the Devil says,
'These are Episcopalians who ate their salads
with the wrong fork!'" The soldiers restrained their mirth
with watchful, roving glances. He could see their nerves,
deep in the enemy wood. Four in number,
one a lieutenant, riding a gorgeous sorrel,
the other horses red and speckled with white.
The Yankees' uniforms were clean and neat, buttons
and buckles shiny. He let the horsemen pass
and lay in broom sedge cover to give them distance.
Catching a whiff of wood smoke, he struck through a hollow,
hearing only cicadas, the sparrows' anfractuous
music keeping its distance. He emerged in a meadow
by a cabin, shaded with dogwood and three greeny yews.
An ancient woman dressed in flour sacks balanced

on the stoop leaning precarious as if to spill her
in the yard. He felt a twinge she'd seen him come,
preferring to steal what she would likely offer
to save time spent on courtesy, and the truth of it stung,
and he was ashamed. She propped herself with a cane
shaking in her grip, her dead eyes skewed away.

"What folk they is around here call me Mother."

"I'm pleased to know you."
                         "You a Southern boy."

"Yessum. How can you tell?"
                         "Because you stink.
And your talk, of course." Her mouth tipped in a smile.
She put out her hand; he came up the steps and took it,
surprised her flesh could be so cool in such
hot weather. She led him halting inside the dogtrot.
The house dark doused his vision, the woman knocking
her cane on walls like the failing beat of a heart.
They entered the kitchen, where an open window cast
penumbral light. A stove, a table and chairs,
the crone felt for her chair back, eased herself down,
leaning her cane on the wall and placing her head
in her palm. He took the other chair. Her flesh
was marred with age spots and bruises; resting between them
was a large bowl, the contents so black it reflected
his face and next to that repast packages of crackers,
printed USA. *The Yankees will surely*
get to hell before me. Savor of food
entranced and his visage, ghost-misted in the bowl.

The woman pushed a spoon underneath his hand,
which he raised quaking. "Feller acrosst the holler
yonder come by this morning and give me a quart
of pig's blood. I had me some oats, so I fixed a pudding.
Hit won't set up in the hot, but hit tastes as good
as it does in winter." He broke the mirror's supple
skin with the shaking spoon and drank the gruel,
viscid and sweet, determined not to raise
the bowl and gulp it, but eat like a dignified man.
With every spoonful he drank, he felt the blood
restoring his empty shade with vital substance.
"My boy, Iddo, he went off to the war.
He was fighting for General Lee. I ain't had a letter
since near the start of September, sixty two.
His name was Iddo Whisonant. I don't suppose
you ever heared tell of such a one?"

                            "No ma'am,
I'm sorry." Letters were stacked in the window, weighted
with a stone. She covered her eyes with her hand, her knuckles
swollen like knots in pine sticks, fingertips tapered.

"A neighbor child reads 'em to me, and I get 'em by heart."

"He was probably killed at Sharpsburg, that's in Maryland.
When the Rebels retreated, they had to leave their dead.
I'm sorry."

                "I know he's gone. Hit's just I've always
wondered where and how. What else is a widder
to do in a day but pick at rags, when the grinders
cease because they are few, the windows be darkened,
the keepers of the house tremble and strong men bow."

Her face was rived like bark, her odor sour.
Her wet eyes shined, blue irises almost clear.
"Where are you from?"
                              "Eufaula, Alabama."

"Is your mother alive?"
                              "Yes'um, she is."
                                                  "Go home."

"All right. I can't do that, Mother."
                                        "Son,
we know the race is not to the swift nor riches
to men of understanding, and a hag in the wildwood
knows when Yankees come to her stoop, the thing
is done. Don't be a fool. Go home and live."

"I've given my word to men and women both.
I have to be a fool. It's that or nothing."

"But men will pass and women will pass." She shook
her head and sucked her gums, forehead still propped.
"The closer we come to God the farther we get
from them we loved. You can't imagine such,
but you grow old, you'll come to savor grief
else death is a perfect nothing. Life is vanity,
and no one can change it. What little they is is home."

"I'll do my best. I promise." Out the window,
the sun was getting low, and he thought of his crossroads
assignation.
                    "When you leave on out of here,

take the path from my stoop and follow down
to the lightning blasted oak fornenst the creek.
A stone's throw to the west, they is a cornfield.
The master won't mind you pulling a shirt tail of ears.
Get on back to the path and when it forks,
bear left to the creek. The nigger there is Tye.
Tye is an honest man, so treat him with good.
He'll ferry you over." He took her leathery hand
with a gentle squeeze, feeling the odd angles,
like holding a bundle of sticks.
                              "Thank you, Mother,
for your hospitality."
                              "What's your name, son?"
                                        "Garland."

"Blessings go with you, Garland, and fare you well."
He strode from the cabin's shadow and frowsy must.
A half hour later, he stood before the Negro,
clasping a generous shirttail full of corn.

"Hyeah, now massuh. I done got me two moccasins
dis mawning. Dey was tangled up together
like dey was fighting, and I wacked 'em both wit my pole."
He had opened the skin of one and was tacking it flat
to a board, the other serpent lying in a bight.
On several frames, muskrat and coon pelts were hanging
cased and drying. Tye put down his hammer
and wiped his hands. "I reckon you done seen Mothuh?"
He nodded. "Now if'n you don't watch out, Mothuh
will commence to preaching to you. Hit's a right strange sermon

what she got," he cocking his head and closing
his eyes in concentration. "I know hit come
from the Bible, but hit don't ever have nothing to do
wit Jesus or saving, like what dem preachers preach
in town. Ain't that peculiar?"

                      "Yes, it is.
Who are you working for?"

                      "I works fo me.
I's a free Negro, massuh. I bought myself
three yar ago off Mistuh Grimes' plantation—
dat's his corn you got, what Mothuh's always
giving away" —he chuckled— "now I's like every
man else, a slave to myself, and call me a fool
if'n I ain't the wustest massuh I ever did have.
The he coon walks 'fore dawn, and Tye's dare waiting.
I fotch two dollah fo every pelt I make
and a fip fo taking gentlemens cross de ribber
and a fip fo dey hosses. Deys fo clean Yankee sojuhs
come through hyeah dis mawning what gimme a quarter
a piece—you'll want to keep yo eye out, massuh.
Dis ribber ain't much—dey can cross it any old wheres."

"I'm obliged. All I got is Confederate script."

"Now massuh, Tye don't charge no Rebel sojuhs,
naw suh. Rebs is fighting the bravest war
what ever been fought by no man. Call me a fool
if Tye ain't helping dem sojuhs what's fighting for him.
Goliath rages, but little David's coming."
The Negro laughed, climbing aboard his vessel,
retrieving his pole, untying the mooring line.

"I'd be obliged if you'd take a little money."

"Un-uh. Naw suh. Not from no Rebel sojuh."
He threw his weight down hard against the pole
and the flat boat moved out breasting summer sky.
The Negro spoke abstracted now, "Naw suh,
not from no Rebel sojuh," then winked at him.
"Don't tell nobody, massuh, but Tye is rich."
Traveling back to encroaching night, he discovered
Caleb standing alone at the crossroads, whose excursion
had turned up nothing but bottom land and marsh,
so he was delighted with a windfall of green corn
and not disposed to regret the blood pudding.
They built a fire large enough to parch
the ears, sumptuous to them as pound cake and champagne.

April 5, 1865

Another day of passing vacant men
staring from fence corners, waiting for Federals to come
and collect them. He passed a soldier sitting back
on his haunches, elbows propped on knees, his empty
hands suspended in air before him, meek eyes
heavy with battles, full of rage and longing
to be in step with comrades. Despair shone
around him. Some called out, the fabulous ruined
who'd marched with Lee to Gettysburg, with Jackson
through the Shenandoah Valley, who'd waged triumphs
at Fredericksburg and Chancellorsville, now skeletal
and bleating in wayside ditches. He would never forget

those surrendered eyes, their staring forlorn eloquence.
They marched into dark and halted he didn't know where.
He eased himself to the ground by Caleb, his body
slack. His heart was knocking insistent rhythm
in fingers, toes, and throat, along his hair line.
He knew why the aged give up their lives for promise
of rest.
      "If death is a perfect nothing, how welcome
a surcease of struggle dying must be," said Garland.

"But what a farce after all to be marched to death."

April 6, 1865 Rice's Station

The night grew frigid, a sudden sleet blew down.
He, like most men, fell asleep in snatches,
awakened often by bone damp, aching cold.
Revolving streaks of mocking dawn appeared,
and once again they strode down desperate byways
and made by morning the rear of Longstreet's corps.
Back toward Saylor's Creek, a many-noted,
musical booming died in ominous silence
as they crossed the Appomattox River at High Bridge.
That night the day time stragglers drifted into camp,
their wearied gestures shadowed among the fires.
One ghost emerged from darkness, his face transparent
in ember glow. He offered the soul their last
nubbin of parched corn, who said,
                    "Three days."
Caleb lifted his hat brim above his eyes.

"Three days till what?"

"He means he ain't et nothing
in three days," said Ainey.

"Is that what you mean?"

"Nome," said another of Longstreet's scarecrows, "He means
we got three days to live. Three days and then
we die."

"Well hail and storm in Beulah Land.
Take that nubbin away from him. I want
a better saying for our offering."

"Well, a prophet
don't cause things to happen; they only says what's gwine
to happen."

"Take his corn, I say. I demand
a better outcome." The phantom seemed oblivious
to protestations and gnawed the bitter ear.
When he was done, he tossed the cob behind him.
He opened his mouth, the men inclining toward him.
He produced a delicate belch, and his left hand, lifting
the right hand sleeve of his blouse, dabbed the corners
of his mouth, Caleb observing him in disdain.

"Now there's prophecy; there's the divine afflatus."
Now he'd eaten, Patty asked,

"What regiment
are you, friend?"

"Kershaw's Division."

"Bejabbers!"
There followed a long and comprehending silence.

"Storm and hail. Three days it is," said Caleb.
The ghost remained mute; however, another eidolon
stepped from darkness and joined their houseless bivouac
and without invitation or greeting began to speak,

"The Yanks done cut us off at Saylor's Creek.
Anderson and Ewell's corps is bagged, snout
and trotters. Ewell is captured, along with Kershaw
and Custis Lee." The look alike soul stretched out
on the ground and continued, "We'uns in a hell of a fix.
A one eyed President, a one legged, general prisoner,
and a played out one horse Confederacy sucking hind tit."
Wet and corpse-frigid in flurries, they slept.

April 7, 1865 Farmville

Stragglers winnowed far behind the march.
At roadside, soldiers had stood their rifles up
on bayonets, clustered in random musket groves.
The order came to halt and fall in for rations.
There was no energy left to cheer, but a great
exhalation like churring from a settling flock let loose
from the whole scarecrow division. The men sat down
in ranks and soon the skillet wagons came,
clanking a grudging mile out of Farmville.
Garland procured their bacon and struck a fire,
and soon from every quarter of the peaceful meadow
aroma of frying pork was rapturous.
                                        "Hot damn,"
said Ainey, "First rations issued in five days,

and I'm so hungry my innards are working outside of me."
Just east, the hum of guns pursuing all morning
like a gnat annoying the ear, began to menace.
An officer spurring a lathered horse came shouting
for the regiment's commander. Patty said,

                                        "I'll be bound.
Would you look and see a filthy officer. We're in it
now, me lads." Rice appeared in a twist.

"Mahone has failed to order his engineers
to fire the spans at High Bridge. That oversight means
that Humphrey's Division has crossed and even now,
just four miles east is breathing down on us.
We must get beyond the junction of Cumberland Church
and High Bridge Road before we are cut off.
I'm sorry, men. We must move out at once."
Like a murder of startled crows, a chorus of eloquent
blasphemies rose and collided. He unsheathed his camp knife,
sharpened the stick he was using to turn the portions
and skewered the meat as men dumped skillets and flung
them in wagon beds as wide eyed teamsters glanced
behind them, hankering to shake the reins.

                                        "Eat it
quick. They's here what'd shoot us for it in a wink."

"Bless yore heart," said Ainey, and he and the others
with delighted looks stripped the meat bare handed
from the stick the way a boy might strip the leaves
of rabbit tobacco from stems, furry and silver.
They chewed in quiet ecstasy and set their flap
soled boots to marching, their shadows leading them west.

April 8, 1865

Tomorrow came one minute after midnight.
A corporal barely able to read stuttered
their orders to sniggering dark. Pickett, Heth,
and Wilcox were assigned to Longstreet. Old Peter's corps
would guard the rear, so they halted, allowing Gordon
to take the lead toward Appomattox Station.
Patty's voice,
         "It's a tinker's breakfast, lads."

"I'd rather be in hell with my back broke than make
another march," said Ainey. His limbs grew light,
he passing hallucinations of farms and fields,
borne on a weary river, comforting and peaceful,
till his head jerked up, his eyes sprang open like jalousies.
The ju-ju bag was out of his shirt and knocking
his chest in pulse rhythm. He tried to imagine
how he might persuade her, filling the dead time
planning their reunion. But his weary mind refused
out right to try and manage thoughts so full
of trouble and complexity and kept on switching tracks
to simple things, prospects of sleep in a bed
or rashers of pork, and his feet kept falling morning
to noon to dewy evening. At last they halted
and fell down where they were in a pasture clearing
about three miles from Appomattox Station.

"I'm so dry I'm whistling for the dogs," said Ainey.
Garland lay stiff as a fencepost. A few stars winked,

Canis Major lunging for Orion's heels.
He closed his eyes. To be without a body
and float among stars. . . . A rhythmic pocking of hooves,
a horse reigned in nearby, a panicked voice.

"Tolliston, sir, reserve artillery, First Corps.
We had our guns in park, near sixty pieces,
in a field at the county seat, when Federal cavalry
burst upon us from out'n the woods. We set
two batteries to work to hold 'em off. Hot damn,
if it waren't the closest fight I ever seen!
Our guns were fought right up to the muzzles, our boys
was jousting Yankees off their mounts with sponge rods.
We fought 'em well past dark."
                                                  "How many pieces
did we lose?"
                        "Two dozen. Orders for tomorrow's march?"
A silence followed, then a belated, "Yes sir,"
and then his horse galloped out of hearing.

"Every which way we turn, the Yankees are there,"
said Caleb. The two heard Colonel Herbert speaking
to Fagan.
                "See the map, this jugged peninsula
between the James and Appomattox Rivers?
There is only one way out, that way is here—
at Appomattox Station. Both armies are heading there
with all due haste. Grant has the shorter road."
Sleep weighed his eyes, a heavy coin on each.

April 9, 1865 Appomattox Station

Camp canard bestirred the line, telling
him what he could have guessed. Little Phil
had beaten the Rebels to Appomattox and must be
swept aside. The dawn was close to breaking.
Longstreet's corps watched Gordon's men go forward,
Louisianans and Georgians driving determined
west on Lynchburg Pike, their road to freedom.
Fitz Lee's guns were catching their breath on the right.
Blue cavalry hunkered in field works, dug last night
and studded with guns. Gordon's division pressed
in rags and audacity, wading fog, raising
their savage exulting made thrilling by desperation,
swamping Federal defenses, and Longstreet's corps
answered the yell in shrilling caterwauls. The blue coats
scattered rearward for cover. Now Gordon wheeled
his corps hard left to hold the Lynchburg open.
The attack surged on, dribbling dead, a gray
and blue detritus behind the atrocious wave.
The wagon train began to roll, the Rebel
door kept swinging left, and fog began
to lift above the trees and—astonishing—on the far
side of fields straddling the cleared road
as far as he could see, as far as they all
could see, rank on rank of infantry, blue flags
snapping in breezes, at ease and facing the sunrise.
Cheering ceased as if every man had dropped
on a hangman's rope. Gordon, nearer the fight,
had seen it already, shook out a picket line,
stepped up artillery, and ordered his men to fall back.

"You lived to hear the final Rebel yell,"
said Caleb.
                    "They've got us. Why don't they come?"
                                                        "I reckon
they ain't no Federal, as I'm sure they ain't no Confederate,
what wants the distinction of those on the field before us,
of dying in the war's last hour. And I reckon it mote be
General Lee's already asked for terms."

"You really think he'd surrender?"
                              "Look at us, Garland."
But neither could take his eyes off the ranked blue serge.
Philistine hordes could not have numbered so many.
They were ordered back to a stretch of defensible ground,
and Gordon's troops passed through them, forming behind,
taking available cover, but no one dug.
The air was charged electric with instinct for destruction,
a reckless thirst for blood, the enemies' or their own.
Longstreet rode between their lines, his right arm
hanging limply at his side.
                          "Say the word,
Old Peter, we'll rile them Yankees good." He tipped
his hat and trotted on. And nothing happened.
Hours crept by, and Caleb got up and milled,
collecting scuttlebutt.
                      "Come on."
                                "What you got?"

"Lee is surrendering now in a private home
on the edge of Appomattox Courthouse a mile
or so down the road."
                    "You mean the war is over?"

"Could be." He wished it to be but couldn't believe it.
They trotted a good two miles, sides stitched and panting,
and reached a scarecrow convention in a shady lane.
A path led up a rise between rail fences
to a neat brick dwelling, with a wrought iron belvedere,
wide front steps, palings, well curb and smoke house.
He thought of the ruined houses he'd seen in towns
and hamlets. But war had entered this house quietly,
with a gentleman's conduct. In the dooryard a butternut officer
stood, holding the bridle of the iron gray horse,
stamping and eyeing two soldiers lounging on the stoop.
The door swung open. The bluecoats sprang to attention
as a man in gray emerged, his uniform plain
and smart, linens clean as new blown cotton,
his boots' high polish throwing off the light.
A sash was tied about his waist in crimson
liquefaction. A dress sword hung at his side.
Blue officers flooded out behind him and gathered
for a moment. A man among them pointed.
                                        "That one
to the left of Lee, that's U.S. Grant." Brown headed,
stooped, even from this far away, they could tell
he'd just gotten out of the saddle, dusty and spattered.
Introductions and shaking of hands ensued.
The man in gray dress paused a moment and spoke
to a dark-skinned officer, then drew his sword, supporting
shank and blade in open palms, and offered it
to the grungy man in blue, who raised one hand
in polite refusal. The officers bowed their respects,
and Lee pulled on his heavy gauntlets, smacked
his right fist in his left palm, mounted

the storm cloud horse tossing its gun metal mane
and spurred from the yard at a gallop. He reined in
when he reached the knot of men and raucous cheers.
They saw his solemn face when he raised his hat.

"General Grant is going to treat us well, men."
At the name of General Grant the cheering withered.

"General, are we surrendered?"
                                    "Are we surrendered?"
They thronged around him now, hemming him in.
He hung his hat on the pommel.
                                    "Men, we have fought
the war together, and I have done the best
I could for you. You are all paroled and free
to go home until you are exchanged." His face
was tracked with wet. His voice seized, and he spoke
an almost inaudible, "Goodbye." His own heart clenched.
Traveler snorted and twitched his tail's dark broom.

"I love you just as I ever did, General Lee!"
a scarecrow veteran shouted, spreading his arms
cruciform above the crowd, a swelling battalion.

"General, we'll fight 'em yet. Say the word
and we'll go in and fight 'em." Lee shook his head,
that mild, reticent gesture quieting all,
and the end came home to them in stupified silence.
He urged Traveler to a slow walk and thousands
of soldiers, heads bowed, many weeping, passed
their open palms along the horse's flanks

as he rode the long gauntlet of hands and adoration
until the general passed them out of sight.
A veteran threw down his rifle.
                    "Blow, Gabriel,
Blow! My God, let him blow. I'm ready to die."
That evening they lined up for dinner. The skillet wagons
stretched at least a mile along the Confederate
campsite on Lynchburg Pike and lines of dusty
scarecrows surrounded them all. A Yankee private,
fat and jocund, served them.
                          "Step up Johnnies,
dinner's on me." The soldier in front of Garland,
too weak to stand, was supported under each arm
by two of his fellows. "Here you go, my friend,"
the Federal bellowed. The Rebel hugged his rations
to his chest like clutching a child.
                          "I'm obliged," he croaked,
"and we'uns is sorry for the late unpleasantness."
The Federal erupted in laughter, and every Rebel
was mesmerized by the astonishing appurtenance, the shivering
abdominous protrusion, belly pregnant with rations,
jerking upwards with every intake of breath.
They turned their charge around, and he saw his bloodshot,
staring eyes, spikes of cheekbones prominent
from weeks of starvation, his uncomprehending smile.
The rations were generous; soon the cook fires blazed,
and victuals helped to ameliorate the gloom.

"Hard to think we've come all this way to have it
end like this."
                "Yeah, it is, but I

for one, am glad the thing is over with,"
said Ainey. "You know Grant's give us our paroles?"

"I reckon he's something of a gentleman, after all."

"Caleb and I moseyed down the road
and watched the surrender. We saw when General Lee
offered Grant his sword and Grant refuse it."

"Well lay me down. That's mighty white o' Grant."

"But they's more to it than courtesy," Caleb observed.
"No man will ever offer his sword again
after that refusal. It wasn't a sword that Grant
was rejecting; it was the aristocrats' high flown notions,
the notions they lived by. Those things no longer apply
in the world the Yankees are going to reconstruct,
and to this work, the Negro will be a mere diversion.
The yeoman must embrace the Negro, rebuild
his values, barns and houses, mills and farms."

"Caleb, in all the war you never sounded
like such a passionate Southron," Ainey said.

"The South is still my home. I struggle and love it."

"You know they gwine to use the Negro agin us."

"Only time will tell, but time *will* tell
if they have been sincere in what they've said
about the war and especially about the Negro.

How will Lincoln birth this second union,
enforce the proposition of Negro freedom,
and not allow oppression's shadow system?
Southern folk will strive so that their dead
shall not have died in vain, and there the impasse
of spilled blood, which always demands allegiance.
But I know this. If the North goes back on its word,
blood of the Union dead will cry from the ground.
If it gives us back our brutal system of class,
the North will reveal itself the face of Empire.
Better for all the North should keep its word."

April 10, 1865

The day was long and nothing to do but wait
in drizzling cold. Since martial matters were always
formal affairs, they were mustered and given instructions
for the surrender's conduct. Herbert read them a farewell
order from Lee, addressing his thanks to his men,
who were then advised to return to bivouac for shelter,
prepare their rations, and wait to meet the Army
of the Potomac, but he could not stay still, his thinking
troubled, knotted like grumous roots, and so ambled
through woods, rhythmic with dripping, loosening tautened
nerves. Back in camp, Caleb was wrapped
in a rubber blanket beneath a shagbark hickory,
abstracted in thought.
                    "Think about it, Garland.
The war's cataclysm, battles at Gettysburg,

Spotsylvania, the Wilderness have been transmogrified
into memories. With us its meaning stands apart
from whatever imputed thing it will come to be.
Now every night across these states in dreams
the shells will screech, the balls will hum, the colors
surge forward on breezes until the marching years
shall flank us out of life, the Blue and Gray,
and one by one, dream by dream, snuff out
our recollections so nothing remains but grass
and trees and hillsides recovered in green shade,
and cradling earth will hold this war forever."

"Caleb, you should get out of that store and be
a schoolteacher, use that fine eloquence of yours."

"Students these days don't appreciate it."

April 11, 1865

The rain was drumming threnody in shelves of branches.
He huddled with Caleb, their backs against the trunk
of a pignut hickory, trying to shelter from the wet.
The Federals posted pickets to avoid the mingling
of soldiers and any attendant misunderstandings,
but Union troops were wandering about their camps,
wanting to meet the enemy and collect souvenirs.
A temper sometimes flared, but most encounters
were cordial. He overheard a Rebel say,

"Success has made them civil." A bluecoat private

ambled around a caisson, the rain's tramp
building, and headed for their hickory's shelter. He watched
his face as he came, crouching and hopping puddles,
a good natured smile beneath his short brimmed kepi.
He wasn't coming to gloat. He slapped his cap
on his thigh to knock out the water.

                           "Hey now, Johnnies.
We been fighting each other four years now.
Give me a Confederate five dollar bill to remember
you by." Garland opened his wallet, offered
a crisp new bill. The Yankee took it in both hands.
"Hey now, thanks!" He placed the money with care
inside his wallet and removed a five dollar greenback.
"We'll make it an even swap."

                         "Even? That shinplaster
warn't never worth the ink they used to print it,
and after Sunday last, it ain't worth nothing."

"You kidding me? I'll show this note to my grandkids
and tell them a Rebel soldier give it me
in the Great American War. It'll make 'em think
the old man's had adventures and didn't spend
his whole life busting sod on an Iowa farm."

"Well I'm obliged."

             "You're welcome. Where you guys from?"

"We both from Alabama. He's from Montgomery,
and I'm from Eufaula down in the Wiregrass."

"The Wiregrass? What's life like in Alabama?"

"Like most folks in Dale County, we work all day
for possum, taters, and sop."
                                    "Is Dale County
in the Black Belt?"
                                    "Just south of that, down
in the coastal plains."
                                    "You going back, now
the war is over?"
                                    "I reckon I will. It's home."

"It's good for a man to have a home to get to,
but this war has given me the travel bug.
Clayville's going to seem pretty slow after this.
I been thinking about the west and Indian Territory.
The army needs some help with the Apaches. I'm sure
they could probably use another rifle out there."

"From what the papers say it's wild country."

"A young man finds adventure in wild country.
And besides, the Indian question must be settled,"
he paused in reflection, staring through sheaves of rain.
"Johnnies, it's an honor having you back in the Union,
men whose courage will ever remain unquestioned.
I got no hard feelings. You knocked us around pretty good,
but that's just war. Now I hope we'll be friends.
One day we'll turn out against the world together,
and when that day comes, the world had better look out."
He extended his hand and Garland shook it, touched
his cap to Caleb, who nodded, then stepped through a curtain
of rain.
                    "Garland, you keep on swapping Confederate

paper even money for greenbacks, you might
just leave on out of here a man of means."

"I doubt that many Yankees will share his hankering
for Confederate money. He seemed a nice enough fellow."

"Nice enough."
                    "What?"
                                        "Awe I don't know.
The Yankee mind just gives me the collywobbles.
They always wanting a little more of everything,
adventure, power, money, where does it end?"

"You sound a mite chafed."
                                        "I'm not chafed."

April 12, 1865

This gray Wednesday, the regiments marched to a field
fronting Appomattox Courthouse. En route,
they passed a cavalry unit sitting their mounts
on a rise of hill by the road.
                                        "Who you fellers?"

"First Virginia Cavalry, at your service, sir."

"Yer mules is starving."
                                        "These are brevet horses
of Confederate issue. They do not require fodder."

A man in the ranks hee-hawed. Laughter sputtered.
A junior officer, a haggard aristocrat,
addressed a young man ambling past,

                           "Say boy,
you got any bacon in your sack?"

                                "Yes sir, a mouthful."

"Well grease up, son, and slide on back in the Union."
The Rebels did their best to dress for parade,
scarecrows with batting knocked out, in tatters too ragged
to hang on a line, most fought out to exhaustion,
staring eyes incongruent and distant, odd
and unmoored from things at hand, the grassy field,
the line of wagons, the tee pee stacks of rifles.
They halted in the midst of the Federal Army, a legion
of clean blue serge and shining buckles and buttons,
some Yankee chin music quickly suppressed by officers,
but they were not ashamed. The Union Army,
magnificent in panoply of appurtenance and arms, stirred
their pride. For Rebels, naked and starving, had held
this host at bay for four long years. A rumor
had it that when their column reached the field,
a unit from Maine saluted, and Gordon leading,
returned the courtesy. He, for one, was relieved
the thing was ending well. He stood among soldiers
rolling up the regimental colors, one saying,

"We'll go home, make three crops, and try 'em again,"
and he heard another telling his brigadier,

"My shoes is gone, my clothes is almost gone.

I'm tired. I'm sick. I'm hongry. My family's kilt,
my children is scattered. I've suffered four yares,
and I would die because I love the South,
but I'm here to say now this war is over,
I'm damned if I'll ever love another country."
Herbert and Regis stood side by side, stacking
their arms. His eyes fell on the black hand leaning
his piece in a loathsome bouquet of bayonets.
He offered Regis his hand.
                              "Of all the men
who made the cause of the South their own, none
deserves more glory than the Negro under arms.
The South is bound to honor such selfless devotion.
Thank you, Regis. It gives me pleasure to shake
the hand of a sovereign man." Regis responded
with embarrassed silence. Herbert turned away.
He and Caleb watched the tattered men,
their haversacks full of Yankee rations, form
in groups of friends or parties destined for the same
towns or hamlets.
                        "I'm heading down to Wilmington,"
said Caleb. "I've got an aunt who'll put me up
and feed me out until I get my strength back.
You come too. I know she wouldn't mind.
The rest would do us good before we start
our journey."
                    "Friend, I appreciate it, I do;
but though I'm hurt and starved, I want to go home,
and I don't reckon I'm going to rest at all
until I get there."
                        "I thought you'd be in a hurry."

"We'll stay in touch. Caleb, you saved my life"—

"I saved your life just once, but you saved mine
every day. I never would have survived
the war without a friend."
                              "Every October
we kill a passel of hogs. All the neighbors
come to help and bring a dinner on the grounds.
It's hard work and good food. I'll expect you."

"I'll be there." The two embraced and parted, Caleb
retracing his steps to Petersburg for the Weldon Railroad,
and he to Lynchburg for an engine bound to Atlanta.
The Union Army was running the railroads now,
loading gray backs in south bound cars, so many
sick and weak, assisted onto trains by healthy
Yankees, it made him think they were being sent
to their doom, instead of home, though home it was.
The Federal quartermaster issued him a pass
to take him all the way to Opelika.
A tuxedoed man was strutting about the platform,
his impatience at regular intervals checking his watch
and barking orders like a brigadier. His mien of pride
might make men think the very earth depended
on the end of his golden chain.
                                  "It's up to me
to make this railroad solvent, sir, and it shan't
be done unless it turn a profit. "You"—
he barked to the sentries, "Tell the quartermaster
to summon another train at once. And you—
order those niggers there to fetch these parcels

and stow them with the baggage. I want to see them skipping!
A million dollars a day to set them free—
we have our claim to a bit of African sweat!"
These orders pleased the guards who hurried away.
As top hat paced the platform and gave commands,
puffing his cigar and directing others to tasks
with his gold tipped cane, he boarded his car, packed
with Rebels, and sat till his head was throbbing with fetid
stink of bodies. The whistle blasted twice,
he jerked forward, and this, this bodily tug
was the palpable sign he was going home at last.
His head cleared, the pain vanished, and his heart,
unclenched. They rode all night with windows opened,
the country breezes cleansing stenches and wafting
in spring odors of things green and blowing.

April 13, 1865

That afternoon, the engine huffed into Columbia,
throttling back, creeping through a city of char.
Passing the platform's head, he saw three haggard
soldiers, cooling their feet in a drinking trough.
He heard a distant church bell tolling, and out
of the coach, the view of the city struck him dumb,
a merciless Sodom purge, the grass and trees
and rubble tainted black, and all the structures
hollow facades. The air was heavy with incinerated
stench and not a window glass in the city.
A platoon of Federal soldiers passed in the street,
and he could sense an instant malice flourish

in Rebels massed on the platform. The lieutenant glanced
their way, but only in passing. The men marching
behind looked straight ahead. Several scorched
structures appeared to be churches. A couple of blocks
away, the columned state house was domeless and pocked.
At the steps he could just make out a statuette
of polished bronze; the clouds shifted allowing
a valley of sunlight, showing a haze of ash
suspended above Columbia's charred heart.
A tow-headed boy appeared among the travelers
pulling a wooden barrel on rickety wheels.

"Mister, you want a glass of cold iced water,
only a nickle?"
                        "I'll give you a dime if you tell me
who the man is standing in front of the statehouse."

"Where's?"
                "The statue there."
                                "At's George Washington,
our first president. The Yankee sojers thowed brickbats
at him when they's attacked us. My momma says
Yankees ain't no Americans and ain't no Christians."

"She's right about that, little feller."
                                "Sholey right,"
two scarecrows laughed sitting on the platform for the benefit
of the Federal stationed guard.
                                "Mister, are you all
Confederate sojers?"
                        "Yes son, here's your dime."

"My momma says Confederate sojers are the bravest
sojers they's ever been. She says we've been
subdued but we ain't been vanquished." The Federal smirked.
On the platform a wounded Rebel lay with no
right leg below the knee, fresh blood staining
the stump bandage. He moved his hand from shading
his eyes and regarded the boy.
                                          "Son, you can tell
your momma Will O'Shea is vanquished." But tow head
gave no notice and drew his squeaking barrel
beside him and ladled a drink. "Take it away.
I have no money." The boy got down on his knees
and lifted the wounded man's head, and all the soldiers
looked away, even the Yankee sentry,
but he watched the boy as he placed the sweating cup
to split and peeling lips and revived the man
with a sweet, cold draught of water and fed the man
some bites of bread.
                         "Say young'un, where's your daddy?"

"My paw was kilt at Seven Pines. He'uz fighting
with General Polk." An engine hissed behind him.
The whistle sounded twice. The Federal stepped forward.

"All right all you heroes—all aboard!"
Sunset dragged the dark behind it, consuming
fields and woods, and the traincar rocked him to sleep.

April 14, 1865

He woke hog in the bed style, his cheek cool

and mashed on window glass, his breath clouding
and unclouding the water tower near which the train
was parked, his drool soaking a sleeve. He swallowed
and stretched. The double shriek. He felt the massive
inertial urge as the wheels began to turn
and wished he could have gotten off to pee.
He was surprised what little conversation
there'd been, the man beside him hardly speaking,
but staring ahead wringing his hands, not
in anxiety, but in meditation, the way a woman
in prayer might finger a rosary. Once he asked,

"I swany if folks back home'll recognize me?"
But folks back home were not the problem; the problem
was war, the deprivations and killing, required
him to fashion a warrior self. That man
was the war's last casualty. His spirit was haunting trenches
in places everyone knew and did not know,
could never know, while his body occupied a coach,
wringing its hands, going home, but home required
him to be the man he'd always been,
and he couldn't recall that man, his life or manners.
Which would enter his house, kiss wife and children?
The train cars raced ahead of familiar dawn.

April 15, 1865 Atlanta

Pitiable, inhuman screaming piercing darkness,
the whistle shrilled, the couplings, caught on the hold back,
now gave the tug, whip-lashed his head backward.

Ten years ago a man in these parts knew
the dawn by the whippoorwill's call, bluejay's exuberance,
but now this shrill mechanic shrieking obliterates
his morning peace. For mile on mile, their way
showed signs the road had recently been destroyed
and then rebuilt—great heaps of char where crossties
and telegraph poles were fired to heat the rails
the Yankees deformed on tree trunks, the irons stacked eight
or nine high and pulled tight—Sherman's neckties.
They rocked by cracker box shacks and lean-to barns.
A lone rail splitter labored in eerie shade.
He straddled his log, ripped end to end, the burnished
heels of wedges bright, he gangling, naked
to the waist, muscles gathering as he raised the heavy
mallet and struck. As the cars passed, he mopped
his brow and raised a hand. Garland waved
and thought him a forlorn man, a creature of shadows
and time, floating past his coach. Some shacks
of up end green pine clapboard passed the window.
The cars began a gentle westward turning,
an appalled silence settling. For miles in every
direction the earth was leveled, no tree or bush,
no fences or cattle, houses or barns, just blackened
squares witnessing ground where these had stood.
Not even a crow could subsist in this ravaged land,
which he imagined stretching all the way
to Savannah. The man beside him spoke again.

"I'd rather have lost. Yes, by God, I'd rather,
than show the world that such an act were possible
for me." Now they were come to the city's outskirts

and more destruction, passing a rubbled, bombed out
engine house. Workmen had cleared away most
of the fallen bricks, and a stoked engine revolved
on the table. The engineers greeted each other with a whistle
blast, and they clattered on past gutted blocks
of charred brick, patches of its facing shot away,
swept with innumerable pocks and drill marks, varied
in size and depth and holes knocked out by shot
and all the windows doused like blinded eyes.
The train pulled up to the famous Atlanta Car Shed,
a waste of brick and a platform in open air.
A porter greeted them.
                           "This train is thirty minutes
for Macon, Millen, and Savannah. This platform at three
boards Columbus and Opelika, Alabama."
Garland cut across the car shed lot,
across a city block of rubble and char,
which must have been a hotel, so many fire dogs
and slop jars among the ashes. He entered a five street
intersection and turned down Peachtree Street.
No hotels, churches, foundries, rolling mills,
or stores, and private homes reduced to bricks
and ashes. East down Line Street blocks were measured
by debris of buildings reduced and poured onto sidewalks.
Northwest up Walton Street three blocks or so,
a girl of twelve or thirteen stood in the road,
shading herself with a parasol. He waved at her.
She made him a slight curtsy and turned away.
A man was stooping by a hodgepodge of brick. A crow,
perched on a remnant wall, was mocking him.
The man did not look up as he approached

though he was surprised and pleased he recognized him.

"Doctor Britt. It's good to see you, sir."
The doctor wore his surgeon's smock, the sleeves
rolled up, the bloodstains faded out to brown.
He did not halt his work, retrieving bricks
and stacking them on a barrow, but gave a furtive
glance at his arms and legs, his eyes corpse-vacant.
"Of course you don't remember me. We met
at Fredericksburg, December sixty two."

"My wife and daughter are dead. I have no home
or practice. I'm sober as an Anabaptist for the past
two months. I find the state is uncongenial.
My winsome girls. How lovely they were to me."

"I'm sorry for your loss, sir. I know it's hard."

"Do you?" The doctor kept on grasping and stacking.
He wondered if there were any point to his labor
or if it were only a mad, mechanic exercise.

"I've lost a few I loved, though none so dear
as wife and child, but at least the thing is over.
The Yankees are going to treat us well, I think."

"The Yankees have made a wilderness and call it union.
My mind is a nightmare choir of anguished cries.
And what was the point? Misery, world without end.
Monstrous coercion! I will never be one with a Yankee."

"Forgive me, but we all inflicted our share of misery.

Men on the Federal side are hearing those cries."

"True enough. I often consider that fact,
 and the thought never fails to give me satisfaction."
A street away a dog began to bark.
"They have razed my house even to the foundation thereof."

"When I was released from hospital in Fredericksburg,
 you offered to requisition me to try
 and keep me safe. Besides a friend or two
 in my company, you were the only man who ever
 expressed a care for my life. I'm grateful, sir."
He offered his hand, but the doctor grasped two bricks,
turned him away with recognition how even
surrendered there was no conquering the suffered past,
the conflict merely shifting to fronts of outrage
in vanquished lives. He turned to go, then heard,

"The Northern Lights. You divined the meaning, prophet."
But Britt was turned away, addressing ruin.
He retraced the devastation of Peachtree Street
and found the platform astir with excitement, each man
animated and talking at once.
                              "What's the news?"
"Ain't chew heard?"
                    "No."
                         "A rebel actor
 in Warshington City done shot the Original Gorilla."

"What?"
        "Lincoln was at the thee-ater, and a Rebel

actor blowed his black Republican brains out."

"That was yestiddy."
                      "They say he died this morning."

"If the Devil don't get Lincoln, you have to wonder
if they's a point in having a Devil at all."

"Don't you boys think this might go hard on us?"

"How could it get any worse—look around?"

"I'm thinking ahead. How will it get any better?"

"Hell, boy, you talk like a repentant Rebel."

"He's talking like he's got some goddamned sense.
You think the North is gonna let this go?"

"Those men saluted us when we surrendered,
and now we've kilt their president. If they warn't hankering
for revenge before, now they sholey will."
He eased around the man speaking to the stubble-chinned,
slack-jawed one who'd called him a repentant Rebel,
confronting him, face to face.
                      "I brought me a limp
from Cemetery Ridge. What you bringing home
from the war?" He bore his gaze on the watery, blood rimmed
eyes, narrowed in hate, regarding for an instant
in the pupils' black bore his twinned face,
and finding a deep, sympathetic connection, he raged

as his heart softened and forced hate in the breach.
He shifted to land a blow, but his arms were seized.

"Now fellers, we Rebels's got to stick together."

"Our battles are fresh. We got to mind our tempers."
Respect and reason bled away his rage,
the hands feeling it too and falling away.
He removed himself to the platform's farther end
and sat. He was only a day or two from the milk
and honey skin of Duessa. He would go and beg her
to come away with him. He would implore her.
Again and again, she had saved him, saved his life
at Gettysburg. If she would give him the chance,
he would make good his word, that some new birth
of love might save them both. After all,
she was free to do her will. Duessa was free.
He liked the sound of that sentence, Duessa was free.
He got off the train, weary from days in the hot,
cradle-rocking car, yet buoyed by prospects.
He thought of renting a room to bathe and freshen
his limbs, but his funds were short, and he was eager,
so he walked a shady lane out of Opelika,
glad to march alone through gentle hills,
where long leaf pine, sumac, and goldenrod
unbloomed satisfied his mind. Mile on mile,
the land betrayed no sign of raids, just unspoiled
Alabama loveliness. He knew from the papers
Wilson's raiders this month had fired Selma
and occupied Montgomery, routing General Forrest
at Montevallo and then at Ebenezer Church.

He was glad the capitol suffered no destruction,
so Caleb's family still might have their living.
He spooked a yellowhammer at a meadow's edge,
the shy bird streaking his sight with a blur of golden
wing, trilling a warning call to his mate
hidden away no doubt in tufts of grasses.
Thickets green with chickasaw plum, he smelled
his grandma's boiling jelly juice, recalled
her face in caressing steam, watching her raise
the wooden spoon waiting for a drop to cling.
The road took up with a murmuring creek and stands
of apple haw and sassafras. He broke some sappy
twigs from the latter, chewed them to keep his spit wet,
enjoying the licorice tang. Now mazzard cherry,
sumac, and possum haw, sure signs of home.
At noon he stopped to rest beneath a white oak
in shade of wagon tracks and dried out flop.
He was glad for his passel of hardtack though he was looking
forward to the time he'd never have to taste
the stuff again. At dusk he turned off the road
and struck a fire on the outskirts of Tuskeega, pleased
by peepers and whippoorwills making exuberant music
and unrelated stars through obscuring clouds.

April 16, 1865 Tuskeega

A twig snapped, his sight cracked open, his hand
reaching for something not there, and pleasant vacancy
of peace surrounded him. An armadillo,
covered in panoply of plate and mail, rooted

his moist nose in black duff, shoveling
earth with manic scratching of forepaws.
            "Scat,
you ironclad possum." The creature did not scare,
but aimed his snout at him, snuffed, and resumed
his grubbing. He stood, pissed on ashes, and memories
came unbidden, the man with steel in his head,
horses without legs, the headless creature spurting
blood, his hand in a man's wound, the wet
heat of his body. He took a drink, feeling
the canteen's mouth trembling against his lips,
then shook his head, forcing nightmares away.
He broke a piece of worm castle cracker, tossed it
at the crater. The earth stained snout popped out, snuffled
about like a hand searching in darkness and found
the morsel. Holding it in forepaws, he made a further
olfactory inspection and established the bit was eatable.
The force required to bite the sheet iron cracker
caused the creature to bare its teeth and squint.
His laughter echoed the forest. Maybe she'd serve
him lunch, perhaps some wine. Midday he turned
right at the rounded stone and quickened pace,
passed abandoned cabins, a stand of pine,
recalling her clean hot lips in October cold.
Stepping out of the trees, he looked up the rise
of hill to the Bateman House. Nothing was there.
But too many things were familiar, the pebbled walks,
bullace arbors sagging across the lawns,
the well curb, a hammock slung between pecan trees,
and then the twin brick chimneys, Sherman's Sentinels,
but Sherman had not been here, nor Wilson either.

It must have burned by accident, yes, for the barn
still stood on its rise of ground behind the razed
foundation. Ducking some dogwood boughs, heavy
with blossoms, pushing wounded petals aside,
he crossed the bare foundation, leaving prints
in leached ashes. The blaze had been hot and unchecked.
At the well curb, he pumped his canteen full, gulped
it down, his knees struck with rubbery weakness,
filled it again, convulsed by panicked rage,
suppressed by the hardest. He went to the barn, a stamping
and nasal shuddering; his shadow drew him inside.
His eyes in a moment adjusted as he breathed in pungent
dung and sweet crisp hay. A filly whickered.
There were three, each in a stall. He took an ear
from the crib, approached the closest, a chestnut mare
with a white crux high on her forehead. Seeing the corn,
she stretched her fleshy lips and grasped the nubbin,
which he held as she stripped the kernels, stroking the velvet
of her muscular neck.
                            "You ain't a mind a making
off with no horses, air you now?" Surprised,
he kept himself from flinching so not to affright
the animals and turned to see a man's silhouette,
standing in evening's blinding door and holding
something, a rifle he presumed, at arms port.

"Such hadn't crossed my mind. Who are you?"
He stepped inside the barn. He was holding a spade,
one hand behind the shoulder, the other gripping
the handle, knuckles white, his eyes alert.

"Name's Pete Newcomb. I work for Master Bateman."
He cocked his head and took another step.
"Well I be dipped in buttermilk. You is a vetr'n
of the CSA. You'd never steal a hen's egg.
I should have knowed it right off, captain," he chortled,
dropping the shovel's blade to the floor by his foot,
"You ain't come here looking to ride no horses."
The man was shorter than he was, his face hard
with the bitten backwoods rough of work and weather.
A thin scar climbed his forehead into his hairline, his nose
bulbous, his eye obsequious, greedy as a crow's.
His two front teeth being absent, he lisped his s's.
He was a starving stray, dangerous and smart
as he needed to be. "Where you coming from, captain?"

"General Lee surrendered me Sunday last
at Appomattox. I'm heading back to Eufaula."

"General Lee. Well shut my mouth. What I
wouldn't give to clap an eye on him. Captain,
the Yankees have ruined us all for nigger freedom."

"Did Yankees raid your place?"
                                        "Oh no, captain.
One of Master Bateman's crazy high yeller
gals, she's the one what burned the house down.
Barricaded herself in her room and burned herself up
with her chit four yar old. The whole damn house.
I used to make two dollar a week helping
the overseer—that feller could make a nigger
skip from can till cain't. Two dollar a week.

Them's was the good old times. Then war come along
and Master Bateman run a little cotton
through the lines. A yar ago, he'd fetch a dollar
a bale—if I'm lying, I'm dying, captain. I drove
his wagons. We'd load a barge on the Chattahoochee
and down she went to Apalachicola
and the blockade runners. One day there and one day
back and I made two dollars, captain. Now all
I git's is a fip a day fer shoveling shit."

"Who was the woman? Why did she kill herself?"

"One a Bateman's crazy nigger whores.
Deuces we called her and Deuces she surely was."

"It was a whorehouse."
                              "Hail, a rippin' one.
Finest stable of gals east of the river."
He closed his eyes in an icy plunging cataract
of stricken sense, he plummeting dizzying moments.
Duessa and her child alone in fire, both of them
wild with suffering. He opened his eyes, a man
the war had made, passion loaded and primed,
soldiers invading her flesh and he transmogrified
into one of her countless partners, a nameless, grinning
stranger. "I tol ole Marster 'at bitch was trouble,
but he warn't gwine to study the likes of me.
'Pete, you tend to what I'm paying you fer,'
he'd say to me, that's what he'd always say."
He remembered eating alone at Bateman House,
the merriment of gentlemen in a farther dining room.

They'd given her to him because he was
a rube. They'd given him to her for punishment.

"When did she do it?"
                                "I can tell the very day.
It happened July thirty, sixty three.
One of them nigger wenches said Deuces read
about the Rebel victory at Gettysburg,
and got cast down because she warn't gone git
no nigger freedom, said she was pining for a husband
in the bayou parish, what was a Rebel officer.
I don't see why she's pining after him
what must have sent her away. But Deuces was haughty,"
he began chortling again, squinting his eyes,
"and hit's hard on a haughty gal, bucking soldiers
when all's they want's a little puppy nose."
A lanyard's haul, he lunged in crimson haze,
seized the throat, felt the shock of his body
against the barn's plank wall, heard the gasp
of shocked surprise and gloried in the surge of strength,
crushing the hollow windpipe through cords of muscle.
Nose to nose with the wretch, his vision's acuity
returned, he saw the blue eyes wide with terror,
terror mounting the longer he went without breath,
his heels telegraphing distress on the ripped pine boards.

"Who knocked your teeth out? Tell me. Was it you?"
His head shook up and down, he hoping confession
might bring reprieve, but the hands did not relent,
the man panicking in suffocation, features writhing,
the lips working a pantomime of speech, desperate

to fashion a word to placate his murderer, tugging
at Garland's wrists and bunching up his sleeves.
At last the eyes rolled upward showing white,
the face purpled like bruised fruit, the tongue
protruding between the missing teeth, and slackness
fell through the body, water pouring from a bucket,
and gripping the dead weight, he slammed the head
on the wall to keep on killing the villain, repeating
in rhythm, *Henry, Count, Papa, Oscar,*
then let the wreckage fall in a heap. The evening
light resumed its cordial hues. The horses
were watching in pure, uncomprehending calm,
silent until one whinnied softly, stamped
a hollow knock against the barn's plank floor.
Outside the stalls was a heap of dung the man
had shoveled. He lay himself down on the soft stink,
I stood in a line of lusting men to tup her.
I fought for her. I fought the war for her.

April 18, 1865

Dawn, embraced deception of a star's rising,
yet nothing more than the planet's rote and weary
rotation, incomprehensible and vain momentum.
An ache, razor winged and insalubrious
lodged in his breast. He'd thought this mayhem emptiness,
this dire battle that always cost everything, was fought,
and if not won, survived, yet marshaled before him
once more were inexorable forces of mocking vanity,
poised to deal a blow and he to receive it.

A midnight gelding leaned his head from the stall
and whickered. He rose with automaton motion, went
to the corn crib, filled his shirt tail with ears, saw
the heap, the green welter of flies in the blood
black face with civic maggots writhing in its eyes.
He tossed the corn into stalls and sat on the dung pile,
hearing horses crunching nubbins, the breathy
sweep as they lipped up fallen kernels from the floor.
He rose, inspected implements, leather harness,
bridles, several coulters, pairs of chains
with manacles. A lantern hung on a nail. He took it
down and carried it back to the dung pile and sat
once more, staring out the barn door, down
the long green slope of hill into empty pasture
filled with sun, where no wind stirred the grasses.
The day moved off the land, and night fell,
his mind insensate as the peeper's croak, the humming
jizzywitches, or the flies' stumbling buzz.
A motion dove beneath the lintel, a gusting
brushed his cheeks, swerved into rafters and settled,
the eyes seeds in a halved apple, a talisman
regarding him with implacable indifference. The orbits
blinked, the body around them puffed and ruffled.
The icon preened then lurched, something patted
on floorboards. He crawled on hands and knees to see
a casting of fur and bones, could just make out
in dark in the gastric mass, a thumb sized skull.
He grasped the lantern, the wings breathed away.
His palm blossomed with yellow petals, the lamp light
showing in equine eyes like stars. He tossed
the lantern into bales, the fire heaving a sigh

of relief, curling grasses, climbing walls.
The horses whinnied, wide eyed, turning anxious
circles in their stalls, the flames lapping rafters,
trundling smoke rolling under the lintel.
The horses were shrieking now, rearing and striking
the air with hooves. At their fears' pitch, he flung
the stall gates open, and they sprinted away from the roar
of fire, clomping the floor then beating the dirt,
half shadows, half luminous animals, eyes aflame,
till they overtook the night with pounding hooves.
He faced the hot gate and stepped inside,
radiance scalding flesh and stabbing eyes,
the conflagration's heat slicking his torso,
as if the fire were raging inside his body.
To stand the sear he covered his face with his arm
till a forged hand grasped his will, turned him back,
forcing him out of the hoarse and groaning structure,
a creature running and weeping a name in the dark,
through lashes of thin twigs and slicing briers.
He splashed through sudden waters, fell on rocks,
gashing knee and forehead. His cries silenced
vibrating insects, frogs chirruping, a lone
whippoorwill's elegant lamentation to fathomless
dark, void of starlight, moonshine, a dark
no hours measure, a wood without reason or faith,
his mind shrieking its rusted axle, making
tighter revolutions to the turn that finally seizes.
He put his foot in a gopher hole, wrenching
his leg, the heat stabbing his knee, he limping
ahead for miles, pushing his way through thickets,
bearing fire and brimstone of bosom perdition.

He felt his heart was lightning's target, jolted
by paralyzing agonies, bolt on violent bolt,
strike of humiliation, strike of naiveté,
of pride, reaming his eyes, of murder, searing
his hands, of loss, crushing sweetness of his longing,
outrage for immolated woman and child, she raped
again and again by laws and customs, by presidents,
congressmen, judges, minsters, masters, and soldiers.
For the slave's fettered life, no choice obtained
but the sovereign act of suicide, the liberty of death.

April 20, 1865 near Union Springs

He woke in cool darkness, his brow streaming,
body exhausted by his mind's unceasing labor,
careening all the night through the trackless wood,
and offering now to his sense its destination,
the idea forming, he clenching himself to accept
the dark, half knowledge he had possessed, seed
of destruction, the way a cannon tube, imperfectly
cast, conceals a flaw which firings weaken
until the breech explodes and kills the men
who serve the gun. *We stood the African woman*
as well as the white on a pedestal. We rallied round her,
the enfleshed artifice of the Southern man's transgression.
We engendered a race of Helens and raped them all.
The only way I could have done her justice
would have been to leave her alone. He gasped and wept,
stretched in leaf mold, his body one dull aching.

He sat up at last. Beside him lay his sack.
He didn't remember picking it up, but he had.
The army had rendered him an expedient madman.
The daylight's prospect wearied him world without end.
But what was there to do but keep on marching
and battle life's cruelty that empties a man and perserves him?
At noon he came to a river with a suitable pool,
a green shade flowing in cumulus. He stripped and entered,
ducking breathless and scrubbing his scalp to dislodge
the lice, his limbs tingling, bathing in mottled
sun light, gorgeous and serene. He pulled himself out
on a rock streaming and combed his hair, crushing
nits, regarding his thigh's white starburst, his Israel
scar, and the fresh gash mending above his knee,
mark of his mad wandering. He moved into sun
and dried, trying to clear his mind of all
expectation, and words unbidden came to him
as he made his way beside the still waters,
Lord, behold, he whom thou lovest is sick.

April 22, 1865

From out of nothingness, breaking free from leaf
shaped shadows, a strangled face, its eyes maligned
in agony of the death throe, his delighted hands
dousing their light, reveling in force, he gasped
awake, in a wallow of troubled sleep, the quiet
sudden and portent as the moment before a charge,
till the high birling of a grackle, and he rolled over,
stared at sky fractured in blue green shadow

as bodily sense and mind's acuity returned
like betrayal in aching joints, gnawed out belly.
He lay for a while. A jay made outraged cry,
and far away, a crow responded, laughing.
How could she have done this, hiding such terrible
purpose to wreck his heart and mind, but he forced
the question away, for he knew it had not one
but a thousand answers, each a churning whirlpool.
A doe emerged from leaf hang nibbling lichens
from trunks. The wind shifted, she caught his scent,
raised her startled head and bounded away,
her white tail and nimble heels vanishing
in unfettered grace. Swaying branches stilled.
He continued south, stumbling hummocks and pine stands,
the broken shade stippling him like a coat
he was always donning and casting off. He relished
peaceful sounds of lambent footfall on leaf mat,
the phoebe's repeated name, the gabbling streams,
whisk of soft whiplash of swamp loosestrife,
pointed and flowerless, on matted pant legs. He strained
to recall whether it bloomed in racemes or panicles,
its hue and fragrance, such thoughts defending his mind
from ruin. He came to a creek, skirted its bank
until he found a railroad trestle and crossed.
The water was clear and peaceful; a squad of garfish
lazed below the leaf hang swaying and flowing,
each one a bolt of muscle sheathed in sunlight.
A cooter paddled by like a stiff old gaffer,
and swifts twittered down on graceful, tapered wings
and rocking flight, betraying a fathomless sky,
skimming widening arrows drifting downstream.

He drank, and though he was refreshed, he was hungry.
The swifts dove up the high blue rungs of sky
once more, plunging and turning to the dizzy verge
of hearing, their swerving planes changing in elegant,
shifting arcs and sudden plummets, precipitous
winging, filling the heavens with meaningless song.
Because he could hear them fade, he knew they persisted.
He'd skirted the road in woods from Union Springs
and arrived that afternoon at Monticello.
Turning left, he would set his steps toward Eufaula.
The attractive power of place assaulted his breast,
love and comfort, family and friends, his home
where no one knew him. He'd wear that life like a mask.
But he turned to the right, skirted the road in the woods,
lurking in shadows, en route to the city of Troy.

April 23, 1865 Troy

Dawn was lost to daylight when he opened his eyes.
He yawned and drowsed, trying to shake off sleep,
then hefted his sack and moved through woods, his boot soles
soft on winter's compress leaf fall compost
when he heard through dappled light the creak of hames
and rasping axles. When he pushed limbs aside,
a field of open light dazzled vision.
He called, his voice catching a stob, croaking
at the driver's sagging back, perched on the bench
in thread bare blouse and straw hat, traces loose
in one hand, stem of sage grass clamped in teeth,
intent on the trudging ox's shifting buttocks.

He was close enough to see the wheel spokes turning
like hands of an agonized clock, felloes lifting
dust, spilling on the upturn in divided tracks.
He fell in behind. The road was full of sun.
In someone else's stories, he'd traveled this way.
He passed an open field, a shady island
of white oak stranded in pasture, around the bend
a foot bridge twined with bullace vines spanned
a freshet, a worm rail fence ahead on the right.
He stood at this crossing and swallowed the last dash
of his hot canteen. The heat was close and throttling.
He couldn't believe he'd gotten so weak so soon.
Where was the will he showed at Appomattox?
In the army he'd felt he could march forever with air
to breath and a promise of rations at the next depot.
Vertigo rocked him; he closed his eyes a moment.
He moved around the bend, landmarks coming
true like prophesies. He came to his road on the left,
but an impulse turned him right toward rising ground.
He meandered through gorgeous sycamores and crested a hill,
and there below him ablaze in the noonday sun,
the city of Troy, its mills and shops and smiths,
its commerce thriving, structures sound, its life
invigorate, wagons and people wending out of town.
His eyes strained at the distance, but the exodus appeared
to be comprised of Negroes. He caught a rancid
scent and followed the noisome air to the forest,
the stink's intensity growing upon his entering
a hanging garden of corpses, wrists and ankles
bound, the heads wrenched by nooses in strained
articulations with shoulders. Under a stout limb

seven tiptoed on air, the killing's nucleus.
Their clothes were shabby, these plantation Negroes,
who'd been free only days or weeks at most.
The forest floor was trodden, a crowd had turned out.
Through leafy boughs between the trunks of trees,
he could see a circle of dangling rotting bodies,
then noticed putrescences mingling, another familiar
acrid stench, which led to a corpse hanged
with a chain, cold embers and ashes beneath, the legs
burned off at the knees, arms raised as if flexing muscles,
the right hand burned to the bone stick, the charred
visage ghastly, only blackened depressions
suggesting what was once a human face,
the commerce of vision, voice's laws of expression,
one body consumed, a civilization in ruins,
and then a faint apprehension intruded—a feeling
he wasn't alone. A short ways off sat a woman
at the base of a shagbark hickory, her hands folded
in her lap, her back against the flayed tree,
her vacant stare directed away from the corpse
beyond the shadow leaves and leafy sunlight.
He knelt beside her. She did not stir at all.
He touched her shoulder as if he might awake her,
but the waking sleep she'd entered was too profound.
She carried war in her eyes like a veteran soldier.
He stood, shouldered his kit, and left the wood,
then took the path describing a gentle rise,
down through needle fractured sunlight, crowded
dogwood and pine, which opened a lane to homestead
acres of a well ordered farm. He approached the house,
a one story dog trot cabin of neat planed boards,

and stood for a time waist deep in clustered hydrangeas,
its flowers painted with sky. By the cabin's footing,
were crimson tulips, like fractured porcelain cups,
and somewhere near the house a wisteria vine.
The man had never mentioned flowers. This fact
flabbergasted him, for the blooms stirred exultation,
the whole house floating on blossoms. A dozen Dominickers
tip toed the side yard, frowning and cluck-squawking
under their breaths. Back of the house, a verdurous
kitchen garden half concealed a woman
hoeing beans. She wore a dress of homespun,
and her hair, as he well knew, was shocking red,
though tucked in a rigolette, her waist slim
as a willow wand. She possessed disarming beauty.
He stood a long time looking until she raised,
putting a hand to her back and spying him there,
a soft trepidation spreading across her face.
She took a step or two to get in earshot,
he recalling a dream kiss she'd given him once.
From a crib on the back stoop, her son stood watching,
making infant music with lips and spittle.

"What can I do for you, sir?"

                              "I'm passing through.
On my way home from Virginia."

                                    "Where're you from?"

"Eufaula."

         "Eufaula? You've come a right ways out
of your way, soldier."

                          "Yessum. I reckon I have.

My name's Garland. Your husband and I were both
in the Eighth Alabama. I thought I'd just drop in
and see how you were faring. From the look of those beans
and that young corn, you seem to be doing fine."
They stood together a while, becoming familiar,
talking of war and weather and corn earworms.
She pulled a knot from her head rag, shaking her locks out,
her hair tangling rioting crimson sunlight.

"If you want to work, I could use a man round here.
You could bunk in the preacher's cubby. I can't pay wages,
but I can feed you out on milk and cornbread."
He looked about the garden, thought how easy
a man could be happy here, but then recalled
the woman alone in the wilderness, starving and suffering.
He'd always assumed the fine plantation houses
bore the moral burden for the Negroes' lot,
but now he knew this house and houses like it—
his own house—bore the burden, had borne the burden.
He caught himself scowling and tried to recover his face.

"I'm truly obliged, but folks are anxious for me.
But I'd be grateful to purchase a swallow of milk."
She went inside and filled his canteen, refusing
his payment.
                    "What would my husband think of me,
taking a soldier's money?" He tipped his cap
and departed, but soon as he turned away, she called,

"Garland."
              "Yes."
                        "Would that be Garland Cain?"

"Yes."

    "The man who wrote to me."

        "Yes."

She watched him closely.

        "I'm pleased to make your acquaintance."

"It's a pleasure to meet you, Lucy."

        "I want to thank you
for writing that difficult letter. I would have suffered
terribly not knowing when John died or how.
Each time I read that page it breaks my heart,
but the touch of your words is gentle and guides my mind
toward solace, knowing my husband held me dear,
knowing he spoke my name." Her eyes were shining.
They stood staring. He recalled the dream kiss.

"I live in Eufaula, route one, beat fourteen.
If you ever need any help, write me there."
Regaining the blackened hill, he knelt by the woman
and lifted her. She had no strength, so he made her shuffle
to the forest edge and sat her against a dogwood.
"You've got to eat." He put a hardtack cracker
in his mess tin and poured a little milk on top.
When the bread was soft, he broke a piece and pressed it
to her lips. The morsel slid in her mouth and rested,
so he placed his fingers under her chin and moved it
up and down. A few tears squinched from her eyes.
Handling her face with caresses, he tilted her head back
and gave her a swig of milk. She sputtered and swallowed.
He fed her half the cracker. When she resisted
more, he ate the rest. "That man, is he

your brother, your husband?" At the word *husband* her face
contorted. Behind her vacant look a violent
grief rose up, a blind and permanent hurt.
He put his hand on her cheek and turned her eyes
toward his. "I'm sorry." She wore a boarded-up
expression, and when he released his touch, her gaze
drifted back to its aimless stare at the wood.
He stowed his kit. The stench was sickening. He hoisted
the rag doll woman, braced her against the trunk,
then draped her over his shoulders, picking his way
across the swale and down the hill. He turned,
looked back at the forest's charred, black hole, thinking
the slaves will have to learn to fight their war.
He limped his burden to the stream of refugees. When he slid
her off his back, her knees buckled, and he caught her,
a revenant embrace, scent of smoke in her clothes.
She lay her head on his shoulder and stroked his face.
A drover saw them, consternation filling
his eyes as he reigned up and spoke to some women
in the bed. "I brought her down off the hill. You know
what happened up there?"
                              "Everybody know.
Black folk wit sense is moving on out of here."
He worked her around to the tailgate and boosted her up,
the women, full of misery and compassion, gathering
her in, but when they touched her, she began to catch
at his sleeves, wailing an animal keening, that swerved
to an eerie threnody; her gaze suddenly animate,
she locked her eyes on his, and her frail grasp slipped
his fingers, and she was borne away in the innumerable
caravan, diminishing toward distance, the still point

all time was marching toward, crowded out
by streaming emigrants, by mules and chairs and chaffticks.
On the corner, a man in tux and top hat, inspected
his watch.

       "Why are the Negroes leaving?" The watch
snapped shut.

        "These Negroes are no longer welcome here.
They betrayed us to Yankee bummers."

          "The whole lot of them?"

"I took no part in the extrajudicial proceedings."

"Where do you think they are going?"

         "Who can say?
Trouble for them, of course, but better for all."
Garland stared at him in incomprehension.
"I do not condone violence if that's what you think."
Garland smiled in his face.

      "Yes you do."

He made Brundidge by four, asked directions
to the only boarding house and paid a dollar
for a plate of cornbread and turnip greens and a platter
of fried eggs. The dining room was dark
and dusty, tang of rancid grease, the mood
at table somber except for a bachelor farmer,
probably a regular, framed by the one window,
his silhouette yammering about the assassination,
how black hearted Lincoln got what he deserved,
on an on, till one of the other two diners,
both veterans, said softly,

        "Yes sir, we see your point."

Then quiet reigned, except for kitchen noises
of a shuffling Negro who cooked and served the guests.
He sat awhile to rest for his journey then left
with the two other soldiers dressed in threadbare butternut.
As one recalled a Sharpsburg cornfield, they noticed
far ahead a drift of dust. The rider,
blue-clad and hell-bent, reined in hard.
                                      "Johnnies,
we've bagged your president down in Georgia, sneaking
away in a woman's dress." And the Rebel shot back,

"Hyar now, Yank, hit looks like the Devil bagged yourn."
The soldier stiffened, his smile warped to a scowl,
and he spurred his horse away at a lazy walk,
speaking back over his shoulder,
                                       "We Union men
are going to make you traitors pay." They watched
the Yankee's kicked up dust clouds waft to the road.

"Gawd help us now them black Republicans is ruling
the South." They walked in silence to the Pea River
where the three men parted company, shaking hands.
Later he passed the road to Carl's house
and hoped he was well. As pine and oak thinned out
to meadows and fields, their wedges and patterns, farms
and fences, all fell into proper place in his grateful
recognition. He was home. His pace quickened,
but he quashed the urge to hurry. Something told him,
even as he took each step to the house where he
was born, he was making something grand, something
he must build meticulously, with careful attention,

something to yield him pleasure, but also useful
for equanimity, shaped by terrible circumstance,
but for all the terror and heartache, ending in joy,
the day that Garland Cain returned from the war.
Sunlight level through trees and shadows long
were delicious to his eyes. He stopped on a rise of hill
that marked the boundary of his father's land. His land,
now, for his family; land that would one day cradle
his bones while his own son plowed above them. The prospect
was satisfying as pleasure of dusk and shadowy trees.
He came to the sprawling dogwood, open crowned,
upon which branches he'd lounged on languorous evenings
as a boy. He dropped his sack, swung himself up
on a branch and climbed, laughing until his leg
brushed a limb and shocked his calf with agony.
He rolled his pant leg up and touched the crimson
edges of an open sore, a stubborn affliction,
dealing him grief for weeks, but home at last,
he could rest and eat and make himself whole again.
His leg throbbed, but he didn't care. Nothing
would curb his joy. He poked his head through the airy
crown, feasted vision on the barn, a field
of standing corn, evidence of promises kept,
hog pens, cistern, dog trot cabin, the stovepipe
giving feathery smoke, the windows cheerful.
He saw no earth was fresh in the family plot.
This pleased him. As far as he could see in the failing
light was peace. The twilight deepened, he felt
himself sway a little, the windows glowing brighter,
and climbed down eager for homecoming and good cheer.
His feet touching the ground, elation seized him.

He felt like Zacchaeus going to ready his house
or a mythic giant drawing strength from the earth.

June 4, 1865 Home

They'd harnessed Dash to drag the corpse of Harriet
to the forest's edge, letting her down in a pit
they'd dug, the old plow mule, succumbed to colic.
They covered her with brush and gave it all to fire,
and flames gasped and leaped to each other's shoulders,
so many voices whispering the June air,
suffused with the clean scent of spring rain
and honeysuckle mingling with odious rot
and acrid fire, whispering *Wilderness,* and his mind
moved through conflagrations, sparks showering,
and anguished cries of suffering. The wind shifted
and brought the heat against his face square
as a forge door. He stood before the burning
barn, daring himself to that desperate gesture,
to love her to the end. With Duessa he had been
a monstrous child. He would live to do right by her.
He would work to be a plain and decent man.
Therefore, he was burning the mule, consuming mulishness
that made men's hearts intractable. The Yankees had visited
already. They had a talk with Levi, ensuring
that he understood his freedoms. He was sure
there was nothing lacking in Levis' understanding.
They read his parole, told him they'd be back.
He told them they were welcome any time.
He recalled the Tar Heel cavalry officer's goading,

Grease up, son, and slide on back in the Union.
This made him smile. His feet were truly slick.
A ways from the fire, Dash was standing, having ceased
his grazing, glum and dreary eyed as a mourner.
He felt the heft of the tow hook in his hands, the awful
swing and shock, splitting the equine skull.
An odd thing to elicit sorrow in the midst
of that vicious struggle, contesting a corner of hell.
He saw the Yankee storming over the breastwork,
his face contorted, felt his hand on the cold
bayonet's shank, saw the rage in the eyes
as his head exploded spewing blood and brains.
He hoped that Moses was getting on up north.
Every day his mind returned to the war.
He'd rather these visions rise on the updraft and vanish,
but he had decided not to struggle against them.
He made himself their vessel, letting them come
and go. Yet in spite of trouble, his heart was reeling
with anticipation. He wanted to find a woman
and sway her affection. Beth Anne was not a prospect,
having remarried, so he'd written a letter to Lucy,
inviting her to visit. Perhaps she'd come,
perhaps he'd even woo her. He had a notion
marriage would give life shape and sustenance, transform
this box of hewn pine logs and clay chinking
to a serious house on serious earth. He would fashion
a home of honest intention, of honest love.
Levi broke his reverie.

                  "Mistuh Garland,
hit's gone to be rat hard fo us to work
on dis here plot wit jes dat old nag Dash."

"Levi, don't talk that way about Dash, you'll hurt
his feelings."
      "Awe, Mistuh Garland, you is
full a too much fun. Dash don't know.
Dash ain't got de smarts a hoss is s'posed to."
He regarded Levi, in many ways inscrutable
as he had always been, but there was a certain
lightness in his bearing and conversation. He chose
to call it happiness, and that was a promise long
denied fulfilled, but Garland held no illusions.
Justice had not rolled down like a mighty stream.
The Negro needed sympathy in the Southern heart,
but the South had wagered blood against his right
and lost, which meant the Negro faced a long,
steep climb before the mind of the South caught up
with the law. It was unconscionable that after all
the Negro had endured, he should be asked for patience,
and yet he must. The whole affair was charged
and primed; the one right touch might set it off.
The thought was sobering. He'd sinned against Duessa,
and justice and nature gave her the right to despise him.
Instead, she'd offered pity and tendered him
a glorious grace that awakened his heart to life.
She'd taught him depth of soul and rich humanity
and challenged his heart to humility; he would be humble.
Her goodness, her suffering would abide with him in that
and make him a better man. And here stood Levi.
Born into slavery, now he was free, free
to live from hand to mouth, to suck his paw,
to scratch out the life of a poor man, but Garland knew
their common blood conferred a common manhood.

The fire sighed and leapt into air. He recalled
the face of the boy who died beside him on the way
to Chambersburg, John Fisher's ruined face,
the Texan's face, that handsome, loquacious boy,
poor Oscar who did not even know he had died
or how, Henry, Eugene, Hiram, Yance,
a fool perhaps, but a good man nonetheless,
the nameless lady he found on the lynching hill.
He'd have to find a way to live up to them all.
He did not know exactly how to proceed,
but it started today, putting a fire brand
to the mulish disposition, burning away
the bonds constraining the soul from perfect liberty,
the gift of God that must be seized and exerted.

"Levi, a barn ain't no place for a man to make
a home. Come this fall, when the corn is in
and the weather is cool, we're going to build you a house."

"Hyar now, massuh"—
                    "Mister."
                              "Mistuh Garland,
you *is* funning now."
                    "No, Levi, I'm not.
We going to build you a house. Up there in the copse
where you go to sit sometimes to watch the creek.
Maybe you'll fool Myra into jumping the broom."

"Ho Lawd! A purty young thang like Myra ain't gwine
to study me. I's a good old wagon oncet,
but I done broke down."
                        "Levi, you ain't broke down.

You got a few loads left to haul. When she finds
you a man of property, it just might turn her fancy.
She just might want to come and set up housekeeping."
The man was quiet for a spell, watching the fire.

"Old slave wit a house and a woman. Sholey de Lawd
has led him out of bonds of de house of Egypt."
In evening, walking to the road, he saw at its vanishing
the day failing with magnificence, horizon's fire
rife in pines. He would make a peaceful life.
In times to come there would be exultation.

About the Author

Scott Ward is the author of two previous books of poetry. He is a professor at Eckerd College and lives in St. Petersburg, Florida, with his wife Jana.

Made in the USA
Middletown, DE
14 March 2021